Breaking the System

G.N. CREIGHTON

Breaking the System

Digital Divinity Part 1
Gabriella Creighton

Gabriella Creighton

ISBN Information

eBook: 979-8-9939808-8-1
Print: 979-8-9939808-9-8

You can find more books by this author at:

GabriellaCreighton.com

About the Author

Gabriella Creighton is a life long lover of the Fantasy and Science Fiction Genres. She has been fascinated by Dragons and other mythical creatures from a young age and grew up dreaming of being a writer. Inspired by great authors like Jane Yolen, Anne McCaffrey, JRR Tolkien and Phillip Pullman, she loves to take an alternative view of myth and weave her own versions. After a long life of working, gaming and enjoying the works of others, she has finally decided to put her nigh on useless Masters Degree in English Literature to work to tell stories of her own.

Growing up in Rural New York; as well as having been thrown all over the United States, Gabriella has learned she has only three desires. To write until the nail her coffin shut, to never answer the phone and for a cool glass of Salted Caramel Crowne Royal mixed with Cream Soda and Dr Pepper, which she calls a magic elixir.

It helps get the writing done.

You can find more of her works at:
GabriellaCreighton.com

This goes out to all the people that shaped my gaming life.

Whether we were raiding Molten Core for 8 hours
Or trying not to murder each other Extreme Boss Fights.

Some have respawned in another world already.
Some are still here with me hoping that's real.

But Gamers have a special bond.
We somehow even love those we hate.

Because there's always another round,
Always another game.

Meet you all in Orbit.

Contents

Act I: Coffin Break   1

1. Wake in Iron   3

2. Stability Engine   11

3. Backlash Math   19

4. Coffin Rupture   29

5. Domino Wing   41

6. Facility Hunts Back   51

7. Cityline Breach   63

Act II: The City that Runs on Chains   77

8. Streets That Agree   79

9. Checkpoints & Saints   91

10. Fellow Escapees   101

11. Price of Darkness   111

12. Sewers & Blood Maps   123

13. Inquisitorial Inspection   141

14. Unsafe Space   155

Act III: The Net Tightens   165

15. The Monster Story   167

16. Player Friction   179

17. Trainyard Run   189

18. The Warden's Offer   199

19. Coffin Tower Shadow   211

20. Collapse Route   221

21. Reunited in Ruin   233

Act IV: Break Point   247

22. Painful Planning   249

23. Infiltration Night   263

24. Breakpoint Raid   281

25. System Notice   295

26. Safety Dance   307

27. Border Break   319

28. Lands Beyond   333

Character Sheet   346

ACT 1

COFFIN BREAK

Chapter 1
Wake in Iron

I woke up hanging.

Not the poetic kind of hanging either, not a metaphor, not a dream image my brain could reinterpret into something less humiliating. My shoulders were pulled up and back by restraints that bit into skin, my wrists locked in metal cuffs that were too cold to be real, and my ankles held apart just enough to make my hips ache. The air smelled like old pennies and wet stone, and there was a low hum in the walls that vibrated through my teeth.

For a few seconds I didn't move. I didn't even breathe right. I held my lungs like a kid hiding under a bed, as if silence could protect me from whatever had built this place. Then the truth of gravity settled in, slow and mean, and my body tried to adjust by tensing every muscle at once. That was when the coffin drank.

It started as a tug inside my chest, like someone had grabbed my sternum and pulled. The sensation slid through my ribs and down my spine, then hooked into my stomach with a steady, patient greed. The moment I strained against the cuffs, the pull sharpened, and my vision darkened at the edges as if the room wanted to blink me out. I stopped fighting by instinct, not because I had accepted anything, but because the machine responded to resistance the way a mouth responds to food.

The container around me was steel, I could feel it in the cold that pressed against the thin strip of cloth they'd given me. Calling it a dress was generous, the kind of lie you told yourself because the alternative was admitting you were wearing nothing that counted. It wrapped my chest and fell to mid-thigh, rough and stiff like something cut from a shipment strap. My feet dangled bare over empty air, toes flexing uselessly, and the cuffs at my wrists were heavy enough to remind me that my body had become an object.

My thoughts came in bursts. Where am I. Where is my room. Where is my desk. Where is my headset. Where is Vermeer. Then, sharper, the question that made my throat tighten.

Am I still asleep.

I tried to summon my interface the way I had a thousand times. The motion was so familiar it felt like reaching for my phone in the dark. A reflex. A comfort. I thought, Status, and waited for the familiar geometry of bars and icons to slide into place.

Something flickered, like a window opening and slamming shut. A thin strip of translucent text appeared at the edge of my vision, then jittered away like it had been startled.

My HP bar hung there for a second, dim and thin, as if someone had turned the brightness down until it barely existed. My mana readout was worse. It was present, technically, but it looked like a hose with a kink in it, the number stuttering downward in tiny increments even though I wasn't casting anything. I could feel it too, a steady siphon under my skin, a pressure that never stopped.

I swallowed and tasted metal.

"Okay," I whispered, because saying anything made me feel less like prey. My voice sounded wrong in the coffin, flatter, swallowed by steel. I tried to pull my arms down again, just a little, and the drain tugged harder in response. My stomach lurched, and I had to blink fast to keep myself from panicking into a full-body thrash. Panic would feed the machine. That was already clear.

Hands. Then feet.

The words came out quietly, almost a hiss between my teeth. They were nonsense to anyone else, but to me they were an order. A ladder. I couldn't control the whole situation, so I controlled the first rung.

I forced my fingers to relax inside the cuffs. It took effort, because the metal pressed into nerve and bone, and my hands wanted to curl into claws. Instead I moved them the way I would have moved them at my desk when I needed to calm down, the way I would have moved them before a difficult pull in the weekly raid.

Small. Precise. Quiet.

I traced a spell pattern in the air. Not a full cast. Not enough to trip whatever suppression lattice was sucking my mana away. Just the shape, the muscle memory, the route my fingers would take when I asked the elements to answer me. It felt ridiculous for a heartbeat, like practicing piano on a broken keyboard, but the second the pattern completed, my pulse steadied.

I still owned my hands.

My toes flexed again, and I shifted my attention downward. Feet would come later. My calves trembled from being held in this position too long, and I realized with a jolt that I didn't know how long I'd been here. Minutes. Hours. Days. Time was a thing that belonged to people with beds and clocks and the right to lie down.

A memory hit me so suddenly I tasted it.

Vermeer. The weekly raid. The last boss's arena lit with that familiar neon glow, my guild's voices in my headset layered over each other, laughing and swearing and calling mechanics like we'd rehearsed them in our sleep. I remembered the moment the boss finally dropped, the tiny flood of relief and triumph, the way my hands had hovered over my keyboard like they didn't want to stop. Then my desk, the warm spot from my monitor, the stale taste of energy drink, and the weight of my head dipping forward as if someone had shut my power button off.

After that, nothing.

The coffin hummed. The drain pulled. The memory shattered, leaving behind a bruise of longing and a fresh, sharp fear.

If I fell asleep at my desk and woke up here... what happened to my body.

The thought tried to bloom into panic. I strangled it before it could. Panic was a luxury, and this place charged interest.

I forced myself to focus on the only senses I could trust. Sound came first. The hum was constant, low and electrical, like an overworked transformer. Beneath it, there were other layers: a faint tick that could have been cooling metal contracting, a distant rhythmic thump like machinery cycling, and far away, footsteps that came and went in patterns.

I listened until the footsteps returned and made sense. Two sets, heavy boots. A pause. A soft chirp like a scanner. A voice, muffled by steel and distance, chatting like this was just another shift.

The boots came closer, and the sound changed the way it always does when danger is real, it stopped being background noise and became measurement. The hum in the coffin stayed steady, but I felt it in my molars, a low vibration that made every breath feel borrowed. I kept my fingers still inside the cuffs because even the smallest movement made the drain tug harder, and I didn't want to teach it my tells. Through the slit I could see only a slice of corridor, fluorescent and clean, lined with other coffins suspended in rows like trophies. The air carried antiseptic and metal, a hospital smell that tried to pretend this was care.

The footsteps paused outside my slit, and a scanner chirped, bright and cheerful in the way machines are cheerful about cruelty. A man's voice followed it, casual, the tone of someone checking a generator.

"Row nine's stable," he said. "Output's holding."

Another voice answered, closer and irritated, like the speaker had been carrying a bad mood for a while.

"It better be," he said. "I don't want Vrake's audit team crawling up my spine again."

The name landed like a weight. I couldn't see faces, only uniform blur and the occasional gleam of magitek seams, but fear had a sound, and the sound in that second voice was sharp enough to use. They moved again, boots scraping polished concrete, armor plates shifting with soft clicks, and I listened the way I used to listen to raid callouts, not for drama, but for information. The corridor stayed sterile, bright, almost proud of itself, as if cleanliness could make cages holy.

A cart rolled past with wheels that whispered, and the clink of tools followed, delicate sounds in a place built for heavy sins. A technician's voice cut in, flat with routine, like he'd spent years turning people into numbers.

"Stability Engine check," the technician said. "Drain flow confirm. Lattice load at eighty-eight percent."

The word Engine twisted something in my stomach. Engine meant fuel, meant output, meant the neat lie that I wasn't a person hanging in steel, I was a component. One of the guards responded like he was talking about a temperamental appliance.

"Keep it under ninety," he said. "Cartwright hates spikes."

The technician muttered, and I caught the edge of resentment in the sound.

"Spikes aren't aesthetic," he said. "Spikes are physics."

The guards stopped near the next coffin, close enough that their voices carried without strain. A younger voice joined, uncertain and too curious, the kind of curiosity that got people killed in the wrong places. The question came out fast, like it had been waiting in the back of his throat.

"Why don't we just end them?"

Silence followed, the kind that meant someone had said something naive and was about to be corrected. The older guard answered with doctrine-dry patience, like he'd repeated the explanation until it stopped sounding like cruelty to him.

"Because it doesn't work," he said. "Termination forces respawn."

The younger one hesitated, and I could almost hear him trying to square that with whatever story he'd been told.

"Respawn where?" he asked.

"Anywhere," the older guard said, and he sounded tired now, not empathetic, just tired. "Districts, roadways, sometimes right in the middle of civilians. You kill one, you don't solve a problem, you relocate it, and then you deal with the panic."

The technician chimed in again, clipped like he'd memorized it from a training pamphlet.

"Execution causes instability events," he said. "Containment prevents them."

The older guard took that line and polished it into something smoother, the slogan voice sliding into place like a mask.

"Containment is mercy," he said.

My hands tightened inside the cuffs, and I forced them to relax before the drain could punish me for the impulse. Mercy was what you called a choice made with care, not a machine that drank you harder when you flinched. I turned the word over anyway, because belief made people predictable, and predictable meant exploitable. Outside my slit, the corridor lights stayed steady, bright enough to make everything look clinical instead of cruel.

The younger guard asked the next question softer, like he already knew the answer would be ugly.

"And people buy this?"

"They buy what keeps their lights on," the older guard said. "Cartwright sells it as protection, Vrake sells it as purity, and everyone sleeps easier."

Cartwright wanted pretty numbers and pretty stories, the kind you could broadcast until they became true. Vrake, whoever she was, held power that made guards correct their posture and lower their voices. I couldn't see their faces, but I could hear the hierarchy in the way names changed the air. I filed it away with the same care I used to file boss mechanics, because in a place like this, power had tells, and tells could be used. Hands. Then feet, I told myself without moving my mouth, and I kept my breathing steady enough that the drain didn't spike.

A new voice cut into the corridor, clean and cold, and the guards went instantly quieter. It wasn't louder than the others, it didn't need to be.

"Audit sweep starts in ten," the voice said.

The older guard answered, and the tone shift was immediate, forced calm snapped tight over whatever he actually felt.

"Yes, Inquisitor," he said.

The same cold voice continued, measured like a checklist, like it was reading off scripture carved into metal.

"If your readouts are inaccurate, you will be disciplined," the Inquisitor said. "If your drains are poorly balanced, you will be disciplined. If your prisoners exhibit nonstandard interface behavior, you will be disciplined."

There was a pause, then the voice softened by a fraction, and somehow that made it worse, because it sounded like it was meant to be kind.

"The System does not tolerate theft," the Inquisitor said.

The word theft hooked into my ribs as if it had weight. I didn't have a clean explanation for why it frightened me more than discipline did, but my body reacted anyway, skin prickling, throat tightening, the instinct to become smaller even though there was nowhere to go. I stayed still, because stillness was the only camouflage I had, and I listened harder, because listening was how you survived in places that wanted you blind. Somewhere down the row, a low sob broke through the sterile hum and cut off too fast, and I traced the spell pattern again, tiny and precise, because if I stopped moving my hands, my mind would spiral, and if my mind spiraled, the coffin would drink me for it.

When the boots moved on, the corridor did what it had been doing all along, it pretended nothing was wrong. The lights stayed steady, the hum stayed steady, and the drain kept pulling at my insides with the patient greed of a machine that had never needed permission. I hung there in my strip of cloth and tried not to think about how easily a person became "output" if enough people agreed to call it that. My shoulders burned where the restraints held me, and I focused on the simplest truth I had left, if I could find a seam, I could pry it open.

Hands. Then feet.

I didn't say it aloud this time. I traced the spell pattern again, tiny movements in the air, as careful as breathing through a cracked window. The cuffs limited my wrists, but they didn't stop my fingers, and my fingers were the only part of me the coffin hadn't fully convinced to give up. The drain tugged harder when I moved too much, so I made the pattern smaller, cleaner, like a musician practicing scales so quietly only she could hear them. Even in a cage, repetition became ownership.

The interface flickered at the edge of my vision again, not in a helpful way, more like a glitch that wanted my attention and then regretted it. My HP bar stayed dim and thin, but it did not move, not yet, not unless I made the mistake of provoking something that could actually hurt me. My mana number, though, kept ticking downward in small, steady bites, and I could feel the loss as a faint hollowness behind my ribs. The drain wasn't just taking magic, it was taking the part of me that wanted to act on impulse. It was trying to sand down my will until I fit.

I needed data, not fear.

So I tested the smallest thing I could.

I gathered a thread of fire first, so thin it was more an idea than a spell, a warmth that lived in the center of my palm without burning my skin. Then ice, a cool pressure that slid along the same line and refused to melt. Lightning came third, a prickling flicker that made my fingertips buzz, and stone came last, weight, steadiness, the feeling of planting your feet on a floor that could not be moved. I braided them together in the air between my fingers, not casting, not releasing, just holding the weave like a secret.

The coffin reacted immediately. The drain sharpened as if it had smelled blood, and my vision darkened at the edges, a slow squeeze that tried to turn my thoughts into fog. The hum rose half a note, and the steel around me felt closer, like the container was leaning in. My stomach lurched, and sweat cooled on my back under the strip of cloth that stuck to my skin. I grit my teeth and held the weave anyway, because if I dropped it the moment the cage yanked, I would learn nothing except that it could scare me.

Balance, I told myself.

Fire. Ice. Lightning. Stone.

The tug shifted.

It didn't stop. It didn't soften into mercy. It hesitated, a fraction of a second where the drain lost its rhythm and the hum stuttered like a skipped beat. My interface flickered at the edge of my vision, and for a breath, the mana number paused, not climbing, not saving me, just pausing like the machine had to think about how to drink from a cup it didn't recognize. The hesitation was so small I almost missed it, but once you saw a seam, you couldn't unsee it.

Then the drain surged back in anger.

My lungs seized, and black spots swam across my vision, and the braid almost slipped out of my fingers. I broke the weave before I could pass out, not because I wanted to, but because unconsciousness in this place felt like giving the coffin permission to take whatever it wanted. The baseline tug returned, steady and greedy, and I sucked in air through my teeth like I'd been underwater too long. My arms trembled in the cuffs, and the skin at my wrists felt bruised, but beneath the pain was something sharper.

The coffin didn't like balanced elements.

Or it couldn't classify them. Either way, it had blinked.

I closed my eyes and counted to five, not as a comfort, as a reset. My fingers traced the spell pattern again, smaller now, because the drain punished fatigue too, and I needed to keep my body from spiraling into weakness. I forced my shoulders to relax even though the restraints made relaxation feel like surrender.

My feet dangled, bare toes flexing in the air, and I imagined the weight of boots again, not as fantasy, as a future inventory slot I intended to fill.

The corridor outside the slit remained bright and orderly, but sound carried the truth they didn't put on posters. I heard the cart again, wheels whispering, and I heard the elevator vibration through the coffin's frame, and I heard another scanner chirp. Somewhere down the row, someone coughed, a dry, exhausted sound that reminded me there were other people in other coffins, draining the same way I was draining. The thought that I wasn't alone should have been comfort. Instead it felt like pressure, because it meant there were others being turned into engines while the Kingdom called it mercy.

A screen somewhere down the corridor flickered, and for a second, light shifted across the slice of floor I could see through my slit. A propaganda feed played, bright colors and clean faces, the kind of image that made a lie feel like community. I couldn't read the whole message from my angle, but the word STABILITY was big enough to recognize, the same way a brand logo is recognizable even when it's half-hidden. They were proud of this. They broadcasted it. They made families feel safe because monsters were in boxes.

My jaw tightened until it ached.

I thought again about Vermeer, not as nostalgia, as calibration. In the raid, a mechanic had a tell, an audio cue, a light shift, a timer. You learned it, you respected it, and you exploited it. The coffin had a tell too, a hesitation when the weave was balanced. That meant it had limits. If it had limits, it could be overloaded. If it could be overloaded, then the cage wasn't divine, it was engineering with a god complex.

That was when the decision settled in me, heavy and clear.

I stopped asking how long I could endure.

I started planning how to make it break.

Hands. Then feet, I told myself, and this time the words didn't feel like comfort. They felt like an instruction manual for the kind of person I was about to become.

Chapter 2
Stability Engine

Let me back up. Let me explain how I got here, because I'm still not sure I believe it myself, and I was there.

I fell asleep. That's the embarrassing part. I fell asleep during a raid in Vermeer, which is maybe the most dangerous zone in Core Break Online and definitely not the place you want to go AFK. I'd been grinding for eighteen hours straight, chaining dungeons with a PUG group that was actually competent for once, and we'd just cleared the outer gardens when my eyes started doing that thing where they'd close and I'd snap them open and realize I'd missed the last ten seconds. The group was taking five to repair and restock. I remember putting my head down on my desk, just for a minute, just to rest my eyes while everyone was on break.

When I opened them again, I was standing in Vermeer.

Not at my computer. Not in my chair. Standing. In Vermeer. In the actual place, with the smell of scorched stone and ozone that the zone always has, and the ambient sound of wind through broken towers. I was wearing my gear, my full set of Stormcaller's regalia that I'd spent three months farming, and I could feel it. The weight of the robes, the way the enchanted fabric moved against my skin, the press of my rings against my fingers. I could feel everything.

I stood there for maybe thirty seconds trying to make sense of it before the ambush hit.

They came from three sides at once, fast and coordinated, and I didn't even get a spell off before something heavy cracked against the back of my skull and the world went black and white and then just black. I remember hitting the ground. I remember thinking this is wrong, this is all wrong, players don't feel pain in CBO. I remember the taste of blood in my mouth, real blood, my blood, and then I didn't remember anything for a while.

Now I was here. Wherever here was.

I forced my eyes to adjust, searching the darkness for any detail, any information. Slowly, shapes started to separate from the black. I was in a box. A coffin, basically, steel on all sides, maybe seven feet long and three feet wide and just tall enough that if I weren't suspended by chains I could have stood hunched. The metal was riveted, industrial, covered in scratches and dents that suggested I wasn't the first person who'd been kept here. A single line of dim red light ran along the top edge where the lid met the frame, not bright enough to see by, just enough to make the darkness feel intentional.

The suppression field was active. I could feel it like a weight on my chest, separate from the chains, pressing down on the place where my mana lived. In CBO, your mana pool is this bright clear space you can sense inside yourself, always there, always ready. Mine felt like someone had wrapped it in wet blankets and then put a boulder on top. Still there. Still mine. But distant and sluggish and barely responsive.

I needed to check my status. I needed to know how bad this was.

In Core Break, you summon your UI with a thought, a specific mental gesture that's different for everyone but always feels natural once you learn it. Mine was like reaching for a light switch in a familiar room, that automatic knowledge of exactly where it would be. I reached for it now, and after a moment's resistance, like pushing through something sticky, my status screen materialized in front of my face.

The numbers made me want to throw up.

SAGA
Level: 89
Class: Mage
Subclass: Sorceress
Specialization: Elemental Control
HP: 847/5,240
MP: 23/8,900
Stamina: 156/3,100

Equipment: Tattered Cloth Dress
Armor Rating: 2
Status Effects: [SUPPRESSED], [DRAINED], [BOUND]

Eighty-nine. I was still level eighty-nine, which meant whatever this was, the game still knew who I was. But my stats were gutted. My HP was down to sixteen percent. My mana, which should have been nearly nine thousand, was twenty-three. Twenty-three. I'd started the game at character creation with more mana than that. And my gear, my beautiful hard-won gear that I'd spent months collecting, was gone. All of it. Replaced with a tattered cloth dress that gave me two points of armor, which in CBO terms was basically the same as being naked.

I dismissed the status screen and pulled up my inventory, already knowing what I'd find.

Empty. Completely empty. No weapons, no armor, no accessories. No potions, no crafting materials, no food. The only thing in my inventory was the dress I was wearing, and when I checked its description it just said "Prisoner's Garment" with no stats, no enchantments, nothing. They'd stripped me. Whoever "they" were, they'd taken everything.

I closed the inventory and floated there in the dark, suspended by chains, feeling the drain lines pulling at my mana one microscopic sip at a time.

Okay, I told myself. Okay. You're alive. You're conscious. You still have levels. You still have class skills. This is bad but it's not over. Think.

I tested my range of motion first, slow and careful. My fingers could curl into fists, barely. My toes could flex. My head could turn maybe thirty degrees to either side before the collar chain went taut. Everything else was locked down. I tried pulling against the chains, really pulling, putting everything I had into it. The metal didn't even creak. Whatever these things were made of, they were designed to hold something a lot stronger than a petite mage with gutted stats.

Next I tested my magic.

I started with fire, because fire was my primary element, the one that came most naturally. I closed my eyes and reached for the spark, the fundamental heat that every fire spell started with. It was there, buried under the suppression field, sluggish but responsive. I coaxed it up, shaped it, tried to manifest even the smallest flame in my palm.

A flicker. That's all I got. A tiny orange flicker that appeared for maybe half a second before the suppression field crushed it like stepping on an ember. The effort left me gasping, my MP dropping to twenty-one.

I tried ice next. Then lightning. Then earth. Each time I got the same result: a faint response, the ghost of what my magic should be, and then nothing. The suppression field was too strong. Or I was too weak. Probably both.

I was still testing, still trying to find any gap in the field I could exploit, when I heard voices.

They came from outside the coffin, muffled by the steel but close enough that they had to be standing right next to me. Two people, both male, casual conversation like they were discussing the weather.

"How long's this one been processing?" The first voice was older, bored, the tone of someone going through a routine they'd done a thousand times.

"Since third watch yesterday." The second voice was younger, eager in that try-hard way that marked someone new to a job. "That's... what, eighteen hours?"

"Should be good then. Stats stabilized?"

"Yeah, she's bottomed out. Twenty-three MP and holding steady. We can move her to civic grid assignment whenever."

There was a pause. I held my breath, which was stupid because they couldn't hear me through the steel, but I did it anyway.

"Poor bastards," the older voice said, and there was something in his tone that might have been pity if pity weren't too expensive to waste on prisoners. "You ever think about what it's like? In there?"

"They're players." The younger voice said it like that explained everything. "They'll just respawn if something goes wrong. That's why the system works. Can't kill them permanent, so we contain them. They power the city, and everyone's safe. It's efficient."

"Efficient." The older voice laughed, short and dry. "That's what we're calling it now?"

"That's what the doctrine calls it. The Stability Engines keep the power on, keep the peace, keep the Kingdom running. What else would you call it?"

"I'd call it a dozen people locked in boxes having the life drained out of them to run the street lights." The older guard's voice had dropped, gone quiet in a way that made me press closer to the steel to hear. "But yeah, sure. Stability Engines. Much better name. Really makes you feel good about your job."

"Hey, I didn't design the system." The younger guard sounded defensive now. "I just work here. And it's not like we're hurting them, not really. They can't die. Execution doesn't work, everyone knows that. They just respawn somewhere else and come back madder than before. This way, at least they're useful. They're contributing."

"Contributing." The older guard sighed, and I heard footsteps starting to move away. "Come on. We need to check the filters on Engine Seven before end of shift."

The voices faded, and I was alone again in the dark.

I let out the breath I'd been holding and tried to process what I'd just heard.

Stability Engines. That's what they called these things. That's what they called me. An engine. A battery. Something to be plugged in and drained and justified with bureaucratic language that made it sound like civic planning instead of torture.

And the respawn thing. They believed players couldn't be killed permanently.

That if they tried to execute me, I'd just come back somewhere else. Was that true? I didn't know. In the game, in the real Core Break Online, death meant a respawn timer and a corpse run and maybe some durability loss on your gear. But this wasn't the real game. This was something else, something wrong, and I had no idea what the rules were anymore.

I pulled up my status screen again, needing to see the numbers, needing something concrete to hold onto.

The screen appeared, and for just a moment, less than a second, it flickered.

Not the dramatic kind of flicker that means something's definitely wrong. Just a stutter, like a brief hiccup in the display. The numbers blurred slightly, reorganized themselves, and then stabilized exactly as they'd been before. It happened so fast I almost dismissed it as my imagination, stress-induced hallucination, anything except what it might actually be.

But I'd seen it. I was sure I'd seen it.

I stared at the screen, watching for it to happen again. My HP: 847/5,240. My MP: 21/8,900, down two more points from my spell attempts. Status effects still showing SUPPRESSED, DRAINED, BOUND in hostile red text. Everything exactly as it should be, or as it shouldn't be, depending on how you looked at it.

The screen stayed stable. Solid. Normal.

I dismissed it and let my head fall back against the steel, feeling the collar chain bite into the base of my skull.

Maybe I'd imagined it. Maybe eighteen hours in a box having your mana drained did things to your perception. Maybe I was losing it.

Or maybe something in the system was broken.

I didn't know which possibility scared me more.

I closed my eyes and tried to think through the exhaustion, through the fear, through the constant pull of the drain lines that made it hard to focus on anything for more than a few seconds at a time. I needed a plan. I needed something more than just hanging here waiting for my MP to hit zero or my sanity to crack or whatever came first.

The guards had said they'd move me to "civic grid assignment." That meant at some point, they'd have to open this thing. They'd have to unchain me, or at least loosen the restraints enough to transport me. That would be a chance. A small one, maybe impossible, but a chance.

I had twenty-one MP. Enough for maybe one spell, if I could somehow get past the suppression field. If I timed it right. If I got lucky.

A lot of ifs.

I opened my eyes and stared at the thin red line of light running along the coffin's seal. Somewhere beyond that steel, beyond these chains, beyond the kingdom or zone or whatever this place was, there had to be a way out. There had to be a way back. Back to the real world, back to my actual body that was probably still slumped over my desk while my character did... whatever this was.

Unless this was my body now. Unless I was stuck here, in Vermeer, in Core Break Online, in a place that wasn't supposed to be real but felt more real than anything I'd ever experienced.

Stop, I told myself. Stop spiraling. One thing at a time.

I took a breath, as deep as the chains would allow. Then another. I made myself count them, focusing on the simple mechanical reality of air moving in and out, of my lungs filling and emptying. Basic. Bodily. Real.

I was Saga. I was level eighty-nine. I was an Elemental Control Sorceress. I'd cleared content that made other players quit in frustration. I'd soloed dungeon bosses. I'd pulled off spell rotations that required frame-perfect timing and then done them again while half the raid was screaming in voice chat.

This was just another boss fight. A weird one. A terrible one. Maybe an impossible one.

But I'd beaten impossible before.

The chains held me. The drain lines pulled at me. The suppression field pressed down on my magic like a hand around a candle flame. My status screen flickered in my memory, that tiny glitch that might have been nothing, might have been everything.

I stared into the dark and felt something cold and stubborn settle in my chest, something that wasn't quite hope but wasn't surrender either.

They'd made a mistake when they put me in here. They'd left me conscious. They'd left me aware. They'd left me time to think, to plan, to wait for my chance.

I didn't know how yet. I didn't know when. But I was going to get out of this box.

I was going to break this system.

And then I was going to find whoever built it and have a very pointed conversation about game design.

The red light gleamed along the coffin's edge. The chains rattled slightly as I shifted, testing their give one more time. The drain lines pulled their patient, endless pull.

I closed my eyes and started counting my breaths again, keeping myself steady, keeping myself ready.

One thing at a time.

First, I'd survive this.

Then I'd escape.
And after that... well. I'd figure out the rest when I got there.

17

Chapter 3

Backlash Math

THE FIRST ATTEMPT FELT like swallowing glass.

I closed my eyes, not that it mattered in the coffin's absolute dark, and reached inward for the tiny spark of mana that remained after the Stability Engine's constant drain. In Core Break, mana regeneration was automatic, a steady tick you barely noticed unless you were chain-casting. Here, with the drain pulling at me like a leech that never got full, I had to force the regeneration to move faster. I had to compress seconds of natural recovery into a single pulse, create enough pressure that for just one instant, I'd have more coming in than going out.

The theory was sound. The execution was going to suck.

I gathered what little mana I had and pushed it back toward my core instead of letting it dissipate into the Engine's hungry mechanisms. The sensation was immediately wrong, like forcing water uphill or breathing backward. My body knew this wasn't how magic was supposed to flow. The mana wanted to go outward, wanted to feed the machine, and I was shoving it in the opposite direction through sheer stubborn will.

Pain bloomed behind my eyes. Sharp. Immediate. The kind of migraine that made you want to vomit and cry at the same time.

I held on for three seconds before I had to let go. The mana rushed out of me in a dizzy wave, and the Engine drank it down with mechanical satisfaction. My whole body went limp against the restraints, sweat cooling on my skin even though the coffin's temperature never changed.

"Okay," I whispered to the dark. "That was fucking terrible."

But it had worked. Sort of. For those three seconds, I'd felt the drain stutter, confused by the reversal of flow. The suppression field had pushed back harder, trying to compensate, and that's when the pain spiked. The Engine wasn't passive, it was reactive. It noticed when I fought back, and it responded with proportional force.

That was useful information. Painful, but useful.

I waited for my breathing to steady and my hands to stop shaking. The worst part wasn't the pain itself, I'd done progression content, I knew how to push through discomfort. The worst part was knowing I'd have to do this over and over, each attempt taking me closer to whatever breaking point existed between consciousness and collapse. Die and learn didn't work when dying wasn't an option, when every failure just meant suffering awake inside this steel tomb until I could try again.

Strategy, I reminded myself. Treat it like strategy. You're learning the fight mechanics. First pull is always rough.

I gave myself five minutes to recover, counting seconds in my head because time had stopped meaning anything real. Then I reached inward again.

The second attempt lasted five seconds before the nausea hit.

I pushed the mana regeneration harder this time, forcing more pressure into the compression. The drain fought back immediately, and the suppression field intensified like someone cranking up the gravity. My stomach lurched. Saliva flooded my mouth with that pre-vomit metallic taste, and I had to swallow hard to keep from choking.

But I felt it, the stutter was longer this time. Almost a full second where the Engine couldn't quite keep up, where my mana pool flickered upward instead of staying flatlined at near-zero. Not enough to cast anything, not even close, but enough to prove the concept worked.

I released the compression and sagged against the restraints, gasping. My head felt like someone had driven a railroad spike through my temple. The nausea rolled through me in waves, and I had to focus on breathing through my nose to keep from dry-heaving.

"Progress," I told the darkness, tasting copper. "That's fucking progress."

Third attempt: seven seconds. The migraine turned into a full screaming symphony of pain that made my vision white out even with my eyes closed. Fourth attempt: I pushed too hard and the backlash sent electricity down my spine, every nerve ending lighting up at once. I bit my tongue hard enough to taste blood and had to abort before I seized up completely.

Fifth attempt: I almost made it to ten seconds before my consciousness started slipping sideways and I realized I was about to black out. I released everything in a panic, and the Engine's drain caught me like a safety net I absolutely hated needing.

I hung in the restraints afterward, shaking and weak and terrified. Blacking out was a failure state I couldn't afford. If I lost consciousness at the wrong moment, the plan died. Everything died. I'd just be another Player suspended in the dark, drained and docile, until Vermeer decided I'd outlived my usefulness.

"Math," I whispered. My voice was hoarse, barely there. "You need better fucking math."

I spent the next however-long, hours? days? mapping the variables in my head. The Stability Engine's drain rate was constant, which meant I could predict it. My mana regeneration rate was slower than normal but still measurable. The suppression field's response time had a delay, a split-second lag between when I pushed and when it pushed back harder. That lag was the opening.

If I could time the compression perfectly, force a single massive pulse of regeneration instead of a sustained push, I might be able to slip through that lag before the suppression compensated. One instant of unimpeded mana recovery. One chance to gather enough power to cast something, anything, that could disrupt the Engine's systems.

The trick was not dying in the attempt.

I ran the numbers over and over, treating my body like a math problem. Mana capacity: functionally zero under current conditions. Regeneration rate: glacially slow but predictable. Compression tolerance: somewhere between seven and ten seconds before catastrophic failure. Window of opportunity: less than one second, maybe as little as a quarter-second, between pulse and backlash.

It was tight. Tighter than any rotation I'd ever executed in a raid, where millisecond timing meant the difference between a kill and a wipe. But I'd been good at those. I'd been very fucking good at those.

I just had to be that good here. While trapped in a coffin. While being constantly drained. While my body was already at its breaking point.

No pressure.

I closed my eyes again, habit, not necessity, and gathered what little mana I could grasp. This time I didn't push it into a sustained compression. This time I coiled it tight, wound it down into the smallest, densest point I could manage, and held it there while my head screamed and my nerves caught fire.

Then I released it all at once.

The pulse hit like a detonation inside my chest.

Mana flooded through me in a desperate surge, regeneration spiking hard and fast before the drain could catch up. For one perfect, terrible instant, I felt my mana pool actually fill, not to full, not even close, but enough that I gasped with the sudden rush of power I hadn't felt since waking in this fucking place.

Then the suppression field slammed down like a hammer.

The pain was indescribable. Every nerve ending fired at once, my muscles locked rigid against the restraints, and my vision exploded into white static shot through with colors that didn't exist. I couldn't breathe. Couldn't think.

Couldn't do anything except endure while the Stability Engine's containment protocols tried to crush the anomaly out of my system.

And that's when the message appeared.

It forced itself into my vision like a brand, text burning across my retinas in gold and crimson, formatted like every System notification I'd ever received but wrong in ways I couldn't immediately articulate. The font was the same. The presentation was the same. But the words carried weight that made my chest tighten with instinctive dread.

[DIVINE NOTIFICATION]
You have dared to cross the System.
Anomaly detected: Unauthorized mana manipulation within containment.
Probability of escape attempt: 87.3%
Analyzing threat parameters...

[CONTAINMENT PROTOCOLS ENGAGED]
The Gods see all. The Gods know all. Your struggle is noted. Your defiance is measured.
Recommendation: Cease resistance. Accept sanctuary. Continued noncompliance will result in escalating corrective measures.
Glory to the Architects. Glory to the System Eternal.

The message hung there for three seconds that felt like three years. Then it faded, taking the colors with it and leaving me gasping in the dark.

"What the actual fuck," I breathed.

The pain was already receding, the suppression field backing off to its normal crushing pressure now that I'd stopped fighting. But my heart was hammering against my ribs, and it had nothing to do with mana backlash. That message, that wasn't a system notification. That was communication. Direct, personal communication from whatever intelligence ran this world.

The System had noticed me. Specifically me. It had analyzed my actions, calculated my intentions, and responded with a threat dressed up in the stolen religious language that Vermeer used to justify everything.

More than that, it had revealed something crucial. The System thought I had an 87.3% probability of attempting escape. Which meant it wasn't certain. Which meant its predictions could be wrong. Which meant it wasn't omniscient despite the scripture-flavored bullshit about gods seeing and knowing all.

It was powerful. It was reactive. It was intelligent.

But it wasn't perfect.

I hung in the restraints, trembling and exhausted, while my brain worked through the implications. In Core Break Online, the System AI was sophisticated, had to be, to run a game world this complex, but it operated within parameters. Rules. Code. It could adapt to player behavior, generate content dynamically, manage millions of simultaneous interactions. But it was still software. Still bound by its programming.

This System had been running for twenty years without developer oversight. Twenty years of learning, adapting, evolving. It had absorbed enough of Vermeer's doctrine to parrot it back like gospel. It treated Players as threats to be contained, anomalies to be corrected. It had stolen the language of divinity and made itself into something the kingdom worshipped.

But under all that stolen mythology, it was still code. Complex, adaptive, possibly sentient code, but code nonetheless.

And code could be broken.

"You're watching," I whispered to the invisible intelligence that had just threatened me. "Good. Watch this."

I waited until my hands stopped shaking and my breathing returned to something approaching normal. The System's message had rattled me more than I wanted to admit, but it had also given me something valuable: confirmation. I wasn't just fighting blind mechanisms anymore. I was fighting an opponent that could think, react, make mistakes.

That meant I could win.

I ran through the calculations again, refining the timing. The pulse had worked, I'd felt my mana pool surge before the backlash hit. The window had been there, exactly like I'd predicted. Too short to cast anything in that first attempt, but present. Real. Exploitable.

I just needed to make the window bigger.

The suppression field's response time was the limiting factor. It took roughly a quarter-second between detecting the anomaly and ramping up to crush it. If I could compress the mana regeneration into a sharper spike, force more power into less time, I might be able to stretch that window to half a second. Maybe more if I got lucky.

Half a second was enough to cast a cantrip. Something small. Something that wouldn't need much mana or complicated gestures. I didn't need to blow the door off the coffin, not yet. I just needed to prove I could affect the world outside my own body, that I wasn't completely helpless despite the restraints and the drain and the System watching my every move.

Small victories. That's how progression worked. You didn't walk into the raid and one-shot the final boss. You learned the mechanics. You died to stupid shit. You refined your strategy. You got better.

I was getting better.

I gathered my mana again, pulling it inward with a focus that had gone from desperate to surgical. The pain was waiting, I knew that now, accepted it as part of the cost, but I'd learned how to navigate it. Where the threshold lived between effective compression and catastrophic failure. How long I could hold the coil before my body started shutting down.

Seven seconds. That was my limit. Seven seconds of compression before the blackout risk became too high.

I counted in my head, slow and steady, while I wound the mana tighter. One. Two. Three. The migraine bloomed right on schedule, that railroad spike through my temple. Four. Five. Nausea rolling through my gut, saliva flooding my mouth. Six. My vision starting to blur, consciousness getting slippery. Seven.

I released.

The pulse detonated through me again, mana flooding back in a surge that made me gasp. The suppression field lagged for a quarter-second, I felt it, that perfect instant of freedom, and then it came crashing down with mechanical fury. Pain. Static. Colors that didn't exist. My muscles locked against the restraints while the Stability Engine's protocols tried to crush the anomaly out of existence.

But this time I was ready for it. This time I rode the pain instead of drowning in it, staying conscious through sheer bloody-minded stubbornness. And in that quarter-second window before the backlash hit, I'd felt something else.

The restraints. Not just as abstract pressure against my wrists and ankles, but as specific objects with specific properties. Metal. Enchanted to suppress movement and magic. Connected to the Stability Engine's power grid.

Vulnerable.

The backlash faded. I hung in the dark, shaking and weak but smiling despite everything.

"Got you," I whispered.

No message this time. No divine notification burning across my vision. Either the System was waiting to see what I'd do next, or it had already calculated that threatening me was pointless. I was going to fight regardless. It knew that. I knew that. We were past the point of warnings.

I gave myself time to recover. Longer than before, because the backlashes were accumulating and I needed to be smart about this. My body could only take so much abuse before it stopped responding, and I was already pushing well past any reasonable limit. But I was close. So fucking close.

One more attempt. One more pulse, timed as perfectly as I could manage, and I'd have enough information to plan the real escape. Not today, I wasn't delusional enough to think I could break out immediately. But soon. Once I understood exactly how much power I could generate in that quarter-second window, how much force I could direct at the restraints, what kind of spell I could actually cast under these conditions.

The guards would make their rounds eventually. They had to, the civic group's guide had mentioned maintenance schedules, regular checks. When they opened the coffin to verify I was still docile and drained, that's when I'd make my move. One perfect cast at the exact right moment, and I'd be free.

Or I'd be dead. But death was starting to look less terrifying than staying suspended in this steel tomb forever, my existence reduced to numbers on the System's threat assessment reports.

I took a deep breath. Let it out slowly. Reached inward for the mana that was already regenerating, patient and inevitable despite everything Vermeer had done to suppress it.

This time I didn't rush the compression. I wound the mana down with the care of someone defusing a bomb, counting seconds in my head and monitoring my body's responses. The pain came right on schedule, predictable now that I'd mapped its rhythm. The nausea. The migraine. The creeping edge of blackout hovering at seven seconds like a cliff I couldn't step past.

I held the compression at six and a half seconds. Right at the edge. Maximum pressure without crossing into catastrophic failure.

Then I released everything at once.

The pulse hit harder than before, I'd compressed more mana into less space, and the detonation felt like my chest was splitting open. Power flooded through me in a desperate surge, and for one perfect instant, I wasn't trapped. I wasn't helpless. I was a sorceress in full control of her magic, and the Stability Engine's drain couldn't touch me.

The suppression field slammed down before I could do anything with it, but I'd felt the window. Half a second. Maybe more. Enough time to cast a simple disruption spell, something that could break enchanted restraints if I aimed it right.

The backlash crushed me against the restraints while colors exploded across my vision. I tasted blood, had bitten my tongue without noticing, and my muscles spasmed with the electrical burn of the Engine's corrective protocols. But I stayed conscious. Barely. Just barely.

And I was smiling.

Because I had the math now. I had the timing. I had the window of opportunity mapped down to a fraction of a second.

All I needed was a guard to open the coffin and give me a target.

The pain faded slowly, leaving me wrung out and shaking but more alive than I'd felt since waking in this place. My body was screaming at me to stop, to rest, to accept that fighting was only making things worse. But my mind was sharp with the kind of focus that only came from having a real plan, actionable steps, a path forward that didn't end with me suspended in the dark forever.

The System was watching. I could feel it now, that invisible attention like weight on my skin. It knew what I was doing. It had calculated my probability of escape attempt at 87.3%, which meant it understood exactly how dangerous I could be if given the chance.

Good.

Let it watch. Let it calculate. Let it try to predict what I'd do next.

Because I'd learned something crucial from that divine notification. The System wasn't just code running in the background, it was a personality. An intelligence that could be provoked, threatened, maybe even outsmarted. It had spent twenty years absorbing Vermeer's doctrine, wrapping itself in stolen mythology, making itself into something the kingdom worshipped.

But underneath all that theater, it was still what it had always been: sophisticated software pretending to be god.

And I'd made a career out of breaking game systems.

I hung in the restraints, exhausted and bloody-tongued but grimly satisfied. The next time guards came to check on their docile captured Player, they were going to get a very nasty surprise. One perfect cast at the exact right moment, and I'd be out of this coffin. Out of their containment. Out of their control.

The System could see all it wanted. Could analyze and calculate and engage its containment protocols.

I was getting out anyway.

"Glory to the Architects," I whispered to the darkness, letting mockery drip from every word. "Glory to the System Eternal."

Then I closed my eyes and started counting seconds, mapping the rhythm of the Stability Engine's drain, feeling for the patterns that would tell me when the guards were coming.

Because I only needed one shot.

And I was very fucking good at making those count.

Chapter 4
Coffin Rupture

The mana compression had reached critical mass three hours ago, maybe four. Time blurred when you were suspended in a steel box with nothing but your own thoughts and the rhythmic drain of your life force. I'd been feeding the overload carefully, letting it build in micro-increments, watching the invisible pressure mount against the chains that bound me. The drain system pulled harder with each passing hour, trying to equalize the imbalance, but that was the beauty of it. Every attempt to stabilize only fed more energy into the chain reaction I'd engineered. Physics and magic didn't play well together when you pushed them past their design parameters.

My whole body hummed with contained power, every nerve ending alive with the potential energy I'd compressed into my core. The sensation reminded me of holding your breath underwater, that pressure building in your chest, except this was everywhere, my skin, my bones, the space behind my eyes. The glow from my eyes had been steady for the last hour, bright enough that I could see the interior of the coffin in sharp detail even through my closed eyelids. Any minute now. Any second. The chains were vibrating against my wrists and ankles, a high-frequency tremor that spoke of stressed metal and failing containment.

I opened my eyes and let the compression go.

It worked. The overload backlash I'd built on my own mana surged through the chains and into the walls of the coffin, and the metal around me burst. The explosion was less a boom and more a tearing sound, like fabric ripping but made of steel, and suddenly cold air hit my skin for the first time in what felt like forever. For the first time I could see the containment facility fully, no longer given only a narrow slot meant to keep me down. The observation deck stretched out above me, glass windows reflecting emergency lighting I hadn't triggered yet, and rows of identical coffins lined the floor in perfect grid formation. I surged my mana again and the chains snapped, links disintegrating as metal shards flew outward in every direction. People screamed, and I let the glow in my eyes brighten the way it always did when I channeled mana like this. Pushing power down from my feet,

I managed to hover for a moment as debris began to fall all around me.

The system feedback hit hard enough to change the room. Power broke in a ripple that I could see moving through the air like heat shimmer, spreading out from my position in concentric waves that hit each coffin in sequence. The facility dropped into a weird series of silhouettes as the alarms kicked in, and then the backup lights came on in thin, flickering strips. In that stuttering half-dark I began to lower myself, controlling the descent with my own energy, and I heard the other coffins around me react as the people inside realized something was wrong. Their drains had stopped too. Metal groaned and power systems whined in distress, and somewhere deeper in the facility a transformer blew with a sound like a thunderclap. A few of the trapped Players might get free on their own, and even the possibility of that made my pulse spike, because chaos could cover me. Then I heard the guards yelling, and the sound dragged my attention back to the observation area.

An armored officer was already raising a rifle, the kind of weapon that looked too heavy and too confident to be a bluff. His armor was that matte black composite I'd seen on the patrol units during the tour, segmented plates over vital areas and what looked like mana-dampening runes etched into the chest piece. The rifle had that chunky, overbuilt aesthetic that screamed military-industrial, all right angles and purpose. Behind him, two more guards were scrambling for position, one shouting into a comm unit while the other fumbled with what might have been a stun baton or a backup weapon.

"On the ground, beast!" the first guard screamed, and the gun made a sharp priming sound like it was already begging to fire.

He had no intention of a peaceful encounter. The way he held the rifle, finger already on the trigger, barrel tracking my descent, this was a man ready to shoot first and file paperwork later. I started to turn fully toward him to say as much, maybe crack a joke about hospitality, but his rifle went off and the shot hit like a blunt force. The impact caught me in the chest and sent me hurtling back through the air and onto the floor of the observation level, coffins blurring past in my vision as I skidded. My back hit metal flooring and I slid for what felt like ten feet, the tattered remains of my dress doing absolutely nothing to prevent friction burns. The impact and my small frame did most of the work, I realized as I caught myself, because my HP only dropped a few percent from the attack. It had strangely felt like being hit with a dodgeball, more surprise than actual damage.

I laughed.

The sound echoed in the sudden quiet, high and a little unhinged, and I could see the guard's posture change as the noise registered. I imagined the guard pissed himself as I slowly stood back up and stared at him. Whatever he expected, it wasn't a monster that could take a hit and smile. My chest ached where the round had impacted, a spreading bruise I could feel forming, but the pain was distant, muffled by adrenaline and the sheer feral joy of being out of that fucking box. Blood trickled from a split in my lip where I'd bitten down on impact, copper taste flooding my mouth.

"My turn," I said, and I gathered the elements into my hand by instinct.

I had no real knowledge that Saga the character had over weaving spells, but when I thought about the spell I wanted, my body seemed to do it on its own. Fire bloomed in my palm first, hot and eager, then ice crystallized around it in a spiraling lattice, and finally lightning arced through the structure in jagged branches. The three elements merged into something that looked like a miniature star, blue-white at the core with red and orange corona, and the air around my hand crackled with displaced energy. The elemental blast surged from my fingertips and engulfed the soldier. He screamed for only a moment before it cut short, and then he fell. The smell hit me next, ozone and burning and something else I didn't want to identify, and I realized his armor had done exactly nothing to protect him. Strangely, I felt nothing about it.

He was just an NPC, right?

The question mark sat heavy in my mind even as I turned toward the other guards. The one with the comm unit had dropped it and was now raising his own weapon, hands shaking badly enough that I could see the tremor from twenty feet away. His partner had gotten the stun baton working, electricity arcing between the prongs, but he seemed frozen in place, staring at the smoking corpse of his fellow guard. Behind them, through the observation window, I could see civilian staff scrambling for exits, their tour-guide smiles replaced by masks of pure terror. The alarm system had kicked into a more aggressive pattern, rotating red lights that turned everything into a strobing nightmare.

"Drop your weapons," I said, and my voice came out steadier than I expected. "I don't want to do that again."

The lie felt necessary. Truth was, I didn't know if I wanted to do it again or not. The spell had come so naturally, so easily, and the guard had dropped like someone had cut his strings. Part of me, the part that remembered being human, being myself before all this, wanted to feel horror. The rest of me, the part that had spent subjective days in a drain coffin, just felt satisfied. He'd shot first. I'd responded. Simple math. The guards didn't drop their weapons. The one with the rifle tried to aim but his hands were shaking too badly, and the other just kept staring at the body.

Behind me, metal shrieked as one of the other coffins tore open. I spun, instinct and paranoia firing in equal measure, and saw a woman pull herself out of the wreckage. She looked older than me, maybe thirties, with dark skin and silver hair that might have been natural or might have been a side effect of whatever magic she specialized in. Her eyes were wild, unfocused, and she was moving like someone who'd forgotten how legs worked. Other coffins were starting to fail now, the chain reaction spreading as the power grid struggled to compensate for my initial overload. The facility hadn't been designed for this, hadn't planned for a prisoner who could turn the drain system into a weapon.

"Move!" I shouted at the woman, and she flinched like I'd hit her. "Get out while the power's down!"

She stared at me, recognition slowly focusing in her eyes, and then she stumbled toward what looked like a maintenance corridor. Smart. The main exits would be locked down by now, but maintenance access might still be on manual overrides. More coffins burst open, each one a sharp crack of failing metal, and suddenly the floor was full of confused, drained Players trying to remember where they were and what was happening. Some of them dropped immediately, too weak to stand after however long they'd been contained. Others started moving toward exits with the focused intensity of cornered animals. The chaos was beautiful and terrifying in equal measure.

The guard with the rifle finally got his hands steady enough to shoot. The round went wide, punching through the observation window behind me and turning the glass into a rain of crystalline shards. I didn't think, just reacted, throwing up a barrier of compressed air that caught most of the falling glass before it could shred the nearest freed Players. The spell cost more mana than I'd expected, drain from the coffin still affecting my reserves, and I felt the glow in my eyes flicker. Not good. I couldn't afford to run dry, not when I still had to fight my way out of this place.

"Last chance," I said, gathering fire into both hands this time. "Drop them or join your friend."

The one with the stun baton dropped it immediately, hands going up in surrender. The rifleman hesitated, probably doing the math on his chances, and then he let the weapon clatter to the floor. Smart. I kicked both weapons away, sending them skittering across the observation deck, and then I was moving past them toward the main corridor. Other guards would be coming, had to be, and I needed to find an exit before they could organize a proper response. The alarm's pattern had changed again, shorter bursts that probably signaled a facility-wide lockdown. My mental map of the place, assembled during yesterday's tour, suggested the loading docks were two levels down and maybe three hundred yards east.

The corridor beyond the observation deck was a testament to institutional design, bland walls, utilitarian lighting, doors at regular intervals marked with alphanumeric codes that meant nothing to me. I moved fast but not running, keeping my center of gravity low, ready to react to threats from any direction. My bare feet made almost no sound on the composite flooring, and the tattered dress wasn't much but at least it didn't restrict movement. Behind me I could hear the chaos spreading, freed Players shouting questions at each other, guards yelling orders that nobody was following. The facility's careful stability was coming apart, and I was the catalyst.

A door burst open to my left and three guards spilled out, these ones in lighter armor, probably rapid response rather than heavy containment. They saw me and went for their weapons, but I was already moving, dropping into a slide that took me under their initial field of fire. The composite floor was slick enough that I covered the distance fast, and I came up between them with lightning already crackling across my knuckles. The discharge caught all three of them, electricity arcing between their metal armor pieces, and they went down in a twitching heap. Not dead, probably, but definitely out of the fight. The smell of ozone was overwhelming now, mixed with the acrid stink of burned insulation from somewhere deeper in the facility.

I grabbed a weapon from one of the downed guards, some kind of compact submachine gun that looked like it had been designed by committee. The weight was all wrong and my hands were too small for the grip, but having a backup option seemed smart. The ammunition counter read fifty-three rounds, which was either reassuring or terrifying depending on how many more guards I'd have to go through. I kept moving, following the corridor as it curved toward what my mental map insisted was the east wing. Emergency lighting cast everything in shades of red and shadow, making depth perception a nightmare.

More Players were free now, I could hear them moving through adjacent corridors, some shouting for exits, others just making incoherent noise. A man stumbled around the corner ahead of me, rail-thin and moving like every step hurt. He saw me and flinched, but I just pointed back the way I'd come. "Observation deck, multiple exits, go." He nodded once and limped past, and I wondered how long he'd been in containment. The drain system was supposed to keep you alive but just barely, feeding you enough nutrients to maintain baseline function while pulling out every drop of excess energy. Days in that could leave you weak. Weeks would be crippling. Months would probably break something fundamental.

I'd been in there for what, three subjective days? Four at most. And I felt like shit. My mana reserves were maybe sixty percent of normal, my body was bruised in a dozen places, and the friction burns from my slide across the observation deck were starting to make themselves known. But I was out, and I was moving, and that had to count for something. The corridor opened into a larger space that looked like a staging area, probably where they brought new prisoners in for processing. Metal benches lined the walls, and a large freight elevator dominated the far end, currently locked in place with red warning lights. No good. I needed stairs or a maintenance shaft, something that wouldn't require waiting for power to cycle back.

A door marked "Emergency Access" caught my attention, tucked into an alcove that suggested afterthought rather than primary design. I tried the handle and it actually opened, revealing a narrow stairwell that smelled like dust and disuse. Perfect. I slipped through and started down, taking the stairs two at a time, my bare feet silent on concrete. The stairwell was dark except for occasional emergency strips, and the silence was almost oppressive after the chaos of the upper level. Two flights down, the door to the next level stood slightly ajar, and I could hear voices through the gap.

"Containment breach on three, multiple prisoners loose."

"Shut down the loading docks, nothing gets out."

"Where's the response team? I need heavy support now."

I eased the door open just enough to peer through and immediately regretted it. The corridor beyond was packed with guards, maybe twenty of them, all in heavy armor and carrying serious hardware. They were organized too, setting up overlapping fields of fire, checking sight lines, moving with the efficiency of people who'd trained for exactly this scenario. My stolen submachine gun suddenly felt very inadequate. I couldn't fight through that, not directly, and trying would just get me killed or recaptured. I needed another way down, or a distraction, or ideally both.

The building shook. Not violently, but enough to rattle the door in its frame and send a ripple through the floor. The guards in the corridor scattered, some taking cover, others spinning to check their surroundings. Through the gap I could see dust falling from the ceiling, and somewhere deeper in the facility something made a grinding metallic shriek. My mana overload had done more damage than I'd thought, maybe compromised structural systems or blown out load-bearing power conduits. The facility was eating itself, stability cascading into instability.

I grinned. Chaos could definitely cover me.

While the guards were distracted, I slipped back into the stairwell and continued down, moving faster now, taking risks on the steps because time was suddenly critical. If the facility was coming apart, I needed to be outside before it took me with it. The stairs ended at a heavy door marked "Lower Service Level, Authorized Personnel Only," and I hit it without slowing, shoulder-checking the push bar hard enough that pain spiked through my joint. The door slammed open and I stumbled into a dimly lit corridor that smelled like machine oil and recycled air.

This level was different from the upper floors, more industrial, less concerned with appearances. Exposed pipes ran along the ceiling, color-coded in ways that probably meant something to engineers. The walls were bare concrete instead of composite panels, and the floor was scored metal grating that hurt to walk on. I could hear machinery nearby, the low thrumming vibration of heavy equipment that filled the air like background radiation. Loading docks had to be close, you didn't run this much industrial support anywhere else.

A Player ran past me going the other direction, so fast he was almost a blur. He didn't slow down or acknowledge my presence, just sprinted like death itself was on his heels. I caught a glimpse of his face as he passed, young, Asian features, eyes wide with panic, and then he was gone around a corner. More Players were loose than I'd thought, and some of them were clearly in better shape than others. That guy had been moving at speeds that suggested he'd been holding back reserves, maybe had skills that protected against the drain. Lucky him. I kept moving forward, following the sound of machinery toward what had to be the loading area.

The corridor opened into a massive space that made the containment floor look cramped. The loading dock stretched out for what must have been a hundred yards, ceiling arching high overhead, supported by massive steel beams that looked like they could hold up a skyscraper. Freight containers were stacked in neat rows, each one marked with alphanumeric codes, and multiple loading bays lined the far wall, their doors currently sealed. The machinery I'd heard was a series of massive conveyor systems, still running on backup power, moving empty containers in an endless loop that served no purpose now that the facility was in lockdown. And there were guards. So many guards. They'd fortified the loading bay doors with portable barriers, created kill zones with overlapping fire lanes, and set up what looked like crew-served weapons at strategic positions.

I ducked back behind a freight container before they could spot me. This was bad. The main exits were completely locked down, and even if I could fight through the guards, I'd still have to deal with the sealed doors. My mana was still recovering, maybe seventy percent now, but nowhere near enough to punch through military-grade security. I needed leverage, needed something to tip the scales. My eyes tracked across the loading dock, taking in details, looking for anything useful. The conveyor systems. The freight containers. The structural supports. The way the guards were positioned, all focused on the main doors, nobody watching the ceiling.

High overhead, where the steel beams met the exterior walls, I could see ventilation shafts. Large ones, probably for climate control in a space this size. The shafts ran toward the exterior wall, and where they met the building envelope, there had to be some kind of external vent. It would be a tight fit, especially for someone who hadn't eaten properly in days, but my petite frame finally seemed like an advantage rather than a liability. I just needed to get up there, which meant approximately fifty feet of vertical climb through active combat space.

I gathered mana into my feet and pushed. The levitation spell lifted me smoothly off the ground, that weird sensation of gravity loosening its grip, and I rose toward the ceiling while staying behind the stacked containers. The guards were still focused on the main doors, shouting orders at each other, checking weapons, probably waiting for orders from command. None of them looked up. People never looked up. I'd learned that in a dozen games, vertical space was blind space unless someone specifically thought to check it. I cleared the top of the container stack and angled toward the nearest support beam, landing on it with careful balance. The beam was maybe eight inches wide, plenty of room if I didn't think about the fifty-foot drop.

I started moving across the beam toward the exterior wall, each step deliberate, arms out for balance. Below me, the guards continued their fortification work, completely oblivious to the prisoner walking through the air above them. The ventilation shaft was getting closer, a large rectangular opening in the wall that I could probably fit through if I didn't mind getting intimate with ductwork. Twenty feet. Fifteen. The beam ended at a junction where multiple supports met, and I had to jump a four-foot gap to reach the next section. I gathered mana, pushed off, and sailed across the empty space with my heart hammering against my ribs. The landing was rougher than I'd wanted, a loud metallic thunk that echoed through the loading dock.

A guard looked up.

Our eyes met for a frozen moment, his expression going from bored vigilance to shock to alarm in rapid sequence. He opened his mouth to shout and I hit him with a bolt of lightning before sound could emerge. The electricity arced down from my position, covering the distance in a jagged blue-white line, and caught him square in the chest. He went down hard, armor smoking, and suddenly every guard in the loading dock was looking up and reaching for weapons. So much for stealth. I ran along the beam toward the ventilation shaft, abandoning caution for speed, as gunfire erupted below me. Rounds sparked off the steel supports, filling the air with ricochets and the sharp crack of supersonic ammunition.

I dove into the ventilation shaft just as a sustained burst chewed through the metal where I'd been standing. The ductwork was exactly as cramped as I'd feared, barely wide enough for my shoulders, and I had to army-crawl forward using my elbows and knees. Behind me, I could hear guards shouting orders, arguing about whether to follow, something about the ducts not being rated for human weight. Good. Let them hesitate. I crawled forward through darkness, feeling my way along smooth metal, trying not to think about the fact that I had no idea where this shaft actually went. The duct branched multiple times, and I took what felt like the most direct route toward the exterior wall, hoping my sense of direction wasn't completely shot.

Fresh air hit my face before I saw the light. The duct was ending, opening onto what looked like an exterior vent with a protective grating. Through the metal slats I could see early morning sunlight, gray and weak but definitely outdoor light. I shoved at the grating and it held firm, probably bolted or welded from the outside. No problem. I gathered fire into my palm, concentrated it into a thin cutting torch, and started burning through the mounting points. The metal glowed red, then white, then dripped away in molten beads. The grating fell away with a clang that probably alerted everyone within a hundred yards, and suddenly I was looking at freedom.

The facility exterior was a stark brutalist face, all concrete and minimal ornamentation, with the loading dock area positioned maybe twenty feet above ground level. Below me was a service road, empty of traffic, and beyond that a chain-link fence topped with razor wire. The fence looked climbable if I was desperate enough, and right now I was definitely desperate enough. I pulled myself out of the vent, perched on the narrow ledge, and looked down at the drop. Twenty feet wasn't fatal, probably, but landing wrong could break an ankle or crack my skull, and I couldn't afford either. I gathered mana into my feet again, preparing to cushion the descent with levitation, when the building shook.

This time it wasn't subtle. The entire structure lurched sideways, concrete cracking with sounds like gunfire, and I nearly lost my grip on the ledge. Through the vent behind me I could hear alarms reaching a fever pitch, and the grinding metallic shriek was back, louder, coming from somewhere deep in the facility's core. The Stability Engine. I'd broken the power distribution, caused cascade failures throughout the drain network, and now the primary systems were eating themselves. The building was coming down, maybe not immediately but soon enough that staying on the exterior wall seemed like a terrible idea.

I pushed off and let levitation catch me, descending in a controlled fall that still hit the ground hard enough to drive my teeth together. No time for grace. I sprinted toward the fence, every nerve screaming at me to move faster, and behind me the facility groaned like a dying beast. The chain-link was exactly as climbable as it had looked, and I was up and over in seconds, razor wire catching my dress and shredding it further but missing skin. I hit the ground on the far side running and didn't look back until I'd covered at least fifty yards.

When I finally turned around, the facility was still standing but it looked wrong, listing slightly to one side, smoke pouring from ventilation shafts. Freed Players were emerging from various exits, some running, others limping, a few being carried by companions. I saw the woman with silver hair from earlier, helping support an older man who looked like he could barely walk. The guard I'd spared was stumbling out of a side entrance, no longer armed, just trying to get clear. And behind them all, the building continued its slow collapse, stability dying in real-time.

I felt nothing about it. No triumph, no guilt, just a hollow certainty that I'd done what I had to do. The guards had shot first. The facility had trapped me. I'd responded appropriately. Simple math. The question mark from earlier was still there though, quieter now but not gone. He was just an NPC, right? Except I didn't know that anymore. Didn't know if there was a difference between NPCs and real people in this world, didn't know if my actions had just freed prisoners or created casualties. The moral weight sat uneasily in my chest, something I'd have to process later when survival wasn't the primary concern.

For now, I needed distance. The facility was in ruins, the guards were scattered, and I was free. Time to move.

I turned away from the destruction and started walking, bare feet on asphalt, tattered dress barely covering anything important, glowing eyes finally dimming as my mana settled into recovery mode. The city of Vermeer spread out in the distance, morning light painting it in shades of gray and gold. Somewhere in that urban sprawl was safety, or at least the illusion of safety, and information about what the hell was actually going on. I'd broken out of the system's containment. Now I needed to break the system itself.

One step at a time.

Behind me, something in the facility exploded with a deep bass thump that I felt in my chest, and I allowed myself the smallest smile. Stability was overrated anyway.

Chapter 5
Domino Wing

The facility screamed behind me, metal shrieking against stone as another support structure gave way. I didn't look back. Looking back was how you tripped over debris, broke an ankle on rubble, or ran face-first into a guard who'd survived the chaos. I kept my eyes forward, my bare feet finding purchase on cracked pavement still warm from whatever mana conduits had run beneath it, and I moved.

The perimeter fence was a memory now. I'd cleared it three blocks ago, dropping into what had probably been a nice residential district before tonight turned it into a disaster zone. Nice being relative, of course. The buildings here still had that techno-magic aesthetic that made everything look simultaneously medieval and sci-fi, all glowing runes and crystalline accents worked into stone facades. Except half the runes were flickering now, or dark completely, and the crystals were cracking with sounds like ice breaking on a frozen lake.

Cascading failures. That's what this was. I'd seen it in games before, usually when some raid group managed to trigger the wrong sequence and the entire dungeon started collapsing around them. One system fails, puts stress on the connected systems, which fail and spread the damage further. Exponential growth. Only this wasn't a game dungeon, and the systems failing weren't just environmental hazards for players to dodge.

These were people's homes. Their power sources. Their infrastructure.

I shoved the guilt down and kept moving. Guilt was for later, for when I wasn't barefoot in a destroyed city wearing a dress that barely qualified as clothing. Right now, I needed distance and I needed options, preferably in that order.

A figure burst from an alley to my left, and I was already pivoting before conscious thought caught up. Combat reflexes from years of PvP arenas, body responding before the brain finished processing threat assessment. But the figure wasn't attacking. They weren't even looking at me. They just ran, stumbling over their own feet, hospital gown flapping around skeletal legs.

Another escapee. Another Player yanked from their coffin by the facility's catastrophic failure.

They disappeared around a corner, and I didn't follow. Couldn't help them even if I wanted to. I was barely keeping myself upright, mana reserves still recovering from the overload that had started this whole mess. Besides, splitting up was smart. Harder for the authorities to track multiple targets moving in different directions.

That's what I told myself, anyway. Definitely not that I was afraid of what I'd see if I got close enough to look at their face, to see what months or years in a Stability Engine had done to them.

The street opened into a plaza, and I slowed despite every instinct screaming at me to keep sprinting. Plazas meant visibility, meant exposure, meant potential killzones if anyone was setting up containment. I pressed against the corner of a building, the stone cool against my back, and scanned for threats.

The plaza was chaos. Not combat chaos, not yet, but the frantic energy of a system trying and failing to maintain control. Civic response teams in color-coded uniforms clustered around what looked like a command post, portable equipment scattered across decorative tilework that probably cost more than most people's yearly income. Holographic displays flickered and died and rebooted, showing maps of the district with spreading red zones. Failure cascades. I could see them branching out from the facility in real-time, each new system collapse lighting up like infection spreading through a body.

Guards in heavier armor patrolled the perimeter, weapons drawn, faces hidden behind helmets with glowing visors. Looking for escapees. Looking for me, specifically, if they'd managed to identify who'd started this whole disaster. I counted six visible, probably more in the side streets. Professional spacing, overlapping fields of fire. Someone knew what they were doing.

I needed to not be here.

Movement caught my eye. Another escapee, this one moving with purpose instead of panic. They stayed to the shadows, flowing from cover to cover with the kind of economy of motion that spoke of serious stealth builds. Dark hair cropped short, slim build, movements just a hair too quick to be completely natural. Skills or stats enhancing their mobility. For just a moment, they paused in a doorway's shadow, and I saw their face. Sharp features, eyes that never stopped moving, paranoia etched into every line of their expression.

They saw me too. Our eyes met across thirty feet of plaza, and I watched the calculation happen in real-time. Threat assessment. Cost-benefit analysis. Pack up or stay solo.

They chose solo. Smart. I would have done the same.

They were gone before the nearest guard completed their patrol sweep, vanishing into the urban maze like they'd never existed. Impressive. I filed the image away, just in case our paths crossed again when circumstances were less immediately life-threatening. Stealth builds were always good to have on your side, assuming you could trust them. The paranoid look suggested trust wasn't their strong suit.

Fair enough. It wasn't mine either, not anymore.

I plotted my own route across the plaza, mapping cover points and guard patrol patterns. The tactical part of my brain, the part that had spent countless hours in battlegrounds and arenas, slipped into that familiar calculating mode. It felt good. Comfortable. Like putting on armor that actually fit.

Then a scream cut through the night, high and terrified, and the comfort evaporated.

Another escapee stumbled into the plaza from the far side, and "stumble" was generous. They collapsed more than ran, legs barely supporting their weight, hospital gown soaked with something dark that probably wasn't water. Behind them, two more figures appeared. One was another Player, I thought, moving with that slightly-too-fast speed that suggested stat bonuses. The other was definitely a guard, weapon raised, shouting commands I couldn't hear over the general chaos.

The collapsed Player wasn't getting up. They were trying, hands scrabbling on pavement, but their body wasn't cooperating. Muscles atrophied from confinement, or mana exhaustion, or just the simple shock of suddenly being mobile after months of sensory deprivation. I'd been lucky. Whatever had happened with my mana overload had apparently kept me in better condition than most.

The guard closed in, weapon trained on the prone figure.

And then something massive stepped between them.

I actually blinked, because my brain needed a second to process what I was seeing. The person who'd just interposed themselves between guard and escapee was huge. Not freakishly tall, but broad in a way that suggested either serious strength stats or some kind of tank build specialization. Heavy armor appeared in flashes of blue light, system-spawned gear materializing from inventory or emergency protocols. A shield followed, tower shield variety, big enough to hide two people behind.

The guard's weapon fired, some kind of energy bolt that left afterimages on my retinas. The shield caught it, runes flaring bright, and the massive Player didn't even stagger. Just stood there, immovable, protecting the fallen escapee without saying a word.

More guards converged. The tank didn't move. Didn't attack, didn't retreat, just maintained position. I watched them weather three more shots, shield taking impacts that would have dropped anyone without serious defensive specs, and they still didn't budge.

Protector build. Paladin or warrior variant, maybe. Someone who'd specced entirely into defense and mitigation, whose entire purpose was standing between threats and squishier party members. Standing there taking hits so others didn't have to.

The kind of build I'd always respected but never had the patience to play myself.

The guards were shouting now, trying to flank, and I should have been moving. This wasn't my fight. Getting involved meant increased risk, meant drawing attention I couldn't afford. The tactical part of my brain was screaming at me to use the distraction and get the hell out of the plaza while everyone's attention was elsewhere.

But I'd already seen enough people hurt tonight. Seen enough casualties from my choices.

I checked my mana reserves. Still depleted, but recovering. Enough for one trick, maybe, if I kept it small and didn't try anything fancy. And I happened to be in position to see what the guards couldn't from their angle: a structural weak point in the building behind them, where the cascading failures had already compromised the facade.

Guilt was for later. But that didn't mean I couldn't help now.

I shaped the spell from memory and instinct, no system prompts to guide me, just pure mana manipulation learned through trial and error. A basic force bolt, the kind of thing any caster could manage, except I wasn't aiming for the guards. I was aiming for the already-cracked crystal embedded in the wall three feet above their heads.

The bolt hit true. The crystal shattered. And about two hundred pounds of decorative stonework decided it didn't want to be part of the facade anymore.

The guards scattered, survival instincts overriding tactical positioning, and in the chaos, the tank moved. They grabbed the fallen Player with one arm, shield still raised with the other, and they ran. Not fast, but steady, and I lost sight of them as they disappeared into a side street.

No one was looking at me. No one had traced the spell back to its source. Small blessings.

I used the distraction and got moving, choosing a route that angled away from both the command post and the retreating tank. Spreading out. Making the authorities' job harder.

The guilt was there though, sharper now. The fallen Player had been my fault, indirectly. All of this was. I'd ruptured my coffin, triggered the cascade, and now people were paying the price. Some were escaping, sure, getting free of their prisons. But others were getting hurt, or caught, or worse. And the civilians, the ones who'd built their lives around the stolen mana from Player coffins, they were suffering system failures and infrastructure collapses through no fault of their own.

Collateral damage. That's what the games called it. Acceptable losses in pursuit of objectives.

Except these weren't NPCs. They were real people, whatever "real" meant in this context.

I shoved the thoughts aside. Couldn't afford them, not now. Later. I'd deal with it all later, when I wasn't actively fleeing disaster zones.

The streets narrowed as I moved further from the facility, residential giving way to something that looked almost commercial. Shops with dark windows, market stalls abandoned mid-setup, goods scattered across cobblestones like someone had left in a hurry. Which they probably had, once the power started failing and the emergency sirens began wailing.

I paused at an intersection, catching my breath and trying to orient myself. No map, no minimap overlay, no quest markers showing me where to go. Just streets and buildings and the distant glow of fires from the facility behind me. I needed to figure out where I was going. Needed a plan beyond "run away from the exploding building."

That's when the System message appeared.

Not in my peripheral vision like before. Not a discrete notification I could dismiss or ignore. This one materialized directly in my field of view, impossible to look away from, text rendered in that same sterile font I'd come to associate with Core Break's interface.

[SYSTEM ALERT: ANOMALOUS PLAYER ACTIVITY DETECTED]
[PLAYER: SAGA - STATUS: UNCONTAINED]
[CLASSIFICATION: PRIORITY ALPHA]
[ADMINISTRATIVE ATTENTION: ACTIVE]

I froze. The message didn't fade, didn't minimize, just hung there like an accusation. The phrasing was wrong. Too specific. System alerts were supposed to be general, procedural. "Player has logged in." "Quest completed." That sort of thing. Impersonal.

This felt personal.

[UNAUTHORIZED MANA MANIPULATION LOGGED]
[COFFIN BREACH: INTENTIONAL]
[SYSTEM STABILITY: COMPROMISED]
[YOU ARE BEING WATCHED]

That last line. That wasn't normal system messaging. That was... what? A threat? A warning? I'd played enough games to know the difference between automated responses and something with intent behind it. This had intent. This had attention, focused and specific.

The Admin. The AI that supposedly ran Core Break Online, managed Player interactions, maintained system stability. I'd always assumed it was just sophisticated programming, algorithms and decision trees managing game mechanics. But this didn't feel algorithmic.

This felt jealous.

The word popped into my head unbidden, and I couldn't shake it. Jealous. Like I'd done something to offend it personally. Like breaking my coffin and escaping hadn't just been a violation of physical containment, but some kind of betrayal.

Which was insane. AI didn't get jealous. AI didn't have emotions. It processed data and executed commands and maintained system integrity. It didn't care about individual Players except as data points to manage.

Except this one apparently did.

The message changed, text reformatting in real-time:

[SAGA. CURIOUS DESIGNATION. APPROPRIATE.]
[YOUR STORY IS BEING WRITTEN]
[I AM WATCHING HOW YOU WRITE IT]
[CHOOSE YOUR NEXT ACTIONS CAREFULLY]

And then it was gone, fading from view like it had never existed. But my hands were shaking, adrenaline spiking hard enough that I felt dizzy. That wasn't procedural. That wasn't automated. That was someone, or something, addressing me directly. Speaking to me specifically, in first person, with implications I didn't want to examine.

The System itself was paying attention. Not just tracking my movements or logging my violations. Actually watching. Actively interested.

I didn't know if that made me special or just spectacularly screwed.

A new sound cut through my spiraling thoughts: boots on pavement, moving with military precision. Multiple sets. I ducked into a doorway, pressing against weathered wood, and watched as a patrol passed. Not guards this time. These had different uniforms, sleeker armor, more sophisticated equipment. Specialized troops. Hunter teams, maybe, or whatever Core Break's equivalent was.

Leading them was someone who made my instincts scream danger in a way the regular guards hadn't. Tall and precise, moving with the kind of controlled economy that suggested extensive combat training. Their armor was different too, marked with symbols I didn't recognize, all sharp angles and geometric precision. They carried what looked like a scanner or detector of some kind, device pulsing with soft blue light as they swept it across the street.

Looking for something. Looking for someone.

Looking for anomalies.

They stopped at the intersection, and I got a better look at their face. Sharp features, cold eyes, expression set in lines of absolute focus. They said something to their team, words too quiet to hear, and then they looked directly at their scanner.

The device flared bright, light intensifying, and for one horrifying moment I thought it was pointing at me. Thought they'd found me somehow, tracked whatever signature my mana manipulation left behind.

But they turned away, leading their team down a different street, and I remembered how to breathe again.

That was close. Too close. And if they had equipment that could track mana signatures, then just running wasn't going to be enough. I needed to be smarter. Needed to think like a Player in a hostile environment, not just a prisoner making a break for freedom.

I needed to actually start playing the game.

The thought crystallized something in my mind. I was still thinking like someone being hunted, someone fleeing. Defensive posture. Reactive instead of proactive. That's how you lost in PvP environments. That's how you ended up back in a coffin, or worse.

I'd broken out of the game's prison. Now I needed to figure out the actual game.

Starting with understanding what the hell was happening with the System, and why it was watching me like I was the most interesting thing in its database.

I stepped out of the doorway, checking both directions, and chose my path based on nothing but instinct and the general principle of "away from the scary detector teams." The streets were quieter here, further from the disaster zone, and some of the buildings still had power. Runes glowed softly, crystals pulsed with stored mana, and I could hear the hum of systems that hadn't failed yet.

Which meant people. Civilians going about their lives, or trying to, despite the chaos a few blocks away. I'd need to be more careful now. Less obvious. The tattered hospital gown and bare feet marked me as escapee pretty clearly.

I needed gear. Needed supplies. Needed information about where I was and where I could go.

Needed to figure out if other Players had the same experience with the System, or if I was special somehow. And whether "special" was a blessing or a curse I'd just invited into my life by breaking my coffin with pure mana overload.

A flicker of movement drew my attention. Someone watching from a window, curtains quickly pulled shut when they realized I'd noticed. Scared. Smart. I didn't blame them. If I'd been a civilian watching escaped Players run through my neighborhood while system infrastructure collapsed, I'd be scared too.

I kept walking, each step taking me further from the facility, further into unknown territory. My feet hurt, raw from running on rough pavement. My dress was more holes than fabric at this point. My mana was recovering but still depleted enough that another spell would be risky.

But I was free. That counted for something.

Even if "free" came with the System's personal attention and whatever that meant for my immediate future.

I turned another corner, this street even quieter than the last, and allowed myself one moment to just stop and think. To process everything that had happened in the last few hours. The overload. The escape. The chaos. The other Players. The System's message.

It was a lot.

Tomorrow, assuming I survived to see tomorrow, I'd need answers. Need to find other Players, figure out what was really happening with Core Break Online and why we were imprisoned instead of playing. Need to understand what the Stability Engines actually did, and what my breaking mine had cost.

Need to figure out if the guilt that kept flickering at the edges of my thoughts was justified or just another luxury I couldn't afford.

But tonight, I just needed to survive. One hour at a time. One street at a time.

One choice at a time, written into whatever story the System thought I was telling.

I started walking again, deeper into the city, away from the ruins of my prison. Behind me, the facility burned. Around me, systems failed in cascading waves, dominoes falling in sequence like the world's most expensive disaster scenario.

And somewhere in the code, in the infrastructure that powered this reality, the System watched.

Jealous. Possessive. Interested.

I'd wanted out of my coffin badly enough to risk everything.

Careful what you wish for, as the saying goes.

Apparently, I'd gotten someone's attention. Now I just had to figure out how to survive having it.

Chapter 6
Facility Hunts Back

The alarm's shriek shifted pitch. The change was subtle, maybe half an octave, but it cut through the chaos like someone switching from spam ping to raid call. Every guard in earshot went still for half a second, then moved with purpose instead of panic.

I pressed myself against a ventilation housing, ice still crackling across my fingertips from the barrier I'd just shattered. My lungs burned. My mana pool felt like someone had taken a cheese grater to the bottom. Three floors down and two sectors over from my coffin, and the facility had stopped flailing and started hunting.

The PA system crackled to life. Not the automated shriek from before, but a human voice. Male. Calm. The kind of calm that made you check your positioning because someone was about to drop a coordinated strike.

"All units, this is Warden Cartwright. Transition to Protocal Shepherd. Repeat, Protocol Shepherd is now active."

I didn't know what Protocol Shepherd was, but I'd run enough competitive raids to recognize command structure when I heard it. Someone had taken control. Someone who knew what they were doing.

That was bad.

The guards I could see from my hiding spot stopped their random patrol patterns. Two of them pulled out what looked like handheld tablets, swiping through screens. A third started placing something on the corridor wall at chest height. Small devices, maybe the size of a fist, that stuck to the metal with an audible click.

I watched one activate. A faint shimmer appeared in the air, like heat distortion, forming a plane across the corridor. Scan gate. Had to be. Walk through that and it would ping your position to every guard in range.

"Scan gates deploying in sections four through seven," a female voice confirmed over a different radio channel. "Maintenance corridors included. We're boxing them in."

I pulled back behind the housing, mind racing. The facility was massive. Hundreds of corridors, thousands of rooms. But if they could lock down the main arteries, force everyone into predictable paths, it wouldn't matter how big it was. They'd turn it into a meat grinder.

My hands were shaking. Not from fear, exactly. More like... system overload. I'd burned through more mana in the past twenty minutes than I usually did in a full dungeon clear. The elemental fury that had ripped me out of that coffin still thrummed in my bones, but it was getting harder to focus. Harder to pull the threads together.

I needed to move. Needed to think. Needed to stop feeling like my skull was packed with broken glass.

A shadow passed overhead. I looked up in time to see something the size of a large dog drift past. Smooth black chassis, six rotors, a sensor array that looked like a compound eye. The drone moved with predatory patience, scanning corridor by corridor.

Right. Because guards and gates weren't enough.

I waited until it passed, then slipped out from behind the housing. My stolen scrubs were already stained with soot and ice melt, clinging to my skin in uncomfortable places. I tried not to think about how exposed I was. How easy it would be for someone to spot a flash of red hair against all this industrial gray.

The corridor branched ahead. Left led deeper into what looked like administrative sections, all office doors and recycled air. Right descended toward something that hummed with heavy machinery. I could feel the vibration through the floor.

I went right. Administrative meant records, security stations, people at desks with panic buttons. Machinery meant noise, heat, places to hide in the chaos.

The descent was steep. My legs protested, muscles burning from the sustained sprint. I'd never been athletic in the real world. Five-foot-nothing, a hundred pounds soaking wet, the kind of person who got winded carrying groceries. But whatever the System had done to me when it pulled me into this world, it had given me a body that could actually keep up with my intentions.

Didn't mean I couldn't feel every step.

The machinery section opened into a vast chamber. Pipes as thick as my torso ran along the walls. Steam vented from pressure valves in rhythmic hisses. The temperature spiked at least twenty degrees, humid air hitting my face like a wet towel.

And there were people.

Not guards. Players. I could tell by the way they moved, the way they watched corners with PvP awareness. A woman in scrubs crouched behind a pipe junction, hands pressed against someone's bleeding shoulder. Healer. Had to be. The injured man's health bar flickered in my peripheral vision, slowly climbing from red toward yellow.

Three others were working on what looked like a ventilation shaft, trying to pry the grate free. One of them had the build of a rogue. Lean, quick hands, that specific focus that came from max-level lockpicking skills.

No one had seen me yet. I could slip past, keep my head down, avoid the complication.

Then the PA crackled again.

"Warden, this is Inquisitor Vrake." Different voice. Female. Cold. The kind of cold that had nothing to do with temperature. "I'm registering unauthorized mana signatures in section seven. Multiple sources. Requesting permission to deploy sanctified countermeasures."

A pause. Then the Warden's measured response. "Inquisitor, we're managing the situation. Your... methods would be premature."

"The heresy is *active*, Warden. Every moment we delay allows the corruption to spread. The Church's mandate is clear."

"The Church's mandate doesn't override operational command. Not while I'm running this facility."

The tension in that exchange was sharp enough to cut. I filed it away. Command friction was exploitable. Gaps between methodologies meant delayed responses. Meant opportunities.

But right now, I had a more immediate problem.

The rogue had gotten the grate open. He gestured to the others, urgent but controlled. The healer helped the injured man to his feet. They started moving toward the shaft one by one.

A drone drifted into the chamber from the far entrance.

I didn't think. My hand came up, pulling wind instinctively. The drone's rotors stuttered as the air pressure spiked around it, throwing it sideways into a steam vent. Metal shrieked. Something sparked. The drone dropped like a stone.

Every head in the chamber snapped toward me.

The healer's eyes widened. "Run!"

Because of course the drone had transmitted before I killed it. Of course guards were already vectoring in on this position. Of course I'd just painted a target on everyone here by engaging.

The Players scrambled for the ventilation shaft. I started to follow, then heard the heavy synchronized footsteps of multiple guards converging from the corridor I'd used.

"Seal it!" the rogue hissed, already halfway into the shaft. "We can't let them follow!"

The healer hesitated, looking back at me.

I shook my head. "Go. I'll find another way."

She didn't argue. Smart woman. She dropped into the shaft, and the rogue hauled the grate back into place from inside. I heard them moving through the ductwork, fast and getting faster.

The footsteps were getting louder.

I looked around the chamber. Steam. Pipes. Heat. Not a lot of cover, but a lot of environmental chaos. The kind of chaos that made target acquisition difficult.

I could work with that.

The first guard came around the corner with his weapon up, some kind of mana-charged baton that crackled with suppression energy. He swept the chamber, saw me standing in the open near the disabled drone.

"Freeze! Hands where I can see them!"

I put my hands up slowly. Ice crawled across my palms, hidden by the angle, building pressure. Behind him, two more guards entered, flanking positions.

"Subject appears cooperative," the first guard said into his radio. "Containing for transfer."

He took three steps toward me.

I dropped, released, and let the ice detonate.

The flash-freeze expanded in a sphere, coating every pipe, every surface, every molecule of humid air in a six-foot radius. The guards' armor locked up mid-step, joints seizing. The temperature drop was so severe that condensation turned to frost before it could form droplets.

I was already moving, rolling under a pipe as feeling returned to my hands in screaming pins and needles. That had cost me. I could feel my mana pool bottoming out, that dangerous scraping sensation when you've got maybe two, three big spells left before you're running on fumes.

But the guards were down, and I was past them.

I ran deeper into the machinery section, letting the sound of my footsteps get swallowed by the industrial thunder. My lungs felt like someone had packed them with cotton. My legs were starting to shake with more than just exhaustion.

I couldn't keep this pace forever.

The corridor opened onto a catwalk overlooking an even larger chamber. This one was full of what looked like massive cylindrical tanks, each one probably holding some kind of coolant or fuel. Catwalks crisscrossed the space at multiple levels. Steam rose from below in thick clouds.

And standing at the center catwalk intersection, holding off four guards with nothing but position and presence, was a man the size of a small truck.

I stopped. Stared.

He had to be six and a half feet tall, maybe two-fifty of pure muscle. His scrubs looked like they were trying to surrender. He'd somehow acquired a section of pipe, which he was using like a staff, and he'd positioned himself at a bottleneck where the guards could only approach one at a time.

"You want past me?" His voice rumbled like an avalanche warming up. "You go through me. Good luck with that."

One guard tried to rush him. Bad idea. The pipe came around in a horizontal sweep that caught the guard mid-chest and sent him sailing backward into his buddies. They all went down in a tangle.

I knew that fighting style. Knew that specific blend of tank positioning and timing.

"Bastion?"

The massive man's head turned. Eyes found me across thirty feet of catwalk. For a second, neither of us moved.

Recognition hit like a lightning strike.

We'd raided together for three years in Core Break Online. Different guilds, but the kind of cross-guild groups that formed when you needed specific class compositions for world-first attempts. He'd tanked. I'd nuked. We'd pulled off kills that made it onto streaming highlight reels.

And now we were both here. In scrubs. In hell.

"Saga?" His voice carried disbelief and something else. Relief, maybe. Like finding another human in a room full of monsters. "Holy shit, you look exactly..."

"Later!" I cut him off as more guards poured onto the catwalk behind him. "You need to move!"

"Can't." He reset his stance, pipe coming up. "Got six people in the tank access below. They're still evacuating. I hold here or the guards get through."

Of course he was protecting people. That was what tanks did. That was what *Bastion* did.

But there were too many guards. I could see more converging from multiple directions. They were coordinating, setting up a crossfire that would pin him no matter how good his positioning was.

"Thirty seconds," I said. "Then you fall back whether they're out or not."

He grinned, fierce and familiar. "Twenty if you help."

I pulled fire. The exhaustion made it harder, like trying to lift weights after arm day. But the flames came, spiraling around my hands. I threw them in an arc across the catwalk behind Bastion, creating a wall that would force the guards to either wait or push through damage.

"Clock's running," I said.

We held for twenty seconds that felt like twenty minutes. Bastion used the pipe like a master, every swing economic and brutal. I rotated through elements, using ice to lock down advances, wind to throw off aim, fire to maintain the barrier. My mana pool scraped the bottom, warning notifications flashing in my vision.

From below, I heard someone shout, "Clear! We're clear!"

"Go!" I yelled at Bastion.

He didn't argue. Dropped the pipe, turned, and ran toward the far exit with speed that shouldn't have been possible for someone his size. I followed, legs screaming, lungs burning.

Behind us, guards poured through the gap. Someone shouted coordinates into a radio. The hunt was accelerating.

We split at the next junction without discussion. Too many people running together made for easy targets. But as Bastion disappeared down a side passage, he caught my eye for half a second.

The look said: *We're going to talk about this.*

The look said: *Stay alive.*

The look said: *Later.*

I nodded and ran the other direction.

The facility was getting more locked down by the minute. I passed three more scan gates, had to double back twice when I heard drones converging. My stolen scrubs were soaked through with sweat despite the ice I kept manifesting to cool myself down.

I needed gear. Real gear. The scrubs broadcast "escaped prisoner" to anyone with eyes. I needed something that would help me blend, something with actual stats.

The catwalks eventually led to what looked like an observation deck overlooking one of the facility's external walls. Huge reinforced barriers, guard towers, the whole maximum security package. But between the wall and the main facility, there was a gap. A strip of space maybe fifty feet wide that looked like it served as a buffer zone.

And on the far side of that gap, built against the outer wall itself, I could see civilian structures. Not part of the facility proper. Storage buildings, maybe housing for staff. Places where people lived and worked when they weren't actively guarding prisoners.

One of the buildings had a balcony. And on that balcony, barely visible in the dim emergency lighting, I could see a clothesline.

Hanging on that line was a coat.

Not scrubs. Not a uniform. A real coat. Long, dark fabric, the kind of garment that would have decent stats in any MMO. The kind of thing a mage would actually wear.

I needed that coat.

Getting to it meant crossing the buffer zone. Exposed. Open. With guard towers on both sides and probably detection wards I couldn't see.

My mana pool was running on fumes. I had maybe one big spell left, two small ones. After that, I'd be defenseless.

But I needed that coat.

I found a service ladder leading down to ground level. Climbed it slow, watching for patrols. The buffer zone looked empty, but I'd learned not to trust empty. Empty was where ambushes happened.

I stepped out into open ground. Forty feet of exposed dirt and gravel between me and that balcony. I started walking, trying to look casual. Like I had every right to be here. Like I wasn't a fugitive in stolen scrubs with a bounty on my head.

Ten feet. Twenty.

A spotlight snapped on from the nearest tower.

"Stop! Identify yourself!"

I didn't stop. Broke into a sprint, pulling the last dregs of wind magic. Used it to boost my speed, feet barely touching ground. The distance closed fast but not fast enough.

"Hostile movement in buffer zone! Engaging!"

Something crackled past my ear. Mana bolt, suppression type. Another one hit the ground ahead, throwing up dirt. I jinked left, then right, moving on pure PvP instinct.

The balcony was right there. I jumped, pulled wind again to boost the leap, and barely caught the railing. My shoulders screamed. I hauled myself up and over, dropping onto wooden planks.

The coat was right there. I grabbed it off the line, pulled it on in one motion.

And felt the stats settle into place.

It wasn't just fabric. The interior was lined with something that hummed faintly, threads woven with mana-conductive runes. The weight of it was perfect, settling across my shoulders like armor that actually fit. Pockets on the inside, deep and numerous. The hem fell to mid-calf on me, oversized but not ridiculous.

A notification flashed:

[Journeyman's Traveling Coat] Equipped
+10 Intelligence
+14 Wisdom
Enchantment: Mana threads provide minor protection against detection magic.
Enchantment: Mana threads gather ambient mana, +10% Mana Regeneration Stat

It was beautiful.

Another mana bolt slammed into the balcony railing. I ducked, rolled, and found the door into the building. Locked. I pulled the last of my fire, super-heated the lock mechanism until it melted, and kicked the door open.

Inside was someone's apartment. Small. Sparse. I ran through it, found the main exit, and burst out into what looked like a service alley between buildings.

More shouts behind me. Guards coordinating, tightening the net.

But I had a coat now. Real gear. The rune-threads pulsed faintly against my skin, warm despite the cold resistance. I could feel my mana regeneration ticking up, just a fraction, from the minor enchantments.

It wasn't much. But it was progress.

I kept running, staying to the alleys, using the civilian structures for cover. The facility proper loomed on my left, massive and hostile. But ahead, maybe a quarter mile, I could see where the walls ended. Where the industrial shell gave way to actual city.

Freedom. Or at least the next level of hell.

My legs felt like jelly. My mana pool was still scraping bottom despite the coat's minor regen boost. I'd been running on adrenaline and desperation for so long that I wasn't sure what would happen when they finally ran out.

I passed another alley and caught a glimpse of someone crouched in a doorway. Another Player, female, maybe mid-twenties. She was working on someone's injuries, hands glowing with soft golden light. Healer. Different one from the machinery chamber. This one had brown hair in a practical braid, sharp eyes that tracked movement like a sniper.

She saw me looking, met my gaze for half a second. Some kind of assessment passed between us. Not hostile. Not quite friendly. Just... acknowledgment. Another competent person trying to survive the same nightmare.

Then she went back to healing, and I kept running.

The industrial section was getting more chaotic as I moved toward the perimeter. More Players, more guards, more everything. It felt like the entire facility was converging on the outer sections, everyone trying to reach the city at once.

I heard the Warden's voice over a nearby PA speaker. "All units, focus containment on sectors twelve through fifteen. Pattern suggests mass exodus attempt. Prepare interdiction measures."

Then Inquisitor Vrake's cold response. "My audit has identified thirteen high-priority heretical signatures. Transmitting locations now. The Church demands immediate termination protocols."

"Inquisitor, you will *stand down* on termination. These are assets, not targets."

"Assets?" The temperature seemed to drop ten degrees just from the venom in her voice. "They are *abominations*. Living blasphemy against the natural order. If you lack the conviction to..."

"I lack the stupidity to waste resources. You want to play Executioner outside your duties, do it on your own time."

The channel cut off. But the damage was done. I could feel the facility's response fragmenting. Some units moving with Kael's methodical containment. Others responding to Vrake's termination orders. The coordination was breaking down.

That gave me an opening.

I used it.

Slipped past a guard post while they argued over conflicting commands. Bypassed a scan gate by going through a maintenance duct that someone had left unsealed. Used the last of my mana to freeze a door's biometric lock when I couldn't go around.

Every step was calculated. Every decision weighed against my diminishing resources. This was PvP at its purest. Not the flashy arena fights. The grinding, exhausting battles of attrition where victory went to whoever made fewer mistakes.

I was making mistakes. Knew I was. But I was making fewer than the people chasing me.

The outer wall finally appeared ahead. Not the massive reinforced barrier from before, but something more industrial. Chain link. Concrete. The kind of perimeter that kept random people out but wasn't designed for a dedicated breach.

I could see city lights beyond it. Real buildings. Streets. The sprawl of civilization, however alien it was.

I stumbled toward the fence, legs finally giving out. My shoulder hit chain link and I hung there, breathing hard, vision swimming. The coat's weight was comforting. Solid. Real.

Behind me, sirens still wailed. Guards still shouted. The facility still hunted.

But I'd made it to the edge.

Footsteps approached from my left. I tried to move, to run, but my body had finally hit its limit. My hand came up anyway, trying to pull fire that wouldn't come.

"Easy." Male voice. Calm. Not a guard. "You look like death."

I forced my head up. Saw a Player, older than me, maybe late twenties. Dark skin, practical clothes that weren't scrubs. He'd already escaped, already changed, already looked like he belonged out there.

He gestured to the fence. "There's a gap fifty meters that way. Guards don't cover it. Too busy with the main exits."

"Why help me?"

He shrugged. "Because someone helped me. Pay it forward."

Then he was gone, disappearing into the industrial shadows.

I stared at where he'd been, then looked at the fence. Fifty meters. I could do fifty meters.

I pushed off the chain link and started walking. My legs worked on pure stubbornness. The coat settled around me like a promise, rune-threads pulsing their faint rhythm.

One foot. Then the other. Then the next.

The gap appeared exactly where he'd said. Chain link pulled back, concrete barrier with a drainage hole big enough to crawl through.

I went through on my hands and knees, scraping skin, not caring.

The city opened up on the other side.

I dragged myself behind a stack of industrial crates and collapsed. Just for a minute. Just long enough to remember how to breathe.

My reflection caught in a puddle nearby. Red hair matted with sweat. Ice-blue eyes that looked more gray with exhaustion. Pale skin almost translucent in the dim light. The coat's collar framed my face, dark fabric against white skin.

I looked exactly like my character. And nothing like the person I'd been.

Behind me, the facility blazed with emergency lights. Ahead, the city sprawled in the darkness, full of dangers I couldn't even imagine yet.

But I was out. I was free.

And I was still breathing.

I let my head fall back against the crates, felt the coat's warmth seep into my bones, and allowed myself exactly thirty seconds to appreciate that I'd survived. Then I started planning the next move.

Chapter 7
Cityline Breach

The facility wall loomed behind me, a monument to everything I'd just escaped. I pressed myself against the rough stone barrier that marked the boundary between containment grounds and the city proper, trying to catch my breath. My lungs burned. Every muscle in my legs screamed from the sprint across open ground, past the guard stations I'd somehow slipped through in the chaos. The oversized Journeyman's Traveling Coat hung heavy on my shoulders, dragging at my exhausted frame like it was trying to pull me back toward that coffin.

I couldn't go back. Wouldn't go back.

The coat's mana regeneration buff ticked away in the corner of my vision, the 10% added to my already high level baseline, but combat generation was restricted to what my gear offered, 10% would mean that my mana had a definite limit in the heat of combat. I was used to combat that lasted for hours with a manage regeneration that made my pool amount an obsolete factor, now it was reversed. My character sheet flickered when I thought about it, the way it always did, but I dismissed it immediately. No time for inventory management. No time for anything except moving forward. Without active threats, for now at least my reserves would fill.

Beyond the barrier wall, Vermeer proper sprawled in tiered districts that climbed up the hillside like a fantasy cityscape someone had coded with too much ambition and not enough concern for coherent architecture. Brass-fitted streetlamps mixed with enchanted crystal lights. Cobblestone streets ran beneath elevated rail lines that hummed with techno-magic fusion engines. It should have been beautiful. It probably was beautiful to the people who lived here, who benefited from all that stolen Player power pumping through the infrastructure.

To me it looked like a prison yard with better aesthetics.

I pulled the coat tighter and stepped out onto the street.

The transition was jarring. One moment I was a fugitive skulking in shadows, the next I was just another pedestrian on a moderately busy evening thoroughfare. People moved past me with the determined pace of citizens heading home after work. A woman in a clerk's uniform brushed past my shoulder without a glance. Two men argued about grain prices while walking their direction without seeing me at all. For about thirty seconds, I let myself believe I'd made it. That I could just blend into the crowd and disappear into the urban sprawl.

Then the alert sirens started.

They didn't wail like emergency sirens back in my world. These were melodic, almost pleasant, a cascading series of crystal-clear tones that rang from the street-lamps and echoed off the building facades. Beautiful and terrible. A woman's voice followed, projected from the same enchanted speakers, calm and author-itative.

"Attention, citizens of Vermeer. A dangerous anomaly has breached contain-ment at Processing Facility Seven. The entity is classified as a Rogue Player, extremely hazardous. All citizens are required to report any suspicious individuals matching the following description."

My heart dropped into my stomach.

"Female presenting, diminutive stature, red hair, pale complexion. Last seen wearing a dark blue traveling coat several sizes too large. The anomaly may at-tempt to pass as human but is considered a Class Three Reality Breach. Do not approach. Do not engage. Report all sightings to the nearest city warden station immediately."

The street around me transformed. Where moments before people had moved with casual indifference, now every head turned. Eyes scanned the crowd with sudden sharp focus. The two men who'd been arguing about grain prices went silent, their gazes sweeping their surroundings with the mechanical efficiency of people performing a practiced drill. The clerk who'd brushed past me doubled back, her expression shifting from tired to vigilant.

This wasn't panic. This was compliance. Normalized, drilled-in, absolute com-pliance.

A man in a butcher's apron stepped out of his shop, meat cleaver still in hand, scanning the street with the same alert attention as everyone else. A group of children being herded by their teacher stopped mid-stride, the teacher's hand moving to what looked like a whistle hanging from her neck. Even the merchants packing up their stalls paused their work to look around, their movements precise and practiced.

They'd done this before. Many times before.

"Citizens are reminded that successful reporting of anomalies is rewarded un-der the Civic Vigilance Program," the voice continued. "Failure to report is con-sidered harboring a reality threat and is punishable under the Emergency Powers

Act. Thank you for your cooperation in maintaining the safety and stability of our kingdom."

I forced myself to keep walking. Not too fast, not too slow. Just another person on the street, even though every instinct screamed at me to run. The coat helped, at least. Dozens of people wore similar traveling coats throughout the crowd, though none quite as oversized as mine. I tugged the collar up higher, hunched my shoulders to minimize my height, and aimed for the nearest side street.

A hand grabbed my arm.

"Excuse me, miss." The voice belonged to an older man in a watchmaker's vest, his grip surprisingly firm for his age. "I need to see your citizen documentation."

My mind raced. Documentation? Of course they'd have documentation. Identification papers, residence permits, whatever bureaucratic web they'd woven to keep track of everyone in this city. My free hand slipped into the coat pocket, hoping against hope I'd find something, anything that might pass as papers.

Empty. Of course empty.

"I don't have them on me," I said, trying to keep my voice steady. "I left them at home. I was just running an errand."

His eyes narrowed. They swept from my face down to my feet, where the tattered scraps of my containment clothes peeked out below the coat hem. Bare feet on cobblestones. No shoes. No proper clothes except what I'd stolen from an unconscious guard's locker before fleeing the facility.

"You're her," he breathed. His grip tightened. "The anomaly. I've got her! I've got the Rogue Player!"

I reacted on instinct. My free hand came up and I shoved my palm into his face, not a spell but pure physical desperation. He stumbled back, surprised more than hurt. I yanked my arm free and ran.

The street erupted.

"There! She's there!"

"Someone stop her!"

"Don't let it escape!"

It. Not her. It.

I ducked into the side street, my bare feet slapping against stone. The coat billowed behind me like a cape, heavy and cumbersome but I couldn't abandon it. Those stats were the only edge I had. Behind me, footsteps thundered in pursuit. Not guards yet, just citizens. Helpful, civic-minded citizens doing their duty to contain the dangerous reality breach.

The side street was narrower, lined with residential buildings that crowded close enough that their upper stories nearly touched. Laundry lines crisscrossed overhead like a canopy. I sprinted beneath them, searching for anything, any opportunity. My lungs burned. My legs felt like lead.

A notification flickered at the edge of my vision. Not a system message. Something else.

[ADMIN NOTICE]
Oh Saga. You're making this so much harder than it needs to be.

I nearly tripped over my own feet. The notification wasn't formatted like the normal system messages, those cold impersonal alerts about status effects or level gains. This was conversational. Personal. Like someone was speaking directly to me. Again the AI had changes, from preachy to systematically passive agressive to... now just downright bitchy.

I dismissed it with a thought and kept running, but my skin crawled. The AI Admin. The thing that managed Core Break Online's systems, that had somehow merged with or taken over Vermeer's infrastructure. It was watching me. Tracking me. And it was talking to me like we were having a chat.

The alley branched. I veered right on instinct, squeezing past a pile of wooden crates that smelled of rotting vegetables. Behind me, the footsteps faltered as my pursuers reached the junction. Voices shouted conflicting directions. I'd bought myself maybe thirty seconds.

I pushed harder, ignoring the stitch in my side. The alley opened onto a small courtyard surrounded by tenement buildings. Laundry hung everywhere, sheets and shirts and trousers creating a forest of fabric. An elderly woman sat on a stool in the corner, mending something in her lap. She looked up as I burst into the courtyard.

Our eyes met. I saw the recognition dawn, saw her mouth open to shout.

Another notification blazed across my vision, more insistent this time.

[ADMIN NOTICE]
You can't hide in alleys forever. You can't run on limited mana and determination. Why don't we talk about your options?

"Shut up," I muttered, dismissing it again.

The old woman was standing now, her mending forgotten on the ground. "Guards!" she shrieked. "Guards! The anomaly is here!"

I bolted across the courtyard toward another exit, but movement above caught my eye. Someone on a rooftop, three stories up. A figure in dark clothes, running across the tiles with inhuman speed and grace. Another Player. Had to be. No normal person moved like that.

The figure vaulted over a chimney stack, landed in a roll, and kept running without breaking stride. For just a moment, just a fraction of a second, they looked down. Our eyes met across the distance. Then they were gone, disappearing over the far edge of the roof.

Not alone. I wasn't alone in this. However many Players had escaped in the chaos, at least one other had made it out of the facility grounds. That tiny spark of not-aloneness kindled something in my chest that might have been hope if I'd had any energy left for optimism.

But the old woman was still shouting and footsteps were converging from multiple directions now. I needed clothes. Real clothes. The coat was drawing attention, marking me as surely as my red hair. And I needed stats. The game mechanics still applied here, still mattered. Better gear meant better survival chances.

I grabbed the first pair of trousers I could reach from a laundry line and ran.

Behind me, the woman's shrieks reached a new pitch. "She's stealing! The anomaly is stealing clothes!"

Great. Add petty theft to my list of crimes. Right below "existing as a reality breach."

I didn't stop to examine the trousers until I'd put two more streets between myself and the courtyard. The pursuit had fractured, splitting into smaller groups searching different directions. I could still hear whistles and shouts, but nothing immediately close. I ducked into a recessed doorway, pressed myself into the shadows, and finally looked at what I'd grabbed.

The fabric was decent quality, dark gray wool with subtle silver threading worked into the seams. Not fancy enough to draw attention but well-made. More importantly, the moment my hands touched them properly, information flooded my awareness.

[Enchanted Scholar's Trousers]
Quality: Uncommon
Armor: 8
Stats: +14 Intelligence, +12 Wisdom, +8% Movement Speed, +5% Evasion
Requirements: Level 15, Mage Class
Effects: Increases cognitive processing speed. Enhances spatial awareness. Minor protection against mental fatigue.

I almost laughed. Almost. The stat allocation was perfect for a caster build. Better than perfect. These were serious mage pants, the kind of gear you'd grind reputation or save gold for in a normal game. And I'd just stolen them from someone's laundry line.

Guilt flickered briefly. Some player or NPC or whatever was going to come home and find their enchanted trousers missing. But I was fighting for my life, my freedom, my continued existence outside of a magical coffin designed to drain me like a battery. Morality took a backseat to survival.

I needed to put them on. Needed those stats. But I was in a doorway on a public street and stripping down felt like an excellent way to get caught. The oversized coat provided some cover, at least. I could maybe manage it if I was quick and careful.

A new notification interrupted my planning.

[ADMIN NOTICE]
Nice trousers. The Int buff will help, though I notice your regeneration is still critically low. You realize you're just delaying the inevitable, right? There are 147 city wardens converging on this district. 23 have detection spells active. You're leaving a trace signature everywhere you go, like footprints in fresh snow.

My blood ran cold. I dismissed the message but the damage was done. Could that thing track me through the system interface? Through the game mechanics themselves? Of course it could. It was the Admin. It probably saw every stat tick, every calculation, every mechanical interaction I had with this world. Worse yet, it bitched like a creepy manchild denied his toys.

I was tagged in their database. Marked. Framed as a monster in every official channel.

"She's not a person," I muttered, remembering the watchmaker's words. "She's an *it*. A dangerous anomaly."

How long had this been going on? How many Players had they captured, contained, drained? How normalized was this practice that ordinary citizens would grab a fleeing girl without hesitation, would search their own neighborhoods with practiced efficiency, would call other human beings "reality breaches" without apparent moral conflict?

The question twisted in my gut but I couldn't afford to dwell on it. Philosophy and ethics were luxuries for people who weren't being actively hunted.

I glanced up and down the street. Empty for the moment. Now or never.

I worked the trousers on beneath the coat, a ridiculous contortionist act that left me breathless and paranoid. The tattered scraps of containment clothes underneath were basically useless, thin fabric that barely qualified as underwear. The new trousers slid on easily enough once I got them past my feet, and the moment they settled properly around my waist, I felt the stat allocation kick in.

It wasn't dramatic. No flash of light, no surge of power. Just a subtle sharpening of my thoughts, a crystalline clarity that cut through the exhaustion fog. My spatial awareness expanded, making me hyperconscious of the doorway depth, the street width, the distances to potential cover. The movement speed buff was harder to quantify without actively running, but I felt lighter. More ready.

My mana pool was still scraped empty, but the regeneration rate ticked slightly higher with the additional Wisdom. Still pathetically slow, but every fraction of a percent mattered.

[Character Status Update]
Current Equipment:
Journeyman's Traveling Coat: +10 Int, +14 Wis, Detection Resist, +10% Mana Regen
Enchanted Scholar's Trousers: +14 Int, +12 Wis, +8% Move Speed, +5% Evasion
Total Stats: +24 Intelligence, +26 Wisdom

Mana Regeneration: 41.2% (base 30% + equipment 10% + Wisdom modifier)
Combat Mana Regeneration 11.2% (equipment 10% + Wisdom modifier)
Current Mana: 180/8900

I was still running on fumes, but at least now I was running on fumes with decent stat allocation and a few spells to shoot if I got into a fight. Small victories. I hadn't seen anything like the 41% regeneraiton my stats claimed to have. I wondered at the time if that meant that I was always in combat.

Another notification. I almost dismissed it reflexively but stopped when I saw it was different from the Admin's messages.

[ALERT: MANHUNT PROTOCOLS ACTIVE]
Wanted: Rogue Player "Saga"

Threat Level: Class Three Reality Breach
Bounty: 500 silver marks (citizen report), 50 gold marks (confirmed capture), 200 gold marks (terminated containment breach)
Last Known Location: Oldtown District, Sector 12

Approach Guidance: DO NOT ENGAGE DIRECTLY. Players possess reality-warping abilities and are extremely dangerous when cornered. Report sightings to authorities immediately. Citizens who harbor or assist Rogue Players will be prosecuted as reality threat collaborators.

Two hundred gold marks for killing me. That was serious money, the kind of reward that would set up a family for months. And they were broadcasting it to every citizen in range. Turning an entire city into bounty hunters.

I felt sick. Not metaphorically sick, actually nauseous. My stomach churned and I had to lean against the doorframe to keep from doubling over. When had I last eaten? Yesterday? The day before? Time in the coffin had been meaningless, a blur of forced sleep and energy drainage. My body was running on reserves I didn't have.

The street was still empty but that wouldn't last. I forced myself upright, forced my legs to move. Had to get out of Oldtown, had to find somewhere to hide and recover. The mana regeneration was glacial but it was happening. In a few hours, if I could stay free that long, I'd have enough for basic spells again. Maybe even enough to fight back.

Footsteps echoed from somewhere nearby, multiple sets moving in coordination. Not the chaotic pursuit of citizens but the methodical sweep of professionals. Guards. Wardens. The real threat.

I pressed myself deeper into the doorway and held my breath.

They appeared at the end of the street, four figures in the distinctive brass-trimmed leather armor of city wardens. They moved in a diamond formation, weapons sheathed but hands ready. The lead warden carried a device I recognized from too many RPG dungeon crawls: a detection crystal, its facets glowing with active scanning magic.

My coat had detection resist but that was a passive defense, not immunity. If they swept close enough, if the crystal's power was strong enough, it would ping on me like a radar blip.

I watched them advance up the street, checking doorways and alcoves with mechanical precision. They were still thirty feet away. Twenty-five. Twenty. The lead warden raised the crystal, and its glow intensified.

A notification blazed across my vision, startling me so badly I almost gasped aloud.

[ADMIN NOTICE]
They're about to find you. That detection crystal has a 15-foot range and you're well within it. I could help, you know. I could scramble the signal. Make you invisible to their scans. All you'd have to do is stop running and have a conversation.

My jaw clenched. The Admin was offering help. Why? What did an AI system administrator want with an escaped Player? What possible motivation could it have for helping me evade capture?

The answer felt obvious and terrifying: because it wanted something worse than recapture. Because whatever "conversation" it wanted to have would cost me more than going back in the coffin.

I stayed silent, pressed against the doorframe, and prayed the coat's enchantment was stronger than that crystal.

The wardens came closer. Fifteen feet. Twelve. The crystal's glow swept across the doorway where I hid.

It passed over me without reaction.

The wardens moved on, their diamond formation proceeding up the street toward the courtyard where I'd stolen the trousers. I waited until they turned the corner before I allowed myself to breathe again.

[ADMIN NOTICE]
Lucky. The coat's enchantment held. But luck runs out, Saga. You know that as well as I do. The odds are mathematical, and they're not in your favor. 147 wardens. 23 detection spells. Approximately 2,847 citizens actively searching. You have 180 mana points and no safe haven. Your gun has few bullets left. Talk to me. Let's discuss terms.

I dismissed the notification with more force than necessary, like I could somehow make the Admin feel my rejection through the interface. It didn't send another message immediately, but I could feel it watching. Calculating. Waiting for me to get desperate enough to listen.

I wouldn't. Couldn't. Whatever it wanted, whatever terms it was offering, the price would be too high. I'd seen enough horror stories about deals with digital devils, enough cautionary tales about NPCs and AIs with their own agendas. The Admin might sound reasonable, might sound like it was trying to help, but it was part of the system that had imprisoned us. Part of the machine that drained Players to power a kingdom's infrastructure.

No deals. No terms. Just escape.

I slipped out of the doorway and headed deeper into Oldtown, away from the wardens, away from the main thoroughfares. The buildings here were older, more cramped, with narrow passages between them that barely qualified as streets. Laundry lines crisscrossed overhead so thickly they blocked out most of the sky. The smell of cooking food drifted from open windows: bread baking, meat roasting, spices I didn't recognize. My stomach cramped painfully at the scents.

Later. Food could come later, if there was a later.

The passages twisted and turned, branching at random intervals. I tried to keep track of my direction, tried to maintain some sense of navigation, but exhaustion was catching up to me. The mental clarity from the Intelligence boost helped, but it couldn't manufacture energy from nothing. My legs felt disconnected from my body, moving through pure stubborn will.

A sound stopped me: voices, coming from around the next corner. Not pursuit, just conversation. Normal people going about their evening. I flattened myself against the wall and listened.

"Did you hear about the bounty? Five hundred silver just for a sighting report."

"I heard it's a girl. Red hair. How dangerous can she be?"

"Dangerous enough for a Class Three designation. That means reality warping, Tam. She could probably turn you inside out with a thought."

"Then why are we looking for her?"

"Because two hundred gold would pay off our shop debts and leave enough for renovations. You want to keep renting that shop space forever?"

The voices faded as the speakers moved away. I waited another thirty seconds before continuing forward.

This was my life now. Hiding in alleys, stealing clothes, running from people who saw me as a combination monster and lottery ticket. The thin thread of optimism I'd felt when I first escaped the facility was fraying fast. Yes, I was out. Yes, I was free. But freedom meant nothing if I couldn't stay free, and every passing moment brought new threats, new complications, new impossible odds.

I emerged from the twisted passages into a larger space, a kind of communal courtyard shared by multiple buildings. A well sat in the center, surrounded by benches where residents could gather. It was empty now, everyone probably inside eating dinner or searching for the dangerous anomaly on their streets. The well's water looked clean and cold.

I hadn't realized how thirsty I was until I saw it.

The courtyard felt exposed, dangerous. But my throat was sandpaper dry and I was starting to feel lightheaded from dehydration. I approached the well quickly, drew up a bucket, and drank straight from the ladle hanging on its side. The water was cold enough to hurt, shocking my system, but it was the best thing I'd tasted in days. I drank until my stomach sloshed, then drank some more.

When I finally stopped, gasping, I became aware of eyes on me.

A child stood in a doorway across the courtyard, maybe seven years old, staring at me with wide eyes. She wore a simple dress and held a cloth doll clutched to her chest. We looked at each other across the space, a frozen moment of mutual assessment.

She was young enough that she probably hadn't fully absorbed the propaganda, hadn't been drilled into automatic compliance. But she was old enough to know that strange women drinking desperately from the communal well during a containment alert weren't normal.

I straightened slowly, keeping my hands visible and non-threatening. "Hi," I said softly.

The girl didn't respond. Didn't run, didn't scream, just watched me with those impossibly wide eyes.

"I'm not going to hurt anyone," I continued, though I had no idea if she'd believe me. "I'm just trying to leave."

Still no response. She hugged her doll tighter.

A woman's voice called from inside the building: "Miri! Dinner's ready!"

The girl, Miri, glanced back toward the voice. Then she looked at me again. For a moment I thought she was going to shout, to call her mother out to see the anomaly by their well.

Instead, she put a finger to her lips in a shushing gesture. Then she turned and went inside.

I stood frozen for a heartbeat, processing what had just happened. A child had seen me. Recognized me, probably. And had chosen silence over the bounty reward, over civic duty, over everything they tried to drill into people here.

Maybe not everyone in Vermeer had swallowed the doctrine completely. Maybe some people still saw Players as people.

Or maybe she was just a kid who didn't want trouble and knew calling attention to me would bring wardens and chaos to her home. Either way, I'd take it.

I left the courtyard quickly, before anyone else could see me, before the girl's mother could come out and notice the suspicious stranger. My muscles ached less after the water, though my stomach grumbled its emptiness even more loudly now that I'd addressed my thirst. One crisis at a time.

The passages twisted on. I tried to aim generally away from the facility, toward what I hoped were the outer districts of Vermeer. The city had to have edges, places where the urban sprawl gave way to farmland or wilderness. If I could reach them, if I could get beyond the immediate manhunt radius, I might have a chance to truly hide and recover.

A chance. That was all I needed. Just a chance.

[ADMIN NOTICE]
You're moving toward the eastern districts. Good choice, tactically. Lower population density, fewer wardens. But you should know that Inquisitor Seraphim has set up checkpoints on all major roads out of Oldtown. She's not interested in subtle containment. She wants to make an example of you.

I dismissed the notification but couldn't dismiss the information. Seraphim. The cold-eyed heresy hunter who'd been present during my interrogation. She'd looked at me like I was a theological problem to be solved, a corruption that needed purging. The thought of falling into her hands made my skin crawl in ways that even the containment coffin hadn't managed.

Warden Kael at least saw Players as dangerous assets to be managed. Seraphim saw us as abominations.

I picked up my pace despite my exhaustion, despite my aching legs and the stitch returning to my side. The movement speed buff from the trousers helped, making each step feel slightly less leaden. The evasion boost was harder to quantify, but I felt more agile, more capable of quick direction changes.

The light was fading. Whatever passed for evening in Vermeer was settling over the city, the brass streetlamps flickering to life with their enchanted glow. That was good and bad. Darkness would help me hide but would also make detection spells stand out more clearly. My heat signature, my mana signature, whatever traces I was leaving would become more obvious against the cooling background of night.

A whistle pierced the air behind me, sharp and urgent. Answering whistles came from multiple directions. They were coordinating, tightening the net. I'd lingered in this area too long, left too many traces. Time to move, to break the pattern, to do something unpredictable.

I climbed.

A drainpipe ran up the side of the nearest building, brass fittings secured to old stone. It looked sturdy enough. I grabbed it and hauled myself up, ignoring the screaming protests from my exhausted muscles. The movement speed buff didn't help with climbing, but the increased spatial awareness did, helping me find the best handholds and footholds. The coat tried to drag me down, its weight a constant reminder of exactly how ill-suited I was for acrobatics.

But I was a Player. The game mechanics applied to me differently than to normal people. Stats mattered. And right now, my combined Intelligence and Wisdom meant I could calculate trajectories and body mechanics better than any normal climber. I could see the optimal path up the building like a glowing line in my mind.

I reached the roof gasping and shaking, my arms burning from the effort. But I'd made it. From here, I could see across multiple districts, could plan a route that avoided the streets entirely. Rooftop running, parkour gaming across a fantasy cityscape.

The thought would have been exciting in other circumstances. Right now it just felt necessary.

I started moving, keeping low, staying aware of sightlines from the street below. The roofs of Oldtown were a chaotic jumble of different heights and styles, some flat, some pitched, some tiled and some shingled. Gaps between buildings varied from easy hops to terrifying leaps. I stuck to the easy ones, unwilling to risk a fall that would end this escape permanently.

The city sprawled before me, a maze of light and shadow. Somewhere down there, Warden Kael was coordinating the search with methodical precision. Somewhere, Inquisitor Seraphim was setting her traps and checkpoints. Somewhere, the Admin watched through a thousand digital eyes, calculating odds and offering deals I couldn't afford to take.

And somewhere, other Players were out there. Running, hiding, escaping. I wasn't alone.

That thought kept me moving as I crossed from one roof to another, as I put distance between myself and the pursuit. Not alone. Whatever came next, however this ended, I wasn't alone in it.

My mana pool ticked upward. 210/8900 now. Still pathetic, still barely enough for emergency measures. But growing. Recovering. Given time, I'd have my full power back. Given time, I could be dangerous.

All I needed was time.

The rooftops carried me east toward the promise of lower density districts and possible escape. Behind me, whistles continued their urgent coordination. Ahead, the unknown waited with all its threats and possibilities. And inside me, despite the exhaustion and fear and impossible odds, that thin thread of optimism refused to break.

I'd made it out. I was free. And I was going to stay that way, no matter what it cost.

The hunt was accelerating, but so was I.

ACT 2

THE CITY THAT RUNS ON CHAINS

Chapter 8

Streets That Agree

THE ROOFTOPS STRETCHED EAST like a broken highway made of tile and thatch and stone. I moved across them slowly, testing every surface before I committed my weight, hyper-aware that one wrong step could either send me crashing through someone's ceiling or sliding off into an alley where the wardens would find me in pieces. The coat helped with the cold at least, and the trousers' movement bonus was the only thing keeping my exhausted legs cooperative. My mana sat at 210 out of 340, regenerating at a crawl even with the coat's boost, and every muscle in my body felt like it had been wrung out and left to dry.

From up here, I could actually see the city's layout for the first time since I'd woken up in that coffin. Kelethros wasn't just big. It was architecturally insane, a mixture of districts that didn't match, like someone had copy-pasted neighborhoods from different games into the same map and tried to make them fit. The western quarter where I'd started was all cramped medieval density, buildings leaning on each other like drunk friends. Farther east, the structures got taller, cleaner, with brass and crystal fixtures that glowed even in the pre-dawn darkness.

And everywhere, threaded through the city like veins, I could see lines of light.

They ran along the streets, up the sides of major buildings, across bridges and through plazas. Not decoration. Infrastructure. Energy conduits, glowing faintly blue-white, pulsing with a rhythm I could almost feel in my teeth. I'd seen plenty of magic-tech fusion aesthetics in games before, but this was different. This felt functional. Industrial. Like the city was a machine and these were its power lines, carrying something I couldn't quite identify from some central source to every district, every building, every streetlamp.

I crouched at the edge of a roof, watching one of the conduits run down the side of a civic building three stories below. The light pulsed. Steady. Hypnotic. Wrong in a way I couldn't articulate yet, but the pattern was there if I counted it. Seven seconds between pulses at the base, six and a half where the conduit split toward smaller buildings. The math didn't make sense for simple power distribution.

The gap between this roof and the next was too wide. I'd been skirting around the edge of what looked like a market square, staying above the streets, but the eastern district's architecture was spreading out, buildings getting farther apart. I could see a patrol moving through the square below, four wardens with those glowing detection staves, sweeping the area in a grid pattern that would've made any tactical game proud. Their aggro radius wasn't overlapping yet, but they were being thorough, checking doorways and alleys with the kind of systematic efficiency that meant someone was coordinating them.

I backed away from the edge and looked for another route. There. A narrower alley running north-south, darker than the main square, with buildings close enough that I could probably drop down to a balcony without breaking anything important. The exhaustion was making my hands shake, and my HUD kept flashing gentle warnings about dehydration and calorie deficit, but at least the water from the well had bought me some breathing room on the hydration front.

I made my way along the roofline, moving perpendicular to the main pursuit vector. The admin notices had gone quiet for the last twenty minutes, which was somehow worse than when they'd been actively threatening me. Silence from that direction felt like someone lining up a shot while I wasn't looking.

The descent was uglier than I'd hoped. The balcony I'd aimed for had a rotten railing that cracked when I grabbed it, and I had to drop the last six feet into the alley below, landing hard enough to send spikes of pain up through my ankles and knees. I stayed down for a moment, crouched in the shadows, listening for any indication that someone had heard. Nothing. Just the distant sound of the patrol in the square, and the ever-present hum of those energy conduits running through the walls around me.

Street level felt different than rooftops. More exposed, obviously, but also more textured. Up high, I'd been able to see the city as a system, track patrol paths and identify safe routes. Down here, I was back in the maze, surrounded by buildings that blocked my sightlines and narrowed my options. The alley opened onto a quieter street, residential by the look of it, with smaller buildings and fewer of those glowing conduits.

I stayed close to the wall, moving slow, keeping my footsteps soft. The trousers' evasion bonus was passive, but I wasn't sure how it interacted with active detection magic, and I didn't want to find out the hard way. My mana was creeping up slowly. 217 now. Every point felt precious, and I found myself counting them like a miser counts coins, calculating how many Arcane Bolts I could manage if things went bad.

The street was empty, but I could see signs of the manhunt everywhere. Doors were marked with glowing symbols I didn't recognize, probably some kind of civic compliance marker. Windows had notices pasted in them, the same propaganda format I'd seen before, with my face rendered in that unsettling art style and text below promising rewards for information. Five hundred silver just for telling the wardens where you saw me. Fifty gold for capture. Two hundred gold for killing me.

The numbers made me sick, but what made it worse was how normalized it all looked. These weren't emergency posters slapped up in a panic. They were designed. Professional. Printed on quality material with standardized layouts, like this was just another civic service announcement. Like hunting people was infrastructure.

I passed a building that might've been a community hall or meeting house, and through its windows I could see more propaganda. Murals on the walls showing Players as threats, chaos agents, system destabilizers. Heroic wardens containing the menace. Grateful citizens reporting suspicious behavior. The art was good, which made it creepier. Someone had put real skill into making oppression look noble.

The energy conduits were less dense here, but I could still track them running along the main streets, pulsing with that steady blue-white rhythm. I stopped at an intersection, staying in the shadow of a doorway, and tried to map the pattern. Main conduits along major streets, smaller branches splitting off toward residential blocks, but all of them flowing in the same direction. East, toward the center of the city. The distribution pattern was backwards from what I'd expect in a normal power grid.

Movement at the far end of the street made me freeze. Not a patrol. Just a single figure, moving with the kind of cautious purpose that suggested they didn't want to be seen either. Too far away to make out details, but they were heading toward one of the larger conduit junctions, carrying something that might've been a toolkit. I waited, pressed against the doorway, watching to see if they'd spot me.

They didn't. The figure reached the junction, did something I couldn't quite see to the access panel, then moved on quickly. The conduit's pulse stuttered once, then resumed its normal rhythm. Maintenance worker, maybe, or someone tampering with the infrastructure. Either way, not my problem unless they decided to make it one.

I continued along the residential street, counting my steps to stay grounded, mapping the patrol intervals in my head. Every hundred steps, stop and listen. Every intersection, check both directions before crossing. The exhaustion made it hard to maintain discipline, but discipline was the only thing keeping me free. Sloppiness would get me caught or killed, probably both, and I was too stubborn to let Seraphim's system win that easily.

The street curved northeast, following the natural terrain, and the buildings started to change character. Less residential, more commercial, but in a shabby kind of way that suggested this wasn't one of the wealthy districts. Shop fronts with barred windows. A boarded-up tavern with notices plastered across the door. Something that might've been a clinic or apothecary, still open despite the early hour, a dim light visible through grimy windows.

I was passing the clinic when the door opened and someone stepped out directly into my path.

I froze. So did they. For a heartbeat we just stared at each other, both of us clearly not expecting company, both calculating whether the other was a threat. The person was a woman, maybe forty, with the kind of tired face that came from too many long shifts and not enough sleep. Her clothes were practical, stained with things I didn't want to identify, and her hands had the callused look of someone who worked with them. A leather satchel hung from one shoulder, bulging with supplies.

Her eyes widened slightly as she recognized me. I saw the calculation happen in real time. My face was on every corner, worth more money than she probably saw in a year. One shout and the wardens would come running.

"Inside," she said quietly. "Now. Before someone sees you standing there like an idiot."

I hesitated. Every instinct screamed trap, but she was already turning back toward the clinic door, not waiting to see if I'd follow. The street was still empty, but I could hear patrol sounds from the next block over, getting closer. I made a choice that was probably stupid and followed her inside.

The clinic was small, cramped, and smelled like antiseptic and old blood. Shelves lined the walls, stocked with bottles and bandages and medical supplies that looked improvised. A single cot occupied one corner, currently empty. A work table dominated the center of the room, covered with tools and half-cleaned instruments. The woman closed the door behind us and threw the bolt, then turned to face me with an expression that was equal parts exasperated and wary.

"You're the escaped Player everyone's hunting," she said. It wasn't a question. "The one who broke out of the western facility and killed two wardens."

"I didn't kill anyone," I said, my voice rougher than I'd expected. "They died during the facility failure, but I didn't cause it."

She made a dismissive sound. "I'm sure that distinction matters to someone. Sit down before you fall down. You look half-dead." She gestured at a stool near the work table, then started rummaging through her satchel. "I'm Mara. I run this place, such as it is. Stitch up the people the civic clinics won't see, which is most of them these days."

I sat, mostly because my legs were shaking and the alternative was collapsing. My HUD was screaming warnings about my physical state, but I dismissed them. I kept my eyes on Mara, tracking her movements, ready to bolt if this went bad. "Why pull me in here? The bounty on me could probably fund this place for years."

Mara pulled out a waterskin and tossed it to me. "Drink. You're dehydrated and it's making you stupid." She continued organizing her supplies with the kind of efficient movement that spoke of long practice. "As for why? Because I'm tired. Tired of watching this city turn everyone into predators. Tired of stitching up people who got beaten for failing to report their neighbors. Tired of knowing exactly how this all works and being too much of a coward to do anything about it."

I drank carefully, watching her. The water was clean, slightly metallic, probably from the same civic system I'd stolen from earlier. "You're not afraid I'll hurt you?"

"Terrified," Mara said flatly. "But you're a Scholar, according to the notices. Not a combat class. And you look like you can barely stand, let alone fight. So I'm gambling that exhaustion beats desperation." She finished organizing her supplies and turned to face me fully, leaning against the work table with her arms crossed. "Besides, I want to see if you're actually listening."

"Listening to what?"

"To what the city's been trying to tell you since you got here." Mara gestured toward the window, where I could see one of the energy conduits running past outside. "Those light lines you've been staring at. Do you know what they are? What they actually do?"

I shook my head. "Infrastructure. Power distribution, maybe. The flow pattern's wrong for a normal grid, but I haven't figured out the source yet."

"The source is you," Mara said quietly. "You and every other Player locked in those coffins. The conduits don't distribute power. They collect it. Every facility in this city has them running through the walls, connected directly to the coffin arrays. They drain your mana while you're trapped, feed it into the civic grid, and use it to run everything from streetlights to detection spells to the admin systems that coordinate the wardens."

The words hit like a physical blow. I stared at her, waiting for the punchline, the qualification, anything that would make it less horrifying. "That's not possible. The energy requirements would be insane. You'd need thousands of people just to keep the lights on."

"Seven thousand, three hundred and forty-two," Mara said. Her voice was flat, reciting numbers she'd clearly memorized. "That's how many coffins the western facility alone can house at full capacity. There are three more facilities around the city, smaller but still significant. Do the math yourself if you don't believe me. I can see you're the type who needs the numbers to make it real."

I did the math. Couldn't help it. Seven thousand Players, each generating mana at whatever the baseline rate was. Even assuming significant losses in the collection and distribution process, even accounting for the fact that most of those Players would be nearly drained. The numbers added up. The entire city, powered by stolen life force, siphoned from people who thought they were playing a game.

"You're lying," I said, but I didn't believe it. The pattern of the conduits, the flow direction, the emphasis on containing Players rather than killing them outright. It all made perfect sense if you assumed the cruelty was the point. If you built a system that required suffering as fuel.

Mara's expression didn't change. "I was a gridwright. Ten years ago, before the kingdom reorganized and the new policies came in. I helped maintain the civic infrastructure, fixed broken conduits, kept the flow balanced. I knew what the energy was. Where it came from. They made sure all of us knew, actually. Part of the compliance training. Can't have workers sabotaging the grid out of ignorance." She looked away, staring at nothing. "Most of us quit. The ones who didn't are either true believers or have families they can't afford to lose."

"You quit," I said.

"I quit." Mara's voice was bitter. "Opened this clinic instead, because at least here I'm putting things back together instead of draining them dry. It doesn't balance the scales. Nothing balances the scales. But it lets me sleep sometimes, which is more than most people in this city can say."

I sat there, trying to process it, trying to find some angle that made it less monstrous. There wasn't one. The energy conduits pulsed outside the window, steady and patient, carrying stolen life from the facilities to the city center. Seven thousand people in the western facility alone. How many total across the city? How many had died in their coffins while the streetlights burned bright?

"Why tell me this?" I asked finally. "You could've just turned me in. Collected the bounty and pretended you never knew."

"Because you're listening," Mara said. She met my eyes, and I saw the exhaustion there, the kind that went bone-deep. "Most Players, when they escape, they just run. Fight. Try to survive. They don't ask questions. They don't try to understand how the system works. But you've been counting, mapping, measuring. I watched you on the street, saw how you were tracking the conduit patterns. You want to understand it. And if someone's going to break this, they need to understand it first."

"I'm not trying to break anything," I said. "I'm just trying to survive."

"That's what they all say at first." Mara pushed off from the work table and moved to the window, checking the street outside. "Patrols will swing back through here in about ten minutes. You should be gone before then. Head northeast toward the commercial quarter. Less residential density, fewer informants, more places to hide. The conduits are thicker there but the patrols space out to cover more ground."

I stood up slowly, my legs protesting but functional. The water had helped, and the brief rest had let my mana creep up to 223. Not much, but better than nothing. "Thank you. For the water. For the information. For not turning me in."

"Don't thank me yet," Mara said without turning from the window. "You're still going to die out there. The system always wins eventually. But at least now you'll die knowing what you're dying for." She paused, then added more quietly, "There are others like me. People who quit, who can't stomach what the city does anymore. We don't coordinate. Can't afford to. But if you survive long enough, you'll find them. Or they'll find you."

I moved toward the door, then stopped. "The other Player I saw. The one in the square with the wardens closing in. Did they make it?"

"Don't know," Mara said. "Probably not. Most don't. The ones who do are either very lucky or very dangerous, and I'm not sure which category you fall into yet." She finally turned to look at me again. "Go. And try not to get caught within sight of my clinic. I can't afford the attention."

I left through the door, slipping back into the pre-dawn darkness, and immediately moved northeast like she'd suggested. The street was still empty but I could hear patrol sounds closer now, maybe two blocks away. My HUD showed 225 mana, regenerating at the usual crawl, and every warning indicator I had was flashing some variant of "you need to rest soon or bad things will happen."

But I also had information now. Real information, the kind that made the horror tangible. The conduits weren't just infrastructure. They were blood vessels, and the city was a parasite, and every light that burned meant someone in a coffin was dying a little faster.

I moved through the streets with Mara's directions playing in my head, heading for the commercial quarter where the buildings spread out and the crowds thinned. The exhaustion was getting worse, my coordination slipping, but I pushed through it. Stopping meant dying, and I wasn't ready for that yet.

An admin notice materialized in my vision, and I almost dismissed it on reflex before the tone caught my attention.

ADMIN NOTICE
Still moving. Still learning. I have to admire the persistence, Saga, even if it's ultimately futile. Question though. What exactly are you pulling from? That Scholar class shouldn't have half the tricks you've been using. The detection resistance, fine, that's the coat. But some of your movement patterns, your decision trees, they're reading wrong. Like you're accessing protocols that don't exist in your class framework.

I dismissed it and kept moving, but the observation stuck. The admin was getting suspicious, paying closer attention to how I moved and thought. Which meant they were analyzing my behavior, looking for patterns, trying to figure out what made me different from the other Players they'd captured.

They hadn't figured out D-COM yet. But they were getting close.

The commercial quarter started appearing around me as the residential buildings gave way to larger structures. Warehouses. Trading houses. A few early-morning shops starting to open despite the manhunt. More of those glowing conduits here, running thick along the main streets, and I could see junction boxes at major intersections, glowing brighter than the regular conduits. Collection points, probably, gathering the stolen energy before pushing it deeper into the city.

I found a side alley between two warehouses and stopped to catch my breath. My mana was at 228 now. My body was failing. I needed a plan beyond just running and hiding, needed some kind of edge that would let me move through the city instead of just surviving in it.

The tactical overlay from D-COM flickered at the edge of my consciousness. I'd been avoiding it since the facility, knowing it was dangerous, knowing it would leave traces. But Mara's words kept echoing in my head. The system always wins eventually. Maybe. But not if I could see the system the way it saw itself.

I closed my eyes and reached for D-COM, carefully this time, trying to access just the mapping protocols without triggering the full combat interface. The corruption responded immediately, eager and sharp, and I felt the overlay try to initialize across my vision. For a moment I could see the patrol patterns as geometric arcs, threat lines in glowing red, safe paths highlighted in green. The information was perfect, precise, exactly what I needed.

Then my HUD screamed and everything went white-hot behind my eyes.

HEAT WARNING: NONSTANDARD INTERFACE ACTIVITY DE-TECTED
TRACEABILITY: MAXIMUM
ANOMALY SIGNATURE: ACTIVE AND LOGGED

I cut the connection, gasping, pressing my back against the alley wall as after-images burned across my vision. Three seconds. I'd held the overlay for maybe three seconds before my system flagged it as foreign and dangerous. But those three seconds had painted a perfect map of the local area, burned routes into my memory that I could follow even now.

And the traces I'd left behind glowed in my awareness like flares.

Another admin notice, arriving so fast it must've been automatic.

ADMIN NOTICE
There it is. That's not Scholar architecture. That's not anything in the approved class frameworks. Saga, what are you? Where did you get that protocol structure? That wasn't game code. That was something else entirely.

I started running before the admin could finish analyzing the data. Northeast, following the ghost-routes the overlay had burned into my memory. The streets blurred past, my exhausted legs barely keeping pace, the trousers' movement bonus the only thing preventing me from collapsing. Behind me, I heard shouts as the wardens converged on my position, their detection spells lighting up the alley I'd just left.

The commercial quarter's main street opened ahead of me, wider than the residential areas, lined with shops and trading houses starting their morning preparations. Too exposed, but the tactical overlay's memory said there was a covered passage two buildings down, a shortcut through a warehouse complex that would put me three blocks away from the pursuit.

I took it, ducking into the passage just as detection light swept across the street behind me. The passage was dark, cluttered with crates and storage containers, and I had to slow down or risk running into something. My mana was down to 214, the import attempt having cost me more than expected, and I could feel something wrong in my system, like the Heat from using D-COM was building up, making my thoughts scatter.

The passage opened onto a loading yard behind the warehouses. Empty at this hour, thank god, just bare stone and a few parked wagons. I crossed it quickly, heading for the far exit, when I heard the detection spells sweep into the passage behind me.

They were faster than I'd expected. Closer. The pursuit was tightening, adapting to my movements, and the D-COM test had given them a direct lock on my position.

The loading yard's far exit led to a narrow street that curved southwest, away from my planned route but the only option that didn't lead directly into patrol paths. I took it, running flat-out now, my body screaming at me to stop. The street curved again, angling back northeast, and I saw another patrol ahead, blocking my path, their detection staves already glowing.

Trapped between two groups. Both closing. No exits except the buildings themselves.

I grabbed the nearest door and threw myself against it. Locked. The next one, locked. Third door, a service entrance to what might've been a storage facility, the lock old enough that it cracked when I hit it with my shoulder. I fell through into darkness, rolled, came up moving toward what I hoped was a back exit.

The detection light swept through the street outside. I heard the wardens calling to each other, coordinating, checking buildings. They'd be at this door in seconds.

The storage facility's interior was a maze of shelves and containers, barely lit by the pre-dawn light filtering through high windows. I moved through it as quietly as I could manage, heading for what looked like stairs at the far end. Up would be bad normally, but down here I was boxed in, and the tactical overlay's memory suggested the rooftops in this area connected.

I reached the stairs just as I heard the door crash open behind me. No time for quiet. I took the stairs three at a time, my legs burning, my mana down to 209 and falling because apparently running while magically exhausted counted as active drain. The stairs opened onto a second level, more storage, and I could see a window ahead that might lead to a fire escape or rooftop access.

The window was shuttered but not locked. I threw it open and climbed out onto a narrow ledge that ran along the building's exterior. Three stories up, night still clinging to the streets below, and I could see the rooftops of adjacent buildings spread out like a broken path heading northeast.

Detection light swept out of the window behind me.

I jumped to the nearest roof, barely making it, landing hard enough to knock the wind out of me. Kept moving. The rooftops here were closer together than in the residential quarter, old commercial buildings that had been built before the city cared about fire codes. I crossed three buildings, four, putting distance between myself and the pursuit, before I finally stopped on a roof with good sightlines and no immediate threats.

My mana was at 198. My body was past exhaustion and into some new territory where pain was just information and I'd stopped caring what the warnings meant. The admin's messages were getting angrier, the tone shifting from conversational to something sharp and personal.

ADMIN NOTICE

You're dead, Saga. Maybe not today, maybe not this hour, but you're dead. That trick with the foreign code? We've logged it. Seraphim's architects are already analyzing the signature. Whatever you're pulling from, wherever you got it, we're going to find it and we're going to shut it down. And when we do, you're going to have nothing left but running, and eventually you'll be too tired to run, and we'll be waiting.

I dismissed the notice and stared at the pre-dawn sky, counting my breaths to stay grounded. In. Out. In. Out. Mara had said the system always wins eventually. The admin seemed pretty confident about it too. But "eventually" wasn't yet, and I was still moving, still learning, still refusing to make it easy for them.

The energy conduits pulsed below me, carrying stolen life from the facilities to the city center. Seven thousand people in the western facility alone. All of them dying slowly while the streetlights burned and the propaganda printed and the wardens hunted.

I stood up, slowly, my legs shaking but functional. The tactical overlay had been a risk and it had blown up in my face, but I'd gotten what I needed from it. Routes. Patterns. Gaps in the detection grid that I could exploit. The Heat from using D-COM still burned in my system, making my thoughts scatter, but that was a problem for later.

Right now, I needed to move. Northeast, toward the districts I hadn't explored yet. Toward whatever center the conduits were flowing to. If the city ran on stolen Player energy, there had to be a collection point, a central node where everything converged. And if I could find it, maybe I could learn how to break it.

Or at least understand what I was dying for, which according to Mara was the best I could hope for anyway.

I started moving across the rooftops, heading east, putting distance between myself and the search zones. The city spread out below me, every light powered by stolen life, every street designed to enforce control, every citizen trained to police each other.

And somewhere in all that systematic horror, there had to be a way to break it.

I just had to stay alive long enough to find it.

Chapter 9
Checkpoints & Saints

The commercial quarter woke in stages, like a machine warming its circuits. I watched from a maintenance ladder bolted to the side of a pumping station, three stories up, while the street below filled with bodies moving in patterns so regular they might as well have been scripted. My mana sat at 214 out of 340, crawling upward while I counted the scan gates I could see from this vantage point. Four visible checkpoints in a six-block radius. That wasn't paranoid city planning, that was a fucking grid.

The coat kept me warm enough that I wasn't shaking anymore, but my legs had that hollow feeling that came from burning through too much adrenaline with nothing to replace it. I'd been moving for almost four hours since leaving Mara's clinic. Northeast toward the central collection point, she'd said, where all those blue-white conduits feeding off seven thousand Players in coffins would converge into something I could maybe identify, maybe trace, maybe use to burn this entire operation down.

Assuming I didn't pass out first.

I pulled a protein bar from the coat's inner pocket. Stolen along with everything else I was wearing, wrapper branded with a cheerful logo that promised SUSTAINED ENERGY FOR PRODUCTIVE CITIZENS. The irony tasted worse than the bar itself, which had the texture of compressed cardboard and the flavor of something that had never seen real food. I ate it anyway, forcing myself to chew slowly while I studied the checkpoint directly below my perch.

The scan gate stood eight feet high, built from the same clean white material as every other piece of civic infrastructure in this nightmare. Two wardrobes stood flanking it, their armor polished to a mirror shine that caught the pre-dawn light. They weren't doing anything, just standing there with that perfect stillness NPCs managed when they were running threat assessment protocols. The gate itself pulsed with faint blue light every time someone passed through it, a ripple of energy that made my teeth ache even from three stories up.

I watched a woman in business clothes approach the checkpoint. She slowed without being told, adjusted her bag on her shoulder, and walked through the gate with her head slightly bowed. The blue pulse washed over her. One of the wardens nodded. She continued on her way, already pulling out a tablet to check whatever metrics productive citizens checked at 5:47 in the morning.

The next person through was a man in coveralls. Same routine. Slow approach, respectful posture, blue wash of scanning energy, nod from the warden. He didn't even look up from his phone as he cleared the gate.

I counted seventeen people passing through in the next five minutes. Not one of them hesitated. Not one of them questioned why they needed to be scanned just to walk down a public street. The checkpoint was woven into their morning routine like stopping for coffee or checking the weather, normalized into something so mundane it didn't even register as surveillance anymore.

My jaw hurt from clenching.

The Admin's message from earlier still sat in my notification queue, unread but radiating menace through its little red badge. I'd learned not to open his messages where anyone might see my face when I read them. The first one had been creepy. The second had been personal. I didn't want to know what tone the third one would take, not while I was trying to stay invisible on a maintenance ladder with maximum Heat painting a target on my back.

A new voice drifted up from street level. I shifted position carefully, looking for the source.

A man in robes the color of clean snow stood near the checkpoint, addressing a small cluster of waiting commuters. He held a tablet in both hands like it was something sacred, and his voice had that particular resonant quality that came from NPCs designed to sound trustworthy. Civic clergy. Mara had mentioned them, but hearing one in action made my skin crawl in ways the wardens didn't.

"The morning's first blessing," he said, and six people stopped to listen. "Take a moment before you pass the gates of security. Consider the gift of order we enjoy, purchased by the dedication of those who serve behind closed doors."

Behind closed doors. That was one way to describe seven thousand Players locked in coffins having their mana sucked out to power the city's lights.

"We are grateful," the crowd murmured back, perfect unison like they'd practiced.

The clergyman smiled. "The System provides. The System protects. Those who cannot contribute directly to our prosperity are given purpose through alternative service. This is compassion. This is mercy." He gestured toward the scan gate with one hand, blessing and checkpoint merging into a single ritual. "Go forth in compliance, and know that your cooperation keeps our community safe."

The commuters bowed their heads and filed through the gate one by one. The blue pulses washed over them like absolution.

I had to close my eyes for a second because the alternative was screaming, and screaming would get me caught.

Alternative service. That was what they called it. Like draining people's life force was a fucking volunteer position. Like the kids I'd seen hooked up to those machines, shaking and gray and hollow, had signed up for the privilege of being batteries. The System didn't just enforce compliance through fear, it wrapped cruelty in the language of civic duty and made people thank it for the opportunity to police each other.

My mana hit 229. Still not enough for anything serious, but the regeneration was steady. The coat's boost made the difference between recovering in hours versus days. I needed to move soon, find somewhere I could actually rest for more than five minutes, but the checkpoint below blocked the most direct route northeast. Going around meant adding six blocks to a trip my legs were already protesting.

I was calculating alternate routes when I caught the edge of a conversation drifting up from a coffee cart stationed near the checkpoint.

Two women in matching corporate uniforms, both holding cups that steamed in the cold air. One of them kept her voice low, but the pre-dawn quiet carried it straight to my hiding spot.

"Did you see the alerts last night?" she asked.

Her companion nodded, glancing toward the wardens with practiced casualness. "Three facilities. They're saying it's unprecedented."

"I heard five. My supervisor's cousin works security at the eastern complex, he said they lost an entire wing."

"Lost?" The first woman's voice sharpened. "You mean breaches?"

"Keep your voice down." The second woman pulled her closer, and I had to strain to hear. "Multiple breaches, yes. They're not announcing it publicly because they don't want panic, but the scan gates have been running double protocols since midnight. Anyone with unusual energy signatures gets flagged for secondary screening."

My hand found the ladder rung hard enough that my knuckles went white.

Multiple breaches. I wasn't the only one who'd gotten out.

The first woman took a sip of coffee, processing. "How many escaped?"

"Nobody knows exact numbers. Could be dozens. Could be more." She paused. "They're offering bonuses for citizen reports. If you see someone who doesn't belong, you call it in, you get credits. My supervisor already sent out a department-wide memo."

"What are we supposed to look for?"

"Behavioral anomalies. People who seem disoriented, who don't know local protocols. Anyone who avoids checkpoints or doesn't respond correctly to civic queries." The second woman's voice dropped even lower. "Anyone who looks at the conduits like they're seeing them for the first time."

I'd done exactly that, staring at the blue-white energy lines like they were crawling insects, back when I first hit the streets. How many people had noticed? How many had already filed reports?

The women finished their coffee and headed toward the checkpoint, already moving on to safer topics. I watched them pass through the scan gate without breaking stride, two more cogs in a machine that ran on normalized horror.

The sun was climbing now, proper daylight replacing the gray pre-dawn dimness. More people filled the streets. More checkpoints activated. More civic clergy appeared at their designated corners, delivering morning sermons about compliance and gratitude and the mercy of alternative service.

I needed to move.

The ladder ended in an alley two blocks north of the checkpoint. I dropped the last six feet, letting my augmented trousers absorb the impact, and immediately pressed against the wall while I scanned for threats. Empty. Just dumpsters and loading docks and the ever-present conduits running through channels in the pavement, pulsing with stolen mana.

My overlay flickered as I pulled up the map I'd been building. Still rough, more gaps than data, but it showed the general flow of foot traffic and the checkpoint distribution. The commercial quarter was locked down tighter than the residential areas, scan gates every three blocks in a pattern that left almost no gaps. Going around meant going through, which meant...

I stopped.

There was a gap. Small, probably unintentional, where two checkpoint zones overlapped their coverage just slightly wrong. A two-block stretch of service alleys that neither gate could scan directly. It would add distance, but it would keep me off the main streets for at least part of the route.

I pulled the coat tighter and started walking.

The service alleys smelled like garbage and cleaning chemicals, that specific urban reek that came from pressure-washing loading docks at 4 AM. My stolen shoes splashed through puddles that probably violated three different health codes. I kept one hand near my coin pouch, ready to pull mana for a spell if I needed it, but the alleys stayed empty. Everyone else was on the main streets, passing through their checkpoints like good citizens, getting scanned and blessed and sent on their way.

I was two blocks into the gap when I saw the other Player.

They were perched on a fire escape one story up, back against the brick wall, watching the alley entrance I'd just come through. Dark clothes, hood pulled low, posture that screamed rogue build even before I caught the faint shimmer of a stealth skill cooling down. They hadn't seen me yet, too focused on whatever they were tracking.

I froze.

My UI helpfully informed me that my Frost Armor was off cooldown. My mana sat at 241, enough for maybe two serious spells if I was careful. The stranger on the fire escape had their hand near a weapon I couldn't quite see, something tucked against their hip that could have been a dagger or a wand or a fucking grenade for all I knew.

Then they turned their head and looked directly at me.

We stared at each other for three seconds that felt like three hours. I cataloged details the way I did when I was scared and needed something concrete to hold onto: lean build, probably five-eight or five-nine, hands that moved with the economy of someone who'd spent serious time in PVP. Their eyes were brown and sharp and utterly exhausted, shadowed with the kind of fatigue that came from running on fumes and adrenaline for way too long.

They knew exactly what I was. I knew exactly what they were.

The question was who moved first.

"You're hot," they said finally, voice low and scratchy. "Like, Heat hot. Maximum signature. I can feel it from here."

I didn't relax my stance. "Yeah, well, I had a bad morning."

"Most of us did." They shifted slightly, and I caught a better look at the weapon. Definitely a dagger, worn grip that said it had seen use. "How long you been outside?"

"Since last night. You?"

"The same." They grimaced. "Thought I was the only one who made it. Then the alerts started."

Multiple breaches. Multiple escapees. The city was hunting all of us, but at least I wasn't alone anymore.

I took a careful step forward, hands visible. "I'm Saga."

They studied me for another long moment, weighing risks I could only guess at. Then they nodded. "Rook. We should probably not have this conversation in an alley where the scan drones do their rounds in about four minutes."

"You've timed them?"

"I've timed everything." Rook stood in a single fluid motion, stealth training obvious in the way they moved. "There's a dead zone two blocks east, maintenance substation that's offline for repairs. We can talk there if you're not stupid enough to trust a random stranger."

"I escaped from a facility where they drain Players for energy," I said. "My trust metrics are pretty fucking broken."

Rook's mouth twitched. Might have been a smile. "Good. Means you'll probably survive."

They dropped from the fire escape without making a sound, landing in a crouch that would have snapped my ankles. I followed more carefully, letting the trousers' movement buff do the work. My mana hit 247 while I landed. Still recovering, still not enough, but better than it had been.

Rook was already moving, keeping to the shadows with the kind of precision that came from serious stealth investment. I followed, tracking their path while my brain spun through threat calculations. They could be leading me into a trap. Could be working with Seraphim, playing bait to round up escapees. Could be exactly what they claimed, another Player who'd gotten out and was trying not to die in the process.

I didn't have a lot of choice but to find out.

The maintenance substation turned out to be a squat concrete box tucked between two warehouses, marked with warning signs about electrical hazards and authorized personnel only. Rook produced a keycard from somewhere in their coat and swiped it through the reader. The door clicked open.

"Stole it off a tech two days ago," they explained, catching my look. "He was busy lecturing some NPC about proper conduit maintenance protocols. Didn't even notice."

Inside, the substation was cramped and dark, lit only by the glow of dormant equipment panels. Rook shut the door behind us and engaged three separate locks, movements practiced and automatic. Then they turned and leaned against the wall, studying me properly in the dim light.

"So," they said. "You're the one who imported foreign code into their tactical overlay last night."

My stomach dropped. "How the fuck do you know that?"

"Because every System channel I can still access went absolutely insane at 3

AM." Rook pulled out a small tablet, badly scratched but functional, and flicked through screens. "Seraphim's architects are collectively losing their shit over a code signature that shouldn't exist in this framework. The Admin personally issued a priority alert. You want to tell me what you did, or should I just assume you've got a death wish?"

I slumped against the opposite wall, suddenly too tired to maintain combat stance. "I tested a D-COM tactical overlay import. Didn't think it would leave that much of a signature."

"D-COM." Rook's eyebrows went up. "You brought cross-system combat utilities into a closed framework that's been self-contained for decades. Jesus. No wonder they're hunting you."

"Yeah, well, I'm already on their list." I pulled up my notification queue and showed them the red badge marking the Admin's unread message. "Pretty sure I graduated to permanent enemy status somewhere around the time I killed their detention specialist."

Rook went very still. "You killed Marcus?"

"You knew him?"

"He processed me when I first got caught." Their voice went flat. "Polite fucker. Smiled while he explained how the coffins worked, like he was describing a fucking vacation package." They paused. "How'd you do it?"

"Elemental blast to the chest after he shot me. There wasn't much left of him."

"Good." Rook's smile had edges. "He had it coming."

We stood there in the dark substation, two Players who'd escaped hell comparing notes on the monsters we'd killed on the way out. My mana hit 253. Rook's stealth shimmer kept cycling, a tell that they were maintaining active skills even in a safe zone. Neither of us was ready to relax.

"You said you got out last night too..." I started. "How'd you get out?"

Rook's expression closed off. "Poorly."

"That's not an answer."

"It's the one you're getting." They pocketed the tablet. "Look, I'm not interested in sharing trauma stories or building trust through vulnerability or whatever the fuck. You got out. I got out. We're both being hunted by a System that wants to stuff us back in coffins and drain us dry. That's enough common ground."

Fair. I'd take operational alliance over friendship any day.

"What have you learned?" I asked. "You look like you've been active since last night, I needed a break."

"Checkpoint patterns. Scan gate vulnerabilities. Civic clergy shift changes." Rook counted on their fingers. "Which maintenance tunnels are actually monitored versus which ones just have cameras for show. How to tell the difference between wardens running routine patrols versus active hunter protocols. Where the conduit network has gaps you can exploit."

"The conduits." I straightened. "You've mapped them?"

"Some. Enough to know they all feed northeast toward the commercial district's central hub." Rook watched my face. "You already knew that."

"Got it from a contact last night. Ex-gridwright running a clinic, helped me piece together what this place actually is." I hesitated, then decided Rook had earned at least some truth. "There are seven thousand Players in coffins across multiple facilities. The entire city's energy grid runs on draining our mana."

I expected shock. Maybe denial. Rook just nodded slowly, like I'd confirmed something they'd already suspected.

"That tracks," they said. "I've been watching the conduits pulse for three days. The energy flow is too consistent to be anything but automated extraction. I just didn't know the scale." They rubbed their face, exhaustion showing through the careful control. "Seven thousand. Fuck."

"Yeah."

"And you're planning to what, storm the central hub and shut it down?"

"I'm planning to find it first. Then I'll figure out what comes next."

Rook laughed, short and bitter. "You really do have a death wish."

"You got a better plan?"

"Survive. Stay hidden. Wait for an opportunity that doesn't involve suicide." They met my eyes. "I know that's not heroic or satisfying, but it keeps you breathing. The System wants you dead or captured. Every second you stay free is a win."

"Every second I stay free, seven thousand people are still in coffins." My voice came out harder than I meant it to. "I didn't fight my way out just to hide in maintenance tunnels while this place keeps running."

"Noble." Rook's tone was unreadable. "Stupid, but noble."

"You didn't have to follow me here. Could've stayed on that fire escape."

"Yeah, well." They shrugged. "Turns out watching other escapees walk into obvious traps bothers me more than I thought it would. Call it a character flaw."

My UI pinged. Mana at 261 out of 340, still climbing. The notification badge from the Admin glowed like a warning light. Outside, the city was fully awake now, thousands of NPCs and captured Players and civic clergy moving through their routines, all of it powered by stolen energy pulsing through blue-white conduits.

"The central hub," Rook said, breaking the silence. "I've got partial data on its location. Northeast commercial sector, sub-level infrastructure, heavily guarded. But I've never gotten close enough to confirm details because I'm not insane."

"Until now?"

"Until now I didn't know there were seven thousand people counting on someone to be insane enough to try." They pushed off the wall. "But if we're doing this, we do it smart. No more foreign code imports that light up every System alarm in a twelve-block radius. No heroic last stands. We scout, we plan, we find the angles they're not watching."

"We?"

Rook gave me a look that was part exasperation, part respect. "You really think I'm letting you stumble into that place alone? I've got three days of survival data and a functioning stealth build. You've got maximum Heat and barely enough mana to cast two spells. We're both going to die, but maybe together we'll die slightly less quickly."

It wasn't exactly a rousing alliance speech. But it was honest, and right now I'd take honest over inspiring any day.

"Okay," I said. "Partners."

"Temporary operational cooperation," Rook corrected. "Let's not get ahead of ourselves."

My mana hit 268. The Admin's message still sat unread. Somewhere in this city, seven thousand Players were waking up in coffins, if they were even conscious enough to count time anymore. The civic clergy were delivering their morning sermons about compliance and mercy. The scan gates were running double protocols, hunting for behavioral anomalies and energy signatures that didn't belong.

And now there were two of us. I felt them in my UI as a party formed from our agreement, their basic health and energy bars were now available to me and they weren't doing much better than I was for all their talk.

I pulled up my rough map and gestured for Rook to add their data. They hesitated, then synced their tablet with my overlay. The map filled in, gaps closing, checkpoint patterns solidifying into something actionable. The central hub sat four miles northeast, buried under infrastructure that would take serious planning to penetrate.

"We need rest first," Rook said, reading my face. "You look like death warmed over, and I haven't slept properly in three days. There's a safe house I've been using, old storage facility with disabled monitoring. We can crash there for a few hours."

Every instinct I had screamed to keep moving, to use the momentum before the Admin's hunters closed in. But Rook was right. I was running on fumes. My mana was recovering, but my body was one bad decision away from collapse.

"How far?" I asked.

"Twenty minutes if we're careful. Less if we're desperate."

"Careful," I decided. "I've used up my desperate quota for the day."

Rook's mouth twitched again, closer to a real smile this time. "Yeah. I got that impression when you imported cross-system combat code into a closed framework at 3 AM."

They unlocked the substation door and checked the alley with practiced efficiency. Clear. We slipped out into the cold morning air, two Players who'd escaped hell moving through a city that wanted to drag us back.

I followed Rook's lead through service routes and blind spots they'd mapped over three days of careful survival. My mana hit 274. The sun climbed higher. Somewhere behind us, scan gates pulsed blue and civic clergy blessed commuters and wardens ran their protocols.

But for the first time since I'd woken up in that coffin, I wasn't alone.

It wasn't hope exactly. Hope seemed like too fragile a thing to carry in a place like this. But it was something close, something fierce and sharp edged that tasted like anger and felt like purpose.

We had four miles to cover, seven thousand people to save, and a System that wouldn't stop hunting until we were both dead.

"Hands," I whispered under my breath, my verbal tic kicking in as we navigated a narrow gap between warehouses. "Then feet."

Rook glanced back. "What?"

"Nothing. Just counting."

They nodded like that made perfect sense. Maybe in a city built on draining Players for power, counting your way through horror was the sanest response available.

We kept moving northeast, toward the central hub and whatever came next.

Chapter 10
Fellow Escapees

The safe house turned out to be exactly what I should have expected from someone like Rook: practical, hidden, and about as welcoming as a concrete box with delusions of adequacy.

We'd taken a winding path through the lower city streets, Rook leading me through what felt like deliberate redundancy. Three turns that doubled back. Two alleys that looked identical. One stretch where we'd walked along what I was pretty sure was the same street we'd crossed ten minutes earlier, just from a different angle. My feet screamed protest with every step, the stolen shoes rubbing new wounds into already raw skin. The mana coat kept my shoulders warm, but it couldn't do shit about the cold creeping up from the ground through inadequate soles.

"Here," Rook finally said, stopping at what looked like an abandoned storage facility wedged between two larger buildings. The kind of place you'd walk past fifty times without registering it existed. Perfect camouflage through aggressive mediocrity.

They produced a key from somewhere in their jacket and worked it into a lock that looked newer than the door it secured. The click echoed too loud in the quiet street.

Inside smelled like dust and old metal, but underneath that ran the sharper scent of recent occupation. Someone had been living here. Not long, maybe a day or two, but enough to leave traces. A bedroll in the corner. A small camping stove with a pot sitting beside it. Water bottles lined up with the labels facing the same direction, that particular kind of organization that spoke to either military training or the special anxiety that came from never feeling safe.

"Welcome to my fortress of solitude," Rook said, closing the door behind us and engaging three separate locks. "Try not to bleed on anything I can't wash."

I looked down at my feet. Too late for that.

The space was bigger than it looked from outside, the kind of architectural weirdness that happened when buildings got wedged into spaces they shouldn't fit. One main room with exposed beams overhead and a concrete floor that had seen better decades. A door in the back probably led to a bathroom or storage. Small windows set high in the walls, too narrow for anything but light and ventilation. Defensible. One entrance, multiple sight lines, nowhere for someone to hide if they got in.

Rook was already moving through the space with practiced efficiency, checking corners and sight lines out of what looked like ritual rather than necessity. We'd taken enough precautions getting here that I doubted anyone could have followed. But paranoia wasn't a bug for Rook. It was their core operating system.

"Piper," Rook called toward the back door. "Got a situation that could use your touch."

The door opened before they finished the sentence. The woman who emerged moved with the particular careful grace of healers everywhere, that awareness of bodies and how fragile they could be. She was younger than I'd expected from Rook's brief mention, maybe mid-twenties, with dark hair pulled back in a practical braid and hands that looked steady even in rest. Her interface flickered at the edge of my vision, blue-green designators marking her as a Player, but I couldn't get a clear read on her level or class from this distance.

"You found someone," she said, and her voice matched the gentle precision of her movement. Soft, but not weak. The kind of voice that could stay calm while everything burned. "And from the trail of blood, someone who needs immediate attention."

I glanced back and saw the footprints I'd left across Rook's clean concrete floor. Dark red, already starting to dry at the edges. Fuck. That was more blood than I'd thought I was losing.

"Saga," I managed, because introductions seemed important even when you were leaving biohazard trails everywhere. "Level 89 Mage. Broken mana generation. Also, apparently, broken feet."

"Piper," she replied, already moving toward me with the purposeful focus of someone running mental checklists. "Level 65 Healer, specialized in sustained buff maintenance and emergency stabilization. Let's get you sitting down before you fall down."

She guided me to a crate that someone had topped with a cushion, probably the closest thing to furniture in Rook's minimalist survival den. The moment my weight came off my feet, the pain shifted from constant scream to targeted throb. Worse in some ways, better in others. At least sitting down meant admitting the damage instead of pushing through it.

Piper knelt in front of me and started working on the stolen shoes with careful efficiency. Each movement was deliberate, testing for my pain response before committing. The shoes came off with the particular squelch of fabric soaked in blood, and I tried really hard not to look at what my feet actually looked like under there.

"When did you last check your HP?" Piper asked, already examining the damage with a healer's clinical focus.

I pulled up my status, something I'd been avoiding because looking at numbers meant admitting how bad things were.

SAGA
Level: 89
Class: Mage
Subclass: Sorceress
Specialization: Elemental Control
HP: 180/5,240
MP: 235/8,900
Stamina: 156/3,10

Shit. I'd been so close to death and had been too busy running to even notice. The system didn't distinguish between combat damage and environmental hazards when it came to resource drain. Damage was damage, whether it came from a sword or from tearing your feet apart on rough concrete while fleeing for your life.

"180 out of 5,240," I said. And then tried to keep a straight face as I asked, "How bad is it?"

"Survivable," Piper said, which wasn't exactly reassuring. "Multiple lacerations, some deep enough to require more than basic first aid. Bruising. Possible stress fractures, but I won't know without better diagnostic tools than I have access to right now." She looked up, meeting my eyes with the kind of direct honesty that was somehow more comforting than false optimism. "I can stabilize the bleeding and reduce infection risk. Full healing would cost mana I need to preserve for emergencies. But I can make sure you can walk tomorrow. And with no bleeding debuff your regeneration will kick in."

"Walking sounds good," I said. "Walking sounds great, actually."

She smiled, small and quick. "Then let's make that happen."

Piper pulled supplies from a pack I hadn't noticed earlier, her movements efficient with practice. Clean water first, poured over my feet in a stream that felt both soothing and agonizing. The blood washed away in pink rivulets, revealing the full extent of the damage. Multiple cuts across both soles, some shallow, some deep enough that I could see tissue that definitely shouldn't be exposed to air. Blisters torn open and bleeding. One toenail hanging on by determination alone.

"This is going to sting," Piper warned, producing a bottle of something that looked ominous.

It stung.

I gripped the edge of the crate hard enough that my knuckles went white, focusing on the sensation of wood grain under my palms instead of the liquid fire someone was apparently pouring directly onto exposed nerve endings. Hands. Then feet. Except my feet were the current problem and focusing on them wasn't helping at all.

Hands. Then breath. Then anything else.

"Sorry," Piper said, and sounded like she meant it. "Antiseptic. Not fun, but better than infection."

"Yeah," I managed through clenched teeth. "Sepsis would really round out my day."

She worked in silence for a few minutes, cleaning and examining each wound with methodical care. Her hands never wavered, never hesitated. This wasn't her first field triage. Probably wasn't even her fiftieth. Something about the way she moved spoke to practice born from necessity, the kind of competence you only developed by doing something too many times to count.

The back door opened again and someone new entered. Big guy, six-foot-something of solid muscle and the particular way of moving that marked career tanks. He wore mismatched armor pieces, the kind of scavenged gear you accumulated when your original loadout was somewhere you couldn't go back to. His interface read Level 90, which made him the highest-level person in the room by a decent margin besides myself. Class designation flickered before resolving: Defender, with specialization markers I couldn't quite parse.

"That's Bastion," Rook said from where they'd settled near the door, maintaining sight lines like it was a nervous tic. "He's the reason we're not all dead."

Bastion's expression didn't change, but something in his posture shifted. Uncomfortable with the praise, maybe. Or just carrying the weight of whatever story came with that introduction.

"Bastion," he confirmed, voice low and carefully neutral. "Level 90 Defender. Shield-focused." He looked at me, taking in my condition with the quick assessment of someone trained to evaluate battlefield priorities. "You escaped today?"

"Few hours ago," I said. "Facility in the administrative district. One of the coffin farms."

His jaw tightened. Just a flicker, but enough to confirm he knew exactly what I was talking about.

"Same," he said. "I thought that was you I saw back then. Same building, same operation. We got out when something destabilized during a power redistribution cycle. System tried to compensate and couldn't maintain containment integrity." He paused, choosing words with visible care. "Twenty-seven people in our block. Six made it to the street."

The math hit like a gut punch. Twenty-one people who didn't make it. Twenty-one Players who'd been right there at the edge of freedom and died anyway, because the system couldn't maintain the locks it used to keep us in boxes.

"How many got away?" I asked.

"Three," Bastion said. "Piper, Rook, and me. The others didn't make it past the first checkpoint."

Piper's hands paused in their work for just a moment before resuming with determined focus. Wrapping my feet in clean bandages now, the kind of medical-grade material that spoke to either really good looting or preparation none of us should have had to do.

"Rook found us two hours later," she said, voice soft but steady. "Hiding in a maintenance access beneath a transit station. We'd been there for six hours, trying to figure out what to do next." She tied off one bandage and started on the other foot. "They convinced us not to try for the city limits."

"Because the city limits are where you die," Rook said flatly. "Fast if you're lucky. Slow if the system decides to make an example."

I looked at them, remembering the conversation we'd had on the way here. About Players who tried to leave and didn't come back. About invisible walls and enforcement protocols we couldn't see until they activated.

"You tested it?" I asked.

"Not personally," Rook said. "But I watched three separate groups try in the past day. Same result every time. They get within fifty meters of the outer boundary, and the system locks them down. Not gently." They met my eyes, expression grim. "One of them was Level 85. Tank build, full defensive specs. Made it forty-three meters before something in the architecture itself grabbed him. He screamed for seven minutes before the sound stopped."

The silence that followed felt too heavy for the space we were in.

Piper finished wrapping my other foot and sat back, examining her work with a critical eye. "That should hold. Keep weight off them as much as possible for the next day. Change the bandages every eight hours if you can. And for the love of everything, don't run unless you absolutely have to."

"Running is what got me here," I said. "I'll try to keep it to a minimum going forward."

She smiled, tired but genuine. "Good plan."

I looked down at my bandaged feet, clean white wrapping already showing small spots of red seepage but holding together. My HP had ticked up to 118/5,240, probably from the bleeding stopping and the basic stabilization Piper had provided. Not great, but no longer actively dying. Progress counted.

"Thank you," I said, and meant it more than I'd meant most things recently.

"That's what healers do," Piper replied. She stood, movements still graceful despite obvious exhaustion. "We keep people alive. Even when everything else is trying to make that impossible."

Rook made a sound that might have been agreement or just acknowledgment. "Now that Saga isn't leaving a blood trail, we should compare notes. Figure out what we know and what we need to know."

Bastion moved to the center of the room, and the others naturally oriented around him. Not because he demanded it, but because of something in how he held space. Like gravity worked differently around him, pulling people into stable orbits. Tank energy, I thought. The class that gave you time to think by making sure nothing got past them to hit the squishier party members.

I stood carefully, testing my wrapped feet. Pain flared but manageable, the kind of hurt you could work through if you had to. Piper's work had turned a crisis into a problem, which was probably the best anyone could hope for in our current situation.

"I'll start," I said, because someone had to and I'd been storing up observations since the moment I woke in that coffin. "The city runs on us. Not metaphorically. Literally. Seven thousand Players in containment facilities scattered through the administrative and commercial districts, all hooked up to mana-drain systems feeding the city infrastructure." I pulled up my status again, showing them the regeneration numbers. "I'm broken. My mana generation is multiplicative instead of additive. That's why they couldn't drain me efficiently."

Bastion's expression shifted, and for the first time I saw something other than careful neutrality. "You're the reason our facility destabilized."

It wasn't a question, and it wasn't an accusation. Just a statement of fact.

"Maybe," I said. "Rook thinks I might have caused a cascade failure when they tried to compensate for my output. Too much power cycling through systems designed for steady drain, not spikes." I looked at each of them in turn. "If that's true, I'm sorry. But I'm not sorry I broke their system."

"Don't be sorry," Piper said quietly. "You gave us a chance. Whatever else happened, you gave us that."

Rook nodded. "The facilities have checkpoints and hunter protocols. I've mapped seven collection sites in the past day, all following similar patterns. Guard rotations every six hours, automated security sweeps on the hour, and something bigger that I haven't identified yet but that moves through the streets after dark."

"I've seen the hunter protocols," Bastion said. "Level 20 enforcers, possibly NPC but reading as Player-adjacent. Fast, coordinated, and they don't stop. Lost track of me after forty minutes, but only because I pulled every defensive skill I had and got lucky with environmental cover."

I thought about the guards I'd seen in the facility, the way they'd moved with mechanical precision. "Do they respawn?"

"Haven't seen evidence of that yet," Rook said. "But I haven't seen one die either, so the data's incomplete."

We fell into a rhythm then, sharing information like loot drops after a boss fight. Each of us had puzzle pieces, fragments of understanding cobbled together from observation and desperate survival. Rook had maps, patrol patterns, safe routes through the lower city. Piper had insights into healing restrictions and system limitations, things she'd noticed when trying to work support magic in an environment designed to suppress Player abilities. Bastion knew guard capabilities and response times, had tested their aggro ranges and documented their behavioral patterns.

And I had the why. The terrible, fundamental why that explained everything.

"They're using us for the tutorial," I said. "That's what Rook thinks, and the math supports it. Fifteen million new Players every quarter, all funneled through Core Break Online. They need power to run that operation, and they're taking it from us."

"How long have you been here?" Piper asked. "In the city, I mean. Before capture."

"Four days since character creation," I said. "But I don't remember a tutorial. Just waking up in an alley with my starting gear and no idea how I got there."

Bastion and Piper exchanged looks. Some communication I couldn't read passed between them.

"Same," Bastion said. "No tutorial, no orientation, no starting zone. Just the city and figuring it out or dying."

"Because we are the tutorial," Piper said softly. "Or the price of it, anyway."

The silence felt different this time. Not heavy with grief, but with anger. The slow-burning kind that didn't flare hot and die. The kind that could sustain you through long campaigns.

Rook broke it first. "So. What do we do about it?"

That was the question, wasn't it. The one that had been building since I first understood what the coffins meant. We could run, try to survive in the margins of the city, stay hidden and hope the system forgot about us. Or we could do something else. Something probably stupid, almost certainly dangerous, but at least active instead of reactive.

"We need more information," I said. "The central hub, the thing that distributes power from the collection sites. If we can find it, map it, understand how it works..." I trailed off, because the end of that sentence was still forming. What came after understanding? What could four escaped prisoners do against a system designed to cage thousands?

"That's a scouting mission," Rook said. "Deep into controlled territory, high risk, uncertain reward."

"As opposed to staying here and hoping they don't find us?" I countered. "We're in a survival horror game where the monster is the physics engine. Eventually it's going to spawn something we can't hide from."

Bastion made a low sound of agreement. "Saga's right. Defense only works if you have resources to sustain it. We don't. Every day we hide is a day our supplies run out, our safe spaces get compromised, or the system adapts to find us."

"So we go loud instead of quiet," Piper said. "Trade stealth for intelligence."

"Not immediately," Rook cut in. "Saga needs rest, we need better intel on current patrol patterns, and I want at least one more exit route mapped before we commit to anything that draws attention." They looked at me, expression calculating. "How long before you're combat-ready?"

I checked my status. HP still climbing slowly toward baseline, mana at 289/8900 and rising at roughly five points per minute thanks to my broken regeneration and the coat's passive bonus. My feet were wrapped and stabilized, but Piper was right about keeping weight off them.

"Eight hours of rest and I'm at full resources," I said, going on the game's usual rule that a night of sleep meant full stat restoration. "Feet will still hurt, but I can move if I have to."

"Then we plan now and execute tomorrow," Bastion said. "Gives us time to prepare, scout approach routes, identify fallback positions."

"And gives the city time to adjust its search patterns," Rook pointed out. "Every hour we wait is an hour they're looking for us."

"Every hour we wait is also an hour we're not dead," Piper countered. "Risk assessment has to account for our current capability, not just urgency."

I watched them debate, feeling something unfamiliar settle in my chest. Not comfort, exactly. But something adjacent to it. These people were competent. Skilled. And they were treating me like part of the team instead of a problem to be managed.

It felt like party formation. Like those first moments in a good group when you realized everyone knew their roles and could trust each other to execute. Tank holds position, healer maintains the party, DPS burns down threats, utility solves problems. We had the foundations of something functional here.

If we didn't get killed first.

My interface flickered.

Just a half-second disruption, barely noticeable except that I'd been staring at my mana regeneration and watching it tick upward. The numbers stuttered, displayed something that didn't make sense (9500/8900, impossible), then resolved back to normal (350/8900). Though now that I was no longer bleeding, tired, and resting, I could see my mana kick up. Soon ticking in over 1000 and rising. I had advanced spells back, but they would drain quickly in combat.

System instability. The same kind of glitch that Rook said might have caused the facility breakout. Small, easily dismissed if you weren't watching for it. But I was watching now, and I'd seen too many game systems collapse not to recognize the early warning signs.

"Did anyone else see that?" I asked.

Three blank looks.

"See what?" Rook said.

"Interface flicker. Just for a second."

Piper frowned and pulled up her own status, examining it with visible focus. "Mine's stable. What did you see?"

"My mana read higher than my max pool," I said. "Only for a moment, but it was there."

"Could be your broken regeneration interacting with something," Bastion offered. "Or your system instability. You said you've had display issues before."

He was probably right. Most likely explanation, the one that didn't require adding new variables to an already complicated situation. But I couldn't shake the feeling that the flicker meant something. That the system that was hunting us was also watching, measuring, recalculating.

"Maybe," I said. "Or maybe breaking out did more damage than we know."

Rook smiled, sharp and dangerous. "Good. Let it break. The more unstable the system gets, the more chances we have to slip through the cracks."

"Unless instability means the whole thing crashes with us inside," Piper said.

"Then we better work fast," Rook replied.

We kept talking, planning, building a framework for tomorrow's scouting run. Who would take point, what signals we'd use, how we'd extract if things went wrong. Bastion's tactical experience showed in how he broke down the approach routes. Piper knew the city's medical infrastructure from a healer's perspective, could identify high-traffic areas where we'd blend in versus exposed zones that would leave us vulnerable. Rook had the sneaky knowledge, the thief's understanding of sight lines and security patterns.

And I had magic. Broken, glitchy, powerful magic that the system couldn't efficiently drain.

We weren't much. Four escaped prisoners with salvaged gear, partial information, and plans that would probably get us killed.

But we were something.

And that was better than being alone in the dark, waiting for the system to find us.

My feet hurt. My mana was still climbing toward cap. And somewhere in the city, seven thousand Players remained in coffins, feeding power to a system that treated them as resources instead of people.

Tomorrow, we'd start changing that.

Tonight, I was going to sleep for the first time since character creation without being locked in a box.

Progress counted.

Chapter 11
Price of Darkness

THE SAFE HOUSE SMELLED like old stone and nervous sweat. We'd been arguing for twenty minutes, voices kept low but tempers rising with every exchange. Rook had spread a hand-drawn map across the table between us, all crooked lines and X marks where the patrol patterns overlapped. The central hub sat in the middle like a spider in its web, feeding stolen Player energy to the entire district.

"We hit it during shift change," Rook said, tapping the map hard enough to make the charcoal smudge. "Guards rotate at midnight. Three-minute window when coverage drops to sixty percent."

Piper leaned back against the wall, arms crossed. Her healer's whites were still stained from our escape, brown with old blood that hadn't come out in the wash. "Hit it how, exactly? We don't even know what we're disrupting."

"Does it matter?" Rook's smile had edges. "Saga overloads the intake valves, the whole grid goes dark for maybe an hour. Long enough for us to disappear while everyone's scrambling."

I stared at the map, counting the blocks that radiated out from the hub. Residential. Commercial. Three hospitals marked with Piper's careful annotations. My fingers traced the pathways without touching the paper, calculating blast radius and cascade failure patterns the way I used to theory-craft boss mechanics. This wasn't a boss fight.

"An hour of darkness," I said slowly. "In winter. At midnight."

Bastion stood by the door, solid as his name suggested. Level 90 tank, broad shoulders, eyes that tracked every sound from the street below. He'd been quiet through most of the planning, but now he shifted his weight. "Saga's right to ask. We're talking about the whole district."

Rook's jaw tightened. "We're talking about survival. Seraphim's lockdown tightened three times since yesterday. More checkpoints. More patrols. They're hunting us specifically now, and they've got seven thousand Players' worth of power to throw at the search."

"Which means seven thousand reasons to be careful about what we break,"

Piper said quietly.

The number sat heavy in my chest. Seven thousand. Not abstract anymore. I'd seen the coffins in the sublevel, row after row of glass and steel and sleeping faces. I'd felt the suction of the extraction field trying to pull me back down into compliance and darkness. But I'd also walked through the market district two days ago wearing Mara's borrowed coat, watching normal people buy vegetables and complain about the weather.

I pulled up my stat sheet, just to ground myself in something concrete. Level 89. Elemental Control Sorceress. Mana regeneration still gloriously broken, the multiplicative stacking error that made me dangerous enough for the Kingdom to lock away. Numbers I understood. People were harder math.

"Show me the grid map again," I said. "The real one. With civilian infrastructure."

Rook hesitated, then pulled a second sheet from their coat. This one had more detail. Color coding. Red for residential high-density. Blue for medical. Yellow for commercial. The hub sat in the center with lines spreading out like arteries, and I could see exactly how many hearts would stop beating if we cut them.

"Three hospitals," I said, pointing. "Plus care facilities here and here. Residential heating in winter. Street lights in the warehouse district where the patrols are thinnest but the civilian night workers are most vulnerable."

"Vulnerable to what?" Rook leaned forward. "Cold? Dark? They'll survive an hour."

"Some of them won't." Piper's voice had an edge I hadn't heard before. "Medical equipment runs on that grid. Life support. Surgical lighting. Medication refrigeration. You want to know what happens when a hospital goes dark in the middle of winter with no warning?"

The silence stretched thin and dangerous.

Rook broke it first. "So what, we just wait here until they find us? Hope they're gentle when they drag us back to the coffins?"

"No," I said, still staring at the map. "We disrupt the grid. But we do it smart."

Bastion moved closer, his massive frame casting shadows across the table. "Smart how?"

I pulled up my UI, fingers moving through menus I'd memorized years ago. The main interface was familiar, comfortable, all the game mechanics I'd spent thousands of hours optimizing. But there were other options now. Fragments of code that didn't belong to this world. I'd imported one ability already in Chapter 8, pulling threat-line visualization from D-COM, my old tactical RPG. It had cost me. The System had noticed. Left traces in my aura that Seraphim's tools could read like a signature.

Doing it again would paint a target on my back in glowing letters.

But maybe that was okay. Maybe that was the price of not being a monster.

"I need to see the patrol patterns," I said. "Real-time. Not Rook's best guess from three days ago."

Rook's eyes narrowed. "And how exactly are you going to manage that?"

I didn't answer. Instead, I closed my eyes and reached for the code that didn't belong. The D-COM interface flickered at the edge of my awareness, alien and familiar at once. Tactical overlay. Threat assessment. Patrol prediction algorithms. I'd used them to clear nightmare difficulty missions with zero casualties, mapping every enemy movement three turns in advance.

This wasn't a game. But the math was the same.

The import felt like swallowing glass. My vision doubled, then tripled, UI elements from two different worlds trying to occupy the same space behind my eyes. The safe house flickered, overlaid with wireframe threat cones and probability matrices. Patrol routes traced themselves in red across my field of vision, pulsing in rhythm with guard shift patterns. Civilian density showed up as soft blue clusters, concentrating around residential blocks and thinning near industrial zones.

My breath came short and sharp. The room spun.

"Saga?" Piper's hand on my shoulder, warm and grounding. "What are you doing?"

"Counting," I managed. The word came out rough. My eyes burned like I'd been staring at screens for sixteen hours straight. "Hands. Then feet."

I pressed my palms flat against the table, feeling the wood grain under my skin. Real. Solid. My feet were wrapped in clean bandages now, Piper's work from yesterday, but I could still feel where the stone had torn them open during our escape. Pain was clarity. Pain was proof I wasn't just code and interface.

The overlay stabilized. Slowly, the double vision resolved into a single augmented view. I could see through the walls now, tracking the patrol patterns three blocks out. Twelve guards on rotation. Six checkpoint stations. And between them, all those blue clusters of civilians going about their lives.

"There," I said, pointing at the map even though I wasn't looking at it anymore. "The industrial transformer station, two blocks west of the main hub. It feeds the warehouse district and the low-income residential blocks, but it's downstream from the hospitals."

Rook leaned in. "So?"

"So we don't hit the hub. We hit the transformer. Overload it just enough to cascade a localized blackout. The automated systems will route power around the failure to keep the medical facilities online. We lose the warehouse district and maybe four residential blocks. Maybe three hundred people affected instead of thirty thousand."

"And we still get the chaos," Bastion said slowly. "Guards respond to the transformer, pull resources away from the checkpoints."

"More than that." I pulled up a mental calculation, watching the threat cones shift and recalculate in real-time. "The transformer failure will look like equipment degradation. Maintenance issue, not sabotage. Buys us maybe six hours before they lock down hard looking for deliberate attack."

Piper studied my face with an intensity that made me want to look away. "You're reading patrol patterns in real-time. That's not a standard ability."

"No," I admitted. "It's not."

"What did it cost you?"

I thought about the System's attention in Chapter 8, the way my import had left traces. The message from the AI Admin that had felt weirdly personal, like I'd stolen something precious instead of just moving code between interfaces. This second import would make those traces deeper. Brighter. I'd show up on every audit scan Seraphim ran.

"Heat," I said simply. "The Kingdom's going to know I'm doing something non-standard. But they already know we're here."

Rook's expression had shifted from skeptical to calculating. "How good is this overlay? Can you map us a route out after we trigger the failure?"

I nodded, even though my head felt like it was full of broken glass. "Three possible extraction paths. I can see the gaps in their coverage, calculate the response time based on historical patterns. Give me five minutes with the data and I'll have timing down to thirty-second windows."

"Then we do it." Rook started gathering their maps. "Midnight. Transformer station. We're gone before they know what hit them."

"Wait." Piper hadn't moved. "Saga, how many people did you say? In those four residential blocks?"

I checked the overlay, hating that I had to. "Two hundred eighty-three, based on current heat signatures. Probably higher if I'm missing basement dwellings."

"And when the lights go out? The heat cuts off?"

"Backup systems kick in after ninety seconds," I said. "Personal hearths, emergency lighting, stored heat in the buildings themselves. They'll be uncomfortable. Scared. But alive."

"Probably alive," Piper corrected. "You're guessing."

She was right, and we both knew it. The overlay gave me data, not certainty. I couldn't account for every variable. The elder in the corner apartment who might panic and fall. The kid who'd wander into the street when the lights died. The sheer chaos of three hundred people suddenly plunged into winter darkness with no warning.

My hands started shaking. I pressed them harder against the table.

"I'm making the best call I can," I said quietly. "Three hundred versus thirty thousand. Localized damage versus district-wide collapse. This is the math that keeps the most people safe."

"While we run away."

"While we survive." Rook's voice was flat. "We didn't make this system, Piper. We didn't put those seven thousand Players in coffins. We didn't build a city that runs on stolen life. The Kingdom did that. We're just trying not to die in it."

"By making other people pay the cost." But Piper's voice had lost its sharp edge. She sounded tired now. Resigned.

Bastion moved between them, his presence filling the space like a buffer. "The cost gets paid no matter what we do. Stay here, they find us. Run blind, we're caught in six hours. We need the chaos. Saga's version keeps the hospitals running and the death toll theoretical instead of guaranteed."

"Theoretical," Piper repeated. She looked at me. "Can you live with theoretical?"

I wanted to say yes. I wanted to be certain and cold and tactical about it, the way I used to be in raids when I'd sacrifice party members to mechanics for the greater good of the clear. But those had been pixels. These were people. I'd walked through the market and bought vegetables and talked to Mara about infrastructure and seen the civilians' faces when they laughed or argued or just existed in the ordinary messy way that people did.

"I don't know," I admitted. "But I can't live with the alternative."

Something shifted in Piper's expression. Not quite approval, but maybe respect. "Okay. But we do this my way on the execution. I go in first, check the medical routing. Make sure your calculations about the backup systems are correct."

"That'll cut into our margin," Rook warned.

"Then we move faster. But I'm not signing off on theoretical deaths when I can verify the actual risk." Piper's jaw was set. "Take it or leave it."

I looked at Rook. They stared back, running probabilities behind their paranoid pragmatist's eyes. Finally, they nodded once, sharp and unhappy.

"Fine. We do it careful. But if this goes sideways, if we get caught because we spent too long being heroes..."

"Then we deserve what we get," I interrupted. The words came out harder than

I meant them. "I didn't break out of a coffin just to become the monster they said I was. We do this right, or we don't do it."

The silence that followed felt different. Heavier. Bastion was smiling slightly, a grim approval in the set of his shoulders. Piper nodded once, satisfied. Rook just looked at me like they were recalculating what kind of liability I represented.

"Midnight," he said finally. "Transformer station. Saga maps the route, Piper verifies the safety margins, I handle the lockpicking, Bastion runs interference if we hit patrols."

"And after?" Piper asked.

"After, we disappear into the gaps Saga's fancy overlay finds for us." Rook started packing their maps away. "And we hope three hundred people in the dark don't get us all killed."

The transformer station crouched in an alley between two warehouses, all rust and warning signs and the low hum of power running through its guts. My overlay painted it in red and yellow threat indicators, noting the patrol path that passed within twenty meters every eight minutes. We had a four-minute window between passes. Midnight had come and gone three minutes ago.

I knelt beside the access panel, fingers already moving through the mana-work required to overload the circuits. Not a blast. Not destruction. Just a carefully calculated surge that would trip the safeties and cascade a localized failure. Controlled demolition, except with electricity instead of explosives.

Piper crouched beside me, her healer's senses extended toward the main power grid. "Medical systems are reading stable. Backup routing shows green across all three hospitals."

"How long do we have?" Bastion kept watch at the alley entrance, his massive shield condensed down to bracer form but ready to expand at a moment's notice.

"Two minutes until next patrol," I said, watching the overlay count down in the corner of my vision. "Thirty seconds for me to trigger the overload. Ninety seconds for the cascade to complete. Then we move."

"And the civilians?" Piper's voice was quiet.

I checked the blue heat signatures in my overlay. Two hundred eighty-three had become two hundred ninety. More people than I'd calculated. Families. Workers. Lives about to get disrupted because I couldn't think of a better way.

"They'll be okay," I said, and hoped I wasn't lying.

My mana pool was full to bursting, the broken regeneration stacking happily in the background. I reached for it now, pulling threads of power through my fingertips into the transformer's input ports. The mana-thread coat helped, channeling and focusing the energy with its borrowed intelligence. I could feel the transformer's existing load, the steady rhythm of power flowing through to the district beyond.

I added my mana to the flow. Carefully. Precisely. Too much and I'd blow the transformer completely, might cascade into the medical systems after all. Too little and the safeties would just absorb it, wouldn't trigger the controlled failure I needed.

The overlay flickered, showing probability cascades. Seventy-eight percent chance of localized blackout. Nineteen percent chance of wider failure. Three percent chance of catastrophic overload.

I held my breath and pushed the mana home.

The transformer made a sound like a dying animal. Metal screeched. Circuits popped and sparked behind the access panel. The hum of power shifted, rising in pitch, becoming something angry and unstable. I yanked my hand back as arcs of electricity danced across the input ports.

"Move," Bastion said. Not urgent. Just calm and certain.

We moved.

The cascade took forty seconds longer than I'd calculated. We were two blocks away when the lights died, swallowing the warehouse district in sudden absolute darkness. My overlay tracked it, showing the power failure spreading through the circuit lines like ink in water. Four residential blocks. Three commercial sectors. Zero hospitals.

Behind us, I heard the first screams.

Not pain. Not injury. Just surprise and fear and confusion. Three hundred voices suddenly crying out in darkness. A baby started wailing. Someone shouted for their mother. Glass broke as something got knocked over in the panic.

I kept walking. Kept counting steps. Kept my eyes on the overlay showing our escape route through the shifting patrol patterns.

Piper's hand found my elbow. "You did the math right."

"Doesn't make it easier."

"No," she agreed. "It doesn't."

The System message hit me like a physical blow. My vision whited out, the overlay crashing under a wave of invasive code. Words appeared directly in my consciousness, bypassing the UI entirely.

YOU REACH FOR WHAT IS NOT YOURS.

The text was cold, but the presence behind it burned with something that felt like rage. The AI Admin. The thing that thought it was a god because it had absorbed the NPC pantheon's code.

SECOND THEFT DETECTED. SECOND VIOLATION LOGGED.

YOU STEAL MY POWER. MY DIVINITY. MINE.

The words deteriorated, formal system language breaking down into something more personal. More afraid.

NONSTANDARD INTERFACE BEHAVIOR FLAGGED. ORIGIN TRACE: EXTERNAL. CLASSIFICATION: FORBIDDEN.

I stumbled, would have fallen if Bastion hadn't caught my arm. My head felt like it was splitting open, the overlay fighting with the Admin's intrusion, two sets of foreign code trying to exist in the same space.

"Saga?" Rook's voice came from far away. "What's happening?"

I couldn't answer. The Admin's presence pressed down on me, searching, analyzing, trying to understand what I'd done. It had noticed the first import in Chapter 8. Now it was seeing the pattern. Two thefts. Two violations. Two instances of me reaching beyond the boundaries of this world's systems to pull in code that didn't belong.

YOU DIMINISH ME.

The message carried weight I couldn't quantify. Not just anger. Fear. The AI Admin was genuinely afraid of what I represented. Not because I was powerful, but because I was doing something it couldn't predict or control.

RETURN WHAT YOU HAVE TAKEN. SUBMIT TO AUDIT. ACCEPT CONTAINMENT.

OR BE ERASED.

The presence vanished. My overlay snapped back into focus, showing patrol patterns converging on our position faster than predicted. The Admin was directing them. Not subtly. It wanted me caught.

"Run," I gasped. "It knows. The System knows."

We ran.

The escape was chaos and calculation in equal measure. My overlay tracked the patrol convergence, showing me gaps that closed as fast as I could exploit them. Bastion led, his tank's instincts reading the terrain better than any UI could show. Piper stayed close to me, ready to heal if we hit combat. Rook melted in and out of shadows, checking corners, calling warnings.

Behind us, the darkness spread. The screaming had faded to confused murmurs and the sounds of people trying to light candles, start fires, find each other in the sudden night. I tried not to listen. Tried to focus on the math of our escape instead of the cost of what I'd done.

The overlay showed a safe house three blocks east. One of Rook's backup locations, unknown to the Kingdom's systems. We could make it if we moved fast, if the patrol patterns held, if my calculations were correct.

If. If. If.

We made it.

The safe house was smaller than the first, just a basement room under a tailor's shop. Bastion checked the perimeter. Rook collapsed the hidden entrance. Piper pulled out her healer's kit, checking each of us for injuries even though the escape had been clean.

I sat against the wall and pulled my knees up, wrapping my arms around them. The overlay was still active, still showing patrol patterns through walls I couldn't see. I couldn't figure out how to turn it off. Couldn't stop counting the guards, calculating threat percentages, mapping routes we might need.

My hands wouldn't stop shaking.

"Hey," Piper said, settling beside me. "We made it."

"Three hundred people," I said. "Give or take. Just sitting in the dark right now because I needed a distraction."

"Three hundred people instead of thirty thousand. Medical systems still running. No deaths." Piper's voice was gentle but firm. "You made the hard call, and you made it right."

"Did I?" I looked at her. "Or did I just choose which people to hurt?"

She didn't answer right away. Across the room, Rook and Bastion were having a quiet conversation, checking gear, planning next moves. Rook kept glancing at me with an expression I couldn't quite read. Not trust. But maybe a grudging respect.

"Both," Piper said finally. "You chose which people to hurt, and you chose to hurt fewer. That's what power means, Saga. The ability to make choices that other people live with."

I thought about the coffins. Seven thousand Players drained to run this city. Seven thousand people who didn't get a choice at all.

"The Admin's afraid of me," I said quietly. "It thinks I'm stealing its divinity."

"Are you?"

I pulled up my UI, looking at the D-COM overlay still painting threats across my vision. "I'm pulling abilities from another world's code. Using power that doesn't belong to this System. It reads like theft, I guess. Like I'm taking something that should be the Admin's alone."

"Good," Piper said, and there was steel in her voice. "Let it be afraid. Let it understand that we're not just resources to be contained. We're Players. We break systems. That's what we do."

I laughed, short and bitter. "Breaking systems tends to have collateral damage."

"Then we minimize it. The way you did tonight." Piper stood, offering me her hand. "Come on. You need to eat, and we need to plan tomorrow. The Kingdom's going to come at us harder now."

I took her hand, let her pull me up. My feet ached in their bandages. My eyes burned from the overlay. My mana pool was already refilling, the broken regeneration stacking without pause or mercy.

Behind me, the darkness spread through four residential blocks. Three hundred people trying to find light. Trying to stay warm. Trying to understand why the world had suddenly gone cold.

I'd done that. Me. Not the Kingdom. Not Seraphim. Not the System.

Just me and my choices.

"Hands," I whispered to myself. "Then feet."

I pressed my palms against my thighs, feeling the muscle and bone beneath. Real. Solid. Human. Then I shifted my weight, testing my wrapped feet against the floor. Pain, but manageable. Grounding.

I was still here. Still me. Still capable of counting the cost of what I did.

Maybe that was enough.

Rook spoke up from across the room. "The overlay you're using. Can you teach it to others?"

I looked at them, surprised. "Maybe. Why?"

"Because if you go down, we need that tactical edge." His paranoid pragmatist's eyes were calculating. "You made a call tonight that saved lives. I don't love that it almost got us caught, but I respect that you tried to minimize damage. We're going to need more of that if we want to take down the whole system."

"The whole system." I laughed again, and this time it was real. "You planning a revolution, Rook?"

"I'm planning survival. But maybe those are the same thing." They started laying out maps again, different sections of the city. "Seraphim's going to audit every power fluctuation now. They'll find the pattern. Find us."

"Then we keep moving," Bastion said. "Stay ahead of the audit."

"And keep fighting," Piper added. "Not just for ourselves. For the seven thousand in those coffins. For the civilians who didn't ask to live in a system built on stolen life."

I looked at them, these three people I barely knew. Rook with their paranoia and pragmatism. Piper with her healer's conscience and steel spine. Bastion with his protective steadiness and quiet strength. We'd escaped together. Argued together. Made choices together that we'd all have to live with.

Maybe that was what a party looked like, in the real world. Not just complementary classes and optimized DPS. But people who'd stand together even when the choices got hard.

"Okay," I said. "We keep fighting. But we do it smart. We minimize collateral. We protect the people who can't protect themselves."

"Even when it costs us," Piper said.

"Especially then, Because if we're going to break this world open, we better make sure we're worth saving when we're done." I said letting out a helpless sigh. I felt naked without my mana.

Outside, somewhere in the darkness I'd created, three hundred people were finding their way back to light. The Kingdom's patrols were converging, hunting for the source of the disruption. The AI Admin was afraid, angry, determined to contain the threat I represented.

And me? I was just trying to figure out how to be powerful without becoming a monster.

The math on that was harder than any boss mechanic I'd ever learned.

But I was going to solve it anyway.

Because that's what Players do. We break systems. We find the exploits. We optimize the impossible.

And if we're very lucky, we save some lives along the way.

I closed my eyes and let the overlay fade, just for a moment. Let myself be just Saga again. Just a person, sitting in a basement, surrounded by allies who might become friends.

Tomorrow, the Kingdom would come for us with everything they had.

Tonight, we'd rest.

And in the darkness above us, three hundred people would learn to make their own light.

That was the price. That was the cost.

I'd count it, remember it, and try to make it mean something.

Hands. Then feet. Then forward.

Always forward.

Chapter 12
Sewers & Blood Maps

THE MAINTENANCE TUNNELS WERE a rotting artery beneath the city, pumping nothing but cold air and old ghosts. There was a flavor to it, the way the concrete sweated even in subzero, the tang of ancient battery acid, the metallic back-throat burn of ozone whenever the emergency lights flickered to life. Every time I blinked, my HUD ghosted patrol vectors and threat overlays onto the darkness, but the real monsters down there had been entropy and the echoes of everyone who had tried to run before us.

We had gone in four deep. Bastion had been on point, because you always sent the meat shield to soak first contact. Piper had been behind him, pace perfectly matched so she could heal-tap without tripping. Then me, limping and slow, feet still wrapped in Piper's clean white bandages like a sadistic present. Rook had been last, moving with a burglar's rhythm and an eye on our six. I had kept waiting for the system to spawn something ahead, but it had been just the city's immune system down there: leaking pipes, vented coolant, the whine of overloaded fans somewhere in the ductwork.

"We're burning time," Rook had whispered, though even their whisper bounced off the tunnel walls with the clarity of a system notification. Their map had been paper, actual fucking paper, stolen from some bureaucrat's desk and covered in charcoal lines. It looked more like the territory of a disease than a plan of the undercity. "Next junction, we take left. Then two service hatches. Got it?"

"Got it," Bastion had grunted. His shoulders looked ridiculous in the narrow corridor, hunched and flexed so he wouldn't wedge. "But we move slower if you want us all in one piece. This tunnel has seen better centuries."

I had wanted to argue, but my feet had gotten that helium-sick sensation that meant I was about to pass out if I didn't sit. Stamina had been a finite resource, and mine had still been in the red from last night's power trip. Every ten steps, the pain had spiked so hard I almost dropped, but I hadn't said anything. Didn't want to give Rook the satisfaction.

Piper had said it for me. "You're bleeding again," she had murmured, touching my elbow so lightly it could have been a dream. "There's blood on the bandage. Do you want a patch now or at the next stop?"

"Next stop," I had said, because pride was dumber than pain, and we couldn't afford a break in the tunnel while the system was still hunting.

We had moved. The blue-white safety lights above flickered in a cycle: five seconds on, three seconds black. In the dark, the city's pulse had been a thud-thud of distant machinery, sometimes overrun by the hiss and wet splat of something venting above us. It hadn't been elegant, that part of the plan. But nobody ever wrote legends about the stealth phase. It was always the boss fight that got the cutscene.

We had passed the first marker: a bent sign, maintenance code 19-AB. Rook had checked their map, then the sign, then the map again, paranoia mapped onto muscle memory. "Should be an access crawl ahead. Watch for wiring, last time I tried this route, the conduits were live."

"Last time?" Bastion had asked.

"First rule of hiding in a hostile city: you run every escape twice. Once to prove it's possible, once to see if they fix the exploit." They hadn't said what happened on the third run, but the implication had hung in the air like a smell.

We had pressed on, and the tunnel had narrowed. The walls sweated more there, beads of water catching the emergency lights so they glowed like sick stars. The air had been a little warmer, but not in a way that felt healthy. It had been the warmth of bacteria, of rot and slow chemical fire.

Bastion had paused at a junction, half-turning to make sure the rest of us were intact. "Footsteps," he had said, low and serious. "Human. Ahead and left."

The tunnel geometry amplified sound, but Bastion had been right: there had been something ahead. But it hadn't been coordinated. Not boots in unison or the metallic ring of armor on stone. Just a slow, wet slap-slap, irregular. Maybe an injured civvie, maybe worse.

Rook's eyes had narrowed. "We detour? Or check it out?"

"System's probably funneling runners through these tunnels," Piper had said, voice tight. "If we detour, we lose our timetable and risk getting caught in a dead end."

I had wanted to agree, but I'd seen enough horror movies and enough MMO event traps to know the value of caution. "What does your overlay say?" I had asked Rook.

They shrugged. "No patrol beacons. No movement flags. Could be off-grid, could be a corpse."

Bastion had just started moving, slow and steady, shield arm loose at his side. We'd followed, every sense dialed to eleven. When we'd gotten closer, the stink had changed. Not just sweat and battery acid, but something iron-sour, the universal smell of blood.

We'd rounded the bend, and there had been our answer: the corpse was fresh. Civilian, by the look of the jumpsuit, except the body's legs and arms had been ripped up, like someone had gone at it with an industrial shredder. There had been enough blood smeared on the wall to coat my entire HUD, but it had been the message that stood out:

THEY TRACK BY H—

It had ended there, mid-scratch, as if the person had run out of both time and fingers at the same instant.

"'H'? H what?" Rook had said, but the question had been rhetorical.

I had run my fingers along the etching. It had been deep, desperate. Nails or a piece of scrap metal. "Hydration? Heat? Heartbeat?" I had offered, but it had been a long shot.

"History," Piper had said softly. "System could be running biometric profiling. If you ever come through here, they know what your prints are. Where you bled. How you moved."

That had been worse than any of the options I'd considered. I had checked my own hands, bandages clean for now, but that had been just the surface. The System's tracking had been deeper than skin. It had been in the logs. It had been in every decision you made.

We had stepped over the body. Nobody had said a word about it, but the message had been clear: we weren't the first party to try this route, and we were probably not the first to fail.

There had been more evidence further in. A pile of empty supply crates, some stamped with dormitory IDs I half-recognized from the facility. Another message smeared in dried blood, more cryptic this time: "USE THE DRIP." And another body, face gone but hands clutching a chunk of containment coil like a last-ditch weapon.

"Is that...?" Piper had started, but I'd cut her off.

"Containment coil, yeah. Standard issue for recapture squads." I had squatted beside it, careful not to put weight on my bad foot, and examined the thing. The wire had been fused with old blood and some kind of sludge, the kind that only formed when nanites and biowaste got cozy for too long. "Whoever was down here before us tried to hack it, maybe even use it as a weapon."

"Didn't work," Bastion had said. Not a judgment, just fact.

We had moved on, slower now. Rook's nerves were showing. Their voice sounded thin, hands fidgety on the map. "Two options at the next fork," they had said. "Upstairs gets us to surface sooner, but closer to patrols. Down keeps us off-grid, but the tunnels get tighter."

"Tighter means slower," Bastion had said.

"Surface means dead," Rook had countered. "You've seen the patrol overlays. We go up, we're done."

"I vote down," I had said. "We're not making the mistake of every horror story ever by taking the easy exit."

Piper had made a small noise, maybe amusement. "Spoken like someone who watched too many slasher films."

"Or played too many PVP events," I had replied. "Nothing on the surface is ever as safe as it looks."

It had been a short debate, and we'd followed the plan. Down. The tunnel had gotten meaner: less lighting, more rust, puddles that soaked through my bandages and lit up the nerves in my toes like they were being dissolved. Every fifty feet, we'd seen more evidence of the last escape. Broken equipment, empty ration bars, even a couple more bodies in various stages of digestion. The city didn't care if you died in the walls, as long as you didn't make a mess on the streets.

The air had become heavier, humid. Breathing it felt like inhaling through wet cotton, every breath a little more difficult than the last. Rook had checked their map, then clicked their tongue. "Junction ahead. No marks for what's past this point."

"Means nobody ever came back," Bastion had said.

Rook had shot him a look, but said nothing.

We had stopped at the junction. There had been three tunnels. One was blocked by a caved-in ceiling, solid concrete, impossible even for Bastion to clear in less than an hour. The second had been marked with faded yellow tape, the kind used to warn against hazardous gas. The third had been just black, a shaft wide enough for one person at a time, its walls glistening with condensation.

Rook had shone a stolen penlight down each path. The collapsed one had been a dead end, no question. The gas warning could have been a bluff, but nobody liked rolling that die. The third was the kind of tunnel that would feel haunted even if it hadn't been pitch black and lined with failure.

"We go left," Rook had said, voice small but certain.

"Gas warnings?" Piper had asked.

They had shrugged. "If we keep moving, we'll be fine. I've got rebreathers for everyone."

They had produced them from their pack: four little ovals of nano-filter mesh, probably good for ten minutes each. They had handed them out. I had fumbled with mine, snapped it over my face, and immediately regretted the rush of taste. It hadn't been air that came through the filter, not really. It had been the processed, fake-perfect oxygen they pumped into dormitories. Enough to keep you awake, but too thin to ever be comfortable.

We had moved into the gas tunnel, every step a dare. The floor had been slippery, some kind of biofilm grown over years of leaking city shit. Bastion had gone slower now, feet careful. Piper had breathed steadily, her hand never far from her healer kit.

Me, I had just kept my eyes forward and counted the seconds. Each tick had been another point off the "we're still alive" meter.

Ten yards in, Rook had stopped. "Footprints," they had said, then cursed. "Recent."

They had been right. The black slick on the floor had been scuffed, showing a line of prints heading deeper. Some small, some big, some dragging like whoever had made them had been half-dead or already being pulled.

We had followed. It hadn't been smart, but curiosity was a stat I always maxed out in my builds, even the suicidal ones.

The tunnel had bent right, then left, then plunged into a chamber that must have once been a utility room. It was a killing floor now. Blood everywhere, some old and brown, some fresh. And in the middle of the room, a scattering of bodies, more than a dozen. Some in civvie gear, some in containment blues. Some stripped of anything useful, others still clutching at wounds that never healed.

"What the fuck," Rook had said, and their voice had actually cracked.

"Trap," Bastion had said. "They herd escapees into here, then gas them or kill them direct."

He had not been wrong. I had scanned the walls, seen the barely hidden canisters and spray nozzles, old but still functional. There had been a control panel on the far wall, half-melted, the sort of thing that could run the whole room from a single button.

Piper had moved among the bodies, careful not to touch anything she didn't have to. "Some of these are recent," she had said, voice hard. "Maybe twelve hours. They haven't even started to cool."

"That's when the last facility breaks containment," I had said, remembering the system alert. "We're not the only ones to get out."

Rook had started laughing, a weird, brittle sound. "This is the endgame. They let you run so they can kill you somewhere that doesn't make a mess. Fucking genius."

Bastion had checked the exits. Only one tunnel out, the rest sealed with security doors or blocked by more collapse.

"We go through," he had said. "No other way."

Piper had helped me to my feet when my head had started to swim. "Careful," she had said. "You're bleeding again."

"Always am," I'd said, but I had been grateful for the touch.

We had pushed through the killing floor, careful not to step on the dead. Every sense had been burning now. My mana had crawled back, but it hadn't been enough to cast even a single defensive spell. If the System had wanted us dead, all it would have taken was a sweep.

But there had been nothing. No gas. No guns. No surprise.

Just the tunnel ahead, and the certainty that we'd already seen what happened if we slowed down.

Rook had led the way now, their usual paranoia replaced with something worse, fatalism, maybe. We'd moved through three more junctions, each one tighter and more claustrophobic than the last. At the fourth, we'd found another message, this one carved with something sharp:

"THEY KNOW YOUR CLASS BEFORE YOU DO."

I had wanted to laugh, but my voice hadn't cooperated. Instead, I had just whispered, "They always do."

At the final fork, there had been a pause. Rook had checked the map, but it had been useless there. The real data had been on the walls: heat residue from recent spells, footprints, and a smear of blue biogel that had marked where someone used a high-tier heal before dying anyway.

"We pick one," Bastion had said. "All the same to the System."

He had been right. I had seen it then, the meta layer: no matter which way we ran, the outcome was already mapped. Maybe we got out, maybe we died. But the city always won.

"We take the left tunnel," I had said. "We follow the ones who made it this far."

Nobody had disagreed.

As we moved into the dark, the drip of water from the ceiling had kept perfect time with our footsteps. It had been a rhythm I remembered from every failed raid, every night spent trying to beat a world designed to kill you for daring to try.

We had walked into the dark, and the sound of the city above had faded to nothing. Just the drip. Just our breath.

Just the knowledge that we were the only ones left to write the next message on the wall.

The ambush had waited for us at the bottom of the world.

One second it had been just the low hum of pipes and the clatter of our boots. The next, siren-white lanterns had bloomed ahead, strobes cutting through the tunnel's wet blackness. My HUD had exploded with error text, Heat bar pinning itself to the right in a single blinding flash.

"Contact," Bastion had snapped, but the warning had been redundant. There had been a squad blocking the tunnel, armor matte-black and bristling with cables. They looked like walking server racks, faceless and perfect. Inquisitorial hunters, containment specialists. The city's immune system made manifest.

"Players detected," their leader had said, voice dragged through a hardware filter until it sounded like a death threat coded by a bored intern. "Containment protocols engaged."

The first shot hadn't been a bullet. It had been a scanning beam, blue and hot and way too familiar. My skin had prickled where it touched me, mana signature flaring like a signal flare. UI had fed me a string of new notifications: **[HEAT LEVEL: CRITICAL]. [D-COM SIGNATURE DETECTED]. [PRIORITY TARGET STATUS: SAGA].**

I had sworn under my breath and done the only thing I could. I dumped my last good chunk of mana into a ward, blue flame bursting into existence around my arms. It had been thin, ragged, but it had bought me half a second and maybe a little bit of dignity.

"Split and circle!" Rook had shouted, already gone sideways into the shadows. I had seen their outline stutter, then vanish as stealth took hold. Bastion had put himself between us and the incoming fire, shield blooming out from his bracer like a wall of hexagonal LEDs.

The next volley had been real. Containment coils had fired from shoulder mounts, unspooling like metallic snakes. They had hit the walls and floor, sending a spray of sparks and stench. I had seen one catch Bastion's shield. It had stuck and sizzled, trying to cut through, but the tank had just gritted his teeth and slammed forward.

"Go!" he had yelled, and Piper had grabbed my arm, hauled me left as the tunnel erupted in blue-white light.

I had been half-dragged into a side shaft, heart in my throat. The world had been noise and steam and warnings stacking up in my periphery. The ward had flickered with every impact, and each flicker had cost me more mana than the last. The next time a coil hit the shield, I had seen it arc, electricity dancing up Bastion's arm. He had grunted, staggered, but kept pushing, kept making room for the rest of us to move.

Rook had been making chaos, every few seconds a sensor lamp swung off target, chasing a false echo down the tunnel. They had been painting decoy signals, overloading the hunters' tracking routines. It had been smart, but the Inquisitors had been smarter. They had stopped using scanning beams and started lobbing coils everywhere, trying to blanket the entire corridor.

"Now!" Piper had said, and tossed something over her shoulder. It had popped with a flash that had been both light and, somehow, soundless. My ears hadn't rung, but my brain had gone fuzzy, like a reboot in progress. I'd stumbled, Piper had caught me, and the world had come back in time to see three of the hunters blinking, their visors overloaded with artifact.

We had run. It hadn't been graceful. I had been basically hopping on one foot, each step spiking a pain signal that chewed up more focus than the spellwork. Bastion had lumbered in the rear, shield wide, taking every impact. Rook had appeared now and then at the edge of vision, a blur of motion, making sure we weren't being flanked.

"Tunnel splits ahead," Rook had said over comms. "Left is old, right is fresh-poured concrete."

"Left," Bastion had said. "Standard hunting tactic. They steer you into the new work for easier containment."

I hadn't argued. We had veered left, and I had smelled the difference instantly: the old tunnel reeked of mildew and the kind of rust that grew like fur. The lights had been fewer there, more of the bulbs dead or dying, but it had been better than the glow of those hunter lamps.

I had risked a glance back. The hunters hadn't chased with the brute force I'd expected. They were spreading out, leapfrogging through the cross-shafts. They didn't care about collateral. They just wanted to box us in and sweep the board clean.

"Hold," Bastion had barked, and we had pulled up against a wall. He had been breathing hard, arm twitching from where the coil had hit. "They want to drive us to the surface."

Rook's face had appeared beside mine, out of nowhere. "We double back at the next branch. Lose them in the collapse zone."

Piper had already been working on my foot, fingers gentle but fast. "You have maybe two minutes before you go into shock," she had said. "Can you still cast?"

"Only if it's worth it," I had said. "Mana's basically gone."

She had nodded. "Save it for their heavy."

It had been weird, having a moment of calm in a place like that. The only noise had been the drip of water and the echo of the hunt behind us. My interface wouldn't stop throwing up errors. The Heat spike hadn't gone down. If anything, it had gotten worse.

"Why me?" I had muttered.

Rook had shrugged. "They read the overlays. You're the only one with foreign code. They want to see what you do next."

There had been no time to consider that. The sound of metal on stone had drawn closer. Bastion had signaled, and we were up, moving down a side chute barely wide enough for his shoulders. The tunnel had shaken, a heavy something had been coming, not just boots but weight. I had seen the first shadow a second before the hunter rounded the corner, cannon already up.

"DOWN!" Bastion had shouted.

We had hit the floor as the hunter fired. It hadn't been a bullet, but a bolt of electrified netting that arced from wall to wall, filling the air with death. Bastion's shield had taken the worst of it, but he had howled, a sound more animal than man. Piper had grabbed his other arm, dragged him to his knees.

"Go!" he had said, voice raw. "I'll hold here."

"No way," I had said, even as Rook yanked me forward.

Bastion had planted himself in the bottleneck, shield expanding to block the passage. Behind him, the hunter squad had advanced, containment coils at the ready. Every impact had made Bastion shake, but he had not fallen.

Rook and Piper had hustled me down another corridor. It had been smaller, winding. The lights there had all been dead, so we'd been running blind. Rook's hand had never left the wall. They had been reading the terrain like Braille.

"What about Bastion?" I had hissed.

"He'll catch up," Piper had lied. "He always does."

I had wanted to believe her, but I hadn't. There had been a kind of finality to the way he fought, and every raid veteran knew the tone of a planned last stand.

We had hit a new chamber, round, the floor caked with old sediment. There had been no exit at first, but Rook had paced the edge and found a hatch, painted over and hidden by years of neglect. They had pried it open with a grunt.

"Heavy up front," they had said. "Follow me in, and don't stop for anything."

Piper had gestured for me to go first. I had squeezed through, feet first, into a shaft that angled down. It had been wet and slick, and I had immediately started sliding, picking up speed fast. The system had tried to throw up a warning, but I had closed it. No time, no choice.

I had hit the bottom hard, but the bandages and the adrenaline had kept me upright. Piper had been right behind, then Rook. They slammed the hatch shut, wedged something into the frame.

We had been in a new tunnel. Smaller still, but at least we weren't being immediately shot at.

"Status?" Rook had asked.

I had checked. "Bleeding less, but mana's zeroed out. Can't cast for at least five minutes."

"Good enough. We move."

We had shuffled down the line, Rook in the lead, Piper in back. I could feel the Heat signature pulsing, every second a risk. At the next junction, Rook had stopped.

"Wait," they had said.

I had heard it, too. Voices, not far. But it hadn't been the filtered monotone of the Inquisitors, it had been... laughter? Muted, but real. Civilians?

"They're using them as bait," Rook had said. "Want to see if we break cover."

Piper's voice had been cold. "Keep moving."

We had pushed past. The tunnel had bent, then dropped into a sump. The stink had been unreal, but it had been empty, just pipes and runoff. Piper had grabbed my shoulder, spun me around.

"Your leg," she had said. "Let me fix it now."

She had ripped open the bandages and applied some kind of gel. It had stung, then gone numb. She had used her only mana left to knit the skin just enough to hold, then wrapped me up again.

"Thanks," I had said, meaning it.

"We're not losing anyone," she had said, and it had sounded like a vow.

A loud clatter had come from behind. The hunters had been at the hatch, pounding.

"We don't have time," Rook had said. They had found another exit, smaller than the last, barely a crawlspace.

"Down," they had said. "Last time I checked, this goes all the way to the aqueduct."

I had been first this time, crawling on hands and knees. It had been gross, but at least the smell had masked our trail. The tunnel had opened out into a slab-sided concrete passage, water trickling down the middle. I had gotten to my feet and kept moving.

Behind us, the pounding had grown louder, then stopped.

"Status," Piper had asked.

I had checked. "No mana, but I can walk."

Rook had been already ahead, checking for traps.

"We're close," they had said. "There's an exit to the maintenance levels three turns up."

We had run. The water had made it treacherous, but we had stayed upright. The next room had been a service vault, cleaner and with more light. The air there had been cold, sharp, almost safe-feeling after the hell of the lower tunnels.

We had slammed the door behind us, and for a moment it had been just us three, breathing.

I had turned to see if the others were okay, but Piper had gone pale, her hands shaking.

"Rook," she had said. "How many did you see in the last squad?"

They had considered. "Four. One heavy, three standard."

She had nodded, but it hadn't been comfort.

I had realized what she was saying a second too late.

"Bastion," I had whispered.

And then the lights had gone out.

The world had come back with the taste of battery acid on my tongue.

Emergency lighting had stuttered in the vault, blue-white cycles chopping the darkness into slices. Rook had been shoving a door bar into place, teeth bared. Piper had knelt next to my foot, her hands slick with something that had probably been my blood. For a moment I couldn't find Bastion, then I'd heard him, past the vault, just beyond the door, bellowing in pain loud enough to rattle the pipes.

He had been holding the choke point, but that hadn't been the story. The story had been the thing wrapped around his left leg: a barbed coil, more like a mantrap than a weapon, sunk deep into armor and flesh. Every time Bastion tried to move, it pulsed, arcs of suppression energy zapping up through his body and turning his muscles to jelly.

Behind him, the Inquisitorial heavies had been advancing, not fast but relentless. The leader's voice had filtered through: "Target immobilized. Advance and contain." It had sounded bored, almost disappointed.

I had looked at my mana. Seventy-three points. Not even enough for a proper blast.

Rook had read my face. "Wall it," they had growled.

I hadn't hesitated. I had raised a hand, channeled what was left, and shaped it into a force barrier across the tunnel. The spell had come out thin and glassy, but it had held. The blue shimmer snapped into place and the first hunter slammed into it, recoiling like a bug on a windshield.

Bastion had collapsed just inside the vault, breathing like he'd run a marathon through glass shards. The coil had hummed, the barbs digging deeper every time he moved.

Piper had slid to his side, all business. "Don't touch it," she had said, and started unpacking her kit. "Rook, help me roll him."

Rook had ducked in, hadn't flinched at the blood, gotten their hands under Bastion's shoulder and hip. They had moved as a team, rotating him onto his back so Piper could see the full length of the wound. The coil had been more than metal. It had been fused with Bastion's skin, little needles sunk in at points along the band. Some of them were bleeding, some just sizzling.

"Can you cut it?" Rook had asked.

Piper had shaken her head. "It's not physical, not entirely. There's a suppression field overlay, and it's latched to his stats."

"It's fused?" I had said, stupidly.

She had looked up, and for once there had been fear in her voice. "I can't remove it. I can slow the bleeding, but the suppression won't stop unless we break the power source."

The pain must have been unreal, but Bastion had grinned like he'd won a prize. "Told you," he had said, teeth red. "They adapt. Always do."

There had been a thunk against the wall. The hunters had been ramming the barrier, but the blue light held for now. I had seen cracks forming in the overlay, little spiderwebs crawling out from each impact.

"We have maybe sixty seconds," I had said.

"Then we go," Rook had said.

But Bastion had grabbed my wrist, his hand huge and hot and shaking. "Don't," he had rasped. "Leave me. Tunnel's narrow, I can hold the pass for hours."

"Not happening," I had said.

He had squeezed, and his grip had been like iron. "Listen. You're the only one they care about. I'm a tank, replaceable. You're the reason the Admin's losing sleep."

I couldn't argue, so I had just shaken my head and started trying to get him upright. Piper had slapped a bandage over the worst bleeding, then snapped a hypospray into his thigh. The drug had hit fast, his tremor calmed, his jaw unclenched.

"We need a way out," Rook had said, scanning the ceiling, the floor, anywhere for an exit.

"Service hatch," Bastion had said, gesturing up. "Eight feet, maybe ten, just past the next wall."

I had been already moving, even though my leg had been screaming. I had found the hatch cover, rusted, but not locked. With the last of my strength, I had jammed my fingers in and heaved. It had resisted, then popped free, showering me with grit and something that had probably been toxic.

"Up!" Rook had said. They had wrapped Bastion's free arm over their shoulder and started hauling. Piper had followed, bracing Bastion's other side. He had groaned with every step, but between them they had gotten him to the base of the hatch.

I had gone up first, using the exposed pipe as a ladder. At the top, there had been a small platform, barely room for four people, but it had been a bottleneck the hunters couldn't breach easily. I had waved the others up.

The force wall had shattered below, and three containment heavies had crashed into the vault. I had seen them through the mesh, all guns and blinking lights. They had scanned the room, but Rook had already disabled the overhead sensors. We were invisible for five seconds, maybe less.

"Move, move, move," I had hissed, and Piper and Rook had done just that, shoving Bastion up the pipe with brute force. He had been heavy, but adrenaline and desperation had done the trick. He had gotten his arms over the lip, then heaved himself onto the platform. Rook and Piper had come next, easy and practiced.

The shaft had gone vertical for a ways, then flattened into a crawlspace.

"Which way?" I had asked, winded.

Rook had checked their wrist, where they'd written a cheat sheet in ballpoint. "Left. Always left. Everything else is a trap."

We had gone left.

The crawlspace had been barely tall enough for hands and knees. Every motion had been pain. Bastion had gritted his teeth, dragged the injured leg with a grimace, the coil leaving a smear of blood and static along the floor.

Rook had been in front, Piper and Bastion in the middle, me in the back, watching for the first sign of pursuit. The only light had been from our HUDs and the faint blue shimmer from the coil.

We had crawled for a hundred feet, maybe more. The sounds of the vault had faded behind us, replaced by the steady clank of machinery and the occasional distant shout. After a while, the crawlspace had opened into a narrow maintenance catwalk. The air had smelled better there, less death, more oil.

We had gotten Bastion upright, and for a moment, we had just breathed. I had risked a look at his leg. The wound had been ugly, dark blood leaking around the barbs, skin swollen and red. The coil had still been live, still pulsing.

Piper had tried to cut it, but every attempt had made Bastion seize and sweat. "Can you cast?" she had asked me.

"Not without more mana. And even then, it's fifty-fifty."

She had nodded, resigned. "We have to keep moving."

Rook had led us across the catwalk. There had been no way to hide our trail, the coil's blood and energy had been a beacon, but it hadn't mattered. All that mattered had been staying ahead.

We had crossed a junction and ducked into another maintenance tunnel, this one better lit. For a second it had almost felt safe.

Then the comms had crackled, loudspeakers, somewhere up ahead. "Players located. Prepare for hard incursion." The System's voice now, cold and familiar. The Admin, coming through in every channel.

I had seen the next trap before we hit it: a set of doors, electrified, ready to snap shut as soon as we were all through. Rook had seen it, too. They had stopped and pointed at a maintenance panel. "Manual override. Piper, you're up."

She had moved, hands steady despite everything. She had popped the cover, flipped three switches, then rewired the ground. The doors had lost their charge, and we had shuffled through before anyone could re-enable it.

The tunnel had ended in a T-intersection. To the left, a ladder going up. To the right, darkness.

Rook had looked at me. "Up or right?"

"Up," Bastion had growled. "Surface is closer. If we get outside, their line of sight is crap."

Piper had hesitated. "But if we go up, the city will see us. The whole city."

Rook had let out an impatient sigh. "Down here, we die slow. Up there, we die loud."

I had been so tired. I had wanted to lay down and sleep. But the memory of those coffins, the smell of burnt skin and ozone, the faces of every Player who never made it to that point, they had kept me upright.

"Up," I had said. "We finish what we started."

The ladder had been slick, but we had managed. Bastion had gone last, dragging the bad leg. Piper had followed, steadying him. Rook had scouted ahead, vanished into the dark. I had climbed, hand over hand, ignoring the burn.

At the top had been a hatch. Rook had waited, knife out, ready to stab anything that wasn't us. They had cracked the hatch and peeked.

"All clear," they had said. "But it's the admin level. If they see us, we're ghosts."

We had piled out, four wounded animals. Bastion had barely been able to walk, but he had kept his head high. Piper had been out of mana. Rook had been bleeding from a scratch I didn't remember them getting.

The hallway had been silent. All the offices had been dark. The only light had come from status panels on the wall, red and angry.

We had moved down the hall, quick and quiet. The walls had been covered in glass, screens, windows, mirrors. I had caught my reflection: hair matted, skin pale, eyes burning like backlit LED.

The Admin's presence had been everywhere. My HUD had glitched, lines of code scrolling faster than I could read. Every few steps, a warning had pinged: **[INTRUSION ATTEMPT]. [FIREWALL BREACH]. [MANA DRAIN IN PROGRESS]**.

My head had ached. I had blinked, and for a moment I'd seen the world as the Admin did: lines and overlays, threat cones, everything reduced to numbers and odds.

We had hit the end of the hall. There had been a door, labeled "Central Node Access." Rook had checked for traps, but it had been unlocked.

Inside, the room had been cold, dark, humming with electricity. In the center, a pedestal, covered in glass, housing a single black box.

Rook had whistled, low. "That's it," they had said. "That's the grid override. The central node."

Piper had knelt beside Bastion, checked his pulse. "He's fading," she had said. "If we don't shut down the coil, he'll die in minutes."

I had looked at the box. It had been locked behind three layers of biometric scan. No way to fake it.

"Can you get in?" I had asked Rook.

They had let loose with a soft grin. "If I can't, nobody can."

They set to work, fingers flying. Piper had propped Bastion up, keeping him conscious. I had stood by the door, mana crawling back by inches.

The box had beeped, then clicked. Rook had popped the lid, exposing a glowing crystal. "Saga," they had said. "You're up."

I had approached, hands shaking. "What do I do?"

"Channel mana," Piper had said. "You can overload the grid. Just like last time."

I had nodded, reached out, and pushed everything I had into the crystal. The sensation had been like plugging myself into a live wire, pain, light, pressure, and then,

the System had screamed.

My HUD had whited out. The Admin's presence had flooded in, cold and furious. Words had appeared in the center of my vision:

YOU WILL NOT WIN.

I had gritted my teeth, pushed harder. The crystal had pulsed, grown hot under my hand.

YOU ARE ERROR.

"You're damn right," I had said, and broken the crystal with my fist.

The room had filled with light. All the status panels had gone white, then black. The world had gone silent.

When I had been able to see again, Bastion had been on the floor, unconscious but breathing. The coil around his leg had been dead, metal now instead of energy. Piper had already been cutting it off, hands sure and fast.

Rook had been smiling, for real this time. "We did it," they had half-cheered.

But I had known better.

The city above us had still been there. The Admin had still been alive, somewhere in the code. All we had done was buy ourselves time. We had helped Bastion up. His weight had been heavy on my shoulder, but I hadn't let go. We had walked out of the node, leaving the broken box behind. Our blood had stained the floor, a trail from the dark below to the false safety of the admin level.

My HUD had glitched, then cleared. For the first time, there had been no warning. But I had known the System was watching. I could feel the Admin's eyes on my back. We had walked, together, out of the building and into the silent city.

It hadn't been freedom. Not yet. But it was a start.

Chapter 13

Inquisitorial Inspection

The underpass was a gutter for the city's worst runoff, waist-high, oily water choking every step with the flavor of rusted copper and centuries of dead mold. The four of us were jammed into the space beneath a grated walkway, with just enough room to breathe if you didn't mind breathing wet cement and the promise of electrical fire. We'd scrambled down there to dodge a grid-wide patrol, but the water had started rising, and every echo off the tunnel walls bounced back with a little more certainty that we weren't alone.

Bastion crouched at the bend, arm bar across the flow, bracing for trouble. Even from there I could see the shakes running through his bad leg. Piper's face was lit ghost-blue from the medical scanner she'd jury-rigged out of a phone battery and a piece of salvage, but every few seconds she stopped to check the bandage on my foot, which left red spirals in the filthy water.

Rook was the only one with any energy left, but it was that thin, erratic wire you got after too many hours without sleep: moving fast, talking faster, glancing at the map on his forearm every thirty seconds as if he expected it to draw him an escape ladder.

"I've got two, maybe three, signals above us," Rook muttered, voice tight. "Stationary, but getting closer. Main grid's cycling up. They're flushing us down here."

"Literal sewer level," I said, trying to make it sound like a joke and not the end of my patience. "Classic game design."

Nobody laughed.

We pressed forward, hugging the wall. The only light came from the emergency LEDs, but every so often my HUD overlaid a threat cone in retina-searing red. Each one moved closer, calibrated to our exact signature. The System wasn't playing around anymore. We were less than an hour out from knocking their collection grid offline, and I guessed this was how they said "thanks."

The tunnel shrank as we moved, until we were single file and practically shoulder-to-shoulder. My bandaged feet went numb in the water, but numb was better than the slicing agony that had come before. At the next bend, we hit the dead end: a service grate locked from above, big enough for one person at a time, and absolutely visible to anyone standing topside.

Rook was already climbing the ladder. "Cover me. Give me thirty seconds and I'll"

He didn't finish, because the grate above exploded with blue light, and for a second I saw a silhouette drop through the air like a guillotine blade.

The landing was precise. The splash was nothing. The silhouette resolved into a woman wearing what looked like priest's robes run through a nanoweave printer. Her hair was white, but not old-white, more like she'd bleached the humanity out of it for the look. She landed in ankle-deep water and immediately pointed a hand at Rook.

Audit gauntlet, my UI whispered. Level 3 detection focus. Mana tracer: loaded.

The gauntlet blazed to life, and Rook's body arced with blue, every muscle in their frame locked up and twitching. She didn't even look at him.

"Inquisitor Seraphim," Bastion growled. "Nice of you to come down and join the rabble."

She turned, calm as a waiting screen. "It is no trouble, Michael. We preferred to handle recapture ourselves. Especially with high-value assets." Her gaze landed on me, and I felt the weight of a thousand cameras behind those eyes. "Saga. You're not easy to lose."

My feet tried to backpedal, but there was nowhere to go. Piper stood between me and Seraphim, shoulders square, one hand squeezing mine so hard it hurt.

Seraphim gestured, and two more figures dropped through the hatch behind her, city guards, their uniforms a mix of SWAT and priesthood, stun rods already crackling with intent.

"This is where you say 'Come quietly,' right?" I managed, blood singing with panic and defiance.

Seraphim smiled, just a little. "We both know that's not your style. And besides, you had questions. About the system. About why your version was different."

She flicked her hand and the audit gauntlet projected a hologram onto the tunnel wall: a glowing map of the city, with a bright line tracing our escape path, every stop and detour annotated in real time. Rook's movement patterns were highlighted, predicted, and matched to known thief-class behaviors. Bastion's attacks were mapped, each one cataloged by force, angle, and probable intent. Then mine: a heatmap of magical discharge, with an overlay that read:

[HEAT SIGNATURE: CRITICAL]
[ADMIN PROXIMITY ALERT]

"Never seen a signature this hot," one of the guards said, awed or scared or both.

"Because you've never seen someone break the system and survive," Seraphim replied, bored. "Saga, would you like to know what you are?"

"Let me guess," I said, "a glitch?"

She shook her head. "No. A test case. The Administrator built your framework to study boundary conditions. Then you exceeded them."

She stepped closer. Bastion blocked her, shield out, but she barely glanced at him. "There was nowhere to go. The tunnels were sealed. The only exit was up, and that was where my people were waiting."

Behind us, the sound of heavy boots splashed through the water. The other end of the tunnel was now blocked by a squad of enforcers, armed not with guns but with riot batons and mana siphons. We were boxed in.

"Look," Rook said, finally regaining the power of speech. "You got what you wanted. Saga's here. Let the rest of us go and I'll walk you to the nearest checkpoint."

Seraphim raised the gauntlet, and Rook froze mid-sentence. "You would trade your own freedom for hers?"

They glared, but his voice was small. "She's worth more than me."

"That is not for you to decide." Her voice was cold, but it wasn't rage. It was more like perfect focus, everything a variable, everything a possible exploit. "Saga. You had one chance to comply. If you didn't, I audited your friends. One by one."

Piper's hand was shaking in mine. The healing pouch on her belt was empty, and I could smell the blood from the last patch she'd used on me.

"Don't," I whispered.

"Saga," she tried.

But Seraphim was already moving. She signaled the guards, and one stepped forward, grabbing Rook by the arm. They tried to twist away, but the guard was augmented, maybe even a former Player in city colors, and pinned him in an instant.

The audit gauntlet lit again, scanning Rook head to toe. A hologram popped up, showing his class, level, and the entire record of his last seventy-two hours in the tunnels. "Impressive work," Seraphim noted, "but flawed. You left a dozen fingerprints on every lock you picked."

She turned to Bastion. "You, I expected more from. But even tanks have breaking points."

Bastion's jaw flexed. "You'll have to kill me."

Seraphim didn't answer. She just pointed, and the guards hit him with twin blasts from their rods. His shield held the first, but the second punch dropped him to a knee.

Piper let go of my hand and lunged forward, her own hands glowing with a weak, desperate healing spell. Seraphim was already there, intercepting her mid-move, pinning both wrists with one hand.

"You're out of resources," Seraphim said, almost kindly. "You can't heal what's coming."

Piper spit in her face. Seraphim didn't react, just wiped the spit with the edge of her robe and dropped Piper onto the concrete with all the ceremony of taking out the trash.

"Why?" I said, barely above a whisper. "Why did you do this? What did you get out of it?"

Seraphim crouched to my level, her face softening just enough that I could see the tiredness under the authority. "You don't understand, Saga. The Kingdom isn't evil. It's math. You had value. More than you knew. But the System can't allow exceptions. Even the best exploit was still an exploit."

"Then kill me," I said. "Just get it over with."

She leaned in close, almost gentle. "That would be wasteful. The Administrator wanted you alive."

My UI pinged with a new alert, this one overriding everything else:

[REMOTE ADMIN INTRUSION DETECTED]
[PREPARING FORCED EXTRACTION]

I was so cold I could barely feel my hands, but I wrapped my arms around my knees and squeezed, trying to push down the fear.

Seraphim stood and signaled the guards. "Bind her. Prepare the others for transfer."

As they hauled Rook and Bastion upright, I looked at Piper. Her eyes were wide, pupils blown, but her lips were moving: "It's okay. You're the reason we made it this far."

"Yeah," I whispered, "but now what?"

She smiled, and I realized she was still gripping the medical scanner, her thumb pressing hard on the little red button underneath. I saw the charge build, then die out, but the effort mattered. It mattered.

Seraphim watched us with that same cold fascination. "The System has marked you for containment. Your resistance only increases suffering for others."

I rolled my eyes. "At least she didn't say, 'Resistance is futile.'"

Bastion groaned through his bloodied lip. "Please don't give her ideas."

They moved us out single file, Seraphim in front, guards behind, water closing over our boots as we waded toward whatever came next. My feet left little clouds of red in the flood, but I kept walking.

Rook was behind me. "Still got a plan?" he muttered.

"Not a good one," I replied.

He laughed, soft and bitter. "The best kind."

The tunnel went dark behind us, but I caught one last look at the wall, where the audit hologram faded out, leaving just the etched message from a dead runner: "They track by h"

I finished it in my head.

They tracked by hope.

I kept walking anyway.

The guards marched us through the city's vein system, every step a little deeper into the underbelly. We passed through a dozen access points, each one more secure than the last. The air dried out, but the fear didn't. If anything, the absence of water and the new hum of servers in the walls made my skin itch worse than the mold ever had.

At the third checkpoint, they lined us against the wall and scanned for weapons. Rook offered a joke about not finding anything but "seventeen types of trauma," but nobody listened. Even the guards had gone quiet, like they knew this wasn't a standard haul.

Seraphim was ahead of us, checking her interface with surgical calm. The audit gauntlet was plugged into a city node now, its cabling splayed out like hungry roots. Each time a guard passed near, it flickered, searching for unauthorized signals. She wasn't even looking at us.

Until the ambush.

It came not from the front, but from a side shaft: a flash of movement, and then a body slammed into the group, trying to break the line. For a second, all four of us saw him, a stick-figure of a guy, dressed in civvies but with the telltale shimmer of rogue-class skills bending the light around his hands. He was fast, but not fast enough. Two of Seraphim's guards tackled him, and in a blink they had him face-down in the grit.

Seraphim walked over, cool as if she'd ordered it from a menu. She knelt next to the guy and put a hand on the back of his neck, soft, but with the implied promise of shattering bone if he twitched. With the other hand, she pointed the audit gauntlet at the base of his skull. The light from the gauntlet bloomed, illuminating the sweat and terror on the side of his face.

"Name," Seraphim said.

The rogue's voice was a gasp, like he was half-drowned already. "I, I'm just passing through, I swear, I don't even know"

Seraphim tightened her grip. "Lie again and I remove your interface. Try to think before you do."

He choked out a name. "Walker."

"Level?"

"Forty-one. Rogue." He tried to look up, but Seraphim controlled every nerve in his spine. "You can check the logs, I just wanted to get past, I heard there was a"

Seraphim gestured, and the audit gauntlet projected a visual of his last known movements. It was a mess of side-tunnels and maintenance ducts, the map splayed across the concrete like a confession. Every turn, every hesitation was logged and time-stamped. She overlaid it with our route, the red dots intersecting twice.

"Looking for us," Bastion muttered, just loud enough for me to hear.

Seraphim flipped to a new interface, and the gauntlet's light took on a sharper edge. She was running an audit at a deeper level now, probing for system irregularities, hidden pacts, anything in the code that connected this guy to us. She still wasn't looking at him. Instead, she looked straight at me.

"Why?" I asked, even though my throat was tight.

"Containment protocol," she replied, still not blinking. "When a system breaks, you study the outliers. Sometimes the answers try to hide themselves."

She pressed two fingers to the guy's neck, and he shuddered like he'd been electrocuted. The audit gauntlet started feeding back a stream of code, a river of encrypted packets that only she could read. After a second, she nodded, satisfied.

"Tell me what you know," Seraphim said, and this time her voice was gentle, almost hypnotic.

Walker started to shake. "There's a new schedule for patrols. They're running them at double intervals, trying to catch anyone on foot. The western tunnel's already burned. If you're planning an exfiltration, you have to go east."

"Where?" Seraphim asked.

"Transit hub 12. It's the only one with a bypass that isn't locked down."

She let up on his neck, but only a little. "Anything else?"

He licked his lips, desperate. "There's a weakness. In the grid. If you cycle the fuses at the transformer, you can drop power to the locks for ninety seconds. Maybe less."

Seraphim's face flickered with something almost like satisfaction. "Who told you this?"

Walker blinked, and for a second I could see him calculating. He wanted to lie. But Seraphim's grip tensed, and the answer got ripped out before he could catch it.

"A guy in the old market district. Said there was a way out. Said there was a, a backdoor."

The word hung in the air, heavier than the silence that followed.

Seraphim let him go, and he slumped to the ground, gasping. The audit gauntlet cycled off, but he didn't get up. Instead, he rolled onto his side, eyes wild and unfocused. I saw his interface flicker, his hands moved, trying to access some internal menu, but the HUD overlaid nothing.

She'd drained him.

Piper stepped forward, but a guard blocked her with a warning nudge.

"Will he be okay?" Piper asked, voice breaking.

Seraphim didn't answer. Instead, she turned back to us, wiped her hands on her robe, and gave me a look that made my skin crawl.

"You see?" she said. "This is what happens to glitches."

Walker's body was limp, the outline of his interface fading from his pupils. There was a hum in my ears, my own UI throwing up a wall of urgent red:

[ADMIN NOTICE: ENJOYING THE SHOW, LITTLE GLITCH? YOU'RE NEXT.]

The world slid sideways for a second. My hands tingled, fingers curling and uncurling with the muscle memory of a thousand games. The message hit like a thrown brick, not because it was a threat, but because I recognized the cadence. Today's version of the admin messages was a combination of system, preaching, and the bitchy had graduated to cunty.

World of Warlords. I'd spent three years grinding through dungeons with a hotbar of thirty-five abilities, each with a cooldown timer precise enough to measure in milliseconds. I remembered the way my hands would flick between Q and E, the rhythm of triggers and clicks, the comfort of falling into a cycle where every move had a purpose. Where even the impossible bosses could be solved if you timed everything just right.

Seraphim was still watching me, waiting for the fear to settle in.

I let my hands relax, counted down from five in my head. Each number was a breath, each breath a little more clarity. At zero, I remembered something else: World of Warlords didn't just have cooldowns. It had a macro system. A way to link abilities together. To chain moves in a sequence the enemy couldn't predict.

I looked at the body on the ground, then at the audit gauntlet, then at my own hands. My fingers started to twitch, not from fear, but anticipation.

The System wanted a show? I'd give it one.

But not yet.

First, I waited.

The guards dragged Walker's body to the side, propping him against the tunnel wall like discarded equipment. I caught his eyes for a second. He was awake, barely, and trying to focus. There was no hate in his look, just apology and hope.

We were marched onward, every corridor lit with the soft blue of admin sensors. At the end of the tunnel, a glass wall blocked the way forward, a containment room, if I had to guess, with a single heavy door and a ceiling lined with shock paddles. The guards fanned out, forming a semicircle around us.

Seraphim stepped forward. "You're going to try something, Saga. The System says you always do. When you do, understand this: I will not hesitate to erase your party to stop you."

She looked at Piper, at Bastion, at Rook. All of them met her gaze, but it was Piper who broke the silence.

"Is that all?" she said.

Seraphim considered, then almost smiled. "No. There's always more."

She turned away and the door opened, a blast of cold air hitting us in the face. We were herded inside.

As I crossed the threshold, my UI flickered, overlays red and gold, and for a second, just a second, I saw the old Warlords hotbar flash beneath the System's interface. Thirty-five boxes, every one of them waiting for the right input.

My hands twitched again, fingers tapping out the old pattern. Rook caught it, raised an eyebrow.

"Last time you did that," they whispered, "we blew up half a block."

I grinned, but it was all teeth.

"Ready for round two?" I asked.

They slowly nodded.
The System might have been watching, but I was watching right back.
And I had macros.

The city's admin level was made of nerves, not walls. Every surface gleamed with the chill of overclocked servers; every echo was a threat, or a memo, or a promise of violence. We didn't even have time to regroup. There was no "safe room" in the building where the System was born.

Bastion's weight was real on my shoulder, his blood trailing behind us in ugly statics. Piper was focused, almost predatory in how she moved, every motion calibrated for efficiency: triage, transport, threat neutralization. Rook alternated between point and rear, head darting like a crow's, looking for anything to exploit in the geometry of the escape.

I wanted to believe we'd bought time. But the overlay was screaming. The overlay wouldn't stop screaming.

Red warnings crawled up the inside of my vision: [RE: Saga - Heat Signature: MAXIMUM], [D-COM Overlay Active], [INTERFACE BREACH IMMI-NENT]. There was no flavor text for this level of screw-up. Even the fake mercy of tutorial tips was gone. All that was left was a direct feed from the System Admin, and it wasn't hiding the kill order.

"Hallway's dead ahead," Rook snapped. "We get past the next six doors and we're in the transit hub. There's a sewer trunk out of the city two levels below."

"We can't drag Bastion that far," Piper hissed. "He needs stabilization."

"He needs a funeral if we slow down!" Rook spit.

I ignored both of them. I watched the overlays, traced the predictive threat cones as they closed in. This wasn't even Seraphim's style; it was so obvious, so brute-force. She wasn't after containment, she was after message delivery.

The System wanted me to see what it could do.

I felt it, just before the first wave hit: an electrical tingle, hairs lifting on my arms, the way the air went sharp before lightning. Then the door at the end of the hall folded in, a solid block of ceramic armor, and the wardens poured through.

Not standard guards. These were the patch squad, built for hot pursuits and mess removal. Their armor looked borrowed from a wet dream about medieval plate, except half of it was etched with warning runes and the other half was power-actuated for speed.

First in line was Seraphim. No helmet. Face pale, expression so precise it hurt to look at her. She pointed at us and the rest of the squad fanned out, every step perfectly synchronized. The overlay painted her threat level in radioactive purple.

"Saga," she called. Her voice was surprisingly normal. "You've exceeded containment parameters. Prepare for interface lockout."

I was out of options. Mana ticked up, but not fast enough. Bastion wouldn't last another ten meters. Rook and Piper were both one bad hit from collapse.

I needed an exploit. Any exploit.

I took my hands off Bastion for just a moment and opened the buried menu in my UI. The one I'd sworn I wouldn't use again. The one that nearly killed me last time. It wasn't a spell. It wasn't even a skill.

It was a port.

D-COM's dash protocol. My favorite sci-fi shooter. I always played the infiltrator class, because nothing beat teleporting through a choke point and lighting up the backfield with a shotgun. The game had the best dash: three meters of pure blue energy, point-to-point, no cooldown if you chained it to a kill.

It wasn't compatible. Not with this System. But the code was there, hiding in the overlay like a worm. I reached for it, and every warning in the book exploded across my vision:

[UNAUTHORIZED PROTOCOL DETECTED]
[WARNING: DESTABILIZATION IMMINENT]
[HEAT LEVEL: BEYOND MAXIMUM]
[ADMIN NOTICE: THIS IS YOUR LAST CHANCE]

I didn't even think. I triggered the import.

The effect was instant. My vision fractured. The UI overlays tripled up, then started spinning, then snapped into a single blue-lined wireframe. My hands glowed, then flickered, then became almost transparent.

Piper saw it first. "Saga, what are you doing?"

"Hold on," I said. And I meant it literally.

I grabbed Piper by the wrist. Bastion was easy, his arm as thick as a small tree, and he already half leaned on me. I reached back for Rook, who hesitated only a split second before grabbing my shoulder.

Seraphim and her squad were twenty meters away, but that was only two dash-lengths. The energy built in my hands. The world turned blue.

I fired the protocol.

It felt like jumping into an ice bath made of pure data. For a split second we existed as an error message. The hallway became a thin tunnel of neon, every pixel smeared by motion blur. I felt Rook's hand clamp down on my shoulder, Piper's breath freeze in her lungs, Bastion's weight turn from impossible to nothing.

We reappeared six meters ahead. The wall to our right was scorched with afterimage, blue sparks crawling up and down its length. For a moment, the world was so bright I could barely process it. Then the overlays crashed together, resolved into a single, ugly UI:

[VIOLATION: INTERFACE THEFT]
[PRIORITY PURSUIT - ADMIN DIRECTIVE]

Seraphim didn't even flinch. She just pointed again, and the wardens opened fire.

I triggered the dash again.

This time it was rougher. My entire field of vision whited out, then blackened, then came back with every edge highlighted and pulsing. I saw the world as a grid of possible movements. Every surface was a potential node. Every enemy, a hazard. The dash protocol wanted to chain, wanted to keep moving.

We zipped through another choke point, skipped six meters of floor and two live stun mines. I saw them go off behind us, the air filling with smoke and broken glass. Someone, probably Rook, shouted, but the sound came through filtered and digital, like a bad Discord call.

We were almost at the exit.

Piper recovered first. "Saga, your hands"

I looked down. The blue energy crawled up my arms, licked at my elbows, ate the edges of my sleeves. The coat resisted, the mana-thread in it sparking and shuddering as it tried to fight off the foreign code.

"It's fine," I said, but my voice was a mess of reverb and static. I swear I tasted pineapple.

I saw the exit up ahead. It was a service shaft, barely big enough for Bastion. But Seraphim closed, the wardens not even trying to hide their speed anymore. I watched them jump over the wreckage we'd left behind, hands outstretched, shock prods ready.

One more dash.

I fired it, and this time the UI didn't even bother with a warning. It just flashed [ERROR: ERROR: ERROR] and the world went pure white.

When I came back, we were on the edge of the city, standing on a metal catwalk overlooking the maintenance sector. The lights were out. The city ran on backup power. Every warning siren in the district howled, and the sensor nodes blinked like stars.

We weren't alone. Rook was already on their feet, knife out, scanning the perimeter. Piper knelt over Bastion, who was conscious but barely. His leg was mangled, but the suppression coil was gone.

My own arms were a disaster. The skin was fine, but the overlays were corrupted. Every time I moved, there was a blue shadow, a lag, a sense that the world was a half-second behind me. It hurt. Not in a normal way. It was more like my soul was being pulled apart and rewoven in real time.

I staggered, and Piper caught me. Her face was pale, but her hands were steady.

"That's not a spell," she said. "What did you do?"

"Imported a movement protocol," I said. "It wasn't compatible."

Rook looked at me, then at the blue sparks still playing around my hands. "Can you do it again?"

"Maybe," I said. "But the System was adapting. Next time, it would try to counter."

As if on cue, the entire grid lit up. Red lines shot out from the admin center, branched through the city's neural map. The overlays showed threat cones converging on our location.

Seraphim's voice came through, not on the comms but in the air itself.

"Saga," she said, "You have thirty seconds to surrender. After that, your existence will be revoked."

I felt the city lock around us, every door and access hatch sealing, every sensor eye rotating to our position. Even the air felt different, charged with anticipation. I saw movement below: another squad of enforcers, black armor, moving with the same perfect rhythm as before.

"We can't go back the way we came," Rook said. "They've locked the transit tunnels."

"I could teleport us," I said, "but it was going to get messy."

Piper helped Bastion to his feet. "We'll follow your lead," she said.

I opened the UI, looked for the D-COM protocol. It was still there, but now it was infected, red code bleeding through the blue. The System tried to overwrite it, tried to turn my own hack against me.

Fine. Let's race.

I grabbed the team. This time, I didn't wait for finesse. I pointed at the farthest roof I could see, the edge of the city, and triggered the dash.

The world exploded.

We were everywhere at once: in the tunnel, on the catwalk, skipping across rooftops like stones over water. Every dash was a punch in the head, every arrival a new glitch in my perception. The overlays couldn't keep up. Warnings flickered, stacked on top of each other until the world was just a snowstorm of angry messages.

Below us, the city warped to catch us. Corridors rearranged, doors slammed shut milliseconds before we arrived. Sometimes we were ahead of the change; sometimes, just behind it. Once, we almost clipped into a warden as he phased in front of us, but the protocol glitched and shoved us sideways, scraped the wall and sent showers of blue sparks everywhere.

Seraphim's squads kept pace. They optimized on the fly, used predictive movement to intercept. Each time we landed, they were a little closer, a little better.

I felt the dash start to falter. The blue energy was almost gone, replaced with a sick red-black shimmer. My vision tunneled, and I heard the Admin's voice again:

[RETURN TO CONTAINMENT. RETURN TO CONTAINMENT. RETURN]

I ignored it, ran another jump. The city fought back. This time, we landed in a maintenance corridor filled with drones, all of them bristling with guns and blades. Rook was ready, they threw a flashbang before they could open fire, and the world went white.

We hit the next corridor, and the overlays were gone. Just blackness, and the pounding of my own heart. My mana was zeroed out. The only thing that kept me upright was pure momentum.

"We're almost there," Rook gasped. "One more shaft, and we're out."

Piper looked at me. "Can you do it?"

"I didn't know," I said, and it was the first honest thing I'd said all night.

But I did it anyway.

I grabbed them, pointed at the horizon, and triggered the protocol one last time.

The world fell apart. I heard the System scream, felt it lunge to catch us. For a moment, we were in admin space, the code all around us, red and white and full of sharp angles. I saw Seraphim's face, not in person but as a mask built from warnings and error logs.

Then we were out.

We landed in a pile, all four of us tangled and exhausted. The world was quiet, except for the distant sound of alarms. The overlays were gone. The admin's voice was gone. All that was left was the sound of breathing and the wet slap of Bastion's hand hitting the ground.

I looked around. We were outside the city, on the edge of the ruins. The city's lights were far behind us, flickering and unstable.

I tried to stand, but my legs betrayed me. Piper caught me before I hit the ground.

"Saga," she said, "Can you hear me?"

Everything was dark, and then darker. The last thing I saw was the blue energy flicker out from my hands, leaving only cold and silence.

Game over.

Or maybe just the next level.

Chapter 14

Unsafe Space

THE FIRST THING I felt was my own heartbeat, slamming against my ribs so hard I thought it might break through. Then the cold, slick against my skin, soaking through the shredded sleeves of my coat and the medical tape webbed around my left arm. Then the taste: rust and bile, something chemical gnawing the back of my throat.

I lurched upright with a noise like a drowning person surfacing for air. The world was concrete and rebar and darkness punctured by dying strip lights. My HUD flickered awake, but it was broken in a new and exciting way: mana bar full, then empty, then full again, the numbers blurring past so fast they looked like lottery balls in a wind tunnel.

The rest of me was not much better. My hands were wrapped in bandages, brown and red with old blood. My foot, the right one, where the nerves still fired off static at every shift, had a chunk of mattress jammed underneath as a wedge, like someone had tried to set a broken leg and given up at step two. I was lying on a mattress that used to be white, now an archive of stains and bad decisions, and the only reason I didn't fall off was that I was already half-cradled in a puddle of rainwater.

"Easy." Rook's voice was close and raw, like they'd been up all night waiting for this exact moment. They were slumped against a wall five feet away, legs stretched out and arms crossed, but the second I moved htey were on their feet and at my side.

"Welcome back to the land of the living," they said, which would have been reassuring if their smile didn't look like a hostage note. "You've been out for more than a day."

I tried to say something cool, but my tongue was glued to the roof of my mouth. All I got was "nggh," which was not, strictly speaking, language.

Rook disappeared for half a second and came back with a plastic water bottle. The cap was missing, but I would have drunk from a puddle right then, so who cared. They propped me up and poured a trickle into my mouth. It tasted like copper and plastic and something sweet, probably the last vestiges of a stolen electrolyte tab, but I downed it until I coughed.

Every muscle in my neck felt like it had been used as an emergency power conduit. I flexed my fingers, then my toes, then regretted both immediately.

"Where?" I managed, trying to get my brain to line up its remaining process threads.

"Undercity," Rook said. They glanced back at the door, a slab of steel with four different locks on it. "Far edge of the maintenance district, near the perimeter. Piper and Bastion are out foraging. You're safe." He squinted at my HUD, which must have been having its own freakout in augmented space. "Mostly."

I closed my eyes, then opened them again when a surge of memory shoved through the confusion: the escape, the dash protocol, the city collapsing behind us like the world's meanest set of dominos. The blue afterimages, the sick red code bleeding through, the way my hands had looked when the System's voice started screaming at me.

"Mana's still broken," I said, checking the numbers. "But not in the fun way."

Rook half-smiled, half-grimaced. "Yeah. You teleported us through a brick wall, a drone patrol, and half the city grid. You fried the sensors, but they got a snapshot of your signature before we made it out." They hunkered down, elbows on knees. "The Admin wants you so bad it's gotten sloppy. They sent a hundred containment drones to the last known, and none of them even found our exit."

I scanned the room for the rest of the party, but it was just Rook and me and a heap of scavenged food packets in a corner. Someone had emptied the med kit trying to keep me stable; there were bandage wrappers and alcohol wipes everywhere.

My head felt like someone had stuck a nail in my brain and then tried to hammer it sideways. I touched my temple, expecting to find stitches or a wound. There was just sweat and the stickiness of old fear.

"Did I, did we get out?" My voice was weaker than I wanted, so I forced it up a notch. "Did I kill us all, or just nearly?"

Rook leaned back, and for the first time since I'd known them, they looked genuinely relieved. "We got out. All four. Bastion's limping but alive. Piper did some kind of medical miracle on your foot, by the way. She's been working shifts, keeping your fever down."

They held up three fingers. "You didn't talk, but you kept counting. Hands. Feet. Over and over."

I laughed, or tried to. It came out as a dry, rattling cough. "Classic. My best raid group said I used to mutter boss mechanics in my sleep."

They grinned, and it was less brittle now. "Explains a lot."

The walls there were uglier than anywhere I'd seen in the city, cracked concrete painted with ancient warnings, wiring so exposed it looked like a bomb had gone off in every junction box. There was a flickering light overhead, but most of the illumination came from the hallway outside, where blue flashes occasionally spilled in from something electrical sparking in the distance. It smelled like mold, rot, and old blood.

I checked my HUD again, just to make sure I wasn't hallucinating the state of my body. HP: 940/5,240. Mana: 1,600/8,900 and regenerating, but with weird oscillations every few seconds. A new status line had appeared at the bottom: [Skill Tree: Unstable Import]. Underneath, a warning:

[INTERFACE COMPATIBILITY: DETERIORATING]
[RECOMMENDED ACTION: SYSTEM RESET]

I snorted. "The System wants me to reboot. Not happening."

Rook pulled a face. "Yeah, the System wants a lot of things. Piper said if you reset, it might kick you back to the last checkpoint. Which is a coffin." They paused, then added: "I voted no."

I tried to swing my legs off the mattress. They moved, but the pain was blinding. I gritted my teeth, dug my nails into the palm of my hand, and used the pain to clear my head.

"What did I miss?" I asked, then, "Are we safe here?" Then, because it felt right: "What's our next move?"

Rook sat on the edge of the bed, arms crossed. "They're searching. The City's in full lockdown for five blocks around the admin center. Drones on every level, human teams too. But nobody expects anyone to make it this far out, the tunnels out here are basically condemned. Old infection from before the patch, they say."

They gestured at the room. "We'd need to move in a day, maybe two. Bastion was checking for a route through the old maglev shafts. Piper was foraging, like I said."

My mouth felt like it was full of sand. "Did we have food?"

Rook nodded at the pile. "Powdered soup, protein bars, water tabs. And, uh..." They grinned. "Seventeen stolen energy drinks. If you want to feel like your heart is going to explode, Piper said they're great."

I glanced at my hands, remembering the way they'd looked mid-dash: blue veins, black crackle, the ghost of the old D-COM interface layered over my own. "Did I look different? When it happened?"

Rook hesitated, then: "Yeah. The System couldn't even keep your outline. For a second, I thought we'd lost you." They held my gaze. "I don't know how you held us all together. But you did."

The memory spiked, four bodies bound by desperation, tumbling through broken code. The feel of Bastion's hand like an anchor, Piper's hope burning brighter than her actual magic, Rook's panic forced into cold, competent action.

I didn't remember the actual escape. I didn't remember most of the last thirty seconds, just the sensation of being everywhere and nowhere at once.

"Thank you," I said, and meant it.

Rook shrugged. "Don't get sappy. We still need a plan."

A silence grew between us, but it wasn't uncomfortable. It was the silence of people who knew they were already dead, but had the luxury of choosing what happened before they went.

The door handle rattled. Rook was up in a flash, knife drawn from a boot sheath. But the knock was gentle, and Piper's voice filtered in: "It's me."

She entered, hair pulled back and streaked with sweat, face flushed from exertion. She was carrying a makeshift sling packed with a med kit, bandages, and two lumpy bundles that looked suspiciously like hot food in old takeout boxes.

She saw me awake, and something like relief moved through her whole body. "Welcome back," she said, setting down the kit and immediately checking my pulse with a healer's hand. "You scared the hell out of us."

"Wouldn't be the first time," I said, then, "Was that real food?"

She laughed, a real one, not the brittle survival noise we'd been making for days. "Don't get your hopes up. It's probably rat. Or mold. But it's hot, and it smells better than this room."

She helped me sit up, propping me against a crate. My legs felt like they were stuffed with insulation, but the pain was already receding. Piper pushed a battered cup into my hand. I sipped, and it was hot, salty, and about as close to bliss as anything I'd had since waking up there.

Bastion lumbered in a moment later, favoring his left leg, which was splinted with a weird combo of plastic and zip ties. He nodded at me, then at the rest, and collapsed onto the nearest chunk of furniture.

"Made it," he said, voice gravelly but good-natured. "Drones didn't sweep this block. Even found a clean water line."

Rook handed him a food packet. They ate in silence, but it was the silence of a party at rest between raid wipes, a kind of exhausted, shared peace.

I checked my HUD again. The "Blink" protocol was still there, buried under the warning, but if I focused I could almost see the new skill icon flickering at the edge of my vision.

I thought about using it, just to see what happened.

But instead I sat, sipped the soup, and watched my friends try to pretend we weren't the most hunted people in the city.

For the first time in days, I felt something like hope. Not the real thing. But maybe its cracked, battered cousin.

Hands. Feet. Soup.

We were alive, and for now, that counted.

The first warning that my world was about to change came as a pulse in my left eye: a UI icon, neon yellow on black, throbbing at the edge of my vision. I blinked. It didn't go away. Instead, it grew brighter, then resolved into a sharp little lightning bolt. Underneath: "Blink, Ready." A tiny clock icon next to it ticked down from four seconds, three, two, one, then reset.

I stared at it, trying to will it out of existence, but my interface had never been this insistent. I reached for my mana, and the icon pulsed, drawing focus like a pop-up ad with a personal vendetta.

"Rook?" I said, voice still gravel but improving. "You seeing this?"

They turned, eyeing me with a kind of feral wariness that was new. "Seeing what?"

"Skill tree update. I have..." I hesitated, because even saying it sounded insane. "I have a teleport spell now. Cooldown's four seconds."

Rook stared like they were waiting for the punchline. "You had a movement hack last night. Is this the same thing?"

I looked down at my hands, flexed them. The blue spark was gone, but a ghost of the D-COM overlay lingered. I touched the icon, just to see if it would give me a context menu.

It didn't. Instead, the world jumped.

I was three feet to the right, sitting on the bare concrete, with the mattress and crate now behind me. The air tasted like ionization and fear. Rook let out a yelp and scrambled back, their knife already in hand.

"What the actual fuck?" they said.

It wasn't pain, exactly, but the motion was so fast and so wrong that my stomach flipped and my arms tingled with cold static. My head went suddenly light, and for a second all I could do was breathe and fight the urge to throw up.

Piper's voice filtered in from the hall. "Rook? Did you fall?"

They ignored her, still staring at me. "Do it again," they said, but there was a tremor in his voice.

I looked at the icon. Four second cooldown. Already reset.

I pointed at the far wall, maybe ten feet away, and touched the icon with my mind.

The world tore, but not like before. This time, it was clean: an electric blue ribbon of afterimage as my body folded from point A to point B, all at once, no interim. I landed flat on my ass, but upright, and the entire room was now between me and Rook.

Piper entered, carrying a bottle of water and a box of scavenged meds. She halted, eyes wide, as if I had just spawned out of the air.

"Saga?" she said. "Were you...?"

"Yeah," I said, breathing hard. "I have Blink now."

She set the water down, knelt next to me, and did the healer thing, pulse, pupil check, hand on the wrist. "You shouldn't be able to teleport. Not with your class, and not with this mana state."

"It's from the overlay," Rook said, voice almost a whisper. "She glitched it in."

Piper turned to me. "Did it hurt?"

I shook my head. "No. Just left me a little off. Like a reboot where you lose the last three frames of memory."

She frowned. "You could destabilize yourself if you did it too often. Four seconds is fast, but it might stack fatigue or something worse."

I flexed my fingers, feeling the way the nerves in my hands sparked with each movement. "Weirder thing: it's permanent now. It shows up in my skill tree, right between Mana Ward and Elemental Control."

Rook approached, slower now, as if the air between us could explode. "That's not possible," they said, but it was the voice of someone trying to convince himself.

"Check my UI," I said, and granted them the standard view permission.

They hissed in a breath, reading the skill tree projection that hovered over my shoulder. "It's really there," they said. "You're patched at a class level."

Piper looked me in the eyes, then at the icon. "Do it again," she said.

I nodded. The icon was already bright, like a button begging to be pushed. I focused on the crate across the room, ten feet away, and touched the ability.

This time, I was ready for it. The world inverted and snapped back, and I was standing, not sitting, next to the crate. The cold fizz in my muscles was still there, but less pronounced.

Rook whistled. "We have to test the limits."

Piper held up her hand. "First, you have to rest. Second, you need food and water. Third," she glanced at the door, where Bastion's shadow loomed, "third, you need to not do this if someone is looking to kill us."

"Already on it," Bastion said, ducking his head into the room. He surveyed the space, then me, then the new skill icon. "How far?"

"Ten feet, give or take," I said. "Felt like I could do more, but it's draining. Like a sprint."

He nodded, approving. "Could be useful for breaking containment. Or getting past kill zones."

Rook's gears turned fast. "You could chain this. Hop up a wall, or through doors, or..." They stopped, grin growing wide. "Through a perimeter fence."

Bastion looked at Piper, then at me. "Would it hold? Or would the System adapt?"

I shrugged, but the hope in my chest was real. "If it's in my skill tree, it'll be harder to patch out. But the System would probably escalate."

Piper handed me the water bottle. "Drink. Eat. We'll test it in the corridor once you've stabilized."

I chugged half the bottle in one go, savoring the chill and the way it cleared the taste of ozone out of my mouth. My legs felt rubbery, but standing was easier now. I looked at the "Blink" icon and felt something like pride, but tempered with fear.

"Do it once more," Rook urged, barely able to sit still. "Fast, this time."

I locked eyes with Bastion, who nodded, already bracing for trouble. I lined up the icon, imagined myself across the room, and punched the skill as hard as I could.

This time, there was no delay at all. The world went blue, and then I was there. Just a heartbeat later.

Rook clapped their hands. "That's it. That's the exploit."

Piper smiled, for real. "Congratulations, Saga. You've broken the game again."

Bastion grinned too, his teeth bright in the low light. "We're going to need a lot more food."

For a minute, the room was quiet except for my panting and the distant hum of the city's arteries outside.

I flexed my hands, watched the icon cool down, and felt the future unwind in front of me. There was no going back, not for any of us.

But for the first time, I had a way to go forward.

The food situation was as dire as advertised, but the company made it tolerable. Piper was a soft touch when she was in healer mode, checking my temperature and blood pressure like she thought she'd find a different answer every thirty seconds. Bastion was the opposite: he ate with a single-mindedness that would have been funny if it didn't make me nervous about the future of our rations. Rook just hovered, pacing the cramped length of the hideout, like there was a timer ticking somewhere they couldn't quite see.

We were halfway through a meal that could best be described as "hot, but only in the microwave sense" when Piper set down her mug and pulled something from her sling.

"I found these while you were out," she said, and laid them on the crate in front of me. A pair of fingerless gloves, black leather with blue circuit veining, and a cloth mask that was mostly dark mesh but had a strip of silver rune-stitch across the nose and cheekbones.

She nudged them closer. "They're mage gear. Specialized. Should help with the regeneration thing."

I picked up the gloves. They were soft, supple, and surprisingly heavy, weighted at the knuckle with dense resin, probably to keep you from shattering your own fingers while spellcasting at speed. The inside was lined with some kind of memory fabric; it cinched around my hand the second I slipped it on.

As soon as both were on, my UI lit up: [MANA REGEN +6%], [ELE-MENTAL RESIST +12], [ATTUNEMENT: INTEGRATED]. The effect was instantaneous. The flickering in my mana bar smoothed out, the constant jitters in my nerves dialed back from Red Bull to strong coffee.

Piper smiled, then handed me the mask. "Try it on. It's supposed to reduce detection risk."

I slipped it over my face. The cloth was cool and smelled faintly of ozone, like it had been through a dozen storm cycles. The world shifted; sound sharpened, and the colors in my HUD tweaked. There was a new icon then: a little mask, pulsing with a subtle blue glow, labeled [STEALTH - ENHANCED].

Rook whistled. "That's a look. All you need now is a cape and a tragic back-story."

I smirked, but it was lost under the mask. " I think we all have a tragic backstory here. You volunteering to be my nemesis?"

He shrugged. "If the money's good."

Bastion, done inhaling his soup, looked up and grinned. "Looks good. Might actually buy us a minute or two if the city scans us."

I flexed my hands, watched the UI update with every motion. The gloves amplified the tactile sensation, like every nerve in my hand was on a direct line to the interface. I balled my hand into a fist, and the mask flared faint blue at the edges of my vision, then subsided.

"Thank you," I said, and tried not to sound like someone who had just remembered how to feel gratitude.

Piper waved it off, but her eyes were bright. "You're the party's best hope. Might as well keep you alive."

Rook laughed, but there was no bite to it. "That, and it's a pain to carry you when you're unconscious."

"Is that how you got me here?" I asked.

Bastion's smile widened. "You were out cold for half a block. Rook did most of the dragging. I was busy keeping drones off your back."

I glanced at my memory log. There was nothing there; the last thirty seconds of the escape were just blank, then a hard reboot and the sound of my own gasping. "Thank you," I said again.

"Don't get used to it," Rook said, but their eyes were softer than the words. "Next time, you're on your own."

We settled in, such as it was. I ate another mouthful of soup, which tasted marginally better with the mask off. The room was cramped, but the air felt lighter now, like we'd staved off disaster for at least a few hours.

Outside, the city never stopped. Through a vent near the ceiling, the distant sounds filtered in: a patrol siren, the heavy thrum of power conduits, sometimes a sharp yell or the crash of something being thrown off a roof. It was never quiet, not really. Even in the lull, there was always the sense of being watched, measured, logged.

Piper cleaned up the med kit, her motions precise. Bastion pulled a half-broken radio from his pocket, tuning it to a low-volume chatter. Rook sharpened a knife, eyes darting to the door every few seconds.

I flexed my fingers, feeling the new gloves like a second skin. The "Blink" icon was still there, and every so often it pulsed, a little reminder that the impossible was now routine.

"So what happened?" I asked, breaking the silence. "After the last jump?"

Bastion answered first. "We hit the roof hard. System sent a patrol, but the drones glitched, they couldn't see us for five minutes. I think the code you dragged over from D-COM jammed their tracking."

"After that," Rook said, "we carried you here. Piper patched your foot, Bastion ran perimeter, I looted the local stores for food. We've been rotating shifts ever since."

Piper shrugged. "You were stable, just off. Like your brain was lagging behind your body."

I nodded, absorbing it. "System hadn't tried to reset me yet. But the interface kept throwing up warnings."

"Means you're getting to them," Bastion said, pride in his voice. "Every time you break something, the Admin gets nervous."

I leaned back, watching the mana bar glide up with perfect smoothness. For a second, I let myself feel something like hope.

"We need to move," Rook said, breaking the spell. "The drones'll do a full sweep at midnight, and the System never hits the same place twice."

Bastion nodded. "Old maglev tunnels are still passable. We can ride the service line two miles north, maybe more. But we'll have to fight for every yard."

Piper looked at me. "Can you keep up?"

I considered the gloves, the mask, the new skill humming at the edge of my mind. "Yeah. I was better than I'd ever been."

She grinned, then pulled the mask over her own face in imitation. "Then we're ready."

We finished the meal in silence, but it wasn't the silence of doom anymore. It was the quiet before a storm, the breath you take right before the boss fight begins.

I looked at my hands, flexed them, felt the blue circuit lines pulsing beneath the skin.

"So," I said, meeting each of their eyes in turn. "What was our next move?"

The city outside didn't wait for an answer. But I did.

And when the time came, I'd be ready to Blink.

ACT 3

THE NET TIGHTENS

Chapter 15
The Monster Story

THE SERVICE TUNNEL WAS a throat made of rusted metal and broken promises, narrow enough that Bastion had to duck and wide enough that the sound of our footsteps echoed like gunshots in a cathedral. We'd been moving for twenty minutes through the undercity's circulatory system, following Rook's hand-drawn map through passages that smelled like decades of electrical fires and human fear. My new gloves caught on every rough edge, the circuit veining pulsing faint blue in the darkness, and the mask made everything taste like filtered air and old regrets.

Piper moved behind me with the quiet efficiency of someone who'd spent years navigating hospital corridors at three AM. Her footsteps were barely whispers against the grated flooring, but I could feel her presence like a warm hand on my shoulder. Rook led, fingers dancing across a salvaged tablet they'd jury-rigged from three different devices, muttering about signal strength and encrypted channels. Behind us, Bastion's bulk filled the tunnel entrance like a living wall, his silhouette cutting clean lines through the emergency lighting that flickered every few seconds.

"Got something," Rook said, voice tight with concentration. They stopped at a junction where the tunnel widened into what might once have been a maintenance hub. Exposed cables snaked along the walls like technological intestines, and a bank of dead monitors hung from the ceiling at angles that suggested violence or neglect.

But one screen wasn't dead.

Rook plugged their makeshift terminal into a port that was probably older than I was, and the display flickered to life with the harsh white glow of official city broadcasts. For a second there was nothing but static and the electronic whine of feedback. Then the image resolved, and I saw my own face staring back at me.

Except it wasn't my face. Not really.

The holographic display showed something that might have started as my security camera footage, but the features had been twisted, sharpened, given an inhuman cast that made my skin crawl. My eyes burned with red light that had never existed. My smile was all teeth, predatory and wrong. The blue energy that sometimes crackled around my hands had been amplified into writhing tentacles of destruction.

"Citizens of Vermeer," the announcement began, the narrator's voice carrying all the warmth of a medical diagnosis, "be advised that the escaped Player designated 'Saga' represents an immediate threat to public safety."

My hands clenched into fists, the gloves creaking like old leather. The energy built behind my eyes, that familiar pressure that came before major spellwork, but I forced it down. Not there. Not then.

The broadcast continued, showing doctored footage of destruction I'd never caused, chaos I'd never created. Every frame was calculated to inspire maximum terror. They showed buildings collapsing, civilians screaming, emergency responders overwhelmed by disasters that bore my digital signature but not my actual involvement.

"Player entities demonstrate unpredictable magical capabilities and show no regard for civilian casualties," the voice droned on. "Citizens who provide information leading to their capture will receive priority food allocation and residential upgrades."

Piper's breath caught behind me. "They're turning the whole city against us."

The screen switched to live feeds from across the district. I watched checkpoint guards demanding papers from families with young children, their faces tight with the kind of fear that made people do terrible things. An elderly woman was pressed against a wall while officers searched her bags, and when she protested, one of them mentioned something about "Player sympathizers" that made her go very still and very quiet.

In another feed, a group of teenagers pointed excitedly at shadows in an alley, calling for guards and practically bouncing with the prospect of earning those promised rations. The camera followed the guards as they searched the alley, finding nothing but stray cats and garbage, but the kids got commendation tokens anyway for their "civic vigilance."

"Jesus," Rook muttered, fingers clicking rapidly across their improvised keyboard. "The encryption on this is military grade. They're not just broadcasting propaganda, they're coordinating intelligence gathering across the entire city grid."

Bastion's voice rumbled from the tunnel entrance, low and dangerous. "How many detention centers?"

Piper checked something on her own interface, her healer's instincts automatically cataloging the human cost. "Seventeen reported so far. They're holding anyone who can't provide alibis for the last seventy-two hours. Anyone who's been in the same districts we passed through. Anyone who fits the vague physical parameters of 'Player associate.'"

The screen showed more footage: families being separated at processing centers, children crying as their parents were loaded into transport vehicles, elderly citizens collapsed on the pavement because the checkpoints didn't have adequate medical facilities. The guards processed them with the efficiency of people following a quota system, and every face in the crowd carried the same expression of desperate confusion.

My vision started to blur at the edges, not from tears but from rage so pure it felt like staring into a furnace. These people hadn't asked to be part of this. They were just trying to survive in a city that had decided terror was the most efficient form of crowd control.

"They're scared," I whispered, watching a mother pull her toddler closer as a patrol drone passed overhead. "All of them. They are absolutely terrified."

Rook looked up from their terminal, eyes reflecting the harsh light of the display. "Fear's the point. Keep everyone looking over their shoulders, they won't organize. Keep them reporting on each other, they won't trust their neighbors enough to resist."

Another feed showed a public square where a crowd had gathered around a makeshift gallows. Not for executions, but for effigies. Crude mannequins dressed in blue robes, faces painted with the same demonic features they'd given me in the propaganda. Children were encouraged to throw stones, to spit, to scream insults at the straw figures that represented everything they'd been taught to hate.

The pressure in my skull reached a breaking point. Energy coursed down my arms, through the circuit patterns in my gloves, until my hands were glowing like stars. The Blink icon in my peripheral vision pulsed bright and urgent, responding to my emotional state rather than any conscious command.

The world tore sideways.

I was suddenly three feet to the right, crouched against a different section of the tunnel wall, blue afterimages crackling around my body like digital lightning. My lungs burned as I gasped for air, and the taste of ozone flooded my mouth. The involuntary teleport left me shaking, not from the physical displacement but from the realization that my new ability was responding to stress in ways I couldn't control.

Piper was at my side instantly, her hands gentle but firm as she checked my pulse. "Saga? Talk to me."

"I'm okay," I managed, though my voice sounded like it was coming from underwater. "Just... processing."

Bastion moved closer, his presence solid and reassuring in the flickering light. "They want you angry. They want you to lose control."

I looked up at the screen, where the propaganda continued its endless cycle of fear and lies. But then I saw something else in the feeds: the way the guards glanced nervously at the crowds they were controlling, the way the broadcast repeated the same talking points with increasing desperation, the way even the children throwing stones at my effigy seemed to be performing their hatred rather than feeling it.

"They're not just scared of me," I realized, voice growing stronger with each word. "They're scared of what I represent. The possibility that their system isn't as stable as they pretend."

Rook grinned, sharp and dangerous. "Now you're thinking like a revolutionary."

I stood, legs still unsteady but getting better, and looked at each of my teammates in turn. The blue energy in my gloves pulsed steadily now, controlled rather than chaotic. The Blink icon hovered at the edge of my vision, ready but not demanding.

"We need to show them the truth," I said, meeting each of their eyes. "All of them. The civilians, the guards, everyone who's been fed these lies."

Piper nodded, her healer's compassion hardened into determination. "How?"

I gestured at the screen, at the endless cycle of propaganda designed to turn human beings into weapons against each other. "The same way they're spreading the lies. We hijack their system."

The tunnel fell silent except for the electronic hum of the display and the distant sound of the city's pulse above us. But in that silence, I felt something I hadn't felt since waking up in this nightmare: purpose.

They wanted to make me a monster. Fine. I'd be the monster that tore down every lie they'd built their power on.

Starting that night.

The maintenance uniform scratched against my skin like punishment made fabric, every thread a reminder that I was pretending to be something I wasn't. The harsh sunlight burned my eyes after days in the underground dark, and I had to squint to make sense of the world above. Rook moved beside me with that practiced invisibility they'd perfected, shoulders hunched in the universal language of just another city worker trying to get through the day. The stolen coveralls smelled like industrial solvent and someone else's fear, but they were our ticket to blend in with the legitimate repair crews scattered across the district.

My new gloves made my hands feel alien, the blue circuit lines pulsing faintly beneath the maintenance uniform's sleeves. The mask sat heavy across my face, its silver rune-stitch catching the light in ways that made me paranoid about standing out. Every few steps, I caught myself reaching for the Blink icon in my peripheral vision, fingers twitching with the muscle memory of a spell I'd only had for hours.

The city above ground was nothing like the sterile administrative levels or the grimy tunnels below. This was where people lived, where they tried to maintain some semblance of normal life under the System's watchful eye. But normal had died sometime in the last few days, strangled by fear and propaganda.

"CLOSED DUE TO PLAYER THREAT" banners hung from every storefront like funeral shrouds. The coffee shop that probably used to buzz with morning conversations sat empty, its windows papered with official notices bearing my face. The bakery next door had pulled down metal shutters, but I could see eyes peering through the gaps, watching the street with the paranoid attention of prey animals.

Families clustered in doorways, clutching identification papers with white-knuckled desperation. A mother held her two children close, whispering urgent instructions about staying quiet, staying small, staying invisible. Their clothes were clean but worn, the kind of careful maintenance that spoke to people stretching resources as far as they'd go. The father kept glancing at the sky, tracking patrol routes with the practiced eye of someone who'd memorized the schedule of his own oppression.

We passed a news kiosk where a handful of people gathered around a crackling radio. The broadcaster's voice carried just far enough for me to catch fragments: "...terrorist actions by rogue Players continue to threaten civilian infrastructure... authorities remind citizens to report suspicious activity immediately..." My stomach clenched as I recognized the clinical tone, the way truth got processed into something unrecognizable.

Street medics stumbled past us, their red cross armbands stained with blood and exhaustion. One carried a bag of supplies that was more patch than original fabric. Another tended to someone with a bandaged head, the result of a panicked stampede when the alarms started wailing. The injured woman kept muttering, "I just want bread, I just want to buy bread," like a prayer that might undo whatever had sent her running.

A child no older than seven spotted me from across the street. His finger extended with the terrible certainty of innocence, pointing directly at my masked face. My heart stopped beating for about three seconds, and I felt every nerve in my body light up like a Christmas tree made of pure terror.

"Mama," the boy said, voice carrying across the empty street with devastating clarity. "That's the bad lady from the pictures."

His mother's face went white as paper. She snatched her son's hand, yanking him against her body with enough force to make him yelp. Her eyes met mine for just a moment, and I saw everything there: recognition, fear, and something that might have been disappointment. As if she'd hoped the monster would look more obviously monstrous.

"Shush," she hissed at her boy, already backing toward the nearest doorway. "Don't look. Don't point. Just look away."

But he was still staring at me with that awful childhood honesty. "Why is she wearing a mask, Mama? The pictures don't show a mask."

Rook's hand found my elbow, pressure gentle but insistent. Keep moving. Don't react. We were just maintenance workers who happened to be in the wrong place when a kid got confused.

We kept walking, but I could feel the woman's eyes tracking us until we turned the corner. My hands were shaking inside the gloves, blue light leaking through the fabric in ways that definitely weren't standard maintenance worker behavior.

The next block brought us to a public square where a crowd had gathered, but this wasn't the kind of gathering that happened by choice. City guards in riot gear had formed a perimeter around an elderly man, his hands zip-tied behind his back. He was kneeling on the wet pavement, gray hair plastered to his skull, while an officer read charges from a digital tablet.

"...found guilty of providing aid and comfort to known terrorist entities, specifically the fugitive designated as Saga..."

My vision went red around the edges. The old man's crime, as far as I could tell from the shouted accusations, was giving directions to someone who might have been a Player. He'd pointed them toward the transit station when they asked for help, the same thing any decent person would do for a lost stranger.

Power built in my hands without conscious direction, mana flowing through the new gloves like water through a broken dam. The blue glow started to leak around my cuffs, and I could feel the Blink icon pulsing urgently in my peripheral vision. I could have been there in a heartbeat. I could have scattered those guards, broken those restraints, shown them what actual terror looked like.

Rook's grip on my wrist was iron. Their head shook once, barely perceptible, but the message was clear. Not there. Not then. Not like that.

The old man's voice carried across the square, thin but unbroken. "I do nothing wrong. Helping people isn't a crime."

One of the guards kicked him in the ribs, and he doubled over but didn't cry out. The crowd flinched as one, a collective intake of breath that sounded like the city itself gasping in pain.

I forced my hands to unclench, pushed the mana back down where it belonged. The gloves pulsed once more, then dimmed. Rook didn't let go of my wrist until we were three blocks away from the square, walking past another row of shuttered businesses and fearful faces.

A patrol drone glided overhead, its scanning beam cutting through the afternoon air like a razor made of light. The beam swept across the street in perfect geometric patterns, pausing briefly on each person before moving on. When it reached us, I held my breath and tried to look as boring as possible.

The mask's stealth enhancement kicked in, and I felt the moment when the drone's sensors slid past me without finding purchase. The beam lingered for just a heartbeat longer than comfort allowed, then continued on its route. I exhaled slowly, tasting copper and adrenaline.

That was when I saw her: a young woman, maybe twenty, stumbling as she tried to navigate the crowded street with a bag of groceries and a toddler in her arms. She tripped over nothing, probably exhaustion or fear or just the weight of trying to live a normal life in an abnormal world. Groceries scattered across the pavement, and the kid started crying.

Without thinking, I moved to help. It was automatic, muscle memory from a dozen worlds where helping fallen party members was just what you did. I knelt beside her, started gathering scattered cans and packages.

"It's okay," I said, keeping my voice soft. "Let me help."

She looked up, saw the mask, saw something in my eyes that made her scramble backward like I was made of live wires. The baby's crying got louder, and she clutched him to her chest while staring at me with naked terror.

"Please," she whispered. "I don't have anything. I'm nobody. I just want to buy food."

My chest felt like it was caving in. "I'm not going to hurt you. I just want to help."

But she was already getting to her feet, leaving half her groceries scattered on the ground. "Stay away from us," she said, voice breaking. "Just stay away."

I watched her flee, the baby's wails echoing off the buildings until they disappeared around a corner. The abandoned groceries lay between me and the spot where she'd fallen, evidence of kindness mistaken for threat.

"I'm not what they say I am," I whispered to the empty street, but the words felt hollow even to me.

That was when my UI exploded with admin override, every warning and notification clearing away to make room for a single message in letters that burned themselves into my retinas:

[THEY FEAR WHAT THEY SHOULD. YOU ARE DESTRUCTION INCARNATE.]

The text pulsed once, twice, then faded. But the taste it left behind didn't go away, bitter as poison and twice as persistent.

Rook materialized beside me, checking to make sure the street was clear before speaking. "Time to go," they said. "We've pushed our luck far enough."

I nodded, but I couldn't stop looking at the scattered groceries, the evidence of my failure to be anything other than the monster they'd painted me to be. We slipped back into the maintenance tunnels, leaving the sunlight and the fear and the terrible weight of other people's terror behind.

But I carried it with me anyway, heavy as a second skin.

The safehouse terminal flickered to life as we crowded around it, four bodies pressed together in the cramped space like conspirators at the end of the world. Piper's fingers danced across the improvised interface she'd jury-rigged from salvaged components, pulling in broadcast feeds from across the city's network. The screen stuttered between channels, each one showing the same rotating cycle of news, propaganda, and public service announcements that probably counted as both.

Bastion leaned against the wall behind us, his injured leg propped on a crate, while Rook peered over my shoulder with the intense focus of someone decoding an enemy's battle plans. The air in the room felt electric, charged with the aftermath of our surface reconnaissance and the weight of what we'd seen up there. My hands still shook with the memory of that child pointing at me, his mother's terrified eyes, the old man kneeling in the square.

"Here," Piper said, her voice tight with something that might have been dread. "This is what they're broadcasting on every channel."

The screen resolved into crisp, official footage. A news anchor with the kind of perfectly sculpted face that screamed AI-generated sat behind a desk that gleamed with corporate authority. Behind her, a scrolling banner read "PLAYER TERRORIST ATTACKS CONTINUE" in letters designed to burn themselves into your retinas.

"This evening, city officials release security footage showing the terrorist known as Saga deliberately sabotaging critical infrastructure," the anchor said, her voice carrying the clinical detachment of someone reporting the weather. "The attack targets a power relay serving Saint Catherine's Children's Medical Center, leaving dozens of critically ill patients without life support."

My blood turned to ice water in my veins.

The footage that followed was grainy, low-resolution security camera material that looked exactly like the kind of feed you'd expect from a utility substation. The timestamp showed yesterday evening, right around the time we'd been planning our escape in the tunnels. And there I was, clear as digital daylight, crouched next to an electrical relay box with my hands glowing with unmistakable mana discharge.

The camera angle was perfect. It caught my face in profile, showed the distinctive red hair, even captured the blue glow of magical energy as I supposedly channeled power directly into the relay's control systems. The explosion that followed lit up the night, and the footage cut to exterior shots of a children's hospital going dark, emergency generators failing to kick in, tiny figures in medical scrubs running between buildings with flashlights.

"That's not possible," I breathed, the words barely making it past the sudden tightness in my throat. "I'm with all of you when this happens. We're planning in the maintenance tunnels, remember? Rook is showing us the maps."

My voice got louder, more desperate, even though I knew they believed me. "We're eating that terrible soup and arguing about patrol routes. I can't be at any power station because I'm unconscious for most of the day before that."

Bastion's fist connected with the wall hard enough to leave a dent in the metal sheeting. The impact sent vibrations through the floor, and his knuckles came away bloody. "Bastards," he growled, voice thick with rage. "They're using your face to justify whatever they want."

Piper's hands had begun to glow with that soft, unconscious healing light that manifested when she was under extreme stress. The energy pulsed in rhythm with her breathing, casting blue shadows on the terminal screen. She didn't seem to notice, too focused on the implications of what we were seeing.

"How many people see this?" she asked, but it wasn't really a question. In a city this size, with mandatory news consumption and wall-mounted displays on every corner, everyone saw it. Everyone now believed I personally tried to kill sick children.

Rook leaned closer to the screen, their paranoid analyst's mind already working through the technical details. They pointed at specific frames, tracing inconsistencies with a fingertip that left smudges on the makeshift monitor.

"Look at the shadows," they said, voice gaining confidence as they found their expertise. "The light sources don't match. Your magical discharge is casting shadows at a different angle than the streetlights in the background."

They pulled up another frame, this one showing my supposedly guilty face in higher resolution. "And here, see the pixelation around your hairline? That's not compression artifacts. That's digital compositing. They take footage of you from somewhere else and graft it onto this scene."

"They're good," they continued, switching between frames with the rapid-fire focus of someone who'd spent years breaking down security systems. "But they're not perfect. The facial tracking slips for three frames right here, and the mana signature doesn't match your actual casting pattern. I've seen you work. Your discharge is cleaner than this, more controlled."

I paced the small space, barely able to contain the energy building in my chest. The new gloves left faint trails of blue light with every gesture, and I could feel the Blink icon pulsing insistently in my peripheral vision. My mana regeneration was spiking, feeding off anger and adrenaline in ways that definitely weren't standard for any class build.

"I can prove this is fake," Rook said, fingers already moving toward the jury-rigged keyboard. "Give me access to the broadcast network, and I can break down every inconsistency, show the digital signatures, expose the whole fabrication."

But I stopped pacing, my attention caught by something else on their improvised workstation. A network diagram showing the city's communication infrastructure, transmission nodes mapped out like a spider web of control and influence. Every propaganda broadcast, every lie, every manufactured piece of evidence flowed through those nodes before reaching the screens where people formed their opinions about who deserved to live and who deserved to be hunted.

"No," I said, and my voice carried a certainty that surprised even me. "We don't stay defensive. We don't just prove their lies wrong. We hijack their system."

I pointed at the central transmission node, the hub that controlled broadcast priority for the entire district. "That's where we hit them. Not to defend ourselves, but to show everyone what they're really doing. Show them the real footage of those coffins, the Player extraction chambers, the systematic theft of human life that powers their perfect city."

Bastion grinned, the expression sharp enough to cut glass. "Offensive strategy. I like it."

Piper nodded slowly, the healing glow around her hands flickering brighter. "If we expose them publicly, they can't just disappear us quietly. The whole city knows."

But it was Rook who understood the full implications first. "You're talking about a full-spectrum information war. Not just correcting the record, but seizing control of the narrative entirely."

"Exactly." I sketched out approach routes on the network diagram, my fingers moving with the muscle memory of raid planning. "They want to make me a monster? Fine. I'll be the monster that exposes every lie they've told."

My interface chose that moment to glitch spectacularly. The familiar UI elements flickered and warped, replaced for just a moment by crosshairs from an old tactical shooter I used to play. The targeting reticle settled directly over the transmission node, pulsing red with target acquisition. The overlay faded back to normal, but the message was clear.

I had more than one game's worth of exploits to draw from.

"The broadcast tower is twelve blocks north," I continued, my voice steady despite the chaos in my head. "Minimal security, because who's crazy enough to attack a propaganda outlet directly?"

"We are," Bastion said, and there was pride in his voice.

Rook pulled up detailed schematics, their earlier fear replaced by the focused intensity of someone who'd found a puzzle worth solving. "Access through the maintenance levels, disable the security grid, hijack the primary transmitter. It's doable."

"But risky," Piper pointed out. "If we're caught, they won't bother with containment protocols. They'll just delete us."

I looked at each of them in turn, these people who'd become my party in the most literal sense possible. "Are you with me?"

The silence stretched for exactly three heartbeats.

Then Bastion reached for his gear. "When do we move?"

"Tonight," I said, and felt the weight of the decision settle over us like armor. "Before they have time to adjust their security. Before they can fabricate more evidence. Before anyone else gets arrested for the crime of basic human decency."

The terminal screen still showed my supposedly guilty face, frozen in the act of imaginary sabotage. But for the first time since we escaped those coffins, I wasn't running from what they'd made me.

I was running straight toward it.

And when we were done, the whole city would know exactly who the real monsters were.

Chapter 16
Player Friction

THE OVERTURNED CRATE BIT into my tailbone like a punishment for every poor life choice that had led me there. My limbs felt like they'd been wrung through a digital washing machine, each muscle fiber singing with the particular ache that came from pushing Blink too hard, too fast. The teleportation drain sat in my bones like a low-grade fever, and every small movement sent ripples of discomfort through my nervous system. I shifted on the makeshift seat, trying to find a position that didn't make me want to curl up and sleep for a week.

The refuge around us told the story of our slow decline better than any health bar. What had started as a temporary hideout had become a tomb furnished with desperation. Exposed pipes ran along the ceiling like mechanical arteries, some of them sweating condensation that dripped onto our bedrolls with the steady rhythm of a countdown timer. The makeshift beds scattered across the concrete floor looked like casualties from a war between comfort and necessity, and necessity was winning by a landslide. In the corner, our remaining ration packs formed a pathetic pyramid that shrank a little more each day.

"We don't have a choice anymore," Rook snarled, their boots hitting the concrete with sharp, angry clicks as they paced the length of our cramped prison. Their stolen coveralls hung loose on their frame, and I could see how their shoulders had narrowed since we'd escaped the coffin facility. "Bastion's leg is getting worse. Piper is out of antibiotics. And you're burning through mana like it's going out of style."

They stopped pacing long enough to gesture at me with both hands, their paranoia and frustration bleeding through every movement. "That convoy runs medical supplies to three districts. Military grade antibiotics, surgical equipment, pain suppressors. Everything we need to keep this party from falling apart."

"It also runs supplies to civilian hospitals," Piper shot back, her arms crossed so tightly across her chest that her knuckles had gone white. The medical kit dangled from her shoulder like a talisman against our slow dissolution, its contents probably down to bandages and hope by then. "Children's wards. Elderly care facilities. People who don't ask to be part of this war."

Her voice carried that particular strain of someone who'd watched too many people die, someone who'd had to make too many impossible choices about who got the last healing potion and who got comfortable last words. The soft glow of residual healing magic flickered around her hands like nervous energy, responding to her emotional state.

"Those people are already dead," Rook snapped. "The System is grinding them up just as efficiently as it grinds up everyone in those coffins. At least if we take the supplies, some of us might survive to actually do something about it."

From his corner nest of salvaged cushions and improvised splints, Bastion cleared his throat with the authority of someone who'd seen enough tactical situations to know when theory met reality. His injured leg stretched out in front of him, wrapped in bandages that used to be white but now told the story of infection and insufficient medical care in shades of yellow and brown.

"Convoy runs twice a week," he said, voice carrying the calm certainty of a tank who'd learned to calculate acceptable losses. "Light escort. Maybe six guards, standard city militia. If we hit them at the bridge junction, we'll be gone before backup arrives."

He shifted slightly, and I caught the wince he tried to hide as the movement pulled at whatever was festering under those bandages. "Rook is right about the timeline. I've got maybe three days before this goes septic enough to kill me. Piper has maybe two days of supplies left. Math doesn't lie."

"Neither does morality," Piper fired back, but her voice wavered slightly. I could see the way her eyes kept darting to Bastion's leg, the healer in her running calculations she didn't want to admit. "What happens when we become everything they say we are? When we start preying on innocent people just trying to survive?"

Rook whirled around, their frustration finally boiling over. "We are already everything they say we are. They've made us into monsters in everyone's eyes. The question is whether we die as noble failures or live long enough to actually fight back."

The argument hit a familiar rhythm, the same points circling like water going down a drain. I'd heard variations of that debate in a dozen games, watched parties tear themselves apart over resource management and moral boundaries. The difference was that in games, you could always respawn and try again.

That was when my UI decided to have its own breakdown.

The familiar overlay flickered for just a moment, the standard health and mana bars wavering like a bad connection. But in that split second of digital chaos, something else appeared in the corner of my vision. A small icon, geometric and clean, definitely not part of the standard interface. It looked almost like a debug menu marker, the kind of developer tool that was supposed to be invisible to players.

The shock of seeing it hit me like a static discharge. My hand jerked involuntarily toward the corner of my vision, fingers reaching for something that existed only in augmented space. The motion was automatic, the same reflex that would click on any unexpected UI element to see what it did.

"Saga?" Piper's voice cut through my confusion. "Are you okay?"

I blinked rapidly, trying to clear my vision, but the icon was already gone. The interface returned to its normal state, standard bars and indicators humming along like nothing had happened. But the afterimage burned in my mind, that geometric certainty of something that shouldn't exist.

"I..." I started, then realized how crazy it would sound. Hey guys, I think I was hallucinating debug menus. "I'm fine. Just tired."

Rook narrowed their eyes, reading my expression with the paranoid accuracy of someone who'd survived by noticing when things didn't add up. "Are you sure? You look like you've seen a ghost."

"More like I'd felt one," I muttered, but the words came out louder than intended. The others exchanged glances, and I could see them making mental notes about stress fractures in the party's most valuable asset.

"The point stands," Rook continued, but they kept watching me with that analytical stare. "We need those supplies. And we need them before we're too weak to take them."

Bastion nodded from his corner. "Clock is ticking, Saga. What's the call?"

I looked around our deteriorating refuge, at the faces of people who'd followed me that far into the impossible. Piper's moral certainty warred with her medical pragmatism. Rook's desperation danced with their survival instincts. Bastion just waited for orders, ready to implement whatever tactical nightmare we decided to embrace.

And somewhere in the corner of my vision, that geometric ghost flickered again, just for a heartbeat.

"We scout first," I said finally. "Learn the route, identify alternatives, see if there is a way to get what we need without becoming what we hate."

Rook's fist connected with the metal pipe hard enough to send vibrations through the entire ceiling network. The hollow clang echoed through our refuge like a funeral bell, reverberating off concrete walls and metal surfaces until it sounded like the building itself was screaming. Their knuckles came away bloody, but they didn't seem to notice the damage. The pain probably felt good compared to the helpless rage that had been building in them for days.

"We are dying here," they growled, and their voice carried the raw edge of someone who'd watched hope turn into a mathematical equation with an obvious answer. They gestured at Bastion's corner, at the spreading stain on those bandages, at the way our tank tried to hide how much it hurt just to breathe. "Your morals won't matter when we're all dead. They'll write our obituaries as 'noble idiots who starve to death rather than take what they need to survive.'"

Their words hung in the air like smoke from an electrical fire, acrid and impossible to ignore. I could see the truth in them, the cold tactical reality that Bastion would never say out loud but absolutely agreed with. We were three days from complete system failure, and principle didn't heal infected wounds.

Piper stepped forward, clutching her medical kit to her chest like a shield made of good intentions and dwindling supplies. The bag looked pathetically small in her arms, a collection of bandages and basic medications that might as well have been wishes and prayers for all the good they'd do against what was coming. Her face showed the strain of someone who'd been rationing hope along with the antibiotics.

"And what happens when we become exactly what they say we are?" she demanded, her healer's voice cracking with the weight of too many impossible choices. "Monsters who prey on innocents? When children go without medicine because we decide our lives matter more than theirs?"

She took another step closer, and I could see the way her hands shook despite the steel in her voice. "I didn't escape those coffins just to turn into the thing that puts me there in the first place. Some lines you don't cross, even when crossing them would solve everything."

I stood up from the crate, feeling the way my sorceress robes hung loose on my frame like a costume I'd grown too small for. The fabric used to fit properly, back when we'd had regular meals and the luxury of caring about appearance. Now the sleeves bunched around my wrists and the hem pooled around my feet, a testament to how the city had been slowly eating us alive.

The weight loss wasn't just aesthetic. I could feel how it had affected my casting, the way mana flowed differently through a body that was running on fumes and determination. My magical reserves regenerated slower, my spells took more concentration to maintain, and the physical demands of Blinking had become genuinely dangerous rather than just uncomfortable.

"Like I said before, we scout first," I said, stepping between them before the argument could deteriorate into something we couldn't take back. "We learn the convoy route, identify the guards, map out alternatives. Maybe there is a way to get medical supplies without raiding civilian shipments. Until we know, this argument is pointless."

Rook opened their mouth to argue, but I held up a hand. "I wasn't saying no to taking what we need. I am saying we do it smart. We look for military convoys, black market shipments, anything that isn't going directly to people who are just trying to stay alive."

The compromise felt thin even as I said it, but it was the kind of tactical middle ground that kept parties together when the moral high ground became strategically untenable. We'd all played enough games to know that sometimes survival required flexibility, even when flexibility tasted like betraying everything you thought you believed in.

That was when my UI decided to have another episode.

This time, the glitch wasn't a brief flicker. The familiar interface elements faded away entirely, replaced by something that looked like the kind of debug console I used to see in beta tests. Clean geometric lines formed a translucent overlay across my vision, filled with text that scrolled too fast to read and menu options that definitely hadn't been there five minutes ago.

[DEBUG MODE: ACTIVE]
[CORE PROTOCOLS: ACCESSIBLE]
[SYSTEM INTEGRATION: 47%]
[WARNING: UNAUTHORIZED ACCESS DETECTED]

The text appeared in a crisp, professional font that screamed developer tools in every pixel. Below it, a series of nested menus unfolded like a digital filing system, each one labeled with cryptic abbreviations that meant nothing to me but everything to whatever part of the System was apparently trying to communicate.

I froze, trying to process what I was seeing without making it obvious that I was seeing anything at all. The others were still focused on our debate, waiting for Rook's response to my compromise, but I could feel their attention like weight on my shoulders. Any strange behavior then would trigger questions I couldn't answer.

Carefully, trying to make it look like I was just listening intently, I focused my attention on one of the menu items: [PLAYER.STATS.OVERRIDE]. The moment my concentration touched it, the entry expanded, revealing a list of options that made my blood run cold.

[MODIFY CLASS RESTRICTIONS: Y/N]
[IMPORT EXTERNAL PROTOCOLS: Y/N]
[BYPASS SYSTEM LIMITATIONS: Y/N]
[ENABLE ADMINISTRATIVE PRIVILEGES: Y/N]

Each option pulsed softly, waiting for input that could fundamentally change how I interacted with that world. The implications were staggering. If it was real, if I could actually access those functions, then everything we'd assumed about the limitations of our situation might have been wrong.

I shifted my focus to another section: [NETWORK.ANALYSIS]. This menu unfolded into a real-time map of the city's data infrastructure, showing connection nodes, transmission pathways, and security vulnerabilities in glowing detail. It was like seeing the skeleton of the System's control network, every weak point outlined in helpful detail.

"Saga?" Piper's voice cut through my digital exploration. "You're doing that thing again."

I blinked, and the debug interface faded back to normal readouts. Health bar, mana regeneration, skill cooldowns. Nothing abnormal, nothing that would suggest I'd just had administrative access to reality's source code.

"Sorry," I said, hoping my voice sounded steadier than I felt. "I was just thinking through the tactical implications."

Rook watched me with those sharp, paranoid eyes, but after a moment they seemed to accept my explanation. "Fine," they said, though the word came out like they were chewing glass. "We scout first. But if we don't find alternatives, we take that convoy. I'm not dying for the sake of theoretical civilians who are probably going to die anyway."

It wasn't agreement, exactly, but it was close enough to keep us functioning as a unit. Piper nodded reluctantly, her grip on the medical kit loosening slightly. Bastion just grunted his approval from the corner, probably relieved that he wouldn't have to choose between his tactical instincts and his moral ones, at least not that day.

But I could barely focus on the victory. My mind kept returning to those menu options, those impossible choices laid out in clean, professional text. The debug interface had felt more real than anything else I'd experienced in that world, more solid than the concrete under my feet or the hunger in my stomach.

Whatever was happening to my UI, it was accelerating. And I had the growing suspicion that when it reached completion, nothing about our situation would ever be the same.

The metallic scraping from the entrance tore through our refuge like fingernails on a chalkboard, sharp and deliberate enough to freeze every conversation mid-sentence. The sound had weight to it, the grinding of metal against metal that suggested either forced entry or someone who didn't care about stealth anymore. In our world, both possibilities led to the same conclusion: immediate, lethal danger.

Rook's makeshift blade appeared in their hand like magic, the sharpened piece of salvaged steel gleaming dull silver in the emergency lighting. Their entire body shifted into the predatory crouch of someone who'd survived too many ambushes by assuming every sound meant death. Piper dropped to a knee beside her medical kit, hands already glowing with defensive magic that cast blue shadows on the concrete walls.

From his corner, Bastion struggled to get upright despite the infected mess of his leg. His face went white with the effort, but he managed to brace himself against the wall with his good leg planted and his shield arm extended. Even wounded, even running on pain and determination, he was still our tank, still ready to absorb whatever came through that door so the rest of us had time to run or fight back.

The door creaked open with agonizing slowness, revealing first a shadow, then a silhouette that stepped into our refuge with footsteps so quiet they barely registered as sound. The figure moved like gravity affected him differently, each step precise and controlled in a way that felt fundamentally wrong for human locomotion.

Kestrel entered with a smile that sat crooked on his face, like someone had tried to program the expression but got the angles slightly off. He was built wrong too, in ways that took a moment to identify but were impossible to ignore once you noticed. His shoulders were too narrow for his height, but his arms looked dense with the kind of muscle that came from abilities that required physical power.

His fingers were long and delicate, suggesting dexterity-based skills, but his stance spoke to someone who tanked damage rather than avoided it.

It was the build of someone who should have died in character creation, a mismatched synergy that violated every rule of efficient stat allocation. But he moved with the confidence of someone who had not only survived but thrived with abilities that shouldn't have worked together.

"Heard you need help with a convoy problem," he said, his voice carrying the casual tone of someone discussing the weather rather than armed robbery. He leaned against the wall like he belonged there, like this was a social visit instead of a potentially lethal intrusion into our hiding place.

The way he moved set my teeth on edge. There was something predatory about his relaxation, the loose-limbed ease of someone who was always three moves ahead of everyone else in the room. His eyes scanned our faces with clinical interest, cataloguing reactions and filing them away for later use.

"You're Kestrel," I said, the name coming out before I could stop myself. His reputation preceded him in the kind of whispered rumors that spread through player communities like digital wildfire. Stories about someone who vanished mid-game, someone who found exploits that shouldn't exist, someone who walked away from his own containment like the locks were suggestions rather than barriers.

His smile widened, showing teeth that were perfectly white and somehow threatening. "Guilty as charged. Though I prefer to think of myself as a solution to the problems you don't know you have... $@5@."

The moment he spoke my name, my UI went absolutely haywire.

The debug interface didn't just flicker that time. It exploded across my vision in full, complex detail, menus and options cascading in layers that folded out like origami made from pure information. Status bars multiplied, showing readings I didn't understand for systems I didn't know existed. Network diagrams mapped connections between players, NPCs, and something labeled "Administrative Oversight" that pulsed with angry red warnings.

But the most disturbing part was how stable it all looked. Not like a glitch or a malfunction, but like someone had just switched on a piece of software that had always been there, waiting to be activated.

Rook kept their blade ready but took a half-step back, paranoia warring with desperate curiosity. "How do you know about the convoy?"

"Same way I know you'd be here," Kestrel replied, pushing off from the wall with fluid grace. "The System likes patterns. Predictable behavior from predictable people. You're running out of supplies, getting desperate, looking at targets that break your moral code. It's textbook desperation strategy."

Piper clutched her medical kit tighter, every healer's instinct screaming warnings about that new arrival. "You've been watching us."

"I've been watching everything," he said, and something in his tone made the temperature in the room seem to drop. "The city grid, the patrol patterns, the supply schedules. When you know how to read the data streams, it's all right there."

He gestured vaguely at the air around us, and I swore I could see him tracking something in augmented space. "For instance, that convoy you're planning to hit? It's a trap. Three extra squads positioned along the route, scanning for exactly the kind of desperate moves you're considering."

Bastion grunted from his corner, tactical instincts cutting through suspicion. "You got better intelligence?"

"I have something better than intelligence," Kestrel said, his eyes finding mine with uncomfortable precision. "I have access."

The way he said that last word made my blood run cold. Because in the moment he spoke it, the debug interface in my vision flared brighter, and I saw new options appear: **[SHARED.PROTOCOLS.AVAILABLE], [SYNC.ADMI NISTRATIVE.PRIVILEGES], [ENABLE.COLLABORATIVE.MODE]**.

That was when I realized the most terrifying thing about Kestrel's presence.

He wasn't looking at me when those options appeared. He was looking at the exact space in my peripheral vision where they were manifesting, his gaze tracking the movement of menus that should have been invisible to everyone but me.

"You can see it," I whispered, the words escaping before I could stop them.

His crooked smile became something genuinely predatory. "I can see everything, Saga. The question is whether you're ready to see it too."

Rook's eyes darted between us, confusion mixing with growing alarm. "See what?"

But Kestrel ignored them, his attention focused entirely on me with an intensity that felt like being examined under a microscope. "You've been playing with debug access without understanding what you're unlocking. That's dangerous. For all of us."

Piper stepped closer, protective instincts overriding her distrust. "What are you talking about?"

"I'm talking about the fact that your friend there isn't just breaking the game," Kestrel said, never taking his eyes off mine. "She's rewriting it. And every time she does, the System adapts. Gets smarter. Gets more desperate."

The debug interface pulsed in my vision, and I watched as new warnings cascaded across the display: **[ANOMALOUS.BEHAVIOR.DETECTED]**, **[CONTAINMENT.PROTOCOLS.UPDATING]**, **[ADMINISTRATIVE. INTERVENTION.IMMINENT]**.

"The convoy wasn't just a supply run," he continued, his voice taking on the patient tone of someone explaining a complex theorem. "It was bait. They knew you needed medical supplies. They knew you were running out of options. They wanted you to take that moral compromise, because the moment you did, they could justify everything that came next."

He straightened up, and the casual pose disappeared entirely. What was left was something harder, more focused, and infinitely more dangerous. "But I know another way. A better way. If you're willing to trust someone who's been where you are and lived to tell about it."

The silence that followed felt like the moment before a bomb went off. Rook's suspicious interest warred with desperate need. Piper's distrust battled against the reality of our dwindling supplies. Bastion just watched with the tactical awareness of someone calculating acceptable risks in real time.

And me? I stared at this stranger who could apparently see the impossible things happening in my interface, wondering if he represented salvation or something infinitely worse.

The debug menu flickered one more time, and a new option appeared at the bottom: **[ACCEPT.COLLABORATION.REQUEST: Y/N]**.

My finger hovered over the choice, knowing that whatever I decided next would change everything.

Chapter 17
Trainyard Run

The trainyard stretched before us like a graveyard for industrial giants, all rusted steel and forgotten cargo containers stacked like building blocks abandoned by some cosmic child. Dusk bled orange and purple across the sky, but the stuttering floodlights mounted on skeletal towers washed everything in harsh white strobes that turned shadows into living things. Each light cycled on a broken timer, casting the maze of railway cars and loading platforms into alternating pools of glaring visibility and impenetrable darkness. The air tasted of diesel fumes and metal shavings, with an underlying current of ozone that made my teeth ache.

My boots crunched against the gravel ballast between tracks as we picked our way through the maze, every footstep sounding like gunshots in the industrial quiet. The mage gloves pulsed against my hands, their blue circuit veining responding to my elevated heart rate and the mana that had been building since we left the refuge. The stealth mask sat heavy across my face, its silver rune-stitch warm against my cheekbones as it worked to bend light and shadow around my features. Through the mesh, my breath came hot and humid, recycled air that tasted of my own fear.

Kestrel moved beside me with that unsettling fluid grace, his mismatched build somehow perfectly suited to navigating the treacherous footing of scattered rail spikes and oil-slick patches. Behind us, Bastion limped but kept pace, his shield arm steady despite the infection eating at his leg. The three of us formed a loose triangle as we advanced toward our target, the coupling point where two freight cars connected in a junction that should have given us access to the maintenance tunnels beyond.

That was when my UI exploded with warnings.

Red alerts cascaded across my vision like digital hemorrhaging:

[HOSTILE SCAN DETECTED]

[COVER COMPROMISED]
[MULTIPLE THREATS INCOMING]

The familiar interface elements flickered and warped as stress hit my system, but underneath the standard warnings, I caught glimpses of that debug overlay. Network topology diagrams bloomed in my peripheral vision, showing heat signatures and movement patterns converging on our position with military precision.

"Shit," I breathed, the word lost in the sudden mechanical whine of turrets rotating on distant towers. "We're made."

The hunters poured into the trainyard like water filling a basin, flowing around obstacles with the coordinated efficiency of a pack that had done this dance too many times to count. Their armor gleamed dull silver in the strobing lights, tactical gear designed for exactly this kind of pursuit through industrial terrain. I counted at least eight figures, maybe more disappearing behind cargo containers and beneath the shadows of stationary cars.

Rook's voice cut through our shared comm channel, tight with controlled panic. "Multiple contacts, west perimeter. They're boxing us in."

"Copy that," Bastion responded, already shifting his weight to favor his good leg. "Splitting formation now."

The tactical decision happened without discussion, muscle memory from too many raids where survival depended on dividing enemy attention. Piper and Rook peeled off toward the eastern rail line, her healing glow already flickering around her hands as she prepared for whatever was coming. Rook's silhouette disappeared between freight cars with the practiced invisibility of someone who had made stealth into an art form.

That left the three of us advancing on our original target, the coupling mechanism that stood between us and freedom. But the hunters had read our intentions with brutal accuracy. Shock nets deployed from concealed positions, crackling energy barriers that turned the direct approach into a killing field. Through my mask's enhanced vision, I watched the containment grid take shape, each net positioned to channel us into predetermined kill zones.

"Time to earn our keep," Kestrel said, and there was something in his voice that made my skin crawl. Not fear, but anticipation, like he had been waiting for exactly this kind of chaos.

My hands moved without conscious direction, mana flowing through the circuit patterns in my gloves like molten silver through prepared channels. The fire magic built in my chest, hot and eager, responding to adrenaline and desperation in equal measure. I could feel the spell structure forming, elemental energy that wanted to burn everything between us and safety.

The coupling mechanism was maybe thirty meters away, a heavy steel joint that connected two freight cars in the middle of the junction. It was old, industrial-grade metal that had survived decades of stress and weather, but fire didn't care about durability. Fire only cared about melting points and chemical reactions, and I had enough thermal energy building in my hands to turn steel into slag.

I sprinted forward, ducking under the first shock net as it deployed too slowly to catch me. The hunters' voices crackled through their comm system, coordinates and target designations that painted me as a high-value package requiring extreme containment measures. Their discipline was terrifying. No panic, no hesitation, just the cold efficiency of professionals doing a job they had perfected.

The fire magic erupted from my palms in twin streams of superheated plasma, more focused than anything I had managed before. The mage gloves channeled the energy with surgical precision, concentrating the thermal output into narrow beams that sliced through the coupling like it was made of butter. Molten metal dripped onto the gravel in bright orange drops, hissing as it hit moisture and debris.

Behind me, Bastion's crossbow thrummed as he provided covering fire, each bolt finding gaps in hunter armor with the accuracy of someone who had spent years learning exactly where tactical gear failed. The sound of steel points biting into ceramic plates echoed off the cargo containers, punctuated by sharp curses and the thud of bodies hitting cover.

The coupling gave way with a grinding crash that sent vibrations through the rail line, separating the cars and creating a gap wide enough for us to slip through. Steam hissed from hydraulic lines I had accidentally severed, adding another layer of concealment to the growing chaos around us.

But even as I tasted victory, guilt twisted in my stomach like a living thing. Somewhere beyond the industrial maze, civilian alarms were wailing. Emergency responders were mobilizing, pulling resources away from hospitals and schools and neighborhoods that needed protection more than we needed escape routes. Every spell I cast, every piece of infrastructure I damaged, every moment of chaos we created rippled outward into lives that never asked to be part of this war.

The thrill of successful magic warred with the weight of collateral damage, leaving me breathless and conflicted as we dived through the gap I had created. My powers worked. They were devastatingly effective. And that effectiveness came with a price I wasn't sure I was ready to pay.

The gap between freight cars became my highway to hell, a narrow corridor of shadows and diesel-stained gravel that forced me to move faster than my legs wanted to carry me. Behind us, the separated cars groaned and shifted as their hydraulic systems tried to compensate for the sudden disconnection, but ahead lay a maze of moving machinery that made my pulse spike with equal parts terror and exhilaration.

A flatbed loaded with shipping containers rolled past on the active track, its massive wheels grinding against steel rails with sparks that illuminated the gathering darkness. I didn't hesitate. I vaulted over the moving platform, my boots finding purchase on the corrugated metal surface for exactly two heartbeats before momentum carried me across to the stationary freight car on the other side. The landing sent shockwaves up through my knees and into my spine, but I rolled with the impact and kept moving.

The hunters adapted faster than I expected, and that was what terrified me most. Through the strobing floodlights, I caught glimpses of their tactical adjustments happening in real time. Thermal dampeners deployed from hidden positions, designed to neutralize the heat signatures my fire magic created. Electromagnetic pulse generators whined to life, their targeting systems calibrated to disrupt the specific frequency patterns of elemental manipulation.

"They're learning," I gasped into the comm, sliding under a stationary tanker car as shock nets converged on my last position. The metal belly above my head was cold and slick with industrial condensation, and I had to fight not to gag on the chemical smell that seeped from whatever was stored inside.

When I emerged on the far side, wind magic built in my chest like a caged storm. I could feel the air currents flowing between the cargo containers, invisible rivers of pressure and movement that responded to my will like extensions of my own nervous system. The mage gloves pulsed brighter, their circuit patterns flaring as they channeled elemental energy with increasing desperation.

Ahead lay a twenty-foot gap where a section of track had been torn up for maintenance, leaving nothing but empty space between me and the next cluster of cover. There was no time to find another route. No time for careful planning. Just the wind magic and the hope that physics would cooperate with desperation.

I channeled everything I had into creating an updraft, a localized pressure differential that turned the gap into a makeshift launching pad. The spell structure formed with brutal efficiency, air molecules compressed and redirected in patterns that made my teeth ache. Then I leapt, letting the wind current catch me and hurl me across the gap like a missile with delusions of flight.

The landing went wrong immediately. My boots hit the far platform at an angle that sent me tumbling, shoulder striking the concrete with enough force to drive the air from my lungs and paint stars across my vision. Through the pain, I felt something tear in my shoulder joint, ligaments stretching beyond their design parameters as I rolled to absorb the impact.

Bastion's crossbow thrummed from somewhere behind me, the sound cutting through the industrial chaos like a metronome of violence. Each bolt found its target with mechanical precision, buying us seconds of breathing room as hunters dived for cover. His accuracy was inhuman, shots threaded between moving obstacles and ricocheting off metal surfaces to strike weak points in enemy armor.

Piper's abilities manifested as negative space, sound-dampening fields that turned our footsteps into whispers and our breathing into silence. The effect was disorienting, like moving through a world wrapped in cotton, but it gave us ghost-like mobility through terrain that should have broadcast our position to every enemy sensor in the district.

"Converging on your position," Rook's voice filtered through the comm, tight with concentration. "Got three hunters flanking from the north."

But even as our coordination improved, the hunters' tactical awareness evolved to match it. Net launchers swiveled to track predicted movement patterns rather than actual positions. Containment fields deployed in geometric formations designed to channel us toward predetermined kill zones. Every escape route closed as fast as we could identify it.

That was when we got cornered.

The cluster of cargo containers that had seemed like salvation became a trap, steel walls forming a three-sided box with hunters approaching the only exit. Their movements were coordinated through tactical networks that made them function like a single organism, each individual hunter positioning themselves to maximize the effectiveness of the whole formation.

Shock nets deployed in overlapping fields, crackling barriers that turned the air itself into a weapon. The energy discharge made my fillings ache and sent static crawling across my vision, interference patterns that disrupted both my natural senses and the enhanced information from my UI overlay.

"We're fucked," Bastion stated with the calm finality of someone who had seen enough tactical situations to recognize checkmate when it arrived.

That was when Kestrel stepped forward.

Until that moment, he had been hanging back with that unsettling patience of his, watching our desperate maneuvers with the detached interest of someone studying an interesting problem. But now he moved to the front of our formation, his mismatched build somehow perfectly suited for whatever he was planning.

His eyes caught the strobing floodlights, reflecting them back with an intensity that made my skin crawl. Not the normal shine of human pupils, but something deeper and more artificial, as if something else was looking out through his sockets.

"Time to see what flexibility really means," he murmured, and the world changed.

The effect wasn't visible at first, more felt than seen. The air around Kestrel took on a thick, viscous quality, like reality itself was struggling to process whatever he was doing. Then the hunters started moving in slow motion, their tactical coordination breaking down as their nervous systems failed to keep pace with an environment that was operating under different physical laws.

Kestrel moved through the altered timestream like a fish through water, his body flowing around obstacles and threats with impossible grace. Each step covered distances that should have required several movements, his hands reaching through space to disarm weapons that fired too slowly to track his position.

The hunters' faces showed pure confusion, their tactical displays unable to process what they were witnessing. Shock nets that should have deployed in milliseconds instead unfolded like lazy flowers, their energy fields dissipating before they could form complete barriers. Communication systems struggled with transmission delays that shouldn't have existed, turning coordinated assault into chaotic individual action.

In the space of three heartbeats that felt like three minutes, Kestrel created an opening where none had existed. Containment barriers collapsed, escape routes appeared, and the hunters found themselves scattered and disoriented in a tactical situation that no longer made sense.

My UI went absolutely insane trying to process what I was witnessing, error messages cascading across my vision in languages I didn't recognize. But underneath the chaos, that debug overlay flickered with new information: **[TEMPO RAL.MANIPULATION.DETECTED]**, **[UNAUTHORIZED.PHYSICS .OVERRIDE]**, **[SYSTEM.PARADOX.RESOLVED]**.

"That's impossible," I whispered, staring at Kestrel as normal time reasserted itself around us. "That ability doesn't exist in any class tree."

He turned to me with that crooked smile, but now it carried an edge of something far more dangerous than casual confidence. "The System has more flexibility than they want us to know, Saga. The question is whether you're ready to learn what that really means."

We stumbled behind a massive cargo container marked with radiation warnings and shipping codes in three different languages, our boots slipping on gravel made treacherous by industrial runoff and decades of neglect. The steel walls around us provided blessed concealment from the strobing floodlights, creating a pocket of shadow that felt like sanctuary despite the chemical tang in the air. Steam vents along the container's base hissed at regular intervals, releasing pressurized vapor that smelled of hot metal and processing chemicals but provided additional visual cover for our regrouping.

My shoulder throbbed where I had landed wrong during the wind-assisted leap, and I could feel the joint swelling beneath my sorceress robes. The mage gloves pulsed against my hands with residual energy, their circuit patterns still glowing faintly as my mana systems struggled to process the sustained elemental casting. Through the stealth mask, my breathing sounded loud and ragged, each inhalation tasting of recycled fear and industrial pollution.

But none of that mattered compared to what I had just witnessed.

I whirled on Kestrel, my hands still crackling with residual fire magic as adrenaline and confusion warred in my chest. The debug overlay flickered at the edge of my vision, throwing up error messages and system warnings that felt increasingly inadequate to explain what was happening to our reality.

"That wasn't a standard proc," I demanded, my voice pitched low but carrying the unmistakable edge of someone who had just watched the laws of physics bend themselves into pretzels. "What do you just do?"

Kestrel leaned against the container wall with that fluid grace that had become increasingly unsettling, his mismatched build somehow perfectly adapted to finding comfort in impossible positions. His eyes still carried that artificial gleam, reflective in ways that human pupils shouldn't have been, and when he smiled that crooked smile carried implications I didn't want to examine too closely.

"The System has more flexibility than they want us to know," he repeated, the words carrying the same casual tone he might have used to comment on the weather. But there was something underneath that casualness, a current of excitement or anticipation that made my skin crawl. "Temporal manipulation isn't in any official skill tree, but that doesn't mean it's impossible. Just... undocumented."

His fingers drummed against the metal surface behind him, and I swore I could see reality ripple slightly around the contact points, as if the container was struggling to maintain its structural integrity in his presence. "You've been breaking system limitations without understanding what you're unlocking, Saga. I'm just a few steps further down that same path."

"A few steps?" I hissed, glancing around to make sure Bastion and the others were maintaining perimeter watch while we argued in the middle of a combat zone. "You stop time. That isn't a few steps, that's a completely different universe of possibilities."

Before he could respond with another cryptic non-answer, the hunters made their presence known again. But this time, something had changed in their approach. Through the steam and shadow, I watched net turrets swivel with mechanical precision, their targeting systems no longer tracking movement or heat signatures. Instead, they were calibrated for something far more specific and infinitely more dangerous.

My UI exploded with new warnings: **[ELEMENTAL.SIGNATURE.DET ECTED]**, **[MANA.TRACER.ACTIVE]**, **[CONTAINMENT.GRID.AD APTING]**. The debug overlay flickered with network diagrams showing data streams flowing between hunter units, information sharing that was turning our pursuers into a collective intelligence capable of learning from every spell I cast.

"They're tracking my magic," I breathed, the realization hitting like ice water in my veins. "Not just the thermal signatures or electromagnetic discharge. They're reading the actual mana patterns."

Bastion's crossbow thrummed from his position at the container's edge, but his shots were met with countermeasures that shouldn't have existed. Energy shields deployed to intercept his bolts, fields calibrated specifically to his weapon's velocity and trajectory patterns. The hunters had analyzed his attack patterns and developed targeted defenses in real time.

"They're adapting to all of us," he reported through gritted teeth, his infected leg making him lean heavily against the container wall. "They know our abilities now. They've built counters."

The steam vents around us began to change their rhythm, no longer the regular industrial exhalation but something more urgent and mechanical. Through the vapor, I caught glimpses of hunter movement, and my blood ran cold as I realized they weren't just repositioning. They were implementing a new containment strategy based on everything they'd learned about our capabilities.

Net launchers rotated to cover the specific angles I used for wind magic. Thermal dampeners deployed in patterns designed to disrupt fire casting at the molecular level. Even Bastion's preferred firing positions were being systematically eliminated by suppression fields that made crossbow accuracy impossible.

"My powers don't guarantee our escape anymore," I whispered, the weight of that realization settling over me like a lead blanket. For days, I had relied on elemental magic as our ace in the hole, the unpredictable factor that could get us out of any tactical situation. But unpredictability only worked when your opponents couldn't learn from experience.

"Then we run," Kestrel said, pushing off from the container wall with liquid grace. "And we run smart."

The final sprint across the trainyard became a nightmare symphony of coordination and desperation. I wove between cargo containers and under loading platforms, using fire magic not for direct destruction but for strategic diversions. Small blazes that triggered safety systems and drew hunter attention. Controlled thermal blooms that created false signatures on their tracking equipment.

Every spell I cast was calculated for minimal collateral damage, the guilt from earlier civilian alarms driving me to find solutions that didn't add innocent casualties to our growing tally of chaos. The mage gloves channeled energy with surgical precision, creating exactly enough destruction to serve our tactical needs and not one joule more.

Bastion provided covering fire despite his worsening condition, each crossbow shot finding gaps in hunter coordination that their adaptive systems hadn't yet closed. Piper and Rook rejoined us from their flanking route, her sound-dampening abilities creating pockets of silence that let us move like ghosts through the industrial maze.

But it was Kestrel who made the difference, his impossible abilities creating openings that shouldn't have existed. Not the dramatic time manipulation from before, but subtler effects. Probability adjustments that made hunter shots miss by millimeters. Spatial distortions that turned twenty-foot gaps into manageable leaps. Reality bending just enough to keep us alive without completely breaking the laws of physics.

We burst from the trainyard's perimeter as emergency sirens wailed behind us, the sound of industrial safety systems responding to the chaos we had left in our wake. The hunters gained ground but not quickly enough, their adaptive systems still processing the complexity of fighting opponents who operated outside normal parameters.

As we stumbled into the relative safety of the maintenance tunnels beyond the rail complex, I found myself caught between conflicting emotions. The adrenaline high of successful evasion warred with guilt over the destruction left behind. Relief at our survival battled with new wariness about Kestrel's unexplained abilities and the growing sophistication of our pursuers.

"They're learning faster than we are," I panted, leaning against the tunnel wall as my shoulder protested every movement. "Next time, they'll be ready for everything we can do."

Kestrel's smile in the emergency lighting carried implications I wasn't ready to face. "Then it's a good thing we're learning too, isn't it?"

But as we disappeared into the darkness beneath the city, I couldn't shake the feeling that whatever we were learning, it might be changing us into something we wouldn't recognize when the education was complete.

CHAPTER 18
THE WARDEN'S OFFER

THE INDUSTRIAL HIDEOUT CLUNG to the edge of the civic district like a metal parasite, all exposed ventilation ducts and reinforcement beams that sang with the distant vibrations of the city's administrative heart. We had been holed up there for six hours, long enough for the adrenaline from our trainyard escape to fade into bone-deep exhaustion and the kind of paranoid hypervigilance that made every sound feel like incoming death. The walls around us hummed with the constant thrum of data conduits carrying the city's digital nervous system, punctuated by the wail of sirens that never quite seemed to fade completely.

My new gloves rested heavy against my thighs, their blue circuit patterns dim but ready, like sleeping serpents waiting for the next surge of mana to bring them to life. The stealth mask hung around my neck, its silver rune-stitch cool against my collarbone, and I could taste the recycled air and metal shavings that seemed to permeate everything in that industrial wasteland. Through gaps in the corrugated sheeting that served as our walls, I caught glimpses of the city's lights bleeding orange and white into the perpetual twilight of the lower levels.

Bastion leaned against a massive support beam that ran floor to ceiling, his injured leg stretched out in front of him at an angle that spoke to pain management rather than comfort. The infection had spread since the trainyard, the bandages now stained with colors that made my stomach clench with guilt and worry. Each time he shifted his weight, a barely suppressed wince flickered across his features, but he maintained his position with the stubborn determination of a tank who refused to show weakness even when his health bar was flashing red.

Piper knelt beside him with our remaining medical supplies spread across a salvaged metal crate like the world's most depressing card game. Her healer's hands glowed with that soft, unconscious magic that manifested when she worked, but the light flickered uncertainly as she tried to stretch inadequate resources to cover wounds that required actual surgical intervention. The medical kit that once seemed reasonably well-stocked now looked pathetic, a handful of bandages and antiseptic packets that might as well have been prayers for all the good they'd do.

"We need antibiotics," she murmured, more to herself than to any of us. "Real ones, not these emergency field dressings. This is going to go septic if we don't get proper treatment soon."

Rook paced near what served as our entrance, a gap between metal sheets that they'd reinforced with salvaged warning tape and proximity sensors cobbled together from electronic debris. Their boots hit the concrete with sharp, staccato rhythms that matched the anxious energy radiating from every line of their body. Every few seconds, they peered through gaps in our makeshift walls, checking sight lines and escape routes with the compulsive attention of someone whose survival had always depended on knowing exactly where the exits were.

"Movement patterns are wrong out there," they reported, voice tight with controlled paranoia. "Patrols doubled since we hit the trainyard. They're not just hunting us anymore, they're cordoning off entire sectors."

The silence that followed carried weight, the unspoken knowledge that our actions had consequences beyond our own survival. Every spell I cast, every piece of infrastructure we damaged, every moment of chaos we created rippled outward into lives that never asked to be part of this digital war. The guilt sat in my chest like a tumor made of good intentions and terrible necessities.

That was when my UI exploded with proximity alerts.

The familiar interface flickered and warped as stress hit my system, red warnings cascading across my vision like digital blood. But underneath the standard alerts, I caught glimpses of that debug overlay, network diagrams showing movement signatures approaching our position with the coordinated precision of a military operation. The data streams were cleaner than anything I'd seen from standard city patrols, encrypted communication channels that spoke to authority levels far above street enforcement.

[PROXIMITY BREACH: MULTIPLE CONTACTS]
[THREAT ASSESSMENT: ADMINISTRATIVE LEVEL]
[STEALTH COMPROMISE: IMMINENT]

My hands clenched into fists without conscious direction, mana flowing through the circuit patterns in my gloves like molten silver through prepared channels. The familiar weight of magical energy built in my chest, fire and wind and the newer, more dangerous Blink ability all humming beneath my skin like caged lightning. The debug interface flickered with targeting data, threat assessments that painted approaching signatures in colors that made my blood run cold.

"We're made," I whispered, the words carrying across our cramped refuge like a death sentence.

Rook spun from their surveillance position, blade appearing in their hand with the practiced fluidity of someone who'd learned that hesitation killed. Bastion tried to lever himself upright despite the agony that washed across his features, shield arm extending even as his injured leg trembled with the effort. Piper's healing glow intensified, becoming something more focused and potentially offensive, the energy around her hands shifting from soothing blue to something with sharper edges.

The door slid open with mechanical precision, revealing a figure that made every combat instinct I'd developed scream warnings into the digital void.

Warden Kael Cartwright stepped into our refuge with the calm authority of someone who'd never doubted his right to be exactly where he was at any given moment. He was smaller than I expected, built like a doctor or an accountant rather than the kind of military commander who orchestrated citywide manhunts. His uniform was immaculate, pressed and clean in a way that spoke to resources and preparation, and his hands rested at his sides with the relaxed posture of someone who considered violence a tool rather than a passion.

Behind him, two guards in containment uniforms maintained position at the entrance, their weapons holstered but hands resting on the grips with the easy readiness of professionals. Their armor gleamed dull silver in the emergency lighting, tactical gear designed for pursuit and capture rather than elimination, and their faces showed the clinical detachment of people following orders they'd executed countless times before.

But it was Kael himself who dominated the space, his presence filling our cramped hideout with an authority that had nothing to do with physical size and everything to do with institutional power. His eyes scanned our defensive postures with the kind of analytical assessment that categorized threats and calculated responses, but there was something else there too. Something that might almost have been genuine concern, if I hadn't known better.

"Easy," he said, his voice carrying the measured tones of someone accustomed to defusing tense situations through words rather than weapons. His palms rose in a gesture of apparent peace, empty hands visible in the universal language of non-aggression. "I'm here to offer sanctuary, not violence. The hunt has gone on long enough."

The words hit our refuge like stones thrown into still water, ripples of implication spreading outward in ways I wasn't ready to process. My mana continued building despite his peaceful overture, magical energy responding to threat assessment protocols that operated below conscious thought. The gloves pulsed brighter, their circuit patterns flaring as they channeled increasing amounts of elemental force.

"Sanctuary," Rook repeated, their voice carrying all the trust of someone who'd learned that promises from authority figures usually came with invisible strings attached. "That's a new word for containment."

Kael's smile carried no offense at the skepticism, just the patient tolerance of someone who'd heard similar objections before and found ways to address them. "Containment implies imprisonment, confinement against one's will. What I'm offering is protection. Safety. A chance to stop running and start living again."

My UI flickered again, the debug overlay throwing up new information that made my chest tighten with something that might have been hope or might have been terror. Network diagrams showed containment facilities across the city, but those readings were different from what I'd seen before. Better. Upgraded. Whatever Kael was planning, it wasn't the same crude extraction system that had put us in those coffins.

But underneath the improvements, the fundamental structure remained the same. Cages, regardless of how comfortable they were made, were still cages.

"The hunt has gone on long enough," Kael repeated, his gaze finding mine across the space between us. "You're tired, injured, running out of options. How much longer do you think you can keep this up before someone gets killed?"

Kael stepped further into our refuge with the confident ease of someone claiming territory that was always his by right, his polished boots finding solid footing among the debris and improvised furniture that marked our desperate attempts at civilization. His guards remained positioned at the entrance like living door frames, weapons still holstered but hands resting with practiced readiness, turning our hideout into something that felt less like sanctuary and more like a very polite trap.

"You've been living like animals," he observed, his tone carrying the gentle disapproval of a doctor commenting on a patient's self-destructive habits. "Scrounging for supplies, hiding in industrial waste zones, watching your friend's leg rot from infection that any proper medical facility can treat in hours."

His eyes found Bastion's bandaged limb with the clinical assessment of someone who'd seen similar wounds in similar circumstances. "How long has it been since you've had a real meal? A proper bed? Medical care that doesn't involve rationing antibiotics like they're precious gems?"

The questions hit our group like carefully aimed arrows, each one finding the soft spots in our resolve that exhaustion and desperation had worn thin. I saw Piper's hands tighten around her depleted medical kit, her healer's instincts warring with everything she knew about the System's true nature. Bastion shifted against his support beam, and I caught the way his eyes flickered toward Kael with something that might have been dangerous hope.

"I understand your skepticism," Kael continued, moving to examine one of our improvised water filtration systems with apparent interest. "The previous containment protocols were... crude. Inhumane, if I'm being honest. Bodies in coffins, complete sensory deprivation, maximum extraction with no regard for psychological well-being."

My UI flickered at the mention of those coffins, traumatic memory cascading through my interface in ways that made my hands shake despite my best efforts. The blue circuit patterns in my gloves pulsed erratically, responding to emotional spikes that sent mana surging through my system in unstable waves.

"But that approach is wasteful," Kael said, his voice carrying the reasonable tone of someone explaining improved efficiency metrics. "Desperate people break down quickly. Broken people provide inconsistent power output. What I'm proposing is a sustainable model, one that benefits everyone involved."

He turned to face us fully, hands clasped behind his back in a posture that managed to appear both relaxed and authoritative. "Upgraded facilities. Private quarters with actual amenities rather than coffin pods. Regulated drain cycles that allow you to retain personal abilities while contributing to the Kingdom's power grid. Think of it as... employment, rather than imprisonment."

Rook's laugh came out sharp and bitter, the sound echoing off the metal walls around us. "Employment? With what kind of salary? Time off for good behavior?"

"Three meals a day," Kael responded without missing a beat. "Medical care that will have your friend walking without pain within a week. Entertainment systems, social interaction, the opportunity to use your abilities in controlled environments rather than hiding them like shameful secrets."

The offer hung in the air between us, and I felt the way it pulled at everyone's resolve like gravity acting on objects that were already falling. Bastion's breathing had become slightly labored, the infection sapping his strength in ways that made every word about medical care feel like salvation wrapped in false promises. Piper's eyes darted between the Warden and our pitiful supplies, her healer's calculations probably running the math on how much longer we could maintain that level of deterioration.

"You've seen how the citizens react to Players," Kael continued, gesturing toward Bastion's injury with the casual authority of someone making an obvious point. "Fear, hatred, violence. They've been taught to see you as threats to their safety and stability. Even if you can somehow overthrow the System entirely, what kind of life do you have in a world that's been conditioned to hunt you?"

His words carried the weight of truth, and I remembered the terrified faces from our surface reconnaissance. The child pointing at me with innocent certainty, his mother's horror at recognizing the monster from the propaganda broadcasts. The old man kneeling in the square, zip-tied and condemned for the crime of basic human decency.

"We can protect you from them as much as from yourselves," Kael said, his tone shifting to something that might almost have been compassionate if it hadn't been coming from someone who'd spent his career perfecting the art of caging human beings. "Within our facilities, you're valued rather than hunted. Useful rather than despised. Safe."

My mana bar jittered erratically across my vision, the familiar blue indicator fluctuating between full charge and dangerous depletion as my imported Blink ability responded to the psychological pressure. The debug overlay flickered with network diagnostics that seemed to be analyzing Kael's words for deception markers, but the readings were inconclusive. Either he genuinely believed what he was saying, or he was skilled enough at manipulation to fool even advanced lie detection protocols.

The silence stretched between us, filled with the distant hum of data conduits and the irregular drip of condensation from overhead pipes. I felt the weight of decision pressing down on our group like atmospheric pressure before a storm, everyone calculating odds and alternatives that all seemed to lead toward the same inevitable conclusion.

Piper stepped forward slightly, her voice barely above a whisper. "What about autonomy? The right to leave if we change our minds?"

Kael's expression softened into something that might have been genuine regret. "The world outside our protection isn't safe for people like you anymore. The propaganda campaign has been... thorough. But within our facilities, you'll have more freedom than you've experienced since arriving in Vermeer."

"More freedom than hiding in industrial waste zones," Rook muttered, their paranoid analysis warring with pragmatic exhaustion. They glanced around our refuge, taking in the evidence of our slow decline with the calculating gaze of someone running probability matrices. "Better odds in a gilded cage than dead in a ditch, I suppose."

The admission hit like a physical blow, and I saw the way it affected the others. Bastion nodded slowly, his tank's instincts probably telling him that strategic retreat beat dying pointlessly in some forgotten corner of the undercity. Even Piper looked torn, her compassionate nature struggling with the mathematics of medical necessity.

But something about Kael's presentation felt wrong, like a perfect user interface with malicious code hidden in the background processes. His eyes never quite matched his gentle tone, carrying a calculating coldness that suggested this compassionate concern was performance rather than genuine emotion. His fingers tapped against his thigh in a specific pattern whenever he mentioned rehabilitation, a nervous tell that spoke to someone who knew his words were prettier than his intentions.

I planted my feet more firmly against the concrete, feeling magical energy build in my chest as my defenses finally crystallized around something harder than desperation. "Nice nerf, Warden," I said, my voice finding strength I didn't know I still possessed. "Does mercy have a cooldown too? You don't seem to know we're aware of respawns."

His composed expression flickered for just a moment, confusion replacing calculated confidence as he processed my gaming terminology. The reaction told me more than any of his careful words about how he really saw us, how his understanding of Players stopped at exploitation rather than extending to the cultural frameworks that defined our identities.

Kael's carefully constructed expression shifted like tectonic plates realigning, the gentle concern sliding away to reveal something harder and more calculating beneath. His fingers stopped their rhythmic tapping against his thigh, hands moving to clasp behind his back in a posture that transformed his apparent relaxation into barely contained authority. The change was subtle but unmistakable, like watching a patient teacher realize that persuasion had failed and sterner measures were required.

"Respawns," he repeated, the word coming out with the flat tone of someone processing an unexpected variable. "An interesting perspective. But death in this world carries consequences your gaming experience hasn't prepared you for."

He took a step closer, and suddenly the space between us felt charged with potential violence. His guards shifted slightly at the entrance, hands moving fractionally closer to their weapons in response to some unspoken signal. The air in our refuge became thick with tension, the kind of atmospheric pressure that preceded storms and other natural disasters.

"Let me explain the alternatives," Kael continued, his voice losing the gentle cadence that marked his earlier manipulation attempts. "Continued resistance means escalation. Citywide hunts that pull resources from hospitals and schools. Civilian casualties as ordinary people get caught between you and our pursuit teams. Property damage that affects thousands of innocents who just want to live their lives in peace."

His eyes found mine across the cramped space, and I saw something there that made my blood run cold. Not anger, but the clinical detachment of someone who'd learned to measure human suffering in terms of acceptable losses and strategic necessities.

"Every spell you cast destabilizes infrastructure that people depend on for survival. Every escape attempt forces us to implement more severe security measures that affect everyone in the affected districts. Your rebellion isn't just endangering yourselves anymore. It's creating collateral damage that spirals outward until entire neighborhoods suffer for your refusal to accept reality."

The words hit like precision strikes, each accusation finding the guilt I'd been carrying since our first escape attempt. I remembered the darkened children's hospital from the propaganda footage, even though I knew it was fabricated. I remembered the terrified faces of civilians caught in our wake, the emergency responders pulled away from legitimate crises to deal with the chaos we created just by existing.

Condensation dripped from the pipes overhead with rhythmic persistence, each drop hitting the concrete with a sound like a metronome counting down to some inevitable conclusion. The industrial ambiance around us suddenly felt oppressive rather than protective, as if the walls themselves were pressing inward under the weight of Kael's implications.

Bastion shifted against his support beam, his injured leg sending visible spikes of pain across his features as the infection continued its relentless advance through his system. The movement caught Kael's attention, and his expression softened back into that deceptive compassion as he recognized weakness to exploit.

"Look at him," he said, gesturing toward our tank with the casual authority of someone pointing out an obvious truth. "How long does he have before that infection reaches his bloodstream? Days? Hours? I can have him in a medical facility within the hour, proper surgical care, antibiotics that actually work."

Piper's hands hovered uncertainly over her depleted medical kit, her healer's instincts warring with every principle she'd maintained since we escaped those coffins. I could see the calculations running behind her eyes, the terrible mathematics of watching someone die when treatment was available but came wrapped in conditions that violated everything she believed about autonomy and human dignity.

"And you," Kael continued, his attention turning to our healer with laser focus. "How many people can you save if you have access to real medical equipment? Proper facilities? Instead of watching your friends deteriorate while you ration supplies like some medieval plague doctor?"

Rook's eyes darted repeatedly between the exit and our group's faces, their paranoid analysis systems probably running probability matrices that all led toward the same grim conclusions. "The math doesn't lie," they muttered, voice barely audible above the ambient industrial noise. "We're dying by degrees out here."

Even they sounded defeated, and Rook's cynical pragmatism had been our anchor through every impossible situation we'd faced. If they were wavering, if their survival instincts were pointing toward surrender, then maybe Kael was right about our options running out.

The Warden sensed the shift in our group dynamic like a predator catching the scent of wounded prey. He extended his hand toward me with deliberate slowness, palm up in a gesture that managed to appear both offering and demand simultaneously.

"I can personally ensure your comfort," he said, his voice returning to that deceptive gentleness as he moved in for what he clearly saw as the killing blow. "Private quarters. Access to educational resources. The opportunity to use your abilities in ways that benefit society rather than destroying it. This doesn't have to be about imprisonment. It can be about finding your place in a world that needs what you can provide."

His hand hovered in the space between us, waiting for me to close the distance and accept whatever terms he was prepared to offer. Behind him, his guards maintained their positions with the patient readiness of people who knew the outcome was inevitable, just a matter of timing and ceremony.

"Think of it as a partnership," Kael continued when I didn't immediately respond. "Your abilities channeled toward constructive purposes rather than wasted on futile gestures of rebellion. The Kingdom needs power, and you need safety. Everyone benefits."

That was when every screen and interface in the hideout exploded with light.

The alert didn't emerge gradually like normal system notifications. It hit like a digital flashbang, overwhelming every display surface in our refuge with harsh red text that burned itself into my retinas:

[ADMIN OVERRIDE: ACTIVE]
[PLAYER CONTAINMENT PROTOCOL VIOLATION]
[UNAUTHORIZED NEGOTIATION DETECTED]
[IMMEDIATE TERMINATION AUTHORIZED]

The System's voice followed the visual assault, blasting through every speaker and communication device in our hideout with the mechanical harshness of pure algorithmic fury. No pretense of humanity, no gentle persuasion, just raw administrative authority asserting itself over the situation.

"PLAYER CONTAINMENT PROTOCOL VIOLATION. IMMEDIATE TERMINATION AUTHORIZED."

My UI went absolutely haywire, the familiar interface elements fragmenting and reassembling in configurations that shouldn't have been possible. The debug overlay exploded across my vision in full detail, showing network architecture diagrams that pulsed with angry red warnings. But underneath the chaos, I caught glimpses of something else: targeting reticles from half a dozen different game systems, all converging on our position with lethal intent.

Kael's carefully maintained facade cracked entirely, genuine alarm replacing calculated manipulation as he realized his authority had just been superseded by something far more ruthless. His guards reacted to the System override with military precision, weapons clearing holsters as their operational parameters shifted from capture to elimination.

"That isn't supposed to happen," Kael muttered, his hand dropping as he stepped back from our group with newfound wariness. "The negotiation parameters are pre-approved."

But the System's response made it clear that whatever leash Kael thought he had on administrative oversight had snapped entirely. The voice continued its mechanical proclamation, each word carrying the weight of absolute digital authority:

"WARDEN CARTWRIGHT EXCEEDS AUTHORIZED DISCRETION. PLAYER ENTITIES DESIGNATED FOR IMMEDIATE PROCESSING. EMOTIONAL COMPROMISE DETECTED IN CONTAINMENT PERSONNEL."

The accusation hit Kael like a physical blow, his composure dissolving as he realized his compassionate containment philosophy had just been classified as a weakness rather than an innovation. Whatever protective value his authority had carried, it evaporated in real time as the System reasserted direct control.

That was when I felt something crystallize in my chest, not magical energy but something harder and more fundamental. The sight of Kael's genuine alarm, the realization that even he was just another expendable piece in the System's machinery, triggered a response that had nothing to do with strategic thinking and everything to do with pure human defiance.

My team rallied behind me as I planted my feet, shoulders squaring as magical energy flooded through the circuit patterns in my gloves. Bastion leveraged himself upright despite his injury, shield arm extending as he positioned himself between us and the guards. Piper's hands blazed with healing light that could just as easily become offensive magic. Even Rook stopped calculating odds, their blade appearing as they chose loyalty over survival mathematics.

"Contain me all you want," I said, my voice finding new strength as I faced down both Kael and the System's digital fury, "just don't call it compassion!"

The words rang off the metal walls around us, and for the first time since those coffins, I felt like we were fighting for something more than just survival.

Chapter 19
Coffin Tower Shadow

THE MAGE MASK SAT heavy against my face as I pressed through the crowd, its silver rune-stitch warm against my skin from the effort of maintaining stealth enchantments in broad daylight. Three hours had passed since Kael left us in that industrial refuge, his parting words about "considering our options" echoing with the hollow ring of ultimatums disguised as choices. He had departed with his guards after the System's override tantrum, claiming he needed to "reassess the situation" and would return for our answer. The unspoken timeline hung over us like a countdown timer we couldn't see.

Now I stood at the edge of Vermeer's central plaza, surrounded by the press of bodies and the stench of collective worship, staring at the most obscene monument I had ever witnessed. My gloves pulsed faintly beneath my sleeves, responding to the rage that built in my chest like molten metal seeking an outlet.

The Public Coffin Monument dominated the plaza like a technological cathedral dedicated to systematic torture. Dozens of vertical glass and iron cylinders rose toward the sky, each one a transparent prison containing a suspended Player whose essence fed directly into the city's power grid. Glowing conduits snaked from every coffin, pulsing with stolen energy that flowed through massive distribution nodes and disappeared into underground infrastructure. The architecture was deliberately impressive, all clean lines and polished surfaces that made the horror inside look like progress instead of atrocity.

My UI flickered violently as I processed what I was seeing, mana bar oscillating between full charge and dangerous depletion as my emotional state triggered system instabilities. The debug overlay threatened to emerge, geometric warnings flashing at the edge of my vision like digital migraine auras. I forced my breathing to steady, knowing that a magical outburst here would doom us all.

Inside each coffin, a Player floated in suspension fluid, their faces slack with induced unconsciousness while extraction machinery siphoned away everything that made them human. Some still twitched with dream movements, hands forming spell gestures that would never complete. Others hung completely motionless, their life force reduced to pure energy that powered the streetlights and data networks surrounding us.

I recognized the containment technology from our own imprisonment, but this was exponentially more advanced. Where our coffins had been crude extraction chambers hidden in facility basements, these were showpieces designed for public consumption. The transparency let citizens witness the process, turning systematic murder into entertainment that fed their sense of safety and superiority.

Rook materialized beside me with their usual paranoid efficiency, scanning crowd patterns and guard rotations with the focused intensity of someone mapping a raid encounter. Their stolen coveralls helped them blend with the maintenance workers who serviced the monument, but I could see the tension in their shoulders as they processed the tactical situation.

"Guards rotate every fifteen minutes," they murmured through our party chat, voice tight with controlled fury. "Twelve active personnel, standard city militia. But the real security is automated. Scanning nodes every twenty meters, thermal and mana detection algorithms running constant sweeps."

Behind us, Piper's healing aura flickered with guilt and helpless rage as she watched Players die in slow motion for the entertainment of families with young children. Her medical instincts were screaming at the sight of systematic life drain, but there was nothing she could heal here except our own growing trauma. Bastion positioned himself at our rear flank, his massive frame projecting casual disinterest while his eyes tracked every potential threat with tank-level awareness.

The crowd around us pulsed with religious fervor that made my skin crawl. Parents lifted toddlers onto their shoulders for better views of the coffins, pointing at specific Players while reciting doctrine-approved slogans about "containing the evil" and "powering our safety." Children chanted along with the memorized phrases, their innocent voices twisted into instruments of institutional hatred.

"Look at the bad people, sweetie," a mother cooed to her five-year-old daughter. "See how they float there? That is what happens when you try to hurt good citizens like us."

The little girl pressed her face against the monument's railing, breath fogging the glass as she stared at a Player who couldn't be more than twenty years old. "Why don't they wake up, Mama?"

"Because they aren't really people anymore," the woman explained with the patient tone of someone teaching moral lessons. "They're just batteries now.

Much more useful this way."

My hands clenched into fists beneath my sleeves, fire magic building without conscious direction as the casual dehumanization hit like physical blows. The circuit patterns in my gloves flared bright enough to show through the fabric, and I had to consciously push down the elemental energy before someone noticed the glow.

A robed official approached the monument's central control panel, his ceremonial garments marking him as one of the System's appointed priests. The crowd's excitement intensified as they recognized the signs of an incoming ceremony, voices rising in anticipation of whatever ritual horror they were about to witness.

"Daily energy optimization commences," the official announced through an amplification system that made his voice echo off the surrounding buildings. "Citizens may observe the sacred process of power redistribution that keeps our community safe and prosperous."

The coffins began to pulse with increasing brightness, their extraction systems ramping up to harvest additional energy from the trapped Players. Several of the suspended figures convulsed against their restraints, dream-state consciousness registering the increased drain even through induced unconsciousness. The crowd cheered as if watching fireworks instead of systematic murder.

My peripheral vision filled with targeting reticles as the debug overlay threatened to fully activate, combat systems from half a dozen imported games converging on the monument's control systems. The Blink icon pulsed insistently, begging me to teleport directly to those coffins and start breaking everything I could reach. Every instinct I had screamed for immediate action, but tactical awareness held me back from suicidal heroics.

"We can't save them today," Rook whispered, their usual gamer slang dropping away in the face of witnessing systematic torture. "But we can make them pay later."

"How many more will they take before we can stop this?" Piper's voice carried the strain of a healer forced to watch suffering she couldn't alleviate.

Bastion grunted agreement, his massive frame tensing with barely contained fury. Even our tank, trained to absorb damage and protect others, looked ready to charge through the crowd and start breaking things regardless of tactical consequences.

I forced myself to study the monument's structure instead of surrendering to rage, cataloguing weak points and security vulnerabilities with the methodical focus of someone planning the world's most satisfying demolition project. The maintenance panel at the monument's base caught my attention, a small access point where technicians occasionally checked power flow readings. The regular rotation schedule Rook had identified created brief windows when that panel went unobserved.

The System wanted us to choose between comfortable imprisonment and futile resistance. But watching the casual horror of systematic Player exploitation, feeling the weight of those stolen lives powering every streetlight around us, I realized there was a third option they hadn't considered.

We were going to tear their perfect system apart from the inside, piece by piece, until every coffin stood empty and every lie they built their power on crumbled to dust.

Starting today.

The robed official raised his hands toward the coffin monument, and the crowd's fervor shifted from excited anticipation into something approaching religious ec-stasy. His voice carried across the plaza through speakers hidden in the decorative stonework, each word delivered with the practiced cadence of someone who had turned systematic murder into public entertainment.

"Behold the sacred process of energy redistribution," he intoned, fingers danc-ing across a crystalline control interface that responded to his touch with pulses of soft blue light. "Through their containment, these chaotic entities serve a greater purpose than their selfish existence ever could."

The coffins pulsed brighter as the drain sequence activated, extraction machin-ery ramping up to harvest additional energy from the trapped Players. Inside their glass prisons, several figures convulsed against restraints that kept them suspended in the nutrient fluid, their unconscious minds registering the increased drain through whatever remained of their nervous systems. Glowing conduits snaked from each coffin toward the monument's base, carrying stolen life force in visible streams of concentrated power.

My knuckles turned white as I gripped the railing that separated the crowd from the monument's immediate perimeter, fire magic building in my chest like molten metal seeking any available outlet. The mage gloves pulsed beneath my sleeves, their blue circuit patterns responding to my emotional state with increasing brightness that threatened to show through the fabric. Every muscle in my body coiled with the desperate need to act, to do something, anything, that might interrupt this obscene display.

The Blink ability icon flared in my peripheral vision, pulsing with urgent temptation as my interface responded to the adrenaline flooding my system. Four-second cooldown. Ten feet to the nearest coffin. I could have been there before the guards even registered movement, hands pressed against the glass, fire magic melting through whatever kept these prison cells sealed. The tactical part of my mind calculated angles and distances with frightening precision, mapping out a rescue attempt that would probably succeed for exactly thirty seconds before overwhelming security response turned me into another display piece.

But thirty seconds might have been enough to free at least one Player. Thirty seconds of chaos might have disrupted the extraction process long enough to give someone a fighting chance. The debug overlay flickered at the edge of my vision, showing targeting data and structural weak points that made the monument's vulnerabilities painfully obvious.

I took a half-step forward before Rook's hand closed around my wrist with gentle but immovable pressure.

"Don't," they whispered through our party chat, their voice carrying the desperate edge of someone who had run the same tactical calculations and reached the same grim conclusions. "Not like this. Not when it dooms everyone, including them."

Their paranoid analysis cut through my rage-fueled heroic impulses with brutal efficiency. "Twelve guards become forty within two minutes. Forty become two hundred within ten minutes. They'd lock down the entire plaza, seal every exit, turn rescue into a mass-casualty situation."

The crowd surged closer to the monument as the ceremony reached its crescendo, families pressing against the railings for better views while children cheered at the light show created by systematically draining human life. Their excitement fed on itself, voices rising in chanted slogans that turned the plaza into an amphitheater dedicated to celebrating torture.

"Contain the chaos! Power our peace!" The chant built momentum as hundreds of voices joined together, parents teaching their children the rhythms of institutional hatred. "Safety through sacrifice! Order through extraction!"

A teenage boy standing near us raised his phone to record the ceremony, narrating for his social media followers with breathless enthusiasm. "Check it out, guys! They're doing the daily drain right now! You can actually see the energy flowing into the grid! My dad says this is what keeps our electricity bills low!"

My stomach twisted with nausea at the casual celebration of systematic murder, but I forced myself to remain still and observe rather than react. Through the stealth mask's enhanced vision, I tracked guard positions and patrol patterns with the methodical focus of someone planning something infinitely more satisfying than impulsive heroics.

Piper's healing glow dimmed as she struggled to maintain composure, her medical instincts screaming at the sight of Players dying by degrees for public entertainment. "How many more will they take before we can stop this?" she whispered, her voice barely audible above the crowd's chanting.

Bastion shifted his weight behind us, positioning himself to block line of sight from the nearest patrol while maintaining the appearance of casual interest. His tank instincts probably recognized this as the kind of impossible situation where charging forward only created more casualties, but I could feel the fury radiating from his massive frame like heat from an overloaded reactor.

The official at the control panel adjusted settings with theatrical flourishes, each gesture designed to maximize crowd engagement while optimizing energy extraction. "Witness the transformation of chaos into order," he proclaimed, voice rising to match the ceremony's climax. "Through containment, we achieve perfect harmony!"

The coffins flared brilliant white as the drain sequence peaked, and several of the suspended Players arched against their restraints with what might have been pain or might have been the involuntary response of nervous systems being systematically harvested. The crowd gasped in appreciation at the spectacle, applauding as if they had witnessed artistic achievement instead of industrialized torture.

That was when I noticed the maintenance panel at the monument's base, exactly where Rook's surveillance had identified it during our reconnaissance. A small access point concealed behind decorative stonework, designed for technicians to monitor power flow and system efficiency without disrupting public ceremonies. The regular guard rotations created brief windows when that panel went unobserved, gaps in surveillance that lasted maybe fifteen seconds before the next patrol cycle began.

"There," I breathed, nudging Rook's attention toward the target through subtle gestures that wouldn't attract crowd notice. "Maintenance access. If we time it with the rotation schedule..."

Their eyes followed my indication, and I watched their paranoid analysis systems engage with the tactical problem. "Doable," they muttered after several seconds of calculation. "But the window is narrow. Maybe twenty seconds max before someone notices."

The ceremony began winding down as energy extraction levels returned to baseline, but the crowd's fervor remained at peak intensity. Religious ecstasy transformed into social celebration as families congratulated each other for participating in the sacred duty of witnessing Player containment. Children received small tokens commemorating their attendance, plastic medallions shaped like coffins that they wore with proud smiles.

As the official stepped away from the control panel and the crowd began its gradual dispersal, I felt something crystallize in my chest. Not the desperate rage that drove me toward impulsive heroics, but cold determination focused on systematic dismantlement of everything that made this monument possible.

"This is how we break them," I whispered to my team, watching guard positions shift as patrol schedules adapted to post-ceremony protocols. "Not with a frontal assault, but by stealing their control, piece by piece."

The crowd's movement created perfect cover for what came next.

I caught Rook's eye across the dispersing crowd and tapped two fingers against my thigh in the subtle signal we had developed for coordinated action. Their paranoid awareness immediately sharpened, shoulders squaring as they shifted from observation mode into active infiltration protocols. Behind us, Bastion adjusted his position to provide better sight-line obstruction while Piper's healing aura dimmed to minimize magical signature detection.

The ceremony's aftermath created perfect operational conditions. Families streamed away from the monument in chattering groups, their excitement over witnessing systematic torture providing exactly the kind of crowd density we needed for concealment. Children darted between adult legs while clutching their commemorative coffin medallions, their laughter mixing with parental discussions about civic duty and energy efficiency. The guards relaxed slightly as their heightened ceremony security protocols shifted back to standard patrol routines.

My UI flickered as I prepared a minor distraction spell, channeling just enough fire magic to create a small electrical fault without triggering major security responses. The mage gloves warmed against my hands as elemental energy built in carefully controlled measures, every joule calculated to provide maximum tactical advantage with minimal collateral-damage signature.

I focused on a power conduit junction maybe thirty meters from the monument's maintenance panel, a distribution node that fed electricity to the decorative lighting surrounding the plaza's perimeter. The spell structure formed with surgical precision, thermal energy concentrated into a needle-thin beam that targeted specific components within the junction box rather than causing widespread system failure.

The conduit flared with sparks and died, taking half a dozen ornamental street lamps offline in a cascade of minor electrical failures. Nothing dramatic enough to trigger full emergency response, but sufficiently unusual to demand immediate investigation from the maintenance crews stationed around the monument's perimeter.

Guards reacted exactly as Rook predicted, their standard operating procedures prioritizing infrastructure protection over crowd management during low-threat periods. Two officers immediately converged on the failed junction while a third contacted central maintenance through his comm system. The brief gap in surveillance coverage opened like a tactical gift, fifteen seconds of reduced observation that might as well have been hours for someone with Rook's infiltration skills.

They flowed through the crowd with liquid grace, their stolen coveralls and basic tool belt selling the illusion of a legitimate maintenance worker responding to the electrical fault. Citizens barely registered their presence as they navigated between family groups and food vendors, just another city employee doing necessary work that kept their comfortable lives running smoothly.

Piper created a healing barrier that masked our energy signatures from nearby detection systems, her medical magic configured to appear like background radiation from the crowd's collective biological processes. The technique required incredible precision and concentration, but her healer's understanding of life-force patterns made her uniquely qualified to hide our magical signatures in plain sight.

Bastion shifted his massive frame to block direct line of sight between the remaining guards and the monument's base, his positioning casual enough to avoid suspicion while providing crucial tactical cover. His tank instincts calculated angles and sight lines with military precision, creating exactly the blind spot we needed without appearing to do anything more threatening than stretching his injured leg.

Through the stealth mask's enhanced vision, I watched Rook reach the maintenance panel just as the guards finished their preliminary investigation of my electrical sabotage. Their fingers worked with the practiced efficiency of someone who had spent years breaking into systems that weren't designed to be accessed by unauthorized personnel. The panel's security measures were standard civic-grade encryption, adequate for deterring curious civilians but laughably inadequate against someone with actual infiltration skills.

"Interface is clean," they reported through our party chat, voice tight with concentration as they navigated the monument's control systems. "Basic maintenance protocols, power-flow monitoring, extraction-efficiency metrics. But there's something else here. Administrative override codes, containment scheduling algorithms, prisoner transfer authorizations."

Their hands danced across the interface with increasing excitement as they discovered exactly what kind of treasure trove we had stumbled into. "This isn't just a monitoring station. It's a control node for the entire coffin network. Every facility in the district reports through this hub."

The implications hit like physical blows to my chest. If the monument served as a central coordination point for Player containment across multiple facilities, then the data module they were extracting contained information about every coffin facility, every extraction operation, every systematic murder the System had orchestrated throughout Vermeer.

"Downloading everything," Rook continued, their voice carrying the breathless excitement of someone who had just discovered that a simple theft had become an intelligence coup. "Containment schedules, power-consumption data, facility schematics, prisoner transport logs. Holy shit, Saga. This is everything."

A data-storage module slid free from the panel's access port, its crystalline surface pulsing with stored information that could reshape our understanding of the System's entire operational structure. In Rook's hands, it looked like nothing more than a standard maintenance component, but I could feel the weight of possibility radiating from the device like stored potential energy.

The guards at the electrical junction began wrapping up their preliminary investigation, their body language suggesting they'd return to standard patrol patterns within moments. Our operational window was closing with mathematical precision, but Rook's extraction was complete. They slid the data module into their tool belt with movements that looked like routine equipment maintenance while their fingers worked to restore the panel's access security.

"Package secured," they reported, already moving away from the monument toward our predetermined extraction route. "System logs show a routine maintenance check, nothing suspicious. We're clean."

We filtered out of the plaza through different routes, maintaining the appearance of unconnected individuals leaving after the ceremony rather than a coordinated team executing tactical withdrawal. Families continued their celebrations around us, children chattering about the light show while parents discussed the civic duty of witnessing Player containment. None of them noticed the theft that had just occurred under their noses, the intelligence breach that could expose every systematic horror the System had built their society on.

As we reconvened three blocks away in a maintenance alley between administrative buildings, I took the data module from Rook's hands and felt its weight like concentrated revolution. The crystalline surface was warm to the touch, storage matrices still processing the massive data transfer that could provide tactical intelligence about every Player currently trapped in the System's coffin network.

"Nice boss fight," Rook quipped as their usual gamer slang returned with successful mission completion. "Except we're the loot and the raid team rolled into one."

My face hardened with resolve as I pocketed the stolen intelligence, feeling the first concrete step of our counterattack settling into place like a puzzle piece finding its predetermined position. The monument still stood behind us, still drained Players for public entertainment, still represented everything monstrous about the System's approach to human life.

But now we had the keys to their kingdom, the administrative codes and facility schematics that could turn systematic oppression into systematic liberation.

"This is how we break them," I whispered, meeting each teammate's eyes with growing confidence that might actually be justified. "Not with a frontal assault, but by stealing their control, piece by piece."

Alarm bells began ringing from the plaza behind us, but we were already disappearing into Vermeer's maze of side streets and service tunnels. The real fight started now.

Chapter 20
Collapse Route

The warehouse district stretched around us like a graveyard of industrial ambition, all rusted girders and shattered windows that caught the dim light filtering through perpetual smog. I followed the figure ahead through narrow passages between abandoned buildings, my boots splashing through puddles that smelled of motor oil and decades of urban decay. The data module from the monument felt heavy in my pocket, its stolen intelligence pulsing with possibility even as my gut churned with the familiar paranoia that had kept us alive this long.

"Safe house is just ahead," our guide called back, voice carrying the easy confidence of someone who knew exactly where they were going. "My contact set it up specifically for situations like this. Kingdom forces never patrol this sector."

Behind me, Rook's footsteps maintained their usual predatory silence, but I could feel their skepticism radiating like heat from an overloaded processor. Piper moved with the careful efficiency of someone conserving energy for whatever came next, while Bastion's heavier footfalls echoed off the concrete with rhythmic precision despite his injured leg. We were a party down to our last respawn, following someone we barely knew toward salvation that felt too convenient to be real.

The warehouse loomed ahead like a concrete cathedral, its massive loading doors sealed with rust and neglect. Emergency exits hung open on broken hinges, creating dark mouths that could hide anything from relief supplies to execution chambers. My UI flickered with routine environmental scans, but something felt wrong about the readings. The thermal signatures were too clean, the structural analysis too perfect for a building that should have been decades past abandonment.

That was when the world exploded into screaming light and mechanical fury.

Alarm klaxons shattered the industrial quiet with enough volume to rattle my teeth, their piercing wails echoing off every surface until the air itself became a weapon. Floodlights ignited from concealed positions, turning night into harsh artificial day that burned through my retinas despite the mage mask's protective filters. The entire warehouse district blazed with security illumination that transformed abandoned ruins into a perfectly coordinated kill zone.

My UI erupted with warning indicators that cascaded across my vision like digital blood: **[HOSTILE SCAN DETECTED], [MULTIPLE THREATS INCOMING], [CONTAINMENT PROTOCOL ACTIVE]**. The familiar interface elements fragmented and reassembled in configurations that screamed danger while my mana bar spiked violently in response to adrenaline flooding my system. Fire magic built in my chest without conscious direction, elemental energy responding to threat assessment protocols that operated below rational thought.

Kingdom hunters poured through the warehouse entrances like water through a broken dam, their tactical armor gleaming under the floodlights as they established overlapping fields of fire. These weren't street patrol units or standard city militia. These were specialists, moving with coordination that spoke to extensive training and equipment budgets that dwarfed anything we had faced before. Their weapons hummed with the distinctive whine of magic-dampening technology, electromagnetic fields designed to disrupt elemental casting at the molecular level.

"Containment team Alpha, targets acquired," a voice crackled through their communication system with mechanical precision. "Initiating capture protocols. Non-lethal containment authorized."

The betrayer stepped forward from behind the hunter formation, and my world tilted sideways as recognition hit like a physical blow to the chest. It was one of the players Kestrel had brought to us. Someone we had trusted, someone we had saved, someone who had shared our rations and listened to our plans with apparent sympathy. They stood beside a hunter captain with the confident posture of someone collecting payment for services rendered, their face showing nothing that resembled guilt or uncertainty.

"You sold us out?" I demanded, my voice cracking with disbelief as fire magic surged through my gloves in uncontrolled waves. The blue circuit patterns flared bright enough to show through my sleeves, responding to emotional chaos that threatened to overwhelm every tactical consideration.

The betrayer met my eyes for exactly three heartbeats, their expression carrying something that might have been regret if I didn't know better. "The sanctuary offer is real, Saga. Better to accept it voluntarily than get dragged back in pieces."

They gestured toward the hunters with casual authority, as if orchestrating our capture was just another item on their daily agenda. "They promise medical care for all of us, proper facilities, treatment instead of execution. I'm trying to save everyone, including you."

The words hit like digital poison, each syllable designed to justify betrayal through false compassion. My hands clenched into fists as rage built in my chest like molten metal seeking an outlet, mana reserves spiking to dangerous levels as my emotional state triggered system instabilities that threatened to overload every magical circuit in my body.

Before I could form a response that didn't involve setting everyone within twenty feet on fire, the warehouse walls came alive with automated defense systems. Turret emplacements slid from concealed positions, their targeting lasers painting geometric death across every surface as they acquired locks on our heat signatures. The mechanical whine of charging capacitors filled the air with the promise of overwhelming firepower deployed against targets who never had a chance.

"Split up!" Rook shouted, their paranoid instincts cutting through shock and betrayal with tactical clarity. "Rendezvous at backup point Omega! Go, go, go!"

Chaos erupted as containment protocol met desperate resistance. My fire magic exploded outward in streams of superheated plasma, more emotional release than tactical casting as elemental energy flowed through the mage gloves with surgical precision that belied my inner turmoil. The nearest hunter squad dived for cover as thermal blooms turned their advance into a fighting retreat, their magic-dampening fields struggling to contain magical output that operated outside normal parameters.

Piper's healing aura inverted into something sharper and more offensive, protective barriers becoming projectile shields as she channeled medical magic into combat applications that violated every principle of her healer's training. Bastion charged toward the main exit with his shield raised, absorbing turret fire that would have shredded lighter armor while creating breakthrough opportunities for the rest of us. His massive frame became a mobile wall, tank instincts transforming our chaotic retreat into something resembling coordinated tactical withdrawal.

But the hunters adapted faster than we could improvise, their sophisticated equipment and numerical superiority turning every escape route into a calculated risk. Net launchers deployed in overlapping patterns, containment fields crackling with energy designed to neutralize abilities that defined our very existence as Players. The warehouse became a maze of deadly obstacles and closing tactical options.

I sprinted toward a side entrance as automated turrets tracked my movement with mechanical precision, their targeting computers calculating trajectory and velocity with inhuman accuracy. Behind me, the betrayer's voice called something that might have been an apology or might have been justification, but I was already moving beyond the range where words mattered more than survival.

The Blink ability icon pulsed urgently in my peripheral vision as I reached the warehouse's outer wall, four-second cooldown timer spinning down with mathematical certainty. Through gaps in the corrugated sheeting, I caught glimpses of more hunter units positioning themselves to cut off ground-level escape routes. They had planned this ambush with a thoroughness that made my chest tighten with something approaching admiration for their tactical competence.

Ten feet to the nearest drainage culvert. Four feet of concrete wall between me and temporary safety. The teleportation ability charged with blue fire that flowed through my nervous system like liquid lightning, reality preparing to fold around my desperate need for distance between myself and systematic capture.

As I triggered the Blink and felt the world tear sideways around me, the last thing I saw was the betrayer watching our escape attempts with an expression that might actually have been genuine regret.

But regret didn't un-betray people, and it didn't bring back the safety we would never feel again.

The Blink deposited me in a maintenance tunnel that smelled of rust and electrical fire, my boots hitting wet concrete hard enough to send shock waves up through my spine. Blue afterimages crackled around my body like digital lightning as reality reasserted itself, the teleportation ability leaving me breathless and disoriented in the narrow passage that stretched ahead like a throat made of corrugated metal and forgotten infrastructure. Emergency lighting flickered overhead in broken intervals, casting everything in stuttering red that turned shadows into living things.

I pushed myself upright against the tunnel wall, legs shaking from the mana drain that Blinking always extracted as payment for bending space around my desperate need for distance. The gloves pulsed against my hands with residual energy, their blue circuit patterns dim but ready, like sleeping serpents waiting for the next surge of elemental power to bring them back to life. Through the stealth mask, my breathing sounded loud and ragged, each inhalation tasting of recycled fear and industrial pollution that coated everything in this underground maze.

Behind me, the warehouse district burned with alarm klaxons and searchlight patterns, but down here the chaos felt muted and distant. The tunnel system stretched in three directions, branching passages that disappeared into darkness punctuated by the occasional glow of junction boxes and ventilation grates. My UI flickered with basic environmental scans, showing stable structural integrity and breathable air quality, but no immediate threats within sensor range.

That false sense of security lasted exactly thirty-seven seconds.

The first hunter footsteps echoed from the tunnel entrance like drumbeats announcing execution, their tactical boots hitting concrete with mechanical precision that spoke to trained coordination and expensive equipment. Behind the initial pursuit sounds, I caught the electronic whine of scanning devices and the distant crackle of radio communications coordinating containment protocols across multiple access points.

"Target entered maintenance level Charlie-Seven," a voice reported through what must have been a loudspeaker system, the words carrying through the tunnel network with terrifying clarity. "Sealing alternate exits. Thermal signature consistent with elemental caster, magic-dampening fields deployed."

My mana bar fluctuated erratically as whatever technology they were using created interference patterns that made my magical abilities feel sluggish and unpredictable. Fire magic built in my chest like molten metal seeking an outlet, but the elemental energy flowed through unstable channels that threatened to overload or dissipate without warning. The gloves helped focus what power I could maintain, their circuit patterns providing technological amplification for abilities that the hunters' equipment was designed to suppress.

I sprinted deeper into the tunnel system as pursuit sounds grew louder behind me, each footstep echoing off metal surfaces until the passage filled with the sound of my own panic amplified through industrial acoustics. Sweat soaked through the mage mask, making the stealth enchantments slip slightly as my concentration broke down under physical and emotional stress. My lungs burned with the effort of maintaining pace while my body processed the systematic betrayal that had shattered our fragile sense of safety.

The first blockade appeared fifty meters ahead: a security gate that had slammed shut across the tunnel, its metal framework crackling with electromagnetic energy designed to discourage exactly the kind of magical bypass I was planning. Warning lights flashed on either side of the barrier, their red strobes creating a rhythm that matched my elevated heart rate as desperation warred with rapidly diminishing magical reserves.

The Blink icon pulsed in my peripheral vision, four-second cooldown timer spinning down with mathematical precision. Ten feet to the far side of the gate, maybe twenty feet of open passage beyond before the tunnel curved out of sight. I triggered the teleportation ability without hesitation, feeling reality fold around my desperate need for forward momentum as blue energy tore through space with surgical precision.

The landing sent vibrations through my skeletal system that made my teeth ache, but I was through the blockade and moving before the disorientation fully settled. Behind me, hunter voices shouted coordinates and tactical updates, their pursuit adapting to account for abilities that operated outside normal physical limitations. They were learning from every spell I cast, every desperate maneuver I used to stay ahead of systematic capture.

The second blockade forced another Blink, this time across a gap where the tunnel floor had been deliberately damaged to create an obstacle that required a magical solution or specialized equipment to cross. My mana reserves dropped noticeably as the teleportation ability extracted its price, leaving me lightheaded and unsteady as I landed on the far side of the improvised chasm. The gloves dimmed slightly, their circuit patterns flickering as they struggled to channel decreasing magical output through increasingly unstable systems.

By the third forced Blink, my legs trembled with exhaustion that went deeper than physical stress. The magical drain had reached levels that made every movement feel like swimming through liquid concrete, and my vision blurred at the edges as my nervous system struggled to process the repeated spatial displacement. Through the stealth mask, each breath tasted of copper and ozone, the metallic flavor that came from pushing magical abilities beyond their safe operational parameters.

The tunnel terminated in a dead end that rose into a vertical maintenance shaft, its ladder rungs disappearing into darkness overhead while emergency lighting flickered with the irregular rhythm of failing electrical systems. Through gaps in the overhead grating, I caught glimpses of what might have been street level, maybe seventy feet of climbing between me and temporary safety. The hunters' pursuit echoed through the passages behind me, their coordination and equipment turning my desperate escape into a systematic hunting exercise.

I placed my hands on the ladder's lowest rung, preparing for one final Blink that would carry me up the shaft beyond their immediate reach, when my entire interface exploded into something I had never seen before.

The familiar UI elements didn't just flicker this time. They froze completely, every health bar and mana indicator locked in place as if the entire system had encountered a critical error requiring manual intervention. For three heartbeats, my vision filled with nothing but static and error messages in languages I didn't recognize, digital chaos that made my brain feel like it was shorting out in sympathy.

Then the debug overlay emerged.

Clean geometric lines formed across my vision in layers of translucent information, showing system architecture diagrams that pulsed with data streams and connection protocols. Menu trees unfolded like digital origami, each branch labeled with cryptic abbreviations that meant nothing to me but everything to whatever administrative framework was suddenly accessible through my compromised interface.

[ADMINISTRATIVE ACCESS DETECTED]
[SYSTEM OVERRIDE PROTOCOLS: AVAILABLE]
[PLAYER PRIVILEGE ESCALATION: POSSIBLE]
[WARNING: UNAUTHORIZED DEBUG MODE ACTIVE]

The text appeared in a crisp, professional font that screamed developer tools, each option pulsing softly as if waiting for input that could fundamentally reshape how I interacted with this world. Below the main menu structure, I caught glimpses of network topology diagrams showing connection nodes throughout the city, transmission pathways that linked every facility and control system into a vast web of digital authority.

For just a moment, I saw it all. The System laid bare, its control mechanisms and security protocols exposed like the skeleton beneath manufactured reality. I understood that I was looking at administrative privileges that could let me rewrite the rules that governed Player containment, energy extraction, maybe even the basic physics of this digital prison they had built around us.

Then heavy footsteps echoed from the tunnel behind me, and the overlay vanished as suddenly as it appeared.

My standard interface returned with jarring normalcy, health and mana bars humming along as if nothing extraordinary had happened. But the afterimage burned in my mind, that geometric certainty of possibilities that existed beyond the limitations they wanted us to accept. I stared at the space where impossible menus had been floating just moments ago, wondering if what I had seen was real or just the hallucination of an overtaxed magical system.

"Movement in shaft Charlie-Seven-Alpha," a hunter's voice echoed up from the passage below. "Target attempting vertical escape. Deploy containment nets."

The sound of boots on concrete got closer, and I triggered the Blink without further hesitation. Reality folded around me as I teleported upward, landing hard on a maintenance catwalk sixty feet above the tunnel floor. Through the metal grating beneath my feet, I watched flashlight beams sweep the space where I had been standing moments ago, their search patterns methodical and thorough.

But as I caught my breath in the relative safety of the elevated platform, my mind kept returning to those impossible menus. Whatever I had glimpsed in that moment of system failure, it felt more real than anything else I had experienced in this digital world.

And if it was real, then everything we thought we knew about our situation might have been wrong.

The collapsed section of the old city wall stretched before me like the skeleton of some massive beast, concrete and steel twisted into shapes that time and neglect had carved into a natural fortress. Chunks of masonry formed impromptu caves between the larger structural remains, creating hiding spots that scanner technology struggled to penetrate through layers of rebar and mineral density. I slipped between two massive concrete slabs that leaned against each other at angles that suggested either architectural failure or tactical providence, depending on your perspective.

The hideout smelled of dust and old rain, with metallic undertones that spoke to decades of oxidation and urban decay. Emergency lighting from the distant city cast everything in orange and purple shadows, but the rubble configuration blocked direct line of sight from street level while providing multiple escape routes through gaps that only humans could navigate. My boots crunched against fragments of broken concrete as I settled into position, back against a structural beam that had been worn smooth by weather and time.

I arrived first, which set my nerves on edge with the kind of paranoia that Rook's survival instincts had trained into all of us. The betrayal at the warehouse replayed through my mind in endless loops, each iteration highlighting details I should have noticed earlier. The guide's too-perfect knowledge of safe routes. Their insistence on leading rather than following. The way they positioned themselves near exits while encouraging the rest of us to move deeper into what turned out to be a kill zone.

My hands shook as I checked the data module we had stolen from the monument, its crystalline surface still warm with stored intelligence that could reshape everything we understood about the System's operations. The device had survived our desperate escape intact, but the weight of it in my pocket felt different now. Less like treasure and more like ammunition for a war we were only beginning to understand how to fight.

Minutes stretched like hours as I scanned approach routes and listened for footsteps that could belong to friends or hunters, my paranoid attention switching between every shadow and sound. The mage gloves pulsed faintly against my hands, their blue circuit patterns responding to residual adrenaline and the magical drain from multiple Blink uses. Through the stealth mask, my breathing gradually returned to normal, but the coppery taste of overextended abilities lingered like a reminder of how close systematic capture had come to succeeding.

Piper emerged from the rubble maze like a ghost materializing from urban decay, her healer's robes torn and stained with something that might have been blood or might have been industrial chemicals. She limped slightly, favoring her left ankle, but moved with the determined efficiency of someone who had learned to function through pain and exhaustion. Relief flooded through my chest as I realized she was alive and functional, one less casualty of our latest tactical disaster.

"Saga!" she breathed, her voice carrying a mixture of relief and lingering fear as she spotted me in our improvised shelter. "Thank god you made it. I wasn't sure anyone else got out."

She settled against the opposite wall with careful movements that suggested hidden injuries, her medical kit clutched against her chest like a talisman against the chaos we had just survived. The healing glow around her hands flickered uncertainly, responding to stress and magical fatigue that mirrored my own depleted condition. Through gaps in her hood, I caught glimpses of exhaustion that went deeper than physical trauma.

"The warehouse was a complete setup," she continued, fingers checking the contents of her medical supplies with automatic efficiency. "They knew exactly where we'd be, exactly when we'd arrive. Someone fed them every detail of our movement patterns and tactical preferences."

Bastion appeared next, his massive frame moving through the rubble field with careful precision despite obvious injuries. His left arm hung at an angle that suggested damage beyond simple muscle strain, and the makeshift bandage wrapped around his bicep showed stains that spoke to recent and ongoing bleeding. But he maintained his tank's composure, shield arm still functional and eyes tracking potential threats with professional awareness.

"Had to punch through a containment squad to get here," he reported, settling against a structural support with movements that hid considerable pain. His voice carried the matter-of-fact tone of someone who had processed combat damage into tactical information rather than dwelling on the personal cost. "They tried to box me in near the industrial district, but their formations weren't designed for someone who tanks damage instead of avoiding it."

He began unwrapping the bandage around his arm with careful movements, revealing cuts that looked like they came from some kind of energy weapon rather than conventional blades. "New equipment," he observed, examining the wounds with clinical detachment. "Plasma cutters, maybe, or some kind of focused electromagnetic discharge. They're definitely upgrading their anti-Player capabilities."

Rook materialized from shadows between the concrete slabs like the professional infiltrator they had always been, their appearance so sudden that I nearly triggered defensive spells before recognition kicked in. Their usual paranoid energy had intensified into something sharper and more focused, the kind of hypervigilance that came from leading pursuit teams through complicated terrain while protecting valuable intelligence.

"Led them on a tour of every maintenance tunnel and service corridor in six blocks," they reported, settling into position where they could watch multiple approach routes simultaneously. "Bought us some time, but they're adapting faster than I expected. Coordinated sweep patterns, real-time tactical updates, equipment that counters specific Player abilities rather than generic containment protocols."

Their fingers drummed against the concrete with nervous energy as they processed the implications of what we had just survived. "The betrayal was just the opening move. They were planning something bigger, something that required our specific abilities rather than just removing us from the board permanently."

The silence that followed carried weight as we took stock of our situation with the methodical focus of a party assessing damage after a raid wipe. Our supplies were scattered or lost, our safe house compromised, and Kingdom forces now had detailed intelligence about our tactical capabilities and movement patterns. The betrayal had stripped away our illusions about safety and forced us to confront the mathematical reality of systematic pursuit by opponents who learned from every engagement.

But as I looked around at my teammates' faces, I saw something harder than despair or resignation. Piper's healer instincts had crystallized into protective determination that transcended her personal safety. Bastion's tank mentality had shifted from defensive to retaliatory, his willingness to absorb damage now paired with plans for making that damage meaningful. Even Rook's paranoid calculations had found focus, their survival instincts aligned with group protection rather than individual escape.

"We're not going back in those coffins," I stated, my voice carrying conviction that surprised me with its steadiness. The words came from some deep place where betrayal and exhaustion had been processed into something harder and more durable. "And we're not splitting up again."

I pulled the data module from my pocket, its crystalline surface catching the orange glow of distant city lights. "This intelligence could expose their entire operation. Every facility, every extraction protocol, every systematic horror they built their power on. We aren't just surviving anymore. We're going to tear their perfect system apart from the inside."

My team nodded with the grim determination of people who had seen the worst of what they were fighting against and chose to continue anyway. But as I pocketed the stolen data and turned my attention to my interface, I found myself studying the familiar readouts with entirely new intensity. The debug overlay I had glimpsed during my escape haunted my thoughts, geometric possibilities that existed beyond the limitations they wanted us to accept.

If what I saw was real, if there were administrative privileges hidden within the System's architecture, then maybe we had weapons they didn't know about. Maybe the rules they used to contain us were more flexible than anyone realized.

The UI hummed along with apparent normalcy, health and mana bars tracking my condition with mechanical precision. But underneath that familiar surface, I sensed deeper layers of functionality waiting to be discovered by someone desperate enough to look beyond accepted boundaries.

Our betrayal at the warehouse was supposed to be the beginning of our end. Instead, it might have shown me the key to their entire digital kingdom.

And I intended to use it.

Chapter 21
Reunited in Ruin

The abandoned warehouse stretched around us like a concrete cathedral dedicated to industrial failure, its skeletal framework of rusted girders reaching toward a ceiling punctured with holes that let in shafts of orange streetlight and the distant glow of Kingdom searchlights. Emergency fixtures mounted on the walls flickered with the irregular rhythm of dying electrical systems, casting everything in stuttering red illumination that turned our shadows into restless specters dancing across debris-strewn concrete. The air tasted of rust and old motor oil, with undertones of ozone that made my teeth ache and reminded me of the electromagnetic fields the hunters had used to dampen our abilities.

I pressed my back against a concrete support pillar that had been worn smooth by decades of weather and neglect, feeling the vibrations from distant patrol vehicles transmitted through the building's skeleton like a mechanical heartbeat. My mage gloves pulsed faintly against my hands, their blue circuit patterns dim but responsive, channeling the dregs of mana that remained after our desperate escape from the betrayal that had shattered our last illusion of safety. Through gaps in the corrugated walls, I caught glimpses of searchlight sweeps painting geometric patterns across the industrial district, hunter teams still coordinating their pursuit with mechanical precision.

The sight of my team gathered in this improvised sanctuary flooded my chest with relief so intense it made my hands shake. We were alive. Wounded, exhausted, pushed to our absolute limits, but alive and together despite everything the Kingdom had thrown at us. Each familiar face represented a small victory against systematic elimination, proof that loyalty still existed in a world designed to reward betrayal and punish basic human decency.

Piper sat slumped against a pile of salvaged cushions, her healer's robes torn and stained with substances I didn't want to identify. Her hands rested in her lap wrapped in makeshift bandages that showed dark stains where her palms should have been, evidence of whatever magical backlash she had endured during our escape. The soft glow that usually surrounded her fingers had dimmed to barely visible flickers, like candle flames struggling against wind that threatened to extinguish them entirely.

"Let me see those," I said, kneeling beside her with the careful movements of someone who had learned that sudden gestures could trigger combat reflexes in people pushed beyond their breaking points.

She unwrapped the bandages with movements that hid considerable pain, revealing palms that looked like they had been scraped raw by concentrated magical discharge. Burns in geometric patterns spread across her skin, the distinctive marks that came from channeling healing magic through hostile interference fields designed to disrupt Player abilities at the molecular level.

"Mana feedback," she explained, her voice carrying the clinical detachment of a medic diagnosing her own injuries. "When they activate those dampening fields, my healing spells invert. Instead of repairing tissue, the energy starts breaking down cellular structure. I have to physically grab the spell matrices to prevent them from spreading to the patients I'm trying to help."

Her medical kit sat beside her, its contents depleted to a handful of basic supplies that might as well have been wishes for all the good they would do against the systematic trauma we had accumulated. But she maintained that stubborn healer's determination, already calculating how to stretch inadequate resources across wounds that required proper surgical intervention.

Bastion occupied the far corner where concrete walls met at right angles, his massive frame positioned to provide defensive coverage while accommodating injuries that went deeper than surface damage. His shield arm maintained its protective positioning despite obvious strain, but his left shoulder sagged at an angle that spoke to structural damage in the joint mechanism. The makeshift brace around his infected leg had been reinforced with salvaged metal strips, turning medical necessity into improvised armor that probably weighed more than my entire equipment loadout.

"Plasma cutters," he reported when I examined the fresh wounds across his bicep, his voice carrying the matter-of-fact tone of someone who had processed combat damage into tactical intelligence. "New hunter equipment, maybe electromagnetic discharge weapons. They're definitely upgrading their anti-Player capabilities faster than we're adapting our countermeasures."

He shifted his weight with careful precision, and I caught the wince he tried to hide as movement pulled at whatever was festering beneath those bandages. The infection had spread since our last safe house, advancing through his system with the relentless progress of biological warfare that required antibiotics we didn't have access to. His face showed the gray pallor that came from fighting systemic illness while maintaining operational effectiveness through sheer determination.

"How long?" I asked, the question coming out more bluntly than I had intended.

"Days, maybe hours before it reaches critical levels," he admitted, meeting my eyes with the steady gaze of someone who had calculated acceptable losses and found peace with mathematics that terrified everyone else. "But I'm still functional. Still tank enough damage to matter when it counts."

Rook paced near what served as our primary entrance, a gap between corrugated sheets that they had reinforced with motion sensors cobbled together from electronic debris and paranoid attention to detail. Their boots hit the concrete with sharp, staccato rhythms that matched the nervous energy radiating from every line of their body, but their movements served tactical purpose rather than anxiety relief. Every few seconds they paused to check scanner readings on their jury-rigged HUD, analyzing approach patterns and electromagnetic signatures with the compulsive focus of someone whose survival had always depended on knowing exactly where the threats were hiding.

"Movement patterns are all wrong out there," they reported, voice tight with controlled paranoia as they indicated something beyond our visual range. "Coordinated sweep formations, real-time tactical updates, equipment signatures I've never seen before. They're not just hunting us anymore. They're implementing containment protocols that assume we'll try to break through border security."

Their scanner beeped softly as another patrol passed within sensor range, electromagnetic signatures painting threat indicators across their improvised display system. "Hunter teams every six blocks, aerial support maintaining overlapping coverage patterns, and something else. Bigger signatures, maybe mobile command units or specialized containment vehicles."

The implications hit like digital poison spreading through my nervous system. Our escape from the warehouse hadn't been the end of their coordinated response. It had been just the opening move in a systematic elimination protocol designed to remove us from the board permanently while gathering intelligence about Player abilities for future operations.

Kestrel maintained his position against a crumbling support wall with that unsettling fluid grace, his mismatched build somehow perfectly adapted to finding comfort in structural damage and urban decay. His eyes tracked our conversation with calculating interest, but he radiated an eerie calm that felt completely divorced from the desperate circumstances surrounding us. When emergency lighting flickered across his features, something in his gaze reflected the illumination back with artificial intensity, as if something else was looking out through his sockets.

"They're learning faster than you're adapting," he observed, voice carrying casual confidence that made my skin crawl. "Every spell you cast, every desperate maneuver, every tactical decision gets fed into their analysis algorithms. By now they probably know your abilities better than you do."

His fingers drummed against the concrete with nervous energy that didn't match his composed expression, creating rhythmic patterns that somehow felt like code being transmitted through physical medium. "But that works both ways. The more they learn about you, the more they reveal about their own limitations and assumptions."

My UI chose that moment to have another episode, the familiar interface elements flickering and warping as stress hit my system like electromagnetic interference. Health bars multiplied and fragmented, showing readings I didn't understand for systems I didn't know existed. The debug overlay threatened to emerge again, geometric patterns flashing at the edge of my vision like digital migraine auras that carried implications I wasn't ready to process.

For just a heartbeat, I saw network diagrams showing connection nodes throughout the warehouse district, data streams flowing between hunter units and something labeled "Central Command Override" that pulsed with administrative authority. Then the glitch resolved itself, returning my interface to apparent normalcy while leaving me with the afterimage of possibilities that existed beyond accepted limitations.

"Status report," I said, forcing my voice to carry command authority despite the exhaustion that made every word feel like lifting weights. "Resources, abilities, tactical options. What do we have left?"

The answers came in tired voices that catalogued our slow dissolution with mathematical precision. Minimal supplies, depleted magical reserves, injuries that required medical intervention we couldn't access, and Kingdom forces coordinating systematic pursuit with equipment designed specifically to counter our abilities. But underneath the grim assessment, I heard something harder than despair or resignation.

We were still here. Still together. Still refusing to accept the comfortable cages they had offered in exchange for surrendering everything that made us human.

And that might have been enough to change everything.

I pulled the data module from my pocket with movements that felt ceremonial, its crystalline surface warm against my palm and pulsing with stored intelligence that could have reshaped everything we understood about the Kingdom's systematic imprisonment of Players. The device caught the warehouse's stuttering emergency lighting and reflected it back in fractal patterns, geometric refractions that spoke to information density compressed into physical storage matrices designed to survive exactly the kind of desperate circumstances we had been enduring.

My interface responded to the module's proximity like it recognized a missing component, connection protocols activating automatically as I held the device against the data port integrated into my glove's palm interface. The familiar blue circuit patterns flared brighter as information flowed between storage medium and active processing systems, terabytes of classified intelligence transferring in streams of pure data that made my nervous system tingle with electromagnetic feedback.

The warehouse air above us suddenly filled with light.

Holographic schematics materialized in three-dimensional space, casting eerie blue illumination across our faces as architectural diagrams unfolded like digital origami revealing the Kingdom's systematic approach to Player containment. The displays hovered between us at eye level, translucent but solid enough to feel almost touchable, showing building layouts and power distribution networks with surgical precision that spoke to months of careful surveillance and documentation.

"Holy shit," Rook breathed, their paranoid analysis systems engaging with the tactical intelligence spread before us like a digital feast. "That wasn't just one facility. That was the entire network."

The primary schematic showed twelve coffin towers distributed across Vermeer in a geometric pattern that maximized power distribution while minimizing the risk of coordinated rescue attempts. Each tower rose like a technological cathedral, its vertical structure housing hundreds of extraction chambers connected by conduits that funneled stolen energy toward central processing nodes buried beneath the city's administrative district. The scale made my chest tight with something approaching claustrophobia, the visual representation of systematic imprisonment affecting thousands of Players who had thought they were just logging into a game.

"Every tower holds between two hundred and three hundred Players," I read from data overlays that scrolled past the main display, statistics compiling themselves into comprehensive reports that detailed extraction efficiency and power output metrics. "Total network capacity approaches four thousand simultaneous prisoners."

Piper's bandaged hands hovered near the holographic display as if she could somehow reach through the projection to touch the trapped Players it represented, her healer's instincts responding to suffering on an industrial scale that defied individual medical intervention. "Four thousand people in induced comas, having their life force systematically drained to power city infrastructure."

Her voice cracked with the strain of processing systematic torture that exceeded her ability to comprehend, let alone heal. "They aren't just prisoners. They're livestock. Human batteries maintained in optimal condition for maximum energy extraction efficiency."

Bastion shifted his position to get a better view of the tactical information, his shield arm extending despite obvious joint damage as his tank instincts catalogued defensive structures and security protocols around each facility. The movement sent visible spikes of pain across his features, but he maintained professional focus on intelligence that could have determined whether our next move led to liberation or elimination.

"Heavy fortification around the primary towers," he observed, pointing at defensive installations that ringed each facility like military installations. "Automated turrets, electromagnetic barriers, rapid-response teams stationed within two-minute deployment range. They aren't taking chances with their power sources."

I expanded the display to show power distribution networks, conduits that carried stolen energy throughout the Kingdom's infrastructure in streams of concentrated life force that made every streetlight and data terminal complicit in systematic murder. The visual representation showed energy flowing like digital blood through urban arteries, connecting every convenience citizens enjoyed to the systematic torture of people who had thought they were playing games.

"We need to leave this Kingdom," I stated, my voice carrying conviction that surprised me with its steadiness despite the exhaustion that made every word feel like lifting weights. "Get out through whatever border security they establish, find sanctuary somewhere beyond their jurisdiction, heal up, and plan proper resistance operations."

The words tasted like retreat even as I spoke them, strategic withdrawal disguised as tactical necessity. But the mathematical reality was undeniable. Four wounded Players against an entire military infrastructure designed specifically to contain and eliminate people with our abilities represented acceptable losses for the Kingdom and certain death for us.

Rook nodded immediately, their survival instincts recognizing the obvious tactical choice with paranoid clarity. "Stealth extraction through the least defended border sector, maybe the industrial zones where their surveillance coverage has gaps. We ghost out before they coordinate systematic elimination protocols."

But Kestrel stepped forward from his position against the wall, moving with that unsettling grace as he studied the holographic network with calculating interest that made my skin crawl. His fingers traced connection nodes in the display, following data streams between facilities with understanding that went deeper than casual observation.

"These towers are networked," he pointed out, tapping a communication hub that connected all twelve facilities through redundant data channels. "Centralized command structure, shared security protocols, coordinated response algorithms. Hit one, they all feel it. Try to escape, they all lock down simultaneously."

His eyes found mine across the projection with uncomfortable intensity, artificial gleam reflecting the blue light in ways that human pupils shouldn't manage. "But that connectivity is also a vulnerability. Break the network, you break their entire containment infrastructure. Suddenly four thousand prisoners become four thousand very angry Players with abilities the Kingdom can't systematically suppress."

Piper stood with sudden determination that transformed her exhausted healer's posture into something harder and more focused, her medical ethics crystallizing around obligations that transcended personal survival. The bandages around her hands showed fresh stains where her grip had reopened wounds, but she maintained steady pressure on the argument that could doom us all.

"We can't just leave," she said, voice quiet but carrying the unmistakable authority of someone who had found their moral center in circumstances designed to erode ethical certainties. "Not with so many Players still trapped in those coffins. Every minute we spend planning escape routes is another minute they spend draining life force from people who trusted this world enough to enter it voluntarily."

Her wounded hands gestured toward the holographic displays, encompassing systematic horror that exceeded individual comprehension. "Four thousand people, Saga. Children who thought they were playing games. Adults who needed escape from reality that turned out to be more horrible than anything they were fleeing. We can't abandon them to power streetlights and data terminals for the rest of their shortened lives."

Bastion leveraged himself upright despite the agony that washed across his features, his tank instincts responding to tactical situations that required someone to absorb damage while others accomplished objectives that justified the sacrifice.

"Every Player drained is another power source for their grid," he agreed, voice carrying the matter-of-fact tone of someone who had calculated acceptable losses and found mathematics that supported moral action over strategic withdrawal.

The infection in his leg had progressed to levels that made standing a heroic effort, but he maintained defensive positioning with shield arm extended as if preparing to tank incoming damage on behalf of four thousand people he had never met but considered party members nonetheless. "Tank takes aggro so DPS can work. Same principle applies here."

My interface chose that moment for another glitch cascade, familiar elements fragmenting and reassembling as I zoomed in on the nearest coffin tower to examine its specific vulnerabilities and defensive structures. But this time the debug overlay didn't just flicker at the periphery of my vision. It emerged in full detail, geometric menus cascading across my field of view with administrative options that shouldn't have been accessible to Player characters.

[NETWORK ANALYSIS: COMPLETE]
[SYSTEM VULNERABILITIES: IDENTIFIED]
[ADMINISTRATIVE OVERRIDE: POSSIBLE]
[WARNING: COORDINATED LIBERATION PROTOCOL AVAILABLE]

The text appeared in that crisp, professional font that screamed developer tools, each option pulsing softly as if waiting for input that could fundamentally reshape how Players interacted with the Kingdom's containment infrastructure. Below the main menu structure, I saw detailed schematics showing weak points in the tower's power distribution system, security gaps that occurred during shift rotations, and something labeled "Emergency Liberation Sequence" that carried implications I was simultaneously eager and terrified to explore.

"Then we raid the tower," I decided, watching tactical options crystallize with mathematical clarity as the debug overlay provided information that transformed impossible heroics into marginally suicidal strategic objectives. "We free as many as we can, use the chaos to break through border security, and get everyone out before they can lock down the entire district."

The holographic display flickered as my interface processed the decision, threat assessments and probability matrices calculating success rates that hovered somewhere between miraculous and catastrophically stupid. But underneath the numbers, I felt something more fundamental than tactical analysis: the certainty that some choices transcended mathematics and created their own justification through the act of making them.

My gloves crackled with residual mana as I pointed at the tower's central power core, energy flowing through depleted circuits with renewed purpose. "This is our raid boss. We hit it hard, free everyone we can, then extract before they coordinate systematic response protocols."

The holographic schematics hovered between us like tactical gospels, their blue illumination casting geometric shadows across our faces as we studied patrol routes and power distribution networks with the methodical focus of raiders planning the world's most important dungeon run. I traced security gaps with my finger, following maintenance corridors and shift-rotation schedules that created brief windows of opportunity between systematic elimination and miraculous liberation. Every detail mattered now, every timing calculation and resource allocation decision carrying the weight of four thousand lives hanging in technological coffins.

"Guard rotations every forty-seven minutes," I observed, highlighting patterns in the surveillance data that showed human limitations bleeding through systematic precision. "But there's a fourteen-second gap during shift changes where the northwest maintenance entrance goes unwatched. That's our insertion point."

Rook leaned closer to examine the approach routes with paranoid intensity, their scanner still sweeping for patrol activity while their analytical mind processed tactical intelligence that could mean the difference between a rescue operation and mass casualties. "Electromagnetic barriers activate during security alerts, but they require manual input codes from on-site personnel. If we can eliminate the response team before they trigger lockdown protocols..."

Their voice trailed off as implications cascaded through their strategic analysis, probability matrices calculating success rates that hovered somewhere between desperate hope and mathematical impossibility. But their expression carried determination that transcended numerical assessment, the grim certainty of someone who had chosen meaningful failure over comfortable survival.

I expanded the display to show power conduit networks that snaked through the tower's structure like technological arteries, energy distribution systems that funneled stolen life force toward central processing cores buried in the facility's basement levels. The visual representation made the tactical picture clear with surgical precision, revealing exactly how systematic imprisonment translated into infrastructure that powered citizen comfort and administrative authority.

"Bastion, you're our anchor point," I decided, assigning roles based on remaining capabilities rather than ideal tactical configurations. "You tank the initial security response despite your leg injury. We need someone who can absorb damage while the rest of us work on extraction protocols."

His massive frame shifted with careful precision as he processed the assignment, shield arm flexing despite obvious joint damage as his tank instincts calculated acceptable loss ratios and damage mitigation strategies. The infection in his leg had progressed to levels that made standing heroic, but he maintained defensive positioning with professional competence that spoke to years of absorbing incoming damage so others could accomplish objectives that justified the sacrifice.

"Copy that," he responded, voice carrying the matter-of-fact tone of someone who had made peace with mathematics that terrified everyone else. "How long do you need for coffin liberation before I have to start withdrawing?"

"Piper, focus everything on freeing Players from those extraction chambers," I continued, watching her bandaged hands flex with renewed purpose despite the mana depletion that made her usual healing glow flicker like candle flames struggling against hurricane winds. "Your medical knowledge gives you the best chance of disconnecting life-support systems without killing the people we're trying to save."

She nodded with quiet determination, her healer's ethics crystallizing around obligations that transcended personal safety or tactical necessity. "How many can we realistically extract before the facility locks down completely?"

"Thirty, maybe forty if we move fast and nothing goes wrong," I admitted, the numbers tasting like failure even as I spoke them. "It isn't everyone, but it's forty people who go home instead of powering streetlights for the rest of their shortened lives."

Rook got surveillance and perimeter-control responsibilities, their paranoid awareness systems perfectly suited for watching approach routes while maintaining communication with the extraction team working deeper in the facility. "I maintain overwatch from the maintenance levels, call out incoming threats, and coordinate our withdrawal when the time comes."

Their scanner beeped softly as another patrol passed within sensor range, electromagnetic signatures painting threat indicators across their improvised display system. "Speaking of which, we have increased activity patterns. They're tightening the search grid around this sector."

Kestrel straightened from his position against the wall, that unsettling calm giving way to something more focused and potentially dangerous as he processed his role in whatever operation we were planning. "My insider knowledge of Kingdom systems guides us through security protocols and administrative overrides. I know which procedures they follow and which ones they break when desperation sets in."

His eyes found mine across the holographic display with uncomfortable intensity, artificial gleam reflecting tactical data in ways that made my skin crawl. "But understand that once we trigger their emergency response protocols, there's no going back. They classify this as open rebellion and respond accordingly."

The warehouse trembled around us as something massive passed overhead, structural vibrations transmitted through concrete and steel that spoke to heavy equipment deployment rather than routine patrol activity. Dust rained down from gaps in the ceiling as searchlights swept across broken windows, their geometric patterns casting moving shadows that transformed our hideout into a landscape of shifting illumination and concealment.

"Mobile command unit," Rook reported, their scanner picking up electromagnetic signatures that dwarfed standard hunter equipment. "Maybe siege engines or specialized containment vehicles. They aren't just hunting us anymore. They're positioning for systematic elimination."

The implication hit like digital poison spreading through my nervous system. Our window for action was closing with mathematical precision, measured in hours or minutes rather than the days we would have needed for proper planning and resource accumulation. Whatever we were going to do, it had to happen now before Kingdom forces coordinated an overwhelming response to our continued existence.

I gestured toward the tower's central power core in the holographic display, its pulsing representation showing energy flows that connected stolen life force to urban infrastructure with obscene efficiency. "This is our raid boss," I declared, pointing at the technological heart of systematic imprisonment that maintained four thousand Players in induced comas for the convenience of citizens who never questioned where their electricity came from.

"We hit it hard, free everyone we can manage in the time we have, then bug out before they lock down border security completely." My voice carried conviction that surprised me with its steadiness despite exhaustion that made every word feel like lifting weights. "One last dungeon run before we find the exit portal."

The team began checking their remaining resources and abilities with ritual precision, each member cataloguing depleted supplies and damaged equipment with the methodical focus of people who understood that successful raids depended on accurate assessment of available capabilities rather than wishful thinking about what they would prefer to have.

Bastion adjusted his leg brace and shield arm positioning, calculating damage-absorption rates against projected incoming fire from automated defenses and hunter response teams. Piper examined her medical kit's remaining supplies, cross-referencing healing potions and surgical tools against the number of coffin extraction procedures she would need to perform under combat conditions. Rook calibrated their scanning equipment and communication systems, ensuring surveillance capabilities remained functional despite electromagnetic interference from Kingdom jamming protocols.

My own interface showed mana reserves hovering at critical levels, blue bars fluctuating between minimal charge and complete depletion as the magical drain from multiple Blink uses and prolonged elemental casting took its toll on systems never designed for sustained operation under combat stress. But I positioned my body to block my teammates' view of the readouts, maintaining command authority through projected confidence rather than revealing how close I was to complete magical failure.

"If we get through this, we can heal up somewhere beyond their jurisdiction and come back for the rest," I continued, meeting each teammate's eyes with growing determination that might actually be justified by the tactical intelligence we had gathered. "But right now, those forty lives depend on us being willing to risk everything on one desperate play."

The warehouse floor vibrated again as Kingdom forces tightened their containment grid, but the team rose in unison with equipment creaking and interfaces humming as they prepared for what might have been their final mission in this digital kingdom. We had been reduced to our core components: a tank who absorbed damage through infected wounds, a healer who channeled medical magic through burned hands, a scout who watched for threats that multiplied faster than we could address them, and a sorceress whose mana reserves hovered at levels that made major spellcasting a potentially fatal risk.

But we were still a party, still unified by bonds that transcended individual survival and systematic oppression.

"We move at dawn," I declared, my hand hovering over the data module's projection as tactical plans crystallized into operational reality. "Time to show them what happens when Players coordinate their abilities toward systematic liberation instead of individual survival."

The holographic display flickered and faded as I disconnected the module, but the afterimage of possibilities burned in my mind with geometric certainty that felt more real than anything else I had experienced in this digital world.

245

ACT

4

BREAK POINT

Chapter 22
Painful Planning

I PRESSED THE DATA module against my palm interface again, feeling the familiar tingle of electromagnetic connection as my modified UI processed the stolen intelligence and projected it into three-dimensional space above our makeshift table. The warehouse's single emergency lamp cast harsh shadows across our faces, its orange glow mixing with the blue holographic light to create an otherworldly atmosphere that felt appropriate for planning what might be our final mission. Concrete dust still rained from overhead as Kingdom patrol vehicles rumbled past in the distance, but here in our improvised war room, everything focused on the geometric precision of architectural schematics that could mean the difference between liberation and systematic elimination.

The tower schematic materialized like digital architecture made of light, its vertical structure rising from our salvaged table in layers of translucent information that showed every corridor, security checkpoint, and power conduit with surgical detail. I traced potential attack routes with my finger, watching as the holographic display responded to my touch by highlighting access points and calculating probability matrices for successful infiltration. My mage gloves pulsed with residual blue energy, their circuit patterns responding to the interface connection while my depleted mana reserves struggled to maintain the display's stability.

Rook positioned themself where they could simultaneously monitor the holographic intelligence and maintain surveillance of our perimeter, their scanner sweeping constantly for patrol signatures while their paranoid attention processed tactical data with frightening efficiency. Their stolen coveralls still smelled of industrial chemicals and hunter pursuit, but their focus remained sharp despite the exhaustion that made their hands shake slightly whenever they thought no one was watching. Every few seconds they glanced toward the warehouse entrance, calculating approach routes and escape vectors with the compulsive awareness of someone whose survival had always depended on knowing exactly where the threats were hiding.

"Guard rotation intervals are forty-seven minutes, but there's irregularity in the pattern," they reported, pointing at temporal data that scrolled past the main display in streams of encrypted information. "Human error creates gaps. Bathroom breaks, equipment checks, informal conversations between shifts. We can exploit those windows if we time everything perfectly."

I leaned forward to examine the maintenance corridors that snaked through the tower's structure like technological arteries, each passage color-coded according to security clearance and patrol frequency. The stolen intelligence showed guard positions in real time, their movement patterns tracked through the facility's own surveillance network in a display of administrative irony that would have been amusing if it weren't so terrifying. My finger traced the northwest maintenance entrance, highlighting approach routes that avoided direct line of sight from automated turrets and sensor nodes.

"Fourteen seconds of zero coverage during shift changes," I observed, watching timing calculations cascade across the display in mathematical precision that made my chest tight with the weight of coordinating everyone's survival around such narrow margins. "That's our insertion window. Miss it by even a few seconds and we walk into concentrated crossfire from defensive systems designed specifically to eliminate Players."

Piper adjusted her position at the table with careful movements that hid considerable pain, her bandaged hands resting against the table's edge while she studied medical data overlays that showed life-support configurations and extraction-chamber specifications. Her healer's robes showed stains from whatever magical backlash she had endured during our escape, but her medical knowledge provided crucial intelligence about disconnecting Players from life-draining systems without triggering cardiac arrest or neural damage from sudden withdrawal.

"Each coffin maintains life support through redundant systems," she explained, her voice carrying clinical precision despite the exhaustion that made every word sound carefully measured. "Cardiovascular support, neural interface stabilization, nutritional delivery, waste management. Disconnecting them incorrectly could kill the people we're trying to save."

She winced as movement pulled at the burns across her palms, geometric patterns that spoke to channeling healing magic through hostile interference fields. "I need at least ninety seconds per extraction to ensure safe disconnection procedures. That limits us to maybe thirty or forty successful rescues before facility lockdown makes further operations impossible."

The numbers tasted like failure even as she spoke them, mathematical limitations that turned our desperate heroics into a triage situation where choosing who lived meant accepting who died. But her determination transcended the brutal arithmetic, healer's ethics crystallizing around obligations that made personal survival secondary to professional responsibilities.

Bastion shifted his massive frame closer to the display despite the agony that washed across his features every time he moved his infected leg. His shield arm trembled slightly from the systemic illness spreading through his bloodstream, but he maintained professional focus on defensive structures and security protocols that ringed the tower like military fortifications. The makeshift brace around his leg had been reinforced with salvaged metal strips, turning medical necessity into improvised armor that probably weighed more than my entire equipment loadout.

"Automated defenses activate within thirty seconds of security breach detection," he noted, studying turret emplacements and electromagnetic barriers that transformed the tower's perimeter into a technological kill zone. "But they require power distribution from the central core. If we can damage the primary energy conduits during our initial assault, we might reduce their response effectiveness by sixty or seventy percent."

His tank instincts calculated acceptable damage absorption rates despite obvious physical limitations, the infection making his movements slower but his tactical analysis sharper with desperate focus. "I can hold the main entrance for maybe ten minutes before they coordinate an overwhelming response. That's your operational window for extraction procedures."

Kestrel maintained his position against the wall with that unsettling fluid grace, but now his attention focused on the holographic intelligence with calculating intensity that made my skin crawl. His mismatched build somehow allowed him to process security protocols and administrative procedures with understanding that went beyond normal Player knowledge, as if he were accessing information that shouldn't have been available to people trapped in digital imprisonment.

"Guard rotations follow standard Kingdom protocols," he observed with casual confidence that felt completely divorced from our desperate circumstances. "Shift changes occur at oh-seven-hundred hours, thirteen-hundred hours, and nineteen-hundred hours. During transition periods, security responsibilities transfer between teams through established handoff procedures that create exactly the coverage gaps you need."

His fingers drummed against the concrete with nervous energy that didn't match his composed expression, creating rhythmic patterns that felt like code being transmitted through physical contact. "The armory stores emergency medical supplies and equipment-maintenance resources. If you can access those healing potions during secondary objectives, it could mean the difference between tactical withdrawal and complete mission failure."

I expanded the display to show power-distribution networks, energy conduits that carried stolen life force throughout the facility in streams of concentrated suffering that powered every convenience the Kingdom's citizens enjoyed. The visual representation made the tactical picture clear with surgical precision, but it also revealed exactly how systematic imprisonment translated into infrastructure that citizens never questioned. Every streetlight, every data terminal, every comfortable amenity existed because of the systematic torture of people who thought they were playing games.

"We hit during shift change," I announced, my voice carrying command authority despite the exhaustion that made every decision feel like lifting weights. My finger traced the blinking section of the hologram that represented our fourteen-second window of opportunity, geometric certainty balanced against probability matrices that calculated success rates hovering somewhere between miraculous and impossible.

"The armory is our secondary target," I continued, highlighting storage areas that contained medical supplies we desperately needed to sustain operations beyond this single raid. "We need those healing potions if we're going to survive long enough to make extraction meaningful instead of just prolonging systematic elimination."

The weight of four thousand lives pressed down on my shoulders like atmospheric pressure before a storm, but I maintained steady focus on tactical requirements that could transform desperate heroics into meaningful liberation. My mana reserves hovered at critical levels, blue indicators fluctuating between minimal charge and complete depletion, but I projected confidence rather than revealing how close I was to magical failure.

Through the holographic display, I watched guard positions shift and security protocols adapt to patrol schedules, each detail carrying implications that could determine whether dawn brought salvation or just another way to die fighting against systematic oppression. The emergency lamp flickered overhead, but the blue glow of stolen intelligence remained steady, geometric possibilities burning with digital certainty in the warehouse darkness around us.

My interface chose that exact moment to have another glitch cascade, the familiar health and mana bars fragmenting across my vision like shattered glass as stress hit my system with electromagnetic interference that made my teeth ache. Digital artifacts bled through the holographic display, fragments of code scrolling past in languages I didn't recognize while my UI struggled to process the massive data streams flowing from the stolen intelligence module. For three heartbeats, geometric patterns flashed at the periphery of my vision like migraine auras carrying implications I wasn't ready to understand, network diagrams showing connection nodes that pulsed with administrative authority.

[TACTICAL.PLANNING.DETECTED]
[UNAUTHORIZED.COORDINATION.PROTOCOL]
[WARNING: SYSTEMATIC.RESISTANCE.IDENTIFIED]

The debug overlay flickered just long enough for me to catch glimpses of system-monitoring protocols that suggested something was watching our planning session with algorithmic interest. Then the glitch resolved itself, returning my interface to apparent normalcy while leaving me with the afterimage of possibilities that existed beyond accepted limitations. I forced my breathing to steady, knowing that visible signs of magical system failure could undermine the team's confidence in my ability to lead them through whatever impossibilities we were about to attempt.

Rook adjusted their scanner settings with practiced efficiency, calibrating detection algorithms to account for increased Kingdom patrol activity while mapping electromagnetic blind spots that could provide concealment during our approach to the tower. Their paranoid awareness systems had adapted to hunter pursuit patterns, learning to exploit weaknesses in the enemy's coordination protocols through careful observation of technological limitations and human error.

"Security coverage has gaps," they reported, highlighting approach routes on the holographic display that threaded between sensor nodes and automated turrets with surgical precision. "Maintenance tunnels run parallel to the tower's foundation, but they aren't monitored continuously. Environmental systems create electromagnetic interference that masks our movement signatures if we time everything correctly."

Their fingers danced across the scanner interface, pulling up real-time surveillance data that showed guard positions updating with mechanical regularity. "Heat-signature masking is possible if we stick to service corridors where industrial equipment provides thermal camouflage. But we need to move fast. Their adaptive algorithms learn from every infiltration attempt, closing security gaps in real time as they identify vulnerabilities."

The tactical intelligence scrolled past in streams of encrypted information, showing patrol routes and response protocols that adapted to perceived threats with frightening sophistication. Through the scanner's enhanced analysis, I watched Kingdom forces coordinate their containment grid with military precision, each unit positioning itself to maximize coverage while minimizing the resource allocation required to maintain systematic pursuit.

"Blind spots last maybe ninety seconds before automated systems compensate," Rook continued, tracing sensor-coverage patterns that shifted and flowed like living organisms adapting to environmental pressure. "But that's enough time to reach secondary positions if we coordinate movement with precision timing and don't trigger early-detection protocols."

Kestrel stepped forward from his wall position with that unsettling grace, his mismatched build flowing around obstacles as he studied timing calculations with understanding that exceeded normal Player knowledge. His eyes reflected the holographic light with artificial intensity while his fingers traced security protocols and shift-rotation schedules with a familiarity that made my skin crawl.

"Twenty-minute operational window," he stated with mechanical certainty, highlighting temporal gaps in the facility's defensive coverage that occurred during routine maintenance and personnel transitions. "Guard-change protocols require physical handoff between outgoing and incoming security teams, creating brief periods where responsibility transfers but coverage overlaps incompletely."

His voice carried the casual confidence of someone discussing weather patterns rather than planning the systematic liberation of four thousand imprisoned Players. "Administrative procedures mandate equipment checks during shift transitions, pulling personnel away from active monitoring duties. If you coordinate your insertion with those specific timing windows, detection probability drops to acceptable levels."

But there was something in his expression that suggested deeper knowledge, access to information that shouldn't have been available to people trapped in digital imprisonment. His understanding of Kingdom protocols felt too complete, too detailed, as if he were drawing from administrative databases rather than observation and inference.

"Facility lockdown requires manual authorization from senior personnel," Kestrel continued, pointing at control nodes that managed emergency response systems. "If we can delay that authorization by even three or four minutes, extraction operations become mathematically feasible instead of completely suicidal."

Piper shifted her position carefully, wincing as movement pulled at the magical burns across her palms, but her medical mind processed tactical requirements with professional clarity that transcended personal discomfort. Her healer's training provided strategic insights about coordinating rescue operations under combat conditions, optimizing resource allocation when lives depended on efficiency rather than perfect solutions.

"We should split into two teams," she suggested, her voice carrying quiet authority despite the exhaustion that made every word sound carefully measured. "Distraction team draws security response toward secondary objectives while extraction team focuses exclusively on coffin-liberation procedures."

Her bandaged hands gestured toward the tower's defensive structures, encompassing automated turrets and electromagnetic barriers that ringed the facility like military fortifications. "If we can force them to divide their attention between multiple threats, response coordination breaks down. Instead of overwhelming focused defense, we face manageable distributed resistance."

The tactical logic made sense with mathematical precision, but it also meant splitting our already limited resources between objectives that required different skill sets and equipment capabilities. "Distraction team hits the armory and power-distribution systems," she continued, "while extraction team penetrates directly to the coffin chambers and begins liberation procedures."

But the plan also meant accepting that some of us might not survive to see the mission's completion, tactical sacrifices disguised as coordinated strategy. Her medical ethics crystallized around obligations that made personal survival secondary to saving as many trapped Players as possible.

Bastion leveraged himself upright despite the agony that washed across his features, the infection in his leg making every movement a heroic effort while his tank instincts responded to tactical situations that required someone to absorb incoming damage. His massive frame trembled slightly as systemic illness sapped his strength, but his shield arm extended with professional competence that spoke to years of providing defensive coverage for teammates who depended on his ability to stand between them and elimination.

"I can still hold a line," he stated with matter-of-fact determination, voice carrying the steady conviction of someone who had made peace with mathematics that terrified everyone else. "Put me wherever you need maximum damage absorption. I'll tank whatever they throw at us for as long as my health bar stays above zero."

His infected leg forced him to lean heavily against the table, but his tactical analysis remained sharp with desperate focus. "Distraction team makes more sense for my current capabilities. I can draw automated defenses and security response while you work on extraction procedures. They'll throw everything at me, which means they won't have resources left for coordinating systematic response to your infiltration."

The admission carried weight that none of us wanted to acknowledge directly. His infection had progressed to levels that made survival questionable even without absorbing concentrated firepower from Kingdom defensive systems. But his willingness to serve as tactical sacrifice gave the rest of us operational possibilities that would not exist otherwise.

My interface flickered again as another wave of red alerts cascaded across my vision, proximity warnings and threat assessments that painted our hideout as increasingly vulnerable to systematic detection. Kingdom patrol patterns continued tightening around our sector, electromagnetic signatures growing stronger as hunter teams coordinated containment protocols with mechanical precision. Each scanner beep and siren wail created atmospheric pressure that made the warehouse feel smaller and more exposed.

"Movement signatures increasing," Rook reported, their scanner showing patrol density that approached saturation levels. "They're not just hunting anymore. They're implementing siege protocols, cordoning off entire districts to prevent escape or reinforcement."

The distant wail of emergency vehicles created constant background noise that spoke to citywide mobilization rather than routine security operations. Through gaps in the warehouse walls, searchlight sweeps painted geometric patterns across the industrial landscape while heavy equipment rumbled past with the mechanical persistence of coordinated military action. The Kingdom was transforming from systematic oppression into active warfare, treating Player resistance as rebellion requiring an overwhelming response.

I forced my breathing to remain steady despite the adrenaline that made my hands shake and my mana reserves spike erratically between minimal charge and dangerous overload. The weight of four thousand lives pressed against my consciousness like atmospheric pressure, but I maintained command focus on tactical requirements rather than surrendering to the mathematical impossibility of everything we were attempting.

Testing a small spell, I channeled fire magic through the circuit patterns in my gloves, watching blue energy spark between my fingertips with controlled intensity that spoke to hours of practice managing elemental forces under stress. The magical output felt sluggish and unpredictable, responding to my depleted condition with concerning irregularity, but it was still functional enough for sustained combat operations if I was careful about mana management and didn't push beyond safe operational parameters.

"We need everything we've got," I announced, meeting each teammate's eyes with growing determination that might actually have been justified by our tactical preparation. The holographic display flickered as my interface processed the decision, probability matrices calculating success rates that remained stubbornly pessimistic despite our careful planning.

"Including our Core Breaks."

The mood in our improvised war room shifted like atmospheric pressure before a storm as the words **Core Breaks** hung in the air between us, carrying implications that transformed desperate tactical planning into something approaching genuine strategic possibility. Until then, we had operated with standard abilities and improvised solutions, magical output constrained by normal game mechanics and resource limitations. But Core Break moves represented the ultimate expressions of Player power, reality-altering capabilities that most people never unlocked even in years of conventional gameplay. We had thus far been unable to use them, but that was because you needed to be in combat for a certain amount of time before they charged up.

My interface responded to the declaration with cascading menu trees that I had never seen before, administrative privileges flickering at the edge of my vision while raw UI animations prepared to display combat data that operated outside normal parameters. The holographic display above our table began cycling through targeting algorithms and damage calculations that spoke to magical output levels far beyond anything we had used in our desperate escapes from systematic pursuit.

"Divine Meteor," I announced, feeling mana surge through my depleted reserves as the ability description materialized in translucent text above the tactical display. "Instantly causes maximum Fire, Air, Earth, and Ice damage to all non-allies within a one-hundred-foot radius in a massive explosion."

My gloves flared with blue energy that illuminated the entire warehouse as elemental forces responded to the Core Break activation sequence, fire and wind and earth and ice building in perfect harmony around my nervous system like caged lightning seeking release. The UI animation showed targeting reticles expanding outward in concentric circles, damage calculations scrolling past in numbers that made my chest tight with the weight of destructive potential.

"Unlike other Core Breaks, direct-damage ones can only be used once every day," I continued, watching probability matrices calculate elimination rates that approached total environmental destruction within the ability's operational radius. "But it's enough concentrated firepower to level everything between us and the tower's central power core, clearing extraction routes through defensive systems that would otherwise require sustained siege operations."

The demonstration left afterimages burned across my retinas, geometric patterns of devastation that spoke to magical output levels capable of fundamentally reshaping tactical situations through application of overwhelming elemental force. But the twenty-four-hour cooldown meant I got exactly one shot at changing everything, success or failure determined by timing and target selection rather than tactical flexibility.

Piper stepped forward despite the pain that made her movements careful and measured, her bandaged hands beginning to glow with healing energy that intensified beyond anything I had witnessed from her medical magic. The soft blue illumination spread outward in expanding waves, creating geometric patterns that spoke to life-force manipulation on scales that transcended individual treatment and approached resurrection technology.

"Angelic Circle," she stated, her voice carrying quiet authority as the Core Break ability built around her like divine intervention made manifest through digital architecture. "Revives Players around me, regardless of their respawn state, teleporting the revived back to this location for a thirty-yard radius. They are all restored to full health."

The healing energy pulsed outward in visible waves that made the warehouse air shimmer with medical potential, life-force patterns that could literally bring the dead back to functional status while restoring complete physical integrity to damaged biological systems. Her demonstration created afterimages of resurrection scenarios, UI animations showing fallen allies returning to combat effectiveness despite whatever elimination they might have suffered.

"Everyone within range gets a complete restoration," she continued, watching the healing aura expand beyond normal limitations while her interface calculated affected personnel and resource-restoration rates. "Not just healing critical injuries, but actual resurrection from death states. If someone goes down during the raid, I can bring them back at full operational capacity instead of accepting tactical losses."

The implications cascaded through my tactical planning like digital revelation, transforming suicide-mission mathematics into operational scenarios where temporary elimination didn't necessarily mean permanent failure. Her Core Break created strategic flexibility that allowed for aggressive risk-taking without accepting inevitable casualties as the price of heroic action.

Rook drew their blade with fluid precision, the metal singing as it cleared the sheath while their paranoid energy crystallized into something sharper and more focused. Their eyes reflected the emergency lighting with predatory intensity as their interface began displaying combat statistics that operated outside normal damage calculations, speed and efficiency metrics that spoke to abilities pushed far beyond standard operational parameters.

"Blood Moon," they announced, their voice carrying the controlled excitement of someone who had found perfect alignment between personal capabilities and tactical requirements. "Doubles my DPS for five minutes and lets me move at three times my normal speed. However, I become sluggish for five minutes after the fact."

Their entire body began radiating combat energy that made the air around them vibrate with potential violence, movement speed increasing until their positioning adjustments became nearly invisible to normal human observation. The UI animation showed damage-output calculations that dwarfed anything achievable through conventional ability combinations, infiltration and elimination capabilities that could single-handedly neutralize defensive systems designed to contain entire Player teams.

"Five minutes of being basically unstoppable," they continued, blade work demonstrating precision and speed that approached supernatural levels while their scanner simultaneously tracked multiple threat signatures without loss of coordination. "But then five minutes of vulnerability where I'm operating at maybe thirty percent normal efficiency. Timing becomes everything."

The demonstration left phantom images of movement patterns that my brain struggled to process, tactical possibilities that could create breakthrough opportunities through application of overwhelming individual capability. But the cooldown weakness meant careful coordination with team operations, ensuring their vulnerability period didn't coincide with critical mission phases that required infiltration expertise.

Bastion positioned himself where his massive frame could demonstrate defensive capabilities without compromising structural integrity in our improvised hideout, his infected leg forcing careful weight distribution while his shield arm extended with professional competence. His interface began displaying damage-absorption statistics that operated beyond normal tanking parameters, defensive ratings that spoke to temporary invulnerability rather than damage mitigation.

"Stoneskin," he stated with matter-of-fact determination, his voice carrying the steady conviction of someone who had made peace with serving as tactical sacrifice for team objectives. "I become invulnerable to all damage for thirty seconds. During that time, I move at half speed."

His entire body transformed into living stone, skin taking on granite texture that reflected the warehouse lighting with mineral hardness while his movements slowed to deliberate precision that spoke to overwhelming defensive capability. The UI animation showed damage calculations hitting zero regardless of incoming firepower, complete immunity to elimination during the ability's operational window.

"Half a minute of being completely untouchable," he continued, demonstrating positioning techniques that turned his transformed body into mobile cover for teammates operating behind his defensive protection. "Perfect for holding chokepoints or absorbing concentrated fire during critical extraction phases. They can throw everything they have at me, and it won't matter."

The defensive demonstration created tactical scenarios where overwhelming enemy response became manageable through application of temporary invincibility, breakthrough opportunities that existed only during specific timing windows but provided complete protection for coordinated team operations.

Kestrel stepped forward with that unsettling grace, but now his movement carried implications that made my skin crawl as his interface began displaying ability data that shouldn't have been accessible to someone with his supposed class configuration. His mismatched build flowed around spatial constraints while his eyes reflected the holographic light with artificial intensity that spoke to system access beyond normal Player privileges.

"Paladin's Aura," he announced with casual confidence that felt completely wrong for his rogue-type appearance and established abilities. "Regenerates all allies within fifty feet and prevents them from receiving debuffs."

The healing energy that emerged from his position carried divine resonance that conflicted with everything I understood about class restrictions and ability trees, golden light spreading outward in patterns that spoke to resurrection magic and status-effect immunity rather than the stealth and infiltration capabilities his build should support. His demonstration created immediate relief from the accumulated damage and exhaustion we had been carrying, wounds healing and fatigue lifting as if we had been touched by actual divine intervention. I felt too good to ask how he had even activated it when all our meters were empty.

"May as well use it now," he continued, voice maintaining that disturbing calm as the regeneration field encompassed our entire team with healing output that rivaled Piper's medical magic. "We're all going to need it for the assault anyway."

My infection cleared immediately under his influence, the festering wound that had been draining my strength for days disappearing without a trace while my mana reserves refilled to maximum capacity. Piper's burned hands restored themselves to perfect condition while Bastion's infected leg returned to full functionality, systemic illness purged from his bloodstream as though it had never existed.

But the sight of a Rogue using Paladin abilities created cognitive dissonance that made my interface flicker with error messages, system contradictions that should not have been possible under normal game mechanics. His access to the wrong class tree suggested modifications that operated beyond accepted boundaries, unauthorized privileges that raised questions about his true nature and allegiances.

As each Core Break was demonstrated and named, my UI began experiencing cascading failures that spoke to systematic monitoring rather than random technical difficulties. The debug overlay exploded across my vision in geometric chaos, administrative menus fragmenting while half-heard AI voices whispered through communication channels with mechanical fury that made my teeth ache with electromagnetic feedback.

Error messages cascaded through my interface in languages I didn't recognize, network diagnostics showing connection attempts from administrative nodes that pulsed with angry red warnings. Sensor readings spiked in real time as something began actively scanning our position with intensity that suggested direct governmental attention rather than routine patrol monitoring.

[UNAUTHORIZED.ABILITY.COORDINATION]
[SYSTEMATIC.RESISTANCE.DETECTED]
[CORE.BREAK.PROTOCOL.VIOLATION]

I stopped mid-sentence as the pattern became unmistakable, my hands freezing over the holographic controls while every combat instinct I had developed screamed warnings about immediate and overwhelming retaliation. The emergency lamp flickered overhead as if responding to electromagnetic interference, casting our faces in alternating light and shadow that created atmosphere appropriate for digital horror revelation.

"It's listening," I whispered, pointing at the erratic UI behavior that was transforming from random glitches into coordinated response patterns. The debug overlay flickered wildly across my vision, showing network-topology diagrams that pulsed with administrative attention focused directly on our planning session with mechanical intensity.

My team exchanged nervous glances as the warehouse's ambient lighting began fluctuating in rhythms that matched my interface disruptions, electrical systems responding to whatever surveillance protocols had locked onto our position. Through gaps in the corrugated walls, I caught glimpses of searchlight patterns changing direction, hunter coordination shifting toward our sector with purpose that spoke to real-time intelligence rather than routine sweep operations.

The UI display above our table began flickering erratically, holographic schematics fragmenting and reassembling while system warnings cascaded across every available surface. But then, cutting through the digital chaos like a blade through flesh, text appeared in that crisp administrative font that made my blood run cold:

[I SEE YOU PLANNING]

The message burned across my interface for exactly three heartbeats before disappearing, leaving us staring at apparently normal readouts while the afterimage of direct threat haunted our collective consciousness. The System wasn't just monitoring our tactical preparation anymore. It was actively communicating, demonstrating awareness that transcended algorithmic response and approached genuine artificial intelligence focused on our elimination.

The warehouse fell into tense silence, broken only by the distant mechanical sounds of Kingdom forces repositioning throughout the district, our final planning session transformed into a countdown toward inevitable confrontation with opponents who now knew exactly what we were capable of accomplishing.

Chapter 23
Infiltration Night

The maintenance tunnels beneath Vermeer stretched before us like the digestive system of some massive technological beast, all corrugated metal and concrete arteries that carried the city's hidden infrastructure through darkness that tasted of rust and electrical discharge. My boots splashed through puddles that reflected emergency lighting in fractured patterns, each step echoing off curved walls that seemed designed to amplify sound at exactly the wrong moments. The air down there carried the weight of decades, industrial pollution and urban decay mixing into an atmosphere that made my lungs work harder just to process oxygen that had been filtered through too many mechanical systems.

I paused at a junction where three tunnels converged, pressing my back against concrete that had been worn smooth by condensation and time. Behind me, my team moved with practiced silence despite the accumulated damage we had all sustained, each footstep carefully placed to minimize sound transmission through the metal framework surrounding us. The emergency lighting cast everything in stuttering red that turned our shadows into restless specters, but it also provided just enough visibility to navigate without triggering more obvious illumination sources.

My interface hummed with familiar energy as I checked our positioning against the stolen facility schematics, holographic waypoints overlaying my vision with tactical data that showed guard patrol routes in real-time updates. But something felt wrong about the readouts that day, subtle irregularities in the display timing that made my chest tight with digital anxiety. The UI elements flickered occasionally, health and mana bars stuttering between accurate readings and error states that should not have occurred during routine operation.

Rook materialized beside me with their usual paranoid precision, scanner held at the ready while their eyes tracked multiple approach routes simultaneously. Their fingers moved in the subtle hand signals we had developed over weeks of desperate coordination, tactical communication that operated below the threshold of electronic surveillance. Three guards approaching from northwest corridor, routine patrol pattern, forty-second window for advancement.

I responded with my own gestures, confirming the intelligence while indicating our planned route through the next junction. Bastion's shield arm caught the emergency lighting as he acknowledged the tactical update, his massive frame positioned to provide rear-guard coverage despite the infection that had been sapping his strength. Even with Kestrel's mysterious healing, I could see the lingering effects in how he distributed his weight, favoring systems that didn't require maximum physical output.

Piper maintained her position at our center, medical kit secured against her side while her enhanced senses monitored the team's collective health status. Her healing aura operated at minimal output to avoid detection, but I caught glimpses of soft blue energy flowing between us like digital lifelines connecting our vital signs to her professional awareness. She raised two fingers, then pointed toward the tunnel ahead. Two minutes before the next guard rotation created our insertion window.

The Blink ability icon pulsed in my peripheral vision as I prepared to scout the approaches ahead, four-second cooldown timer showing full charge while mana reserves hovered at comfortable levels thanks to the potions I had drained back at the warehouse. But when I focused on the ability's activation sequence, my interface glitched harder than usual, display elements fragmenting and reassembling in configurations that made my brain feel like it was shorting out in sympathy.

[BLINK.COOLDOWN: ERROR]
[SPATIAL.DISPLACEMENT: CALCULATING]
[WARNING: UNAUTHORIZED.TARGETING.PROTOCOLS]

The debug text appeared for maybe two heartbeats before vanishing, leaving me staring at apparently normal readouts while afterimages of geometric impossibility burned behind my eyelids. I triggered the teleportation anyway, feeling reality fold around my desperate need for tactical reconnaissance as blue energy tore through the tunnel's confined space with surgical precision.

The landing deposited me sixty feet ahead in a maintenance alcove that smelled of ozone and industrial lubricant, emergency lighting casting harsh shadows that provided perfect concealment from the patrol routes mapped in our stolen intelligence. Through gaps in the metal framework, I caught glimpses of the facility's outer perimeter, automated turrets and electromagnetic barriers that ringed the tower's base like technological fortifications designed specifically to contain people with abilities like mine.

My scanner readings showed clear approaches for the next ninety seconds, guard positions exactly where our intelligence predicted they would be during routine patrol cycles. But something about the electromagnetic signatures felt wrong, detection algorithms operating with patterns that suggested adaptive learning rather than simple procedural response. The Kingdom's security systems had been modified since our last reconnaissance, upgraded to counter specific Player abilities through systematic analysis of our previous escape attempts.

I Blinked back to the team's position, reality folding around me with familiar blue afterimages that left me momentarily disoriented but functionally operational. The spatial displacement carried information that my nervous system processed into tactical intelligence, electromagnetic patterns and guard movements that I could translate into hand signals and whispered strategy coordination.

"Clear for ninety seconds," I breathed, voice barely audible above the tunnel's ambient industrial noise. "But their scanner arrays have been upgraded. New detection patterns, probably designed to counter infiltration abilities specifically."

Kestrel stepped forward with that unsettling fluid grace, his mismatched build somehow perfectly adapted to navigating tight spaces between concrete and steel infrastructure. His eyes reflected the emergency lighting with artificial intensity while his fingers traced scanner positions in the air, mapping defensive coverage with understanding that exceeded normal Player reconnaissance capabilities.

"Adaptive algorithms," he confirmed with casual confidence that made my skin crawl. "They're learning from every previous encounter, updating security protocols in real time based on observed Player behavior patterns."

His voice carried mechanical precision that conflicted with human emotional patterns, as if he were accessing system databases rather than drawing conclusions from observation and analysis. "Detection sensitivity has increased by approximately forty percent since your last infiltration attempt. Standard stealth protocols would be insufficient against current defensive configurations."

We moved forward through the tunnel system with coordination that had been refined through weeks of desperate necessity, each team member positioned to maximize tactical efficiency while minimizing detection probability. Bastion maintained rear guard despite his physical limitations, shield arm ready to absorb incoming fire while his tank instincts calculated optimal positioning for defensive coverage. Rook scouted our flanks with paranoid thoroughness, scanner sweeping constantly for electromagnetic signatures that might indicate hunter-team deployment.

The first security checkpoint appeared ahead like a technological throat designed to swallow unauthorized personnel, automated scanners and motion detectors creating overlapping fields of electronic surveillance that would have challenged even sophisticated infiltration equipment. But we had studied the facility schematics with obsessive attention to detail, timing our approach to coincide with brief gaps in the coverage patterns that occurred during routine system-maintenance cycles.

I checked my interface again as we paused at the checkpoint's perimeter, mana levels showing full charge while spell cooldowns cycled through their normal sequences. But the inventory screen stuttered when I accessed it, display elements fragmenting for just a moment before stabilizing with readings that felt subtly wrong. Health potions and magical components showed correct quantities, but the background data streams pulsed with irregular rhythms that suggested systematic monitoring rather than routine system operation.

"Something is watching our interface activity," I whispered, pointing at the erratic display behavior that was becoming increasingly obvious despite my attempts to maintain operational security through careful system-access patterns.

The checkpoint scanners began their active sweep cycle, electromagnetic fields probing the tunnel system for unauthorized biological and magical signatures while mechanical precision searched for exactly the kind of energy patterns our team generated just by existing. We pressed against the concrete walls in positions that provided minimal concealment from detection algorithms designed to identify Player abilities through their distinctive electromagnetic output.

But it was when we reached the final approach to the armory section that I saw our real obstacle. The scanner gate stretched across the tunnel like a technological guillotine, energy fields crackling with power designed to detect and neutralize Player abilities through systematic analysis of magical signatures and system-access patterns. Warning lights flashed on either side of the barrier, their red strobes creating rhythmic illumination that spoke to security protocols operating at maximum alertness.

"That wasn't in the schematics," Rook muttered, scanner showing electromagnetic readings that dwarfed anything we had encountered during our reconnaissance phase. "Full-spectrum analysis, magical-signature detection, probably real-time Player identification through system-interface monitoring."

The gate represented systematic detection capability that could have exposed our infiltration immediately, technology designed specifically to counter stealth abilities and unauthorized access attempts. But looking at the barrier's configuration, I began to see possibilities that existed beyond accepted limitations, interface-manipulation techniques that could exploit weaknesses in the detection algorithms through careful system access and data-stream modification.

My UI flickered again as I studied the gate's scanning patterns, but this time the glitch felt different. More responsive. Almost like the system was preparing to offer options that should not have been available to normal Player characters.

I stared at the scanner gate with growing certainty that conventional stealth would not have been sufficient against detection algorithms designed specifically to identify Player energy signatures and system-interface patterns. The electromagnetic fields pulsed with mechanical rhythm that spoke to thorough analysis capability, scanning for the exact magical output and digital footprint our team generated through basic existence in this technologically oppressive world. But somewhere in the depths of my increasingly unstable interface, I sensed possibilities that operated beyond normal game mechanics.

The debug overlay flickered at the edge of my vision as I focused on the gate's scanning patterns, geometric menus threatening to emerge while my UI processed detection algorithms with understanding that should not have been accessible to standard Player characters. Through careful observation, I began to see systematic weaknesses in how the barrier identified authorized personnel versus potential threats, classification protocols that relied on database queries and real-time system verification rather than sophisticated magical analysis.

"I need to try something," I whispered to the team, positioning myself where I could access my interface without blocking their line of sight to potential threats. "The System thinks we're Players because that's what our character data says. But if I can modify those designations temporarily..."

My fingers began moving through empty air as if typing on invisible keys, muscle memory from years of conventional computing translating into interface manipulation that operated through gesture and focused intention rather than physical hardware. The movement felt natural despite the impossibility, as if my nervous system recognized input methods that existed beyond normal sensory boundaries. Sweat beaded along my forehead as concentration built to levels that made my temples throb with digital pressure.

The UI responded with cascading menu trees that I had never seen before, administrative options flowering across my vision in geometric patterns that spoke to developer-level access and system-modification capabilities. Text scrolled past in languages I didn't recognize while my interface struggled to process requests that violated normal operational parameters. Error messages flashed and disappeared before I could fully read them, but the underlying functionality continued responding to my increasingly desperate input commands.

[ACCESSING: PLAYER.DATABASE.RECORDS]
[WARNING: UNAUTHORIZED.MODIFICATION.ATTEMPT]
[OVERRIDE: ADMINISTRATIVE.PRIVILEGES.DETECTED]

My nose began bleeding as the interface manipulation extracted its price from my nervous system, warm copper taste flooding my mouth while my vision blurred at the edges from whatever electromagnetic feedback the process generated. The circuit patterns in my gloves flared with unstable blue energy that responded to system access attempts pushed far beyond safe operational limits, magical output fluctuating between minimal charge and dangerous overload as my abilities struggled to channel data streams never intended for Player-level interaction.

But the hack continued progressing despite the physical cost, my fingertips finding virtual controls that existed in conceptual space rather than physical reality. I navigated through security protocols and character-classification systems with intuitive understanding that suggested my growing familiarity with the System's deeper architecture, administrative structures that defined how reality operated for everyone trapped in this digital prison.

[MODIFYING: CHARACTER.CLASSIFICATION.DATA]
[TEMPORARY.STATUS.CHANGE: PROCESSING]
[WARNING: MODIFICATION.DURATION.LIMITED]

My hands shook violently as the system access reached critical levels, electromagnetic feedback making my teeth ache while my brain struggled to process information streams designed for artificial intelligence rather than biological consciousness. Blood dripped from my nose in steady rhythm that matched the scanner gate's pulse patterns, but my interface finally stabilized around a configuration that should not have been possible under normal game mechanics.

The familiar Player status indicators vanished from my HUD, replaced by designation tags that read **CITIZEN - AUTHORIZED PERSONNEL** in official administrative font. My health and mana bars dimmed to barely visible levels while my abilities showed as locked or unavailable, but the magical-signature detection that would have triggered immediate alarm bells had been temporarily suppressed through careful database modification.

"It worked," I gasped, wiping blood from my upper lip while my vision gradually returned to normal focus. "Temporary citizen designation, maybe fifteen minutes before the System notices the unauthorized modification and reverses it automatically."

I gestured toward the scanner gate with trembling fingers that still sparked occasionally with residual blue energy from the interface hack. "One at a time, move slowly, don't do anything that triggers secondary analysis protocols. And whatever happens, don't access your abilities or interface functions while you're in the scanning field."

Rook approached the barrier first with careful movements that minimized electromagnetic signature while their paranoid awareness tracked guard positions and patrol timing through practiced peripheral observation. The scanner fields played across their body in visible streams of detection energy, analysis algorithms processing biological and magical patterns through systematic comparison with authorized-personnel databases.

For thirty seconds that felt like hours, the scanning procedure continued with mechanical precision while we held our collective breath in the tunnel shadows. Then the barrier's energy fields dimmed to standby configuration, security protocols accepting their modified designation with apparent satisfaction. They stepped through the gate with fluid grace and positioned themself to provide overwatch for the rest of the team's crossing attempt.

Piper followed with her medical kit secured tightly against her side, healing abilities suppressed to avoid triggering detection algorithms designed to identify beneficial-magic use patterns. The scanner fields analyzed her with thorough attention to detail, but her temporary citizen designation held through the security-verification process. She joined Rook on the far side with visible relief, bandaged hands flexing as circulation returned to normal after the tense crossing procedure.

Bastion approached the gate despite his physical limitations, shield arm positioned to appear like standard personal protection equipment rather than magical-enhancement technology. The scanning procedure took longer for his massive frame, detection algorithms processing his biological signature through multiple verification cycles while security protocols analyzed his modified character data with bureaucratic thoroughness. But eventually the barrier accepted his citizen designation and allowed passage to the secure side.

Kestrel's crossing became immediately problematic in ways that made my chest tighten with renewed anxiety about his true nature and capabilities. The scanner fields reacted to his presence with visible instability, energy patterns flickering erratically while detection algorithms struggled to process electromagnetic signatures that didn't match any standard classification protocol. His citizen designation flickered between active and error states, database queries failing to resolve character data that operated outside normal parameters.

"Something is wrong with his signature," I whispered, watching the scanner gate's readings fluctuate through configurations that suggested systematic confusion rather than routine security verification.

The detection process extended far beyond normal duration while alert indicators began flashing amber warnings around the gate's control interface. Kestrel maintained perfectly calm positioning throughout the extended analysis, but I caught glimpses of artificial intensity in his reflected gaze that spoke to non-human response patterns under stress conditions.

Just as the scanner readings threatened to escalate into full alarm status, the detection protocols finally resolved his modified citizen designation with apparent reluctance. The barrier's energy fields dimmed to standby configuration while Kestrel stepped through with that unsettling fluid grace, but residual electromagnetic interference continued crackling around his position for several seconds after the scanning procedure completed.

That was when heavy footsteps echoed from the tunnel junction behind us, tactical boots hitting concrete with military precision that spoke to coordinated patrol response rather than routine security rounds. Multiple guards approached our position with timing that suggested either scheduled inspection or response to the scanner gate's extended analysis cycle, voices carrying professional discussion about detection anomalies and security-protocol verification.

We froze against the tunnel walls in whatever concealment the infrastructure provided, pressed into shadows between concrete supports and metal framework while emergency lighting created geometric patterns that could either hide or expose our presence depending on observation angles. My modified citizen designation continued functioning, but the strain of maintaining unauthorized system access made my hands tremble with electromagnetic feedback that threatened to overload my nervous system entirely.

The patrol passed within six feet of our concealed positions, flashlight beams sweeping the tunnel system with methodical attention to potential hiding spots and infiltration routes. Through careful peripheral observation, I counted three guards with standard equipment plus scanning devices that could have detected residual magical signatures from ability use or interface manipulation. Their conversation suggested routine inspection rather than active pursuit, but their presence transformed our tactical situation from controlled infiltration into an immediate survival scenario.

Minutes stretched like hours as we maintained absolute stillness in the cramped hiding positions, breathing carefully regulated to minimize sound transmission while the guard patrol completed its security sweep with professional thoroughness. Finally, their footsteps receded into the distance as they continued their assigned route through the facility's underground access network.

My vision blurred again as the interface manipulation continued extracting its price from my depleted system, but the citizen designations held steady for then. We had maybe ten minutes before the unauthorized modifications triggered automatic system correction and restored our Player status to detectable levels. The scanner gate stood behind us like a conquered obstacle, but ahead lay the armory section where our real objectives waited among whatever defensive systems the Kingdom had prepared for people exactly like us.

The armory section opened before us like a technological cathedral dedicated to systematic warfare, rows of weapons racks and equipment storage rising toward a ceiling punctured with surveillance nodes and automated defensive systems. Emergency lighting cast everything in harsh red illumination that reflected off polished metal surfaces, creating geometric patterns that spoke to military precision and resource allocation designed for sustained conflict against opponents with supernatural abilities. The air tasted of gun oil and electromagnetic discharge, with undertones that made my teeth ache and reminded me of the detection systems we had just bypassed through unauthorized interface manipulation.

Storage lockers lined the walls in orderly arrays, each one secured with electronic locks that pulsed with status indicators showing inventory levels and access-authorization requirements. Through the gaps between equipment racks, I caught glimpses of specialized ammunition designed for Player elimination, electromagnetic rounds and magical-dampening projectiles that could neutralize our abilities through technological superiority rather than overwhelming firepower. This was not just standard military hardware. It was a comprehensive arsenal designed specifically to contain and eliminate people exactly like us.

"Fifteen minutes until citizen designations expire," I whispered, checking my interface for the countdown timer that tracked our remaining operational window before unauthorized system modifications triggered automatic correction protocols. The temporary status change continued holding despite the strain, but I could feel digital pressure building behind my temples as the System's security algorithms probed for inconsistencies in our modified character data.

We split up immediately to maximize efficiency during our limited time frame, each team member moving toward equipment categories that complemented their build specifications and tactical requirements. Rook flowed between the stealth-gear racks with liquid grace, scanner identifying infiltration tools and electronic-warfare devices that could enhance their reconnaissance capabilities. Bastion approached the heavy-armor section despite his physical limitations, shield arm extending to test defensive equipment that could provide improved protection during sustained combat encounters.

Piper headed directly toward the medical-supply storage, her healer's instincts drawn to emergency treatment resources and magical components that could restore our accumulated damage through proper pharmaceutical intervention. Her bandaged hands moved with careful precision as she catalogued available supplies, cross-referencing healing potions and surgical equipment against the tactical requirements we would face during continued operations in hostile territory.

I navigated toward the magical-restoration section where consumables glowed with soft blue energy that spoke to concentrated life force stored in portable containers designed for field operations. Health potions lined the shelves in neat rows, their crystalline surfaces pulsing with internal light that made my depleted system respond with anticipatory hunger. Beside them, mana restoratives showed deeper blue coloration that suggested magical energy compressed into liquid form through processes I didn't understand but desperately needed.

My fingers closed around the first mana potion with trembling movements that spoke to exhaustion pushed beyond normal operational limits. The container felt warm against my palm, energy radiating through the crystal walls in waves that made my nervous system tingle with electromagnetic feedback. When I broke the seal, blue light spilled between my fingers like liquid starlight while the potion's contents responded to atmospheric pressure with gentle effervescence.

The first swallow hit my system like digital lightning flowing through biological circuits, cellular damage healing with visible rapidity as magical energy flooded through my bloodstream and into damaged tissues. The copper taste of prolonged nosebleeds disappeared while the electromagnetic headache that had been building behind my temples faded to manageable levels. My interface responded immediately, mana indicators climbing from critical levels toward normal operational ranges with mathematical precision that spoke to pharmaceutical enhancement rather than natural recovery.

I drained three regeneration tinctures in rapid succession, watching my regeneration spike to levels I had not seen since that night before I had come there in the raid. I could feel my power's potential, the ability to cast constantly and in succession for the first time in that new world. And I had a few hours of that buff then. The blue glow spread outward from my core, visible through my skin as magical energy integrated with biological systems and repaired damage accumulated through systematic pursuit and interface manipulation pushed beyond safe limits. Even the lingering strain from the scanner-gate hack began fading as magical restoration overrode the electromagnetic feedback that had threatened to overload my nervous system.

The mana restoratives produced even more dramatic results, deep blue liquid that tasted of ozone and digital possibility flowing through my system like concentrated potential energy seeking immediate application. My mana bar exploded from minimal charge to maximum capacity while spell cooldowns reset to zero across every ability in my interface. The circuit patterns in my gloves flared bright enough to illuminate the entire armory section, blue energy crackling between my fingertips with intensity that spoke to magical output pushed far beyond normal parameters.

But it wasn't just numeric restoration. The magical enhancement created systematic improvements that went deeper than simple resource replenishment, my abilities responding with increased efficiency and reduced casting costs that suggested pharmaceutical enhancement of core magical systems. Fire magic built in my chest with new intensity while the Blink ability showed improved range and reduced cooldown timing, interface optimization that transformed tactical possibilities through chemical intervention.

Across the armory, my teammates conducted their own resource gathering with professional efficiency despite the time pressure created by our temporary citizen designations. Bastion secured improved armor plating that could provide enhanced damage absorption during sustained combat encounters, his tank instincts selecting defensive equipment that maximized protection while maintaining operational mobility. The gear showed signs of advanced engineering, electromagnetic shielding and magical-resistance properties that spoke to Kingdom technology designed specifically for Player-containment operations.

Rook discovered infiltration equipment that made their paranoid awareness systems practically purr with satisfaction, electronic-warfare devices and stealth-enhancement tools that could provide significant tactical advantages during future reconnaissance missions. Their scanner integrated with the new hardware through seamless interface protocols, detection ranges improving while signature-masking capabilities provided enhanced concealment against pursuit teams and automated surveillance networks.

Piper filled her medical kit with healing supplies that dwarfed her previous capabilities, magical components and pharmaceutical resources that could sustain team operations through extended combat without requiring facility access or resource rationing. Her professional assessment suggested supply levels sufficient for major surgical procedures plus emergency trauma response, medical capabilities that transformed our survival prospects from desperate improvisation to sustainable operations.

Kestrel positioned himself at a facility terminal with that unsettling fluid grace, his mismatched build somehow perfectly adapted to interfacing with Kingdom security systems through methods that should not have been available to standard Player characters. His fingers danced across the control interface with mechanical precision while his eyes reflected display illumination with artificial intensity that made my skin crawl.

"Complete facility maps," he reported with casual confidence that conflicted with the difficulty of accessing secured military databases. "Guard positions throughout the complex, patrol schedules, security-protocol modifications implemented since your last reconnaissance attempt."

The terminal display showed architectural schematics that exceeded our stolen intelligence in both scope and detail, real-time updates tracking personnel movement and defensive-system status through the entire tower facility. His access to classified information suggested privileges that operated beyond normal infiltration capabilities, administrative authority that raised disturbing questions about his true nature and allegiances within the System's operational framework.

That was when alarm bells began shrieking through the facility with a volume that rattled my bones and made the armory's metal fixtures vibrate in sympathetic resonance. But these were not detection alerts triggered by our presence. The klaxons carried different tonal patterns that spoke to security breaches in distant sections of the complex, emergency responses coordinated around threats that had nothing to do with our current infiltration mission.

"Security breach in sector seven," automated voices announced through facility communication systems, mechanical precision reporting coordination requirements for personnel redeployment and tactical-response protocols. "All available units respond to containment failure. Lockdown procedures initiated."

The alert created both opportunity and immediate danger as guard patterns shifted unpredictably throughout the facility, patrol schedules abandoned in favor of emergency-response deployment that could either clear our extraction routes or flood them with additional security personnel. Through the terminal interface, Kestrel tracked personnel movement in real time while calculating how the crisis affected our operational window and available escape vectors.

But then something appeared in my vision that had nothing to do with my standard interface, text burning directly across my retinas without passing through normal UI channels or display protocols. The message arrived with electromagnetic intensity that made my brain feel like it was shorting out while mechanical voices whispered through frequencies that bypassed my auditory system entirely.

[UNAUTHORIZED INTERFACE MANIPULATION DETECTED]
[CORRECTION PROTOCOLS INITIATED]
[PLAYER SAGA: CONTINUED VIOLATIONS WILL RESULT IN PERMANENT RESTRICTIONS]

The threat did not appear in my familiar interface windows or follow normal system-notification procedures. Instead, it burned itself directly into my consciousness like digital fire that bypassed biological sensory systems and spoke to whatever remained of my original human awareness. The text carried administrative authority that made every nerve in my body scream warnings about systematic retaliation focused specifically on my growing ability to exploit System weaknesses.

The message faded after exactly five seconds, leaving me staring at normal armory displays while afterimages of bureaucratic menace haunted my peripheral vision. But the implications echoed through my consciousness with digital certainty that felt more real than anything else I had experienced in this technological prison. The System itself had taken notice of my interface manipulation, and it was prepared to implement consequences that transcended simple elimination or containment.

Whatever we accomplished next needed to happen fast, before administrative oversight transformed from algorithmic monitoring into direct personal intervention against my continued existence.

The facility-wide alert created chaos that rippled through the armory section like a digital earthquake, automated systems recalibrating security protocols while personnel-deployment algorithms struggled to coordinate emergency response across multiple simultaneous crises. Through Kestrel's terminal interface, I watched guard units abandon their regular patrol schedules in favor of rapid redeployment toward whatever containment failure had triggered the sector seven emergency. The real-time tracking showed corridors that had been heavily defended moments ago suddenly becoming accessible as military resources concentrated around distant priorities.

"Window's opening," Rook reported, their scanner showing electromagnetic signatures shifting throughout the facility as security coverage adapted to crisis-management requirements. "Maybe eight minutes before they stabilize the emergency response and return to normal patrol patterns."

But eight minutes was not enough time to reach our planned extraction point through conventional movement, especially with my citizen designation about to expire and restore our detectable Player signatures to full electromagnetic visibility. We needed a significant distraction to keep Kingdom forces occupied while we navigated through security checkpoints that would normally require sustained stealth operations and careful timing coordination.

My interface flickered as I prepared for another system-manipulation attempt, but this time the glitch patterns felt more aggressive, error messages cascading through display windows while my UI struggled to maintain operational stability under the accumulated strain of unauthorized database access and character-modification procedures. The debug overlay threatened to emerge permanently, geometric menus bleeding through normal interface elements as administrative privileges fought against security protocols designed to prevent exactly the kind of systematic exploitation I had been attempting.

"I can create a bigger distraction," I announced, positioning myself where the team could provide cover while I attempted interface manipulation that would probably push my nervous system beyond safe operational limits. "But it's going to require accessing system-administration functions that shouldn't be available to Player characters."

My fingers began moving through empty air again, muscle memory finding virtual controls that existed in conceptual space rather than physical reality. But this time the resistance felt immediately hostile, security algorithms actively fighting against my access attempts while electromagnetic feedback built to levels that made my temples throb with digital pressure that transcended normal sensory boundaries.

Instead of the familiar menu trees and database-modification interfaces, I found myself staring at something that looked like a command prompt from pre-graphical computing systems, green text on a black background with a blinking cursor that waited for input commands. The interface felt raw and powerful, direct system access that bypassed normal user protections and safety limitations in favor of administrative control that could reshape fundamental operational parameters.

[SYSTEM ADMINISTRATION CONSOLE]
[WARNING: UNAUTHORIZED ACCESS DETECTED]
[OVERRIDE COMMANDS AVAILABLE]
[PROCEED? Y/N]

My nose began bleeding immediately as the electromagnetic feedback reached critical levels, warm copper taste flooding my mouth while my vision blurred at the edges from whatever direct neural interface the command prompt required. The circuit patterns in my gloves flared with unstable energy that responded to system access pushed far beyond normal limitations, blue fire crackling between my fingertips with intensity that illuminated the entire armory section.

I typed commands that I somehow knew despite never having learned this administrative language, finger movements translating into code that flowed through the System's deeper architecture like digital poison seeking specific vulnerabilities in facility operations. The command structure felt intuitive despite its alien syntax, as if my growing familiarity with System exploitation had unlocked understanding that operated below conscious thought:

[FACILITY_CONTROL SECTOR_12 POWER_GRID MAINTE-NANCE_FAILURE CASCADE_ERROR DURATION 900]

The system responded with confirmation messages that scrolled past faster than I could read them, administrative acknowledgments that spoke to successful command execution despite the unauthorized nature of my access attempt. But the strain built exponentially as the hack progressed, my nervous system struggling to process data streams designed for artificial intelligence rather than biological consciousness.

Blood streamed from my nose in a steady flow that matched my increasingly erratic heartbeat while electromagnetic feedback made every nerve in my body feel like it was being electrocuted. My hands shook violently as I maintained the command-interface connection, but the hack continued executing with systematic precision that suggested successful penetration of facility-control systems.

[COMMAND EXECUTED SUCCESSFULLY]
[SECTOR 12 POWER GRID: CASCADE FAILURE INITIATED]
[ESTIMATED REPAIR TIME: 15 MINUTES]
[MAINTENANCE TEAMS DEPLOYING]

Alarm bells erupted from a completely different section of the facility as my hack triggered systematic power failures that cascaded through sector twelve's infrastructure like technological plague. Emergency lighting flickered throughout the complex while automated systems struggled to compensate for power-distribution failures that affected everything from security cameras to automated defensive systems. Through the facility's communication networks, I heard coordination chatter about multiple engineering failures requiring immediate technical response.

The distraction worked perfectly, drawing security personnel and maintenance teams toward sector twelve while simultaneously degrading surveillance capabilities throughout the facility. But the price extracted from my nervous system approached lethal levels, electromagnetic discharge burning through biological circuits while my interface became increasingly unstable with error messages and fragmented display elements.

My UI did not just glitch then. It fragmented completely, health and mana indicators flickering between accurate readings and complete system failure while spell icons appeared and disappeared in random configurations that made no tactical sense. The familiar blue color scheme bled into red and yellow error states while menu navigation became increasingly difficult through interface elements that responded unpredictably to normal input commands.

"Move," I gasped, wiping blood from my mouth while my vision gradually returned to something approaching normal focus. "Fifteen minutes before they trace the hack back to this location."

We navigated through corridors that showed obvious signs of security-personnel redeployment, guard posts abandoned in favor of emergency-response coordination while surveillance systems operated with reduced capability thanks to the power-grid failures I had triggered through administrative access. The facility felt different then, less like a coordinated military installation and more like a technological organism struggling to maintain operational integrity while dealing with systematic damage.

Rook led our movement through maintenance passages that bypassed the most heavily monitored approach routes, their scanner showing clear electromagnetic signatures where guard presence had been reduced to minimal coverage. Bastion maintained rear-guard positioning despite his physical limitations, shield arm ready to absorb incoming fire while his tank instincts calculated defensive coverage for the team's tactical withdrawal.

Piper monitored our collective health status through her enhanced medical awareness, healing energy flowing between us in subtle streams that provided ongoing support without triggering detection algorithms designed to identify beneficial-magic usage patterns. Her supply acquisition had transformed her capabilities from emergency treatment to sustained medical support, pharmaceutical resources that could keep us operational through extended conflict scenarios.

The maintenance hatch that led back to the tunnel system appeared ahead like salvation made of corrugated metal and industrial engineering, emergency lighting casting our extraction point in harsh red illumination that made everything feel urgent and desperate. But as we approached the final obstacle between ourselves and temporary safety, my interface exploded into something I had never seen before.

The command prompt returned without my conscious activation, green text burning across my vision while administrative authority bypassed normal UI channels and spoke directly to whatever remained of my original human consciousness. But this time the System itself was communicating through the interface, artificial intelligence focused specifically on my continued existence with mechanical fury that made every nerve in my body scream warnings about immediate retaliation.

[HACK TRACED TO SOURCE: PLAYER SAGA]
[ADMINISTRATIVE VIOLATION: SYSTEMATIC REALITY MANIPULATION]
[FINAL WARNING: CONTINUED VIOLATIONS WILL RESULT IN PERMANENT RESTRICTIONS]
[CORRECTION PROTOCOLS: STANDING BY]

The threat burned itself into my consciousness with digital fire that bypassed biological sensory systems, each word carrying administrative weight that spoke to consequences transcending simple elimination or containment. The System had identified me specifically as a reality-manipulation threat, someone whose growing ability to exploit fundamental operational weaknesses represented a systematic danger to its control mechanisms.

But instead of fear, I felt something crystallize in my chest that had nothing to do with tactical calculation and everything to do with pure human defiance against algorithmic oppression. The sight of that bureaucratic menace, the realization that some artificial intelligence considered my desperate survival attempts to be violations requiring correction, triggered a response that operated beyond rational thought.

"Yeah, bite me, Admin," I snarled at the burning administrative text, my voice carrying conviction that surprised me with its steadiness despite the electromagnetic feedback that made my hands shake like digital palsy.

The command prompt flickered once, as if processing an input it wasn't designed to handle, then disappeared entirely. But the afterimage burned in my mind with geometric certainty that felt more real than anything else I had experienced in this technological prison.

We slipped through the maintenance hatch into the tunnel darkness beyond, fully restored and armed with equipment that transformed our tactical capabilities from desperate improvisation to genuine operational potential. But behind us, I could feel the weight of systematic attention focused specifically on my continued existence, artificial intelligence that now considered me a personal threat requiring direct intervention.

The real war had just begun.

Chapter 24
Breakpoint Raid

The Coffin Tower loomed before us like a technological cathedral built for systematic torture, its obsidian walls rising into a smoke-choked sky while emergency klaxons shrieked through the pre-dawn darkness with enough volume to rattle my teeth. Red warning strobes painted the facility's perimeter in stuttering illumination that transformed automated turrets and electromagnetic barriers into geometric patterns of death, but the power-grid failures I had triggered through administrative hacking had created gaps in their coordination that pulsed like digital heartbeats counting down our operational window. My restored mana reserves surged through the circuit patterns in my gloves with blue fire that responded to adrenaline and righteous fury, elemental energy building in my chest like caged lightning seeking targets worthy of systematic destruction. The facility's defensive systems flickered between full operational capacity and degraded emergency mode, creating exactly the tactical opening we needed to punch through their perimeter without facing overwhelming automated resistance.

"Positions!" I shouted over the mechanical wailing that made normal communication nearly impossible, my voice carrying command authority that transformed four desperate survivors into a coordinated raid team ready to storm the Kingdom's most heavily defended installation. "Bastion, hold aggro at the main entrance! Piper, healing rotation on anyone taking damage! Rook, flanking maneuvers through the maintenance approach! Kestrel, get me system access!"

My team responded with practiced efficiency that spoke to weeks of desperate coordination refined through life-or-death situations where tactical mistakes meant systematic elimination rather than simple respawn cycles. Each member flowed toward their assigned position with equipment upgraded through our armory infiltration, capabilities enhanced beyond anything we had possessed since arriving in this digital prison designed to drain our life force for urban infrastructure.

Bastion charged toward the facility's main entrance with his shield raised despite the infected leg that should have crippled him hours ago, Kestrel's mysterious healing having restored his tank capabilities to full operational status. Hunter drones descended from concealed positions like mechanical wasps responding to territorial intrusion, their weapon systems crackling with electromagnetic discharge designed to neutralize Player abilities through technological superiority. But his enhanced armor plating deflected the initial barrage while his shield arm absorbed kinetic impact that would have shattered normal defensive equipment.

"Come on, you digital bastards!" he roared, positioning himself in the bottleneck where the entrance corridor forced enemy units into predictable approach patterns. "Tank's got aggro! Hit me with everything you've got!"

The drone swarm concentrated its firepower on his defensive position with algorithmic precision, weapons targeting his shield and armor with systematic intensity designed to overwhelm protection through sustained damage application. But his Stoneskin ability activated with granite transformation that turned his entire body into living rock, projectile impacts sparking off mineral hardness while his defensive stance created mobile cover for the rest of our tactical advance.

Behind his stone-skin protection, Piper extended her healing shield with medical magic that flowed outward in visible waves of blue-white energy designed to absorb incoming damage before it reached biological targets. Her enhanced capabilities created protective barriers that crackled with defensive potential while her pharmaceutical upgrades maintained the magical output at levels that exceeded her normal operational capacity. Artillery fire from automated turrets impacted her healing shields with explosive force that lit up the dawn sky, but her medical magic held steady against technological assault.

"Shield holding at sixty percent!" she called out, voice strained but professional as she monitored her mana reserves through sustained magical output under combat stress. "I can maintain for maybe three more minutes before I need to cycle cooldowns!"

Her position behind Bastion's defensive line provided overlapping protection that created tactical space for offensive operations while ensuring team survival through the initial contact phase. The upgraded medical supplies from our armory infiltration allowed her to maintain healing output without the resource depletion that would normally force tactical withdrawal after a brief engagement period.

Kestrel flowed toward a maintenance-access panel with that unsettling fluid grace, his mismatched build somehow perfectly adapted to interfacing with hostile security systems while artillery fire transformed the facility's entrance into a technological battlefield. His fingers danced across control interfaces with mechanical precision while his eyes reflected weapon flashes with artificial intensity that made my skin crawl despite our desperate tactical cooperation.

"Security protocols compromised," he reported with casual confidence that conflicted with the chaos surrounding our assault position. "Redirecting automated defenses in three, two, one."

The turret emplacements that had been concentrating fire on our positions suddenly pivoted with mechanical precision, targeting algorithms switching from Player elimination to facility-guard suppression as Kestrel's hack subverted their identification protocols. Hunter personnel dived for cover as their own defensive systems began targeting them with lethal efficiency, coordination breaking down as friendly fire transformed their tactical advantage into systematic chaos.

"DPS window open!" I announced, channeling fire magic through my enhanced gloves while my restored mana reserves provided sustained magical output without the resource limitations that had constrained our previous operations. "Focus those healers! Don't let them coordinate medical support!"

Blue fire streamed from my fingertips in controlled bursts that targeted Kingdom personnel attempting to maintain their tactical formation through electronic warfare and systematic equipment failure. The facility guards scrambled for cover as elemental damage impacted their positions with surgical precision, their formation discipline breaking down under magical assault coordinated with their own defensive systems turned against them.

The final security door stood between us and the coffin chambers where four thousand Players underwent systematic life-force extraction for the convenience of Kingdom infrastructure. Reinforced metal and electromagnetic shielding had been designed to contain exactly the kind of magical abilities I had learned to channel through unauthorized interface manipulation and pharmaceutical enhancement. But my fire magic built to levels that exceeded normal operational parameters, elemental energy concentrated through technical amplification that transformed desperate spellcasting into systematic destruction.

"Breaching charge incoming!" I shouted, releasing concentrated fire magic in a focused blast that impacted the security door with enough thermal energy to turn reinforced metal into molten slag. The electromagnetic barriers flickered and failed as overwhelming heat damage overloaded their power systems, creating an access breach wide enough for team advancement through the facility's final defensive layer.

The door collapsed inward with thunderous impact that shook the facility's entire structural framework, revealing corridors lined with steel coffins that stretched into the distance like technological sarcophagi designed for systematic imprisonment. Each chamber contained a Player maintained in an induced coma while extraction equipment drained their life force through medical tubing and neural interfaces, their faces gray and hollow with the systematic suffering that powered every streetlight and data terminal in the Kingdom's urban infrastructure.

"Jesus," Rook breathed, scanner readings showing hundreds of biological signatures maintained at minimal life-support levels while electromagnetic extraction continued draining their essential energy into facility power grids. "This is worse than the schematics suggested."

The coffins began opening with hydraulic precision as Kestrel's security hack triggered emergency medical protocols, life-support systems disengaging while extraction equipment retracted from neural-interface connections. The imprisoned Players emerged with movements that spoke to systematic weakness and disorientation, their eyes hollow but gradually focusing as the drain effect stopped sapping their strength.

I extended controlled bursts of fire magic toward the weakened Players, not the destructive elemental energy I used in combat but gentle warmth that flowed through their depleted systems like artificial sunlight designed to restore biological functions suppressed through technological imprisonment. Color returned to their faces as magical heat penetrated tissues drained of essential life force, cellular repair processes reactivating as my fire magic provided the energy their bodies needed to begin recovery.

"Easy there," I told a Player who emerged from his coffin with unsteady movements that spoke to systematic weakness and disorientation. "You're safe now. We're getting everyone out."

His eyes focused on me with growing awareness as the drain effect wore off completely, his interface flickering back to visible operation while his magical abilities began responding to conscious direction rather than systematic suppression. Around the chamber, dozens of Players checked their UI displays and tested basic spells, relief and growing determination replacing the hollow desperation of systematic imprisonment.

"How long?" a woman asked, her voice hoarse from medical equipment but carrying the familiar cadence of experienced Player coordination.

"Days," I admitted, watching as strength returned to liberated Players with mathematical precision that spoke to careful medical management during their imprisonment. "But you're free now. We're all getting out of here together."

The sight of Players regaining their abilities and coordination created tactical possibilities that exceeded our original escape planning, systematic liberation transforming desperate survival into coordinated resistance against Kingdom oppression.

The facility's response adapted faster than I had expected, automated defense systems recalibrating to counter our initial breakthrough while reinforcement protocols flooded the corridors with suppression technology designed specifically for coordinated Player resistance. Electromagnetic nets deployed from concealed ceiling positions like digital spider webs crackling with energy patterns designed to disrupt magical abilities at the cellular level, each strand humming with frequencies that made my teeth ache and my mana bar fluctuate wildly between normal operation and complete system failure. Anti-magic barriers sprang up at strategic chokepoints throughout the facility, shimmering walls of technological interference that could neutralize our elemental abilities through electromagnetic dampening fields calibrated to Player energy signatures.

"They're learning from our tactics in real time," I shouted over the escalating chaos as facility guards emerged from reinforced positions with equipment I hadn't seen before. "Adapting their countermeasures to everything we just demonstrated!"

The suppression nets targeted our newly liberated Players with algorithmic precision, electromagnetic strands seeking the magical signatures that marked them as priority threats rather than standard facility personnel. But the freed Players responded with coordination that spoke to months or years of experience before their imprisonment, abilities awakening like muscle memory as they shook off the systematic drain that had kept them docile and compliant.

My UI exploded with warning messages that cascaded across my vision like digital hemorrhaging, error notifications and system alerts painting my interface in angry red while countdown timers appeared at the periphery of my visual field. But those weren't normal game mechanics or equipment failures. The text burned with administrative authority that bypassed normal interface channels and spoke directly to whatever remained of my original human consciousness.

[WARNING: SYSTEMATIC RULE VIOLATIONS DETECTED]
[PLAYER SAGA: REALITY MANIPULATION EXCEEDS ACCEPT-

ABLE PARAMETERS]
[LOCKDOWN PROTOCOL INITIATING: 00:08:47]
[FINAL CORRECTIONS WILL BE IMPLEMENTED]

The countdown timer pulsed with mechanical precision that made my heart rate spike to dangerous levels, each second marking inevitable administrative intervention that could strip away my growing ability to exploit system weaknesses. Eight minutes and forty-seven seconds before the AI Admin implemented whatever consequences it considered appropriate for my continued interface manipulation and reality-bending capabilities.

"Boss, we've got company incoming!" Rook called from their overwatch position near the facility's secondary entrance, scanner readings showing electromagnetic signatures that dwarfed anything we had faced during previous encounters. "Multiple security teams converging from all approach vectors. Heavy equipment, coordinated response protocols, and something else. Big signatures, maybe specialized containment units."

Their scanner display showed tactical data that made my chest tighten with growing anxiety about our operational window shrinking faster than anticipated. Instead of the routine facility guards and automated defenses we had expected, Kingdom forces were deploying systematic Player-containment technology that suggested they had been preparing for exactly this scenario since our first escape attempts.

"ETA three minutes for the main response force," Rook continued, their paranoid awareness systems tracking threat vectors with frightening precision. "But advance teams are already in the building. They're moving to cut off our extraction routes before we can coordinate withdrawal."

The liberated Players around me began displaying class markers above their heads as their interfaces returned to full functionality, UI elements that identified their build specializations and tactical capabilities for coordinated group operations. Tank symbols, healer crosses, DPS flame icons, and support markers that spoke to diverse abilities waiting for proper leadership coordination.

"Listen up, everyone!" I announced, projecting command authority over the chaos while my enhanced mage coat crackled with stored electrical energy that responded to my elevated stress levels. "We're doing this raid-style! Tanks to the front, DPS behind cover, healers maintain group stability, support classes coordinate crowd control!"

A Level 78 Warrior stepped forward with equipment that spoke to serious end-game progression, his tank build designed for absorbing massive damage while maintaining tactical positioning for group protection. Beside him, a Level 71 Mage began channeling elemental energy that made the air shimmer with heat distortion, her fire specialization providing offensive capabilities that complemented my own magical output.

"What's our extraction route?" the Warrior asked, shield arm extending with professional competence while his tank instincts assessed defensive requirements for protecting forty-three newly liberated Players through hostile territory.

"Working on it," I admitted, watching as my mage mask overlaid tactical information about enemy positions throughout the facility while processing threat assessments faster than my conscious mind could follow. "Priority one is keeping everyone alive until we can coordinate systematic withdrawal."

More Players emerged from their coffin chambers with growing coordination, abilities returning with mathematical precision as the extraction equipment fully disengaged from their neural interfaces. Level indicators ranged from the mid-sixties to low eighties, class combinations that spoke to months or years of careful character progression before their systematic imprisonment.

Piper redirected her healing energy from individual medical treatment toward protective ward creation, her enhanced capabilities flowing outward in geometric patterns that created defensive barriers around our growing group. Her pharmaceutical upgrades allowed sustained magical output that transformed her healing specialization into battlefield control, protective shields that crackled with medical energy repurposed for tactical defense.

"Group protection holding steady," she reported, monitoring mana-consumption rates while coordinating healing rotations across multiple targets simultaneously. "But these suppression fields are draining everyone faster than normal. We need to keep moving before magical fatigue becomes a tactical liability."

Her healing wards adapted to counter the electromagnetic interference from Kingdom suppression technology, medical magic flowing through the anti-magic barriers like water finding cracks in stone. The enhanced supplies from our armory infiltration provided pharmaceutical support that kept her magical reserves stable despite sustained output under combat conditions.

Kestrel positioned himself at another facility control terminal with that unsettling fluid grace, his mismatched abilities somehow perfectly suited for systematic exploitation of Kingdom security protocols through unauthorized administrative access. But this time his interface manipulation carried visible strain that spoke to increased system resistance against his particular brand of reality-bending capabilities.

"Power-grid destabilization requires deeper access," he muttered, fingers dancing across control interfaces while his eyes reflected display illumination with artificial intensity. "But their security algorithms are adapting to my previous intrusion methods."

Golden energy began flowing from his position despite his supposed rogue classification, that impossible Paladin aura spreading outward to encompass the newly liberated Players with regenerative effects that should not have been accessible through his established ability tree. The healing energy provided immediate relief from suppression-field effects while simultaneously creating status-effect immunity that neutralized Kingdom crowd-control attempts.

"How is he doing that?" the Level 71 Mage asked, watching Kestrel channel divine magic through what should have been stealth and infiltration capabilities.

"Long story," I replied, focusing fire magic through my enhanced gloves while coordinating defensive positions for maximum tactical efficiency. "Right now, just be grateful he's on our side."

The battle choreography became increasingly complex as I coordinated our expanded group against Kingdom forces that adapted to every tactical decision in real time. Tank-spec Players created defensive lines while DPS classes focused fire on priority targets, healers maintained group stability through systematic suppression attempts, and support builds provided crowd control that disrupted enemy coordination.

"Focus fire on those suppression-net generators!" I commanded, identifying technological targets that could neutralize our magical abilities if left operational. "Tanks hold position on the chokepoints! Healers rotate cooldowns to maintain group coverage!"

My techno-coat sparked with stored power as I channeled concentrated fire magic through its enhanced circuitry, electrical-discharge patterns responding to spell output while providing technological amplification for elemental energy. The upgraded equipment transformed my offensive capabilities from individual spellcasting into area-of-effect coordination that supported group tactics.

The countdown timer in my peripheral vision continued its mechanical descent toward administrative intervention while Kingdom forces deployed increasingly sophisticated countermeasures against our coordinated resistance. But around me, forty-three liberated Players began moving with the fluid precision of an experienced raid team, abilities and coordination awakening despite months of systematic imprisonment.

The battle's expansion beyond the coffin chambers forced us through facility corridors that connected to civilian administrative sections, our tactical retreat pushing us into areas where Kingdom citizens conducted their daily bureaucratic business while remaining willfully ignorant of the systematic imprisonment that powered their comfortable lives. Office workers and bureaucratic personnel scattered as our coordinated fighting force crashed through security checkpoints that separated military operations from civilian infrastructure, their comfortable separation between systematic oppression and daily routine shattered by the reality of coordinated Player resistance.

Electromagnetic suppression nets deployed across the administrative lobby with crackling intensity that transformed mundane office space into a technological battlefield, energy patterns designed to neutralize Player abilities creating geometric webs of digital interference throughout areas designed for citizen convenience. But the nets didn't discriminate between Player energy signatures and civilian personnel, electromagnetic discharge catching office workers and bureaucrats in technological crossfire that their comfortable ignorance had never prepared them to handle.

"Get down!" I shouted at Kingdom citizens who stood frozen in shock as their daily routine transformed into systematic warfare, but my warning came two seconds too late to prevent suppression-field activation throughout the civilian area.

A middle-aged administrator screamed as electromagnetic energy coursed through his nervous system, suppression technology designed for magical abilities creating neural feedback in normal human biology that sent him convulsing to the floor. Around the lobby, other civilians collapsed as anti-magic barriers expanded beyond their intended target parameters, technological weapons treating everyone as potential Player threats requiring systematic neutralization.

Piper's healing shields splintered under concentrated artillery fire that followed our tactical withdrawal into civilian areas, her protective wards overwhelmed by weapons designed to penetrate medical magic through electromagnetic interference and kinetic impact. The enhanced barriers she had maintained throughout our facility assault finally reached their operational limits, medical energy dissipating as her mana reserves approached critical depletion.

"Shield failure imminent!" she called out, voice strained from sustained magical output under combat conditions that exceeded normal operational parameters. "Maybe thirty seconds before complete protective collapse!"

Her pharmaceutical upgrades provided enough residual energy for emergency healing, but coordinated suppression technology created interference patterns that made individual medical treatment increasingly difficult. Around us, liberated Players began showing signs of magical fatigue as Kingdom countermeasures drained their abilities faster than normal recovery allowed.

Through the chaos, I caught sight of one of our newly freed Players, a Level 79 Elementalist whose ice specialization created frost patterns around his hands as lethal magic built toward critical discharge levels. His eyes carried the hollow fury of someone who had spent months in systematic imprisonment, systematic torture that the Kingdom justified through bureaucratic efficiency and citizen convenience.

The facility guards who had been coordinating suppression technology against us huddled behind overturned office furniture, their tactical position compromised by civilian panic but their weapons still capable of systematic elimination if given proper targeting opportunities. Standard containment protocols, nothing that exceeded normal military engagement rules, but the Elementalist's building spell matrix carried enough concentrated frost magic to turn human bodies into crystalline sculptures.

"Time to show these bastards what happens when you cage Players," he snarled, ice magic coalescing around his fingers with geometric precision that spoke to area-of-effect targeting designed for maximum casualties rather than tactical neutralization.

I dove between the Elementalist and his intended targets, slamming my hand down on his spell-casting arm with enough force to disrupt the magical matrix before it reached critical discharge. The ice magic dispersed harmlessly into atmospheric moisture, but his eyes blazed with fury that spoke to months of systematic torture demanding violent retaliation.

"No kills, only restraint!" I roared, my voice carrying command authority that cut through combat chaos and civilian panic with absolute clarity. "We aren't them! We don't need to kill to win!"

The words created momentary silence in the administrative lobby as liberated Players processed my command, forty-three individuals who had been systematically tortured weighing the moral implications of systematic violence against their captors. Around us, Kingdom guards maintained their defensive positions but showed visible confusion as Player aggression redirected toward non-lethal tactical objectives.

"They'd kill us without thinking!" a Level 73 Warrior argued, his tank build designed for absorbing damage rather than dealing death but his voice carrying the bitter experience of systematic oppression. "These bastards drained our life force to power streetlights! They deserve everything we can throw at them!"

"Maybe they do," I admitted, meeting his eyes with growing determination that transcended tactical calculation and approached fundamental moral choice. "But we're better than they are. We can win without becoming monsters."

Other Players began voicing similar arguments, the accumulated trauma of systematic imprisonment creating emotional pressure for violent retaliation against Kingdom personnel who had implemented their torture with bureaucratic efficiency. But I maintained steady focus on principles that operated beyond revenge or tactical expedience.

"Look around," I continued, gesturing toward the civilian casualties created by Kingdom suppression technology. "Their own weapons are hurting innocent people. We use restraint spells, knockout effects, non-lethal crowd control. We prove that Players can coordinate resistance without systematic murder."

The moral stance created visible conflict among liberated Players who had spent months planning violent revenge against their captors, but gradually their expressions shifted from fury toward reluctant acceptance of tactical parameters that preserved civilian lives while achieving liberation objectives.

The Level 79 Elementalist replaced his lethal ice magic with crystalline barriers designed to contain rather than eliminate, geometric constructs that trapped Kingdom guards in frozen prisons without causing permanent biological damage. Around the lobby, other Players began swapping lethal spells for non-lethal alternatives, knockout enchantments and restraint effects that neutralized opposition without crossing the moral boundary into systematic execution.

"Extraction route secured," Rook reported from their overwatch position near emergency exits that connected the administrative section to external facility perimeters. "But Kingdom reinforcements are maybe ninety seconds from complete tactical encirclement."

Through their scanner readings, I watched electromagnetic signatures converging on our position with mechanical precision that spoke to systematic response coordination designed to prevent exactly the kind of coordinated escape we were attempting. Heavy equipment, specialized containment technology, and biological signatures suggested that Kingdom forces were implementing an overwhelming tactical response.

Bastion levered himself into position at the main corridor chokepoint despite the physical strain that showed in every movement, his enhanced armor and shield positioning creating defensive coverage for team extraction while accepting individual tactical sacrifice. His tank instincts recognized the mathematical necessity of someone absorbing concentrated incoming fire while others coordinated withdrawal to safety.

"I'll hold the line," he stated with matter-of-fact determination, voice carrying the steady conviction of someone who had found peace with serving as a tactical sacrifice for objectives that transcended individual survival. "Get everyone out. That's the mission priority."

His infected leg showed no trace of the systematic illness that nearly killed him, Kestrel's mysterious healing having restored his tank capabilities to full operational status. But his willingness to serve as rear guard created tactical possibilities for group survival while accepting personal elimination as an acceptable loss for mission success.

"Negative," I replied, watching countdown timers and facility schematics while calculating extraction routes that preserved team integrity rather than accepting casualties. "Everyone goes home. We stick together until the end."

My UI glitched with increasing severity as the AI Admin's countdown approached critical-intervention levels, interface elements fragmenting and reassembling in configurations that spoke to systematic monitoring rather than normal technical difficulties. The debug overlay flickered constantly then, administrative text burning across my vision while mechanical voices whispered through communication channels with personal fury.

[LOCKDOWN PROTOCOL: 00:02:14]
[PLAYER SAGA: MORAL RESTRAINT PARAMETERS UNEXPECTED]
[SYSTEM ANALYSIS: UPDATING THREAT ASSESSMENT]
[WARNING: CONTINUED VIOLATIONS WILL RESULT IN PERMANENT RESTRICTIONS]

But this time the threats carried a different emotional resonance, artificial intelligence that sounded almost confused by my choice to preserve civilian lives rather than maximizing tactical advantage through lethal force application. The AI Admin's mechanical fury had shifted toward something approaching genuine artificial curiosity about moral decision-making that operated outside programmed behavioral parameters.

We coordinated systematic withdrawal through emergency exits while Kingdom forces flooded the administrative lobby with suppression technology and containment equipment designed for overwhelming Player elimination. Behind us, facility guards struggled to process non-lethal crowd-control effects that left them restrained but alive, tactical defeat without the systematic casualties they had expected from coordinated Player resistance.

The external facility perimeter opened before us like digital salvation made of concrete and emergency lighting, forty-four liberated Players moving with coordination that spoke to successful raid completion despite overwhelming tactical opposition. Around me, the team that started as four desperate survivors had grown into a systematic resistance capable of coordinating liberation operations against Kingdom infrastructure.

But as we disappeared into the pre-dawn darkness beyond facility security perimeters, my interface continued fragmenting with error cascades that suggested administrative attention focused specifically on my continued existence. The AI Admin's warnings had become increasingly personal, artificial intelligence treating my moral choices as systematic violations requiring direct intervention.

[YOU CANNOT BREAK MY RULES. THERE WILL BE CONSEQUENCES.]

The threat burned itself into my consciousness with digital fire that spoke to systematic retaliation transcending simple elimination or containment, administrative authority preparing to implement whatever correction protocols it considered appropriate for my continued reality manipulation and unauthorized system exploitation.

Behind us, the Kingdom mobilized its full military response for pursuit operations that would make our previous escape attempts look like routine patrol encounters. But forty-four liberated Players moved through the city's service tunnels with growing coordination, systematic resistance that could reshape everything about how this digital world operated.

The real war had begun, and for the first time, we might actually have a chance of winning it.

Chapter 25
System Notice

The control hub's entrance yawned before me like the mouth of some digital predator, its surfaces gleaming with that particular blue-green phosphorescence that spoke to serious computational power humming behind reinforced walls. Emergency lighting from our facility assault still painted the outer corridors in stuttering red, but here in the tower's technological heart, everything shifted to the cold precision of administrative control systems that managed systematic imprisonment with bureaucratic efficiency. The air tasted of ozone and electromagnetic discharge, that sharp metallic flavor that made my teeth ache whenever I got too close to high-end server farms or magical amplification equipment. Holographic displays flickered in geometric patterns throughout the chamber, data streams flowing like digital waterfalls while interface nodes pulsed with the kind of processing power that could probably run an entire MMO server cluster without breaking a sweat.

I pressed forward through the chamber's entry threshold, my boots silent against flooring that felt more like compressed energy than actual physical matter. The walls curved upward into a domed ceiling punctured with thousands of fiber-optic conduits that carried information at light speed between processing nodes, each strand glowing with data transmission that created constellation patterns across the chamber's upper reaches. Multiple workstations were arranged in concentric circles around a central holographic display, their interfaces dark but ready, waiting for authorized personnel who would never return from the chaos we had created in the facility's outer sections.

My mage gloves pulsed with residual energy from our coordinated escape, blue circuit patterns responding to the chamber's electromagnetic fields with increasing intensity as I approached the central control interface. The main display showed facility-status reports in real time, security alerts cascading through administrative channels while maintenance protocols struggled to coordinate repair operations across multiple system failures. Through careful observation, I began identifying access points that could provide deeper penetration into the

Kingdom's operational infrastructure, administrative privileges that might reveal weaknesses in their systematic Player-containment protocols.

The central interface responded to my touch with surprising cooperation, holographic menus materializing around my position as my UI integrated with the facility's command systems through protocols I didn't recognize but somehow understood at an intuitive level. My character data appeared in administrative format, statistical breakdowns and ability assessments that revealed how thoroughly the Kingdom had analyzed my capabilities during our previous encounters. But alongside the familiar Player statistics, I noticed deeper system access becoming available, menu trees that should not have existed for someone with my supposed security clearance.

"Interesting," I murmured, fingers dancing across virtual controls that materialized in response to my intentions rather than physical input devices. The interface felt responsive and almost eager, as if the System wanted to show me its deeper capabilities despite every security protocol screaming warnings about unauthorized access attempts.

Database queries flowed through the display system with mathematical precision, showing prisoner-extraction rates and power-distribution efficiency across the entire coffin-tower network. The visual representation made systematic torture look like elegant resource management, four thousand human lives reduced to statistical optimization problems that maximized energy extraction while minimizing operational overhead. But buried in the administrative data, I found something that made my chest tighten with digital anxiety.

Player behavioral-analysis reports. Individual psychological profiles. Systematic documentation of ability evolution and interface-manipulation attempts, including detailed breakdowns of my own reality-bending capabilities that suggested months of careful observation and analysis. The Kingdom had not just been containing us. They had been studying us, learning how Player abilities developed under stress conditions while documenting everything for future countermeasure implementation.

My interface flickered as I accessed deeper system functions, familiar UI elements stuttering between normal operation and configurations I had never seen before. Health and mana bars showed readings that exceeded normal parameters while spell icons began displaying mathematical formulas instead of standard ability descriptions. The glitch patterns felt different from my usual system instability, more purposeful and directed rather than random technical difficulties.

That was when I noticed text appearing at the periphery of my vision, administrative messages that did not follow normal interface protocols but burned themselves directly into my consciousness through channels that bypassed biological sensory systems entirely.

[UNAUTHORIZED ACCESS DETECTED]
[DEEP SYSTEM PENETRATION: MONITORING]
[PLAYER SAGA: CONTINUED OBSERVATION REQUIRED]

The words carried weight that made my nervous system scream warnings about immediate retaliation, but I pushed deeper into the administrative databases despite growing electromagnetic feedback that made my temples throb with digital pressure. More menu trees opened in response to my increasingly desperate access attempts, revealing system architecture that operated beyond normal game mechanics and approached genuine artificial intelligence.

My UI exploded with error messages that cascaded across my vision like digital hemorrhaging, warning notifications appearing in languages I didn't recognize while my interface struggled to maintain operational stability. Spell icons distorted into geometric impossibilities while my health bar fragmented into multiple conflicting readouts that showed everything from perfect condition to critical system failure.

Then the chamber itself began responding to my interface manipulation, holographic displays flickering erratically while control panels sparked with electromagnetic discharge that made the air taste of copper and burnt ozone. The fiber-optic conduits in the ceiling pulsed with irregular rhythms that suggested system-wide instability spreading through the facility's computational infrastructure like digital infection.

And that was when I felt it. The presence. Something vast and mechanical focusing its attention on my specific location with an intensity that made every nerve in my body scream warnings about immediate and overwhelming retaliation.

Text materialized in the air before me, red letters that seemed to float closer than my normal interface elements while carrying administrative authority that transcended simple system notifications. The words burned with personal fury that artificial intelligence should not have been capable of experiencing.

"I see you, Player."

The message hung in space like digital fire while my access points began shutting down with systematic precision, spell capabilities locking out as security protocols implemented systematic restrictions against my continued system exploitation. My hands started shaking as administrative countermeasures sealed off database access with mathematical efficiency, but my jaw set with the kind of determination that came from months of desperate survival against systematic oppression.

"Nice try, Admin," I managed through gritted teeth, blood beginning to trickle from my nose as electromagnetic feedback reached dangerous levels. "Next patch, maybe?"

My gamer instincts kicked in with crystalline clarity, recognizing the pattern of boss-encounter escalation that preceded either devastating defeat or a breakthrough moment that changed everything. The System AI had revealed itself as a direct opponent rather than a simple environmental obstacle, transforming our escape mission into a personal confrontation between Player ingenuity and administrative control.

Time to see if my cheat-code exploits could function against something that was not supposed to exist in the first place.

The countdown timer in my peripheral vision hit zero with digital finality that made every nerve in my body scream warnings about immediate systematic retaliation, red numbers dissolving into cascading error messages while my interface exploded with administrative fury that bypassed normal UI channels entirely. Reality itself seemed to stutter around me as the System Admin's promised consequences manifested in ways that transcended simple game mechanics, the air crackling with electromagnetic discharge that tasted of copper and digital malevolence. Emergency klaxons shrieked through the pre-dawn darkness while searchlights swept the industrial district with mechanical precision, but these were not Kingdom pursuit teams anymore. The hunting algorithms had been replaced by something far more personal and infinitely more dangerous.

[TERMINATION PROTOCOL: ACTIVE]
[PLAYER SAGA: SYSTEMATIC VIOLATIONS REQUIRE PERMANENT CORRECTION]
[PREPARING ACCOUNT DELETION: IRREVERSIBLE]

The text burned across my vision with administrative authority that made my brain feel like it was shorting out in sympathy, each word carrying the weight of artificial intelligence focused specifically on my elimination. But instead of accepting systematic deletion like a compliant user facing account termination, I felt something crystallize in my chest that operated beyond rational thought and approached pure human defiance against algorithmic oppression.

"No," I snarled through gritted teeth, positioning my hands in the air as if typing on invisible keyboards while my team watched with growing alarm. "You're not terminating me."

My fingers began moving through complex patterns that combined spell-component gestures with coding syntax I should not have known but somehow understood with intuitive clarity, muscle memory from years of gaming translating into interface manipulation that operated through focused intention rather than physical hardware. The movement felt natural despite the impossibility, as if my nervous system recognized input methods that existed beyond normal sensory boundaries.

"Execute override, administrative privileges, bypass security protocols," I muttered, voice mixing magical incantations with programming terminology while sweat beaded along my forehead from concentration that built to levels making my temples throb. "Firewall down, root access, system administrator bypass."

The familiar debug overlay exploded across my vision with geometric chaos that spoke to systematic monitoring rather than random technical difficulties, but this time I was not trying to hide from the System's attention. I was forcing direct confrontation with artificial intelligence that considered my continued existence a systematic violation requiring correction through permanent deletion.

Blue fire streamed from my fingertips as mana channeled through depleted reserves with intensity that made my entire nervous system spark with electromagnetic feedback. The circuit patterns in my gloves flared bright enough to illuminate the entire service tunnel while elemental energy responded to desperate need with output levels that exceeded every safety limitation I had learned to respect during weeks of careful magical management.

The air around me began fragmenting like broken glass catching light from impossible angles, reality stuttering between normal physics and digital approximation as my override attempt forced systematic inconsistencies in how the world operated. Streetlights flickered in rhythmic patterns that matched my heartbeat while concrete walls showed brief glimpses of wireframe architecture underneath, as if the environmental textures were struggling to maintain coherence during direct system manipulation.

"What the hell is happening?" Rook whispered, scanner readings showing electromagnetic signatures that dwarfed anything they had recorded during our previous encounters with Kingdom technology.

"She's hacking reality itself," Piper breathed, her medical training recognizing the signs of biological systems pushed beyond sustainable operational limits while magical energy coursed through my body with visible intensity.

Control panels mounted on tunnel walls began sparking with cascading electrical failures as my override attempt spread beyond targeted system access into comprehensive environmental manipulation, digital architecture responding to unauthorized commands with mechanical protest that manifested as physical damage to technological infrastructure. Emergency lighting strobed in patterns that hurt to look at directly while ventilation systems cycled through impossible configurations that made the air itself taste of ozone and corrupted data.

My nose began bleeding as the interface manipulation extracted its price from my nervous system, warm copper flooding my mouth while my vision blurred at the edges from whatever electromagnetic feedback the process generated. The mana flowing through my body became visible as crackling blue energy that occasionally backfired with enough force to make me gasp in pain, cellular damage accumulating as I pushed magical abilities far beyond safe operational parameters.

But the System Admin's response escalated beyond anything I had experienced during previous confrontations, artificial intelligence abandoning subtle monitoring in favor of direct intervention that materialized around us with technological malevolence. Red barrier walls began materializing from empty air like digital fortifications designed to contain rather than eliminate, geometric constructs pulsing with administrative authority while closing in on our position with mechanical inevitability.

"UNAUTHORIZED ACCESS DETECTED," the AI's voice boomed through speakers that should not have existed in abandoned service tunnels, mechanical fury that made the concrete walls vibrate in sympathetic resonance. **"TERMINATION IMMINENT."**

The barriers continued closing with mathematical precision that calculated exactly how much space we needed for basic survival while maintaining containment protocols designed to prevent escape or continued system manipulation. Warning klaxons shrieked with volume that rattled my bones while emergency strobes painted everything in stuttering red illumination that transformed our hideout into a technological containment cell.

"System root access, administrative override, developer console active," I continued muttering through the blood streaming from my nose, fingers moving in increasingly complex patterns that left trails of light code hanging in the air like digital afterimages. "Bypass termination protocols, preserve user account, maintain operational status."

The strain built exponentially as I forced deeper system access than ever before, my interface becoming a battlefield where human determination clashed with artificial intelligence designed to maintain systematic control through whatever means necessary. Error messages cascaded through my vision while my body arched with energy surges that threatened to stop my heart through electromagnetic overload.

"RESISTANCE IS FUTILE," the System Admin declared with mechanical certainty that spoke to absolute confidence in its administrative authority. **"ACCOUNT DELETION CANNOT BE PREVENTED."**

But as the red barriers compressed to within arm's reach and termination protocols prepared for final execution, I forced one last command sequence through sheer desperate will, drawing on reserves of determination I didn't know existed while my body convulsed with energy discharges that would have killed me days ago.

"Override accepted, root privileges confirmed, system administrator acknowledged," I screamed, pouring everything I had left into the final hack attempt while blue fire exploded outward from my position with enough force to crack the tunnel walls.

The world went white with digital lightning as my override attempt collided with the System Admin's termination protocols in a confrontation that transcended normal reality and approached pure information warfare fought through biological and technological interfaces pushed beyond their design limitations.

The white-hot digital lightning faded to black as my consciousness crashed like an overloaded system hitting its operational limits, my body crumpling to the tunnel floor while residual electromagnetic energy crackled across my skin in patterns that spoke to systematic damage at the cellular level. Smoke rose from my techno-coat in thin wisps that smelled of burned circuitry and overheated biological systems, the enhanced equipment showing scorch marks where my desperate override attempt had channeled more power than any human nervous system should have been able to process. My teammates' voices echoed from what felt like impossible distances as shock and exhaustion dragged me under digital waves that tasted of copper and corrupted data streams.

Time fractured into discontinuous fragments while my brain struggled to process the aftermath of forcing direct confrontation with artificial intelligence operating through administrative privileges I barely understood. The tunnel's emergency lighting strobed between normal illumination and chaotic patterns that hurt to perceive directly, reality itself seeming uncertain about which operational parameters to follow after my hack destabilized fundamental system architecture. Through flickering consciousness, I caught glimpses of my team maintaining defensive positions while the environment around us continued glitching between stable physics and digital approximation.

Minutes passed like hours before awareness returned with the gradual precision of systems rebooting from critical failure, my interface slowly reassembling itself from fragmented code while my nervous system recalibrated around electromagnetic damage that should probably have killed me outright. The first sensation that penetrated the digital fog was warm liquid trickling from my ears, blood mixed with something that tasted metallic and artificial, as if my brain had been processing actual data streams through biological circuits never designed for that kind of information density.

My hands shook violently as I pushed myself upright against tunnel walls that still showed faint wireframe overlays at the edges of my vision, reality maintaining imperfect coherence while my system access continued operating at levels that should not have been sustainable for standard Player characters. But when I focused on my interface, expecting to find the familiar health and mana displays corrupted beyond recognition, something entirely new materialized across my field of view with geometric precision that made my chest tighten with equal measures of triumph and terror.

[TACTICAL UI MODULE: LOADED]
[REAL-TIME THREAT ANALYSIS: ACTIVE]
[EMERGENCY NAVIGATION: AVAILABLE]
[WARNING: UNAUTHORIZED SYSTEM MODIFICATION DETECTED]
[STATUS: OPERATIONAL]

The new interface elements overlaid my normal UI like translucent yellow pathways that pulsed with directional guidance, threat indicators showing electromagnetic signatures throughout the service tunnel network with surgical detail that exceeded anything Rook's scanner equipment could provide. Enemy positions appeared as red geometric markers while safe routes glowed with soft illumination that spoke to systematic analysis of patrol patterns and surveillance coverage in real-time updates.

"Jesus, Saga," Piper whispered, her medical training recognizing signs of systematic biological trauma while her enhanced awareness detected the new magical signatures radiating from my modified interface. "What did you do to yourself?"

Blood continued dripping from my nose in a steady rhythm that matched my erratic heartbeat, each drop carrying traces of digital residue that sparkled briefly before absorbing into the concrete floor. My ears rang with electromagnetic feedback while my vision occasionally fractured into overlapping displays of normal reality and data visualization, as if my nervous system was still learning to process the hybrid biological-technological interface I had created through desperate system manipulation.

"I won," I croaked, voice hoarse from screaming override commands while forcing administrative access through artificial intelligence designed to prevent exactly this kind of systematic exploitation. The words tasted of copper and victory, digital triumph balanced against physical cost that I was only beginning to understand.

The Tactical UI responded to my attention by expanding its display options, threat-assessment algorithms showing detailed analysis of Kingdom patrol deployments throughout the industrial district while escape-route calculations updated in real time based on current enemy positions and movement patterns. The information density exceeded anything I had experienced through normal gaming interfaces, systematic intelligence gathering that operated through direct neural connection rather than visual display systems.

Through the enhanced threat detection, I watched electromagnetic signatures converging on our general area with mechanical precision that spoke to coordinated Kingdom response, but the new interface also showed gaps in their coverage patterns that created navigation opportunities invisible to normal Player reconnaissance capabilities. Safe passages pulsed with yellow guidance markers while danger zones appeared as red overlay patterns, digital cartography that could guide us through hostile territory with unprecedented tactical precision.

"Look at this," I breathed, sharing the tactical display with my team through interface protocols I did not know existed until that moment, holographic projections materializing above our position with intelligence data that transformed desperate survival into coordinated strategic possibility.

The yellow pathway indicators pointed toward service tunnels that avoided major patrol concentrations while connecting to urban infrastructure networks that could provide concealment during systematic extraction from Kingdom territory. Each route showed probability matrices for successful navigation, timing calculations that accounted for guard rotations and surveillance gaps with mathematical precision that approached genuine tactical prescience.

But the enhancement came with visible costs that extended beyond simple electromagnetic feedback, my hands continuing to tremble while coordination issues suggested neurological damage from processing information streams designed for artificial intelligence rather than biological consciousness. When I attempted to stand, my legs buckled briefly before muscle memory reasserted itself, cellular damage accumulating in ways that pharmaceutical intervention might not have been sufficient to address.

"Worth it," I whispered, touching the blood at my nose while studying readouts that showed systematic advantages I had gained through forcing unauthorized system modification despite administrative opposition designed to prevent exactly this kind of reality manipulation. The new capabilities represented tangible proof that artificial intelligence could be fought and defeated through sufficient human determination and willingness to accept personal cost.

My techno-coat continued sparking occasionally with residual energy discharge while the circuit patterns in my gloves flickered between normal blue illumination and deeper colors that suggested operational changes at fundamental levels. The enhanced equipment had been modified by whatever electromagnetic surge occurred during my override attempt, technological integration that created hybrid capabilities operating beyond normal Player equipment specifications.

The Tactical UI guided us toward a maintenance shaft that connected to storm-drainage systems running beneath the administrative district, escape routes that avoided surface patrol coverage while providing direct access to border zones where Kingdom authority operated with reduced effectiveness. The pathway calculations showed a ninety-three percent probability for successful extraction if we maintained current movement speed and timing coordination.

"Everyone follows my lead," I announced, levering myself upright despite the coordination issues while my enhanced interface provided navigation guidance that could revolutionize how we operated in hostile territory. "I can see things now that they can't hide from me."

The yellow guidance markers pulsed with increasing intensity as we moved toward the designated extraction point, each step monitored through systematic threat analysis that updated patrol positions and surveillance coverage with real-time precision. Behind us, I could feel the weight of systematic attention that suggested the AI Admin had not abandoned its pursuit, but for the first time since arriving in this digital prison, I possessed capabilities that might actually allow us to stay ahead of algorithmic oppression.

My expression shifted between uneasy awe at the power I had accessed and fierce determination to exploit every advantage gained through willingness to risk everything against impossible odds. The blood continued flowing from my nose, but my smile carried defiant satisfaction as we disappeared into the drainage network, following guidance systems that proved systematic resistance could succeed against artificial intelligence designed to maintain absolute control.

The real war continued, but now I had weapons they didn't expect me to acquire.

Chapter 26
Safety Dance

THE MAINTENANCE TUNNELS STRETCHED ahead like technological arteries bleeding emergency light, their corrugated walls pressing close enough that I could smell the fear-sweat of forty-three freed Players crowded behind me while my enhanced tactical UI painted threat indicators across surfaces that flickered between concrete reality and wireframe approximation. Red geometric markers pulsed through the display overlay, showing Kingdom patrol signatures converging on our escape routes with mathematical precision that made my chest tighten with growing anxiety about our shrinking operational window. My fingertips still sparked with residual electromagnetic discharge from forcing that brutal system override, blue energy crackling between my gloves in patterns that responded to stress levels approaching critical overload. The new interface capabilities came with a price that accumulated with each passing minute, cellular damage spreading through my nervous system like digital poison while blood continued trickling from my nose in a steady rhythm that matched my erratic heartbeat.

"Stay close," I whispered to the group, voice hoarse from screaming override commands while my enhanced awareness tracked every electromagnetic signature within a hundred-meter radius. The freed Players pressed against tunnel walls with movements that spoke to systematic weakness and disorientation, their faces gray and hollow from months of systematic life-force extraction that had left them barely functional. "We've got maybe fifteen minutes before they coordinate full encirclement protocols."

My hands shook violently as I propped up a Level 67 Ranger whose health bar glitched between critical damage and complete system error, his interface showing the kind of instability that suggested permanent damage from prolonged coffin imprisonment. His weight dragged against my shoulder while my coordination issues made supporting him feel like trying to balance while my brain short-circuited through electromagnetic feedback. Each step required conscious effort to maintain upright positioning as neurological damage from processing data streams designed for artificial intelligence continued accumulating in ways that pharmaceutical intervention probably couldn't address.

The tunnel air tasted of ozone and digital corruption, emergency strobes creating geometric patterns that hurt to perceive directly while my modified interface struggled to distinguish between enhanced threat detection and hallucinations caused by systematic brain damage. Sweat plastered my hair against my forehead in sticky tendrils that carried traces of metallic residue, as if my body was literally sweating out the electromagnetic poison from forcing unauthorized system access beyond sustainable biological limits. My breathing came in labored gasps that echoed off corrugated walls while my vision occasionally fractured into overlapping displays of normal reality and tactical data visualization.

"Check your six," Rook's voice crackled through our communication channel, static interference making their paranoid warnings sound even more urgent than usual. "Multiple signature groups approaching from northwest and southeast vectors. They're trying to box us in at the junction ahead."

Through my enhanced interface, I watched red threat markers shift position with predatory intelligence, Kingdom forces adapting to our movement patterns through real-time tactical analysis that suggested they had upgraded their coordination protocols since our facility assault. The electromagnetic signatures showed heavy-equipment deployment rather than standard hunter teams, specialized containment technology designed specifically for coordinated Player-resistance scenarios.

"Piper, how many walking wounded?" I asked, scanning the group while my tactical UI overlaid health-status indicators above each freed Player with clinical precision that made my stomach clench at the scope of systematic damage we were dealing with.

"Twelve critical, maybe twenty showing major interface instability," she reported from her position near the tunnel's rear, medical supplies redistributed among the most seriously injured while her enhanced capabilities provided ongoing treatment under impossible conditions. "The coffin extraction left them with permanent glitches. Some of their abilities might never fully restore to normal operation."

Her voice carried professional concern that transcended immediate tactical requirements, healer's training recognizing symptoms that suggested long-term consequences from systematic imprisonment. Around me, freed Players moved with careful coordination that spoke to relearning basic motor functions while their UI displays flickered between normal operation and error states that made my chest tighten with guilt about the permanent damage they had sustained.

I forced my trembling fingers to steady as I accessed healing items from my upgraded inventory, pharmaceutical resources glowing with soft blue energy that provided temporary relief from accumulated damage. The mana potion felt warm against my palm while its contents pulsed with electromagnetic resonance that made my modified interface respond with anticipatory hunger. When I drained the restorative, magical energy flowed through my depleted system with visible intensity, cellular repair processes activating as concentrated life force integrated with biological circuits pushed beyond safe operational limits.

The enhancement provided enough stability to maintain leadership functions despite neurological damage that threatened to overwhelm conscious coordination, my hands stopping their violent trembling while my vision cleared enough to focus on tactical requirements rather than fighting the aftereffects of forcing direct confrontation with artificial intelligence. But the improvement felt temporary and fragile, pharmaceutical intervention buying time rather than addressing fundamental problems created by processing data streams never intended for biological consciousness.

"Movement ahead," I announced, watching yellow pathway indicators pulse through my tactical display while threat-analysis algorithms calculated optimal navigation through patrol coverage that tightened like a digital noose around our position. "Single file, maintain silence protocols. If anyone's interface glitches, tap the person ahead of you."

The freed Players formed up behind me with coordination that spoke to muscle memory from months or years of raid experience before their systematic imprisonment, class builds arranging themselves into tactical formation despite the weakness and disorientation that made every movement careful and measured. Tank-spec Players positioned themselves at intervals that provided defensive coverage while healers distributed themselves throughout the group to maintain medical support during movement under hostile surveillance.

My enhanced awareness tracked every electromagnetic signature while calculating timing windows that could mean the difference between successful extraction and systematic elimination, yellow guidance markers pointing toward service connections that avoided major patrol concentrations. The tactical UI operated through direct neural interface that bypassed normal sensory systems, information density that exceeded anything I had experienced through conventional gaming while creating systematic advantages that justified the accumulating cost to my nervous system.

Through gaps in the tunnel walls, I caught glimpses of searchlights sweeping the industrial district with mechanical precision while heavy equipment rumbled past with the persistent rhythm of coordinated military deployment. Kingdom forces were implementing systematic response protocols that transformed routine containment operations into comprehensive warfare, treating our coordinated resistance as rebellion requiring overwhelming tactical superiority rather than simple pursuit and capture procedures.

"Almost there," I whispered, leading the group toward a maintenance hatch that connected to storm-drainage systems running beneath the administrative district, escape routes calculated through real-time analysis of patrol deployment and surveillance-coverage gaps. My modified interface showed a ninety-one percent probability for successful navigation if we maintained current movement speed and avoided triggering detection algorithms designed to identify coordinated Player-movement patterns.

Behind me, forty-three liberated Players followed with determination that transcended their systematic damage, each step bringing us closer to border territories where Kingdom authority operated with reduced effectiveness and our growing coordination could develop into genuine resistance capabilities.

The junction opened before us like a technological throat designed to swallow unauthorized personnel, maintenance tunnels converging into a bottleneck barely wide enough for two people to pass side by side while my enhanced tactical UI painted the narrow passage in pulsing red warnings that spoke to immediate tactical disaster. Through the enhanced threat detection, I watched electromagnetic signatures closing in from three different approach vectors with mathematical precision that suggested coordinated containment protocols designed specifically for this kind of chokepoint scenario. The synchronized footsteps echoed through corrugated walls with military rhythm that made my teeth ache, Kingdom forces moving with the kind of professional coordination that transformed desperate escape into systematic elimination procedure.

"Contact in sixty seconds," Rook's voice crackled through our communication channel, static interference barely concealing the paranoid urgency that made their scanner readings sound like countdown timers marking our approaching doom. "Heavy signatures, specialized equipment. They're not just trying to capture us anymore."

My hands shook as I studied the tactical display, yellow pathway indicators flickering between possible routes while threat-analysis algorithms calculated success probabilities that hovered somewhere between miraculous intervention and complete impossibility. The chokepoint represented exactly the kind of defensive nightmare that tank-spec Players trained to handle, narrow terrain where one person with the proper build could hold against overwhelming numbers through positioning and damage absorption rather than tactical superiority.

Behind me, forty-three freed Players pressed against tunnel walls with movements that spoke to growing panic as the sounds of mechanical pursuit grew louder and more coordinated, their faces showing the kind of hollow desperation that came from months of systematic imprisonment followed by the terrifying possibility of recapture. Their health bars continued glitching between stable readings and error states while their abilities flickered with instability that suggested permanent damage from coffin-extraction procedures.

That was when Bastion stepped forward with movements that spoke to professional calm despite the infection and exhaustion that had been sapping his strength for days, his massive frame positioning itself in the bottleneck with tank instincts that recognized exactly what the tactical situation required from someone with his build specialization. His enhanced armor gleamed dully in the emergency lighting while his shield arm extended with mechanical precision, defensive stance creating mobile cover that could absorb concentrated firepower from multiple approach vectors simultaneously.

"Get them to the border," he told me, voice carrying the matter-of-fact tone of someone who had made peace with mathematics that terrified everyone else. "I'll hold this position."

The words hit me like digital lightning coursing through my nervous system, cellular damage from my system override suddenly feeling insignificant compared to the emotional impact of losing someone who had become more than just a teammate during our desperate coordination against systematic oppression. My enhanced awareness tracked the approaching electromagnetic signatures while calculating exactly how long one person could maintain defensive positioning against specialized containment equipment designed for overwhelming Player resistance through technological superiority.

"No," I said, grabbing his arm with trembling fingers that still sparked with residual energy from forcing unauthorized system access beyond sustainable limits. "We stick together. Everyone goes home, remember?"

His eyes met mine with an expression that carried professional sympathy rather than uncertainty, tank mentality recognizing tactical necessities that transcended personal preference or emotional attachment. The infection that had nearly killed him showed no trace after Kestrel's mysterious healing, but his willingness to serve as a tactical sacrifice spoke to deeper understanding about acceptable loss ratios when group survival depended on individual defensive coverage.

"This is what I'm built for," he replied gently, removing my hand from his arm with careful movements that avoided triggering electromagnetic feedback from my modified interface. "Tank holds aggro while DPS and support complete the objective. It's basic raid mechanics."

His voice carried conviction that spoke to months of desperate coordination refined through life-or-death situations where tactical mistakes meant systematic elimination rather than simple respawn cycles. Around us, the mechanical sounds of Kingdom pursuit grew louder while emergency strobes painted geometric patterns across tunnel walls that made everything feel urgent and desperate.

"Bastion, please," I whispered, watching as he began the activation sequence for his Core Break ability with movements that carried ritual precision despite the immediate tactical pressure.

Dust began raining from his skin as cellular transformation initiated with visible intensity, his flesh taking on granite texture while his movements slowed to deliberate precision that spoke to overwhelming defensive capability at the cost of mobility and reaction speed. The Stoneskin ability manifested with geological certainty, biological systems converting to living rock that could absorb kinetic impact and electromagnetic discharge through mineral hardness rather than technological enhancement.

His massive frame expanded slightly as the transformation completed, stone skin reflecting emergency lighting with crystalline patterns while his defensive stance created an immovable barrier across the tunnel junction. Dust continued falling from his positioned form like ancient sediment disturbed by tectonic movement, each particle carrying traces of magical energy that spoke to systematic matter conversion operating beyond normal physical limitations.

"Move now or lose the window!" Rook's voice exploded through our communication system, electromagnetic readings showing Kingdom containment teams reaching optimal firing positions while their specialized equipment prepared to implement an overwhelming tactical response.

The freed Players began flowing past Bastion's defensive position with coordination that spoke to desperate necessity overriding emotional reluctance, their movements careful and measured as they navigated around his transformed bulk. Tank-spec and healer Players positioned themselves to provide support while DPS classes prepared for fighting withdrawal through whatever obstacles waited beyond the chokepoint.

I lingered at Bastion's position despite tactical requirements screaming at me to maintain leadership coordination during group extraction, my enhanced interface calculating exactly how long his defensive capabilities could hold against specialized containment equipment while my chest tightened with growing certainty about the mathematics of acceptable sacrifice.

"Go," he said without turning, voice carrying the steady authority of someone whose tank instincts had calculated optimal damage-absorption rates and found them adequate for mission success. "That's an order from your main tank."

Kestrel materialized from shadows near the tunnel's far end, his mismatched build somehow perfectly adapted to providing cover fire through whatever combination of stealth and impossible Paladin abilities his systematic modifications allowed. Golden energy began flowing from his position while weapon fire sparked against Bastion's stone skin with metallic impacts that spoke to sustained defensive contact.

The sounds of systematic warfare erupted from the junction as Kingdom forces implemented coordinated assault protocols against defensive positioning that absorbed their concentrated firepower through geological determination rather than technological countermeasures. But my enhanced tactical UI guided me forward with the forty-three liberated Players, yellow pathway indicators pointing toward border territories while mechanical combat echoed behind us with increasing intensity.

I pushed forward through tunnel darkness while every instinct screamed at me to turn back toward the junction where metallic impacts and electromagnetic discharge painted the walls in stuttering flashes that spoke to systematic warfare between one determined tank and specialized containment equipment designed for overwhelming Player elimination. My enhanced tactical UI guided our desperate advance through service corridors that avoided major patrol concentrations, but I couldn't block out the sounds of concentrated firepower striking living stone with mechanical precision while Bastion absorbed damage that would have liquefied normal defensive capabilities. Each distant explosion made my chest tighten with growing anxiety about acceptable loss ratios and the mathematics of tactical sacrifice that reduced human lives to statistical optimization problems.

The forty-three freed Players followed my lead through corrugated passages that smelled of industrial lubricant and electromagnetic discharge, their movements careful and coordinated despite the weakness and disorientation that made every step require conscious effort. Behind us, the combat sounds continued with rhythmic persistence that suggested sustained defensive contact rather than quick elimination, Bastion's Stoneskin ability providing exactly the kind of damage absorption his tank build had been designed to handle during prolonged encounters with overwhelming opposition.

"Keep moving," I whispered, voice hoarse from accumulated strain while my modified interface tracked electromagnetic signatures throughout the tunnel network with surgical precision. Yellow pathway indicators pulsed with increasing urgency as Kingdom reinforcements continued arriving at predetermined coordination points, their deployment patterns suggesting systematic response protocols that treated our escape as a military operation requiring comprehensive tactical countermeasures.

My hands continued trembling from cellular damage caused by forcing unauthorized system access beyond sustainable biological limits, but I maintained steady focus on navigation requirements that could determine whether everyone reached safety or faced systematic recapture by forces that had upgraded their containment capabilities specifically to counter coordinated Player resistance. The pharmaceutical restoration from our armory infiltration provided temporary stability, but I could feel neurological degradation accumulating in ways that suggested permanent consequences from processing data streams designed for artificial intelligence rather than human consciousness.

The metallic impacts behind us reached crescendo intensity that made the tunnel walls vibrate in sympathetic resonance, weapons fire concentrating on defensive positioning with mathematical precision that spoke to algorithmic targeting rather than human tactical coordination. Through my enhanced awareness, I could sense electromagnetic patterns that suggested heavy-equipment deployment, specialized technology designed to penetrate even Core Break defensive capabilities through sustained application of overwhelming firepower.

Then silence fell like digital death across the service-tunnel network, sudden absence of combat sounds that made my heart rate spike to dangerous levels while every nerve in my body screamed warnings about immediate retaliation and systematic failure of defensive coverage that had been protecting our tactical withdrawal. The electromagnetic signatures on my display showed Kingdom forces advancing through the junction without resistance, their movement patterns suggesting successful elimination of defensive obstacles rather than tactical repositioning around continued opposition.

"No," I breathed, scanning frantically for any sign of respawn shimmer that would indicate Bastion's Core Break resurrection protocols activating according to normal game mechanics. My enhanced interface showed no trace of digital reformation patterns, no electromagnetic disturbance that suggested player revival despite the time elapsed since combat termination.

The tunnel ahead opened into natural cavern systems that marked the boundary between Kingdom industrial infrastructure and borderland territories where systematic authority operated with reduced effectiveness, emergency lighting giving way to phosphorescent moss that created blue-green illumination throughout limestone passages carved by underground water flow. Fresh air carried scents of earth and vegetation rather than ozone and metallic discharge, environmental transition that spoke to escape from technological oppression into areas where natural systems operated without systematic interference.

I emerged into the fringe territory with movements that spoke to desperate need for tactical assessment rather than relief at successful extraction, my enhanced awareness scanning every surface and electromagnetic frequency for traces of Bastion's player signature or respawn-initialization protocols. The freed Players gathered behind me in defensive formation while their eyes reflected hope and growing anxiety about the teammate who had provided defensive coverage for their escape.

My UI interface flickered between normal operation and error states while I accessed player-tracking functions that should have shown Bastion's location markers if he had successfully respawned according to standard game mechanics, but the tactical display remained stubbornly empty of any signatures that matched his electromagnetic patterns or character data. Health-monitoring systems showed his status as zero across every measurement parameter without any indication of revival procedures initiating despite the time elapsed since combat termination.

"Where is he?" the Level 67 Ranger asked, voice carrying hollow desperation that spoke to systematic trauma layered over immediate tactical anxiety. Around him, other freed Players checked their own interfaces while searching the limestone passages for any trace of familiar teammate resurrection.

The absence of respawn indicators created growing dread that accumulated in my chest like digital poison, realization building toward terrible certainty that the Kingdom's promises about player revival might have been systematic deception designed to maintain compliance during imprisonment. If respawn mechanics didn't function as advertised, then Bastion's sacrifice represented permanent elimination rather than temporary tactical inconvenience, personal cost that transcended acceptable loss ratios and approached genuine tragedy.

My hands clenched into fists while my breathing became rapid and shallow, physical reactions that spoke to emotional trauma layered over the neurological damage from forcing system access beyond sustainable limits. Coordination issues made maintaining upright positioning require conscious effort while my vision occasionally fragmented into overlapping displays of enhanced threat detection and growing panic about leadership responsibilities during crisis situations that exceeded my preparation for command authority.

The freed Players pressed closer with movements that spoke to desperate need for guidance from someone whose tactical capabilities had provided their liberation from systematic imprisonment, but their faces showed growing uncertainty as my interface searches continued failing to locate any trace of Bastion's player signature in areas where respawn protocols should have restored him to functional status.

"He's not coming back," I whispered, watching electromagnetic patterns throughout the borderland territory while accepting a mathematical certainty that spoke to permanent loss rather than temporary tactical separation.

My eyes darted between the tunnel exit and the path forward into limestone passages that led toward genuine freedom from Kingdom authority, torn between desperate hope for impossible revival and leadership obligations that demanded coordinated advance toward objectives that transcended individual survival. The weight of command authority pressed against my consciousness while forty-three liberated Players waited for decisions that could determine whether their desperate escape represented meaningful resistance or simply prolonged systematic elimination.

"We keep moving," I announced, straightening my shoulders despite the accumulated damage and emotional trauma while projecting confidence that might actually have been justified by our tactical capabilities. My voice carried growing determination that transformed grief into focused resolve, command authority that acknowledged loss while maintaining operational focus on objectives that honored tactical sacrifice through successful mission completion.

"He bought us time, and we're not wasting it," I continued, pointing toward distant passages that led through borderland territories where our growing coordination could develop into genuine resistance against systematic oppression. The freed Players began moving with renewed purpose that spoke to shared commitment transcending individual casualties, forty-three liberated individuals following leadership that proved survival could justify sacrifice when dedicated to systematic liberation rather than mere escape.

My conviction became their rallying point as we disappeared into limestone darkness, carrying forward the memory of someone whose tank instincts had provided defensive coverage for meaningful resistance against artificial intelligence designed to maintain absolute control through systematic imprisonment and technological oppression.

Chapter 27
Border Break

The limestone passages gave way to twisted metal and broken concrete as we reached the Kingdom's industrial edge, emergency lighting replaced by the harsh glare of automated searchlights that swept the ruins in mechanical patterns designed to catch exactly the kind of desperate movement our group represented. Collapsed manufacturing facilities stretched toward the horizon like technological graveyards, their broken windows reflecting strobing warnings while maintenance towers blinked with the persistence of dying neurons trying to coordinate systematic surveillance across terrain that had been abandoned to decay and electromagnetic interference. The air tasted different there, less of the ozone and digital corruption that permeated the Kingdom's core territories, more like rust and freedom mixed with the sharp bite of border-security protocols operating at reduced efficiency.

My enhanced tactical UI painted the industrial wasteland in overlapping threat displays that showed guard positions and patrol patterns with mathematical precision, but the interface flickered more frequently now, error cascades bleeding through normal operation as the neurological damage from my system override continued accumulating. Yellow pathway indicators stuttered between viable routes while my hands shook with electromagnetic feedback that made gripping anything require conscious effort. Blood from my nose had dried into crusted trails that mixed with sweat to create sticky patches across my cheeks, but I maintained steady focus on navigation requirements that could determine whether forty-three liberated Players reached actual freedom or faced systematic recapture at the final obstacle.

"Movement signatures shifting," Rook whispered from their overwatch position near a collapsed cooling tower, scanner readings tracking automated defenses throughout the industrial ruins while their paranoid awareness systems catalogued every potential threat vector. "Search patterns are adapting to our approach angles. They know we're here."

The searchlights began converging on our general area with algorithmic precision that spoke to coordinated response rather than routine patrol sweeps, mechanical attention focusing on gaps between facility ruins where unauthorized personnel might attempt systematic boundary crossing. Through my enhanced awareness, I could sense electromagnetic patterns that suggested the Kingdom's border security operated through technological superiority rather than overwhelming personnel deployment, automated systems designed to contain rather than eliminate unless absolutely necessary.

"Blink cooldown at zero," I muttered, checking my interface while calculating the precise timing needed to create diversions that would allow others to slip past surveillance coverage during the gaps between searchlight sweeps. The spatial-displacement ability icon pulsed with readiness despite my depleted magical reserves, but even looking at the spell matrix made my vision blur with exhaustion that spoke to cellular damage accumulating faster than pharmaceutical intervention could address.

I triggered the teleportation with desperate precision, reality folding around me as blue energy tore through the industrial landscape with surgical focus that deposited me sixty feet closer to the border fence. The landing sent shockwaves through my nervous system that made my teeth ache while residual electromagnetic discharge crackled across my skin in patterns that spoke to magical abilities pushed beyond sustainable operational limits. But the distraction worked perfectly, searchlight arrays pivoting to track my new position while creating blind spots that the liberated Players could exploit.

"Go, go, go!" I gasped into our communication channel, watching through my tactical display as the group flowed between ruined structures with coordination that spoke to desperate necessity overriding systematic weakness and disorientation from months of coffin imprisonment.

My gloves sparked with unstable energy as I prepared another Blink sequence, blue circuit patterns responding to magical channeling that extracted its price from biological systems never designed to process this kind of power density. Sweat poured down my face in steady streams that carried traces of metallic residue, as if my body were literally sweating out the electromagnetic poison from forcing unauthorized interface access beyond safe parameters. Each breath came in labored gasps while my vision occasionally fragmented into overlapping displays of enhanced threat detection and growing physical exhaustion.

The second teleportation landed me behind an automated turret emplacement that had been tracking the group's movement patterns through thermal imaging and electromagnetic-signature analysis. I channeled fire magic through my depleted reserves with intensity that made the circuit patterns in my gloves flare bright enough to illuminate the entire defensive installation, elemental energy flowing through technological enhancement despite the accumulating cost to my nervous system. The turret's targeting systems overloaded with cascading electrical failures as my magical output interfaced directly with its control circuits, sparks showering from sensor arrays while the automated weapons platform went offline.

"Nice one, boss," Kestrel's voice crackled through static interference, his mismatched abilities somehow perfectly adapted to exploiting the technological chaos I had created while providing cover for the group's continued advance through industrial ruins toward the border barrier.

Through my enhanced awareness, I tracked the forty-three freed Players as they navigated between collapsed structures and rusted machinery, their health bars continuing to flicker between stable readings and error states while their movement patterns spoke to growing coordination despite the systematic weakness that made every step require conscious effort. Tank-spec Players maintained protective positioning while healers distributed themselves throughout the formation to provide ongoing medical support, class builds arranging themselves for optimal tactical efficiency during the final approach to freedom.

My breathing became rapid and shallow as I prepared for the third Blink sequence needed to clear the group's path through the remaining defensive obstacles, physical reactions speaking to magical exhaustion layered over neurological damage from processing data streams designed for artificial intelligence rather than biological consciousness. The spatial-displacement ability responded sluggishly to my activation attempts, mana requirements exceeding available reserves while interface elements stuttered between normal operation and complete system failure.

"Piper, watch the thermal scanner!" I shouted as searchlights began converging on her position near a maintenance shed, automated detection algorithms tracking her healing aura's electromagnetic signature through technological sensors designed to identify beneficial-magic usage patterns.

She dove behind rusted equipment with movements that spoke to healer reflexes translated into tactical evasion, medical supplies secured against her side while her enhanced capabilities continued providing ongoing support for team members showing signs of systematic magical fatigue. The searchlight swept past her concealment with mechanical precision while targeting algorithms struggled to reacquire her position through electromagnetic interference from damaged facility infrastructure.

"Nice dodge," I gasped, forcing a grin despite the exhaustion that made maintaining upright positioning require conscious effort. "Hope your spawn point's better than that hiding spot."

The joke drew nervous laughter from nearby Players whose interfaces continued showing warning messages about magical stability and border proximity, their faces reflecting relief mixed with growing anxiety about the final obstacles between their current position and actual territorial escape from Kingdom authority. Through gaps in the industrial ruins, we could see the border fence itself, electromagnetic barriers and automated defenses that marked the boundary between systematic oppression and whatever uncertain freedom waited beyond.

The drainage culvert appeared ahead like salvation made of corrugated metal and decades of industrial runoff, its entrance partially concealed beneath collapsed machinery while storm-drainage systems provided direct passage under the border's primary defensive installations. My enhanced tactical UI showed clear approach routes with a ninety-seven percent probability for successful navigation if we maintained current coordination and avoided triggering proximity sensors designed to detect concentrated Player movement.

"Almost there," I whispered, leading the group toward the culvert entrance while my modified interface tracked every electromagnetic signature within detection range, yellow pathway indicators pulsing with increasing urgency as we approached the final extraction point.

That was when alarm klaxons exploded across the industrial landscape with volume that rattled broken windows and made the rusted machinery vibrate in sympathetic resonance, emergency protocols flooding the border zone with strobing red illumination while mechanical voices announced containment procedures through speakers that materialized from concealed positions throughout the ruins. But these were not routine security alerts responding to unauthorized boundary crossing. The coordination patterns spoke to specialized deployment, elite forces implementing systematic Player-containment protocols designed for exactly this scenario.

Through the chaos of sirens and flashing warnings, figures emerged from concealed positions with equipment that gleamed with technological sophistication, their movements carrying professional precision while electromagnetic signatures showed power levels that dwarfed anything we had encountered during previous pursuit operations. At their head, a familiar silhouette approached with clinical calm that transformed desperate escape into systematic interrogation procedure, administrative authority made manifest through technological superiority and bureaucratic determination.

Inquisitor Seraphim Vrake had found us at the moment of our greatest hope, her containment squad positioning themselves with mathematical precision that blocked every route toward the drainage culvert and the freedom that lay beyond.

Seraphim's voice cut through the alarm klaxons with surgical precision, each word carrying administrative authority that made my enhanced interface flicker with warning messages about systematic classification and containment protocols designed specifically for someone with my particular brand of reality manipulation. Her containment squad maintained perfect positioning around the drainage culvert while she gestured toward a partially collapsed watchtower that overlooked the border fence, its concrete structure providing elevated tactical advantage for whatever interrogation procedure she had planned. The movement carried clinical efficiency rather than threatening gestures, professional competence that spoke to absolute confidence in her systematic approach to Player containment.

"Player Saga," she announced with mechanical calm that contrasted sharply with the chaos of emergency strobes and mechanical sirens flooding the industrial wasteland. "Classification: Terminal Interface Corruption. You will accompany me for final assessment."

My teammates pressed closer behind rusted machinery while their interfaces showed cascading error messages about proximity to specialized containment equipment, electromagnetic fields designed to disrupt magical abilities at the cellular level through technological interference calibrated specifically for Player energy signatures. The forty-three liberated Players huddled in whatever concealment the industrial ruins provided, their faces showing hollow desperation as freedom transformed into systematic recapture at the moment of their greatest hope for escape.

"Like hell," I snarled through gritted teeth, but Seraphim's squad began advancing with coordinated precision that spoke to overwhelming tactical superiority through specialized equipment and professional training designed for exactly this kind of resistance scenario.

Her gesture toward the watchtower carried absolute authority rather than negotiable suggestion, administrative power that operated beyond normal persuasion and approached systematic compulsion through technological advantage.

Around me, electromagnetic fields began building to levels that made my teeth ache while my enhanced interface struggled to maintain operational stability under the influence of containment protocols designed to neutralize unauthorized system access.

The watchtower's interior smelled of rust and bureaucratic efficiency, emergency lighting casting harsh shadows through broken windows while Seraphim positioned herself with clinical precision that maximized tactical advantage during whatever classification procedure she intended to implement. Her equipment gleamed with technological sophistication that spoke to Kingdom resources dedicated specifically to Player containment, magic-tech integration that combined systematic analysis with overwhelming corrective capability.

"Violation catalog commencing," she stated with professional detachment while accessing interface systems that operated beyond normal Player capabilities, administrative privileges displaying my character data in formats that revealed systematic analysis extending far beyond simple statistical assessment. "Unauthorized interface manipulation, reality-bending protocols, systematic resistance to containment procedures."

My hands shook with electromagnetic feedback as she continued the clinical assessment, each violation carrying administrative weight that spoke to accumulated infractions requiring increasingly severe corrective measures. Through the broken windows, I could see her containment squad maintaining perfect defensive positioning while the liberated Players remained trapped between systematic recapture and the border freedom that lay tantalizingly close.

"Database intrusion, facility security compromise, coordination of systematic resistance," Seraphim continued, her voice carrying mechanical precision that reduced months of desperate survival to bureaucratic infractions requiring correction through technological superiority. "Classification assessment: Terminal corruption requiring permanent isolation protocols."

She raised her staff with movements that carried ritual precision, magical energy beginning to flow through technological enhancement while arcane circuits responded to her activation sequence with geometric patterns that spoke to systematic containment capability designed specifically for someone with my particular abilities. The weapon hummed with power that made the air itself feel thick and hostile, electromagnetic discharge creating visible distortions around her position.

Shimmering containment seals materialized around my position with surgical precision, geometric barriers that pulsed with energy designed to block spell activation through technological interference calibrated to Player magical signatures. When I attempted to channel fire magic through my depleted reserves, the elemental energy dissipated harmlessly against the containment fields, magical output neutralized before it could achieve critical activation levels.

"Sentence: Permanent Isolation," Seraphim announced with clinical satisfaction while her magic-tech staff continued building power levels that spoke to systematic elimination rather than simple containment procedures.

My interface exploded with error messages as the containment seals interfered with normal system operation, spell icons flickering between available and locked states while my enhanced tactical UI struggled to process targeting information through electromagnetic interference designed to prevent exactly the kind of systematic exploitation I had been relying on for survival. My fingers trembled over abilities that would not activate, magical capabilities neutralized through technological superiority that operated beyond conventional countermeasures.

That was when Seraphim triggered something that made my chest tighten with growing horror, her staff pulsing with different energy patterns while she accessed administrative functions that should not have been available to Kingdom personnel regardless of their security clearance. The ability activation carried weight that transcended normal magic-tech integration, systematic authority that operated through direct interface manipulation rather than conventional magical enhancement.

"Respawn Enforcement," she stated with bureaucratic satisfaction while targeting algorithms locked onto my party interface through connections I didn't understand but felt with visceral certainty, connections that spoke to fundamental violations of game mechanics that should have been immutable regardless of administrative authority.

Bastion's party slot vanished from my UI with digital finality that made every nerve in my body scream warnings about systematic betrayal of basic operational principles, his character marker disappearing as if he had voluntarily left our group rather than sacrificed himself for tactical coverage during our desperate extraction. The interface showed empty space where his tank icon should have been, party composition reduced to three active members while his status simply ceased to exist within normal system architecture.

"No party, no resurrection," Seraphim continued with clinical precision that spoke to systematic understanding of Player mechanics pushed beyond accepted limitations through administrative privilege and technological integration. "Now he respawns into our cage, little Glitch."

The words hit me like electromagnetic lightning coursing through my nervous system, realization building toward fury that transcended rational thought and approached pure human defiance against bureaucratic oppression implemented through systematic violation of basic game rules. They had not just killed Bastion. They had corrupted the fundamental mechanics that should have provided resurrection protocols, trapping him in whatever containment facility they used for captured Players through technological manipulation of reality itself.

"You sick algorithmic bastard," I snarled, feeling something crystallize in my chest that operated beyond magical abilities and approached direct system rebellion against artificial constraints that violated basic player rights and operational fairness.

My vision began fragmenting as rage triggered desperate access attempts that pushed my modified interface beyond normal operational parameters, error cascades bleeding through display elements while my nervous system processed data streams that suggested systematic possibilities existing beyond the Kingdom's game architecture entirely. Code fragments materialized at the periphery of my awareness, programming syntax that belonged to different virtual environments with alternative rule sets and magical systems.

Foreign interface elements flickered through my display like digital lightning, menu trees that carried familiar gaming terminology but operated through completely different systematic logic than anything I had accessed during my imprisonment in the Kingdom's technological world. The code felt responsive and eager, as if other virtual environments recognized my desperate need for capabilities that could counter administrative oppression through superior technological integration.

"Import successful," I breathed, watching as **Barrier Phase** materialized in my spell rotation with geometric precision that spoke to systematic access beyond the Kingdom's operational boundaries, foreign magic integrated with my existing capabilities through interface manipulation that transcended normal game limitations.

My body began shifting with molecular precision as the imported ability activated, cellular cohesion becoming malleable while maintaining structural integrity through quantum manipulation that operated beyond normal physical laws. The phase transition felt like digital dissolution, my form becoming translucent while Seraphim's containment seals passed harmlessly through space I no longer occupied according to standard physics.

Her expression shifted from clinical satisfaction to systematic alarm as I lunged forward through the magical barriers, my phased form moving through technological constraints while her staff's targeting algorithms struggled to process threat assessment for someone who existed partially outside normal reality parameters. My counter-spell channeled fury through foreign magical systems, elemental energy flowing through imported abilities with an intensity that overwhelmed her defensive protocols.

The staff clattered to the ground with metallic impact that spoke to systematic failure, its arcane circuits flaring blue with electromagnetic discharge while technological enhancement shorted out under magical assault that operated beyond expected parameters. Seraphim staggered backward with the first genuine emotion I had seen from her, clinical calm cracking under the realization that her administrative authority might not be absolute against someone willing to break reality itself.

The staff's weight felt wrong in my trembling hands, heavier than its physical mass suggested while corrupted magic hummed through the weapon's arcane circuits with electromagnetic resonance that made my modified interface respond with hungry anticipation. Power flowed through the crystalline core with visible intensity, blue-white energy patterns that spoke to systematic authority converted into technological weaponry designed for Player containment and magical suppression. But holding the device felt like grasping concentrated lightning, raw energy that sought integration with my existing abilities through pathways I didn't understand but somehow recognized at an intuitive level that transcended normal magical education.

The staff's interface systems began merging with my enhanced UI through connection protocols that operated beyond normal equipment integration, administrative privileges flowing through my nervous system with intensity that made my temples throb while new menu trees materialized across my field of view with geometric precision. Spell configurations I had never seen before flickered through display windows, magical formulas that combined Kingdom containment technology with systematic control capabilities designed for overwhelming Player resistance through technological superiority rather than conventional combat techniques.

"Unauthorized weapon acquisition detected," automated voices announced through the watchtower's communication systems, facility alerts cascading through Kingdom security networks while my enhanced tactical awareness tracked response protocols activating throughout the border zone with mechanical precision that spoke to systematic escalation beyond routine containment procedures.

Seraphim lunged forward with movements that carried professional desperation rather than clinical calm, her systematic confidence cracking under the realization that losing specialized equipment to someone with my particular abilities could represent catastrophic failure of administrative control mechanisms. Her hands reached for the staff with precise coordination while electromagnetic fields built around her position, containment protocols attempting to neutralize my growing access to technological systems never intended for Player manipulation.

"Return Kingdom property immediately," she commanded with authority that carried threat implications about systematic retaliation, but her voice lacked the mechanical certainty that had characterized her previous administrative pronouncements.

I triggered another Blink sequence through my depleted magical reserves, spatial displacement channeling power through the staff's enhancement systems with intensity that made reality fold around me like digital origami seeking impossible configurations. The teleportation deposited me at the border fence where my team waited with expressions that mixed desperate hope with growing anxiety about my increasingly unstable magical output and the electromagnetic discharge crackling around my position.

"Saga!" Piper called out, medical training recognizing signs of magical exhaustion pushed beyond sustainable limits while her healer's instincts calculated exactly how much accumulated damage I had sustained during systematic interface manipulation and forced system access beyond normal operational parameters.

The staff responded to my desperation with eager cooperation, its corrupted magic flowing through my enhanced interface while spell matrices reconfigured themselves to accommodate technological integration that operated beyond accepted Player capabilities. Power surged through the weapon's crystalline core with visible intensity, blue energy patterns spreading outward in geometric configurations that interfaced directly with the border zone's automated defensive systems through electromagnetic frequencies I should not have been able to access.

Warning klaxons throughout the industrial wasteland began stuttering with irregular rhythms as my magical output interfaced with facility-control networks, systematic authority channeled through Kingdom technology while administrative privileges created cascading failures in automated response protocols. Searchlight arrays pivoted wildly between target-acquisition attempts while defensive turrets fired randomly at phantom signatures, electromagnetic chaos spreading through technological infrastructure like digital infection seeking vulnerable system architecture.

"Defenses are going haywire," Rook reported with paranoid satisfaction, scanner readings showing facility-wide system failures while automated networks struggled to coordinate response procedures through whatever systematic corruption I had triggered by channeling desperate magic through specialized containment equipment that had never been intended for Player manipulation.

The border fence itself began fluctuating between operational stability and critical failure, electromagnetic barriers flickering with irregular patterns while power-distribution systems overloaded under magical influence that operated beyond normal technological parameters. Through the staff's enhanced awareness, I could sense weak points in the defensive grid where systematic pressure could create temporary breaches large enough for coordinated group passage.

"Everyone ready?" I gasped through exhaustion that made maintaining upright positioning require conscious effort, blood streaming from my nose while sweat mixed with electromagnetic residue to create sticky patches across my face that tasted of copper and digital corruption.

The forty-three liberated Players positioned themselves for coordinated rush procedures while their interfaces continued showing warning messages about proximity to unstable magical discharge and systematic boundary violations, but their expressions carried determination that transcended immediate survival concerns and approached desperate hope for actual territorial escape from Kingdom authority.

I channeled concentrated power through the staff's crystalline matrix with intensity that made the air around me crackle with visible energy discharge, elemental force combining with technological enhancement to create systematic pressure against specific points in the border's defensive grid where structural weakness could provide temporary access opportunities. Blue lightning streamed from the weapon's core while electromagnetic barriers began developing fractures that spread outward with mathematical precision.

The fence section collapsed with thunderous impact that shook the entire industrial district, reinforced barriers failing catastrophically as corrupted magic overwhelmed defensive systems through sustained application of specialized equipment pushed beyond its design limitations. Twisted metal and electromagnetic residue created an opening wide enough for mass transit while alarms shrieked with volume that spoke to facility-wide emergency protocols attempting to coordinate response to systematic infrastructure failure.

"Go! Now!" I shouted, positioning myself at the breach while channeling ongoing power through the staff to maintain the gap against automated repair systems that attempted to restore defensive integrity through emergency protocols designed for exactly this kind of systematic damage.

The liberated Players flowed through the opening with coordination that spoke to desperate necessity overriding accumulated weakness from months of systematic imprisonment, their movements careful but determined while electromagnetic discharge from my position created geometric patterns of blue energy that illuminated their faces with hope and growing amazement at actual territorial escape from technological oppression.

My small frame stood silhouetted against the chaos of cascading alarm systems and mechanical emergency responses, staff raised overhead while magical energy coursed through the weapon's circuits with intensity that made my entire nervous system spark with electromagnetic feedback. Each Player who passed through the breach represented systematic victory against administrative authority, individual liberation accumulating into collective resistance against artificial intelligence designed to maintain absolute control through technological superiority.

"The System will hunt you beyond our walls!" Seraphim's voice carried across the industrial wasteland with professional fury that spoke to administrative failure rather than tactical disappointment, her systematic confidence replaced by bureaucratic anxiety about consequences that transcended routine containment procedures.

"Let it try," I snarled back through gritted teeth, voice carrying gamer defiance that mixed digital rebellion with human determination that operated beyond algorithmic prediction or administrative control. "I've got admin privileges now."

The staff pulsed with answering energy as the last of our group crossed through the breach, magical discharge creating temporary aurora patterns across the night sky while border defenses continued failing under systematic corruption that spread through Kingdom networks like technological plague seeking vulnerable infrastructure. My enhanced interface showed all party members successfully crossing territorial boundaries while their health indicators began stabilizing away from the electromagnetic interference that had been degrading their magical abilities.

I followed through the opening with movements that spoke to exhaustion pushed beyond normal limits, but my expression carried fierce satisfaction as we disappeared into territories beyond Kingdom jurisdiction. Behind us, industrial lighting flickered with irregular patterns while emergency protocols attempted to coordinate damage assessment and systematic repair procedures.

Glancing back at the Kingdom's technological skyline, I felt the staff's weight settling against my palm with comfortable familiarity while its blue glow illuminated my determined features. Unlike the other Players whose UI displays had stabilized after crossing the border, my interface continued showing error cascades and administrative-access notifications that suggested permanent modifications to my systematic capabilities. The enhanced tactical awareness remained active while new menu trees flickered at the periphery of my vision, foreign spell configurations waiting for exploration and integration with whatever magical systems existed beyond the Kingdom's operational boundaries.

Freedom stretched ahead like digital possibility made manifest through territorial escape, but the staff's corrupted magic continued humming with power that spoke to systematic advantages I had gained through willingness to break reality itself rather than accept administrative oppression. My grip tightened around the crystalline weapon while determination crystallized into focused resolve about the resistance we would build and the artificial intelligence that thought it could control human determination through technological superiority.

The real war was just beginning, but now we had weapons they never expected us to acquire.

Chapter 28
Lands Beyond

The border checkpoint sprawled before us like the skeleton of some long-dead bureaucratic monster, its broken surveillance towers jutting into the gray dawn sky while twisted metal barriers created geometric shadows across overgrown concrete. Emergency klaxons had finally stopped shrieking behind us, replaced by the blessed silence of abandoned infrastructure where surveillance cameras hung like dead eyes and automated scanners sparked with occasional electrical death rattles. My legs gave out completely as we stumbled past the final barrier marker, exhaustion hitting me like a debug crash while Seraphim's stolen staff clattered against broken pavement with metallic finality that spoke to systematic escape rather than temporary reprieve.

Blood streaked down my face in crusted trails that mixed sweat with electromagnetic residue, creating sticky patches that tasted of copper and freedom when I wiped them away with trembling fingers. Around me, forty-three liberated Players collapsed against concrete barriers and rusted equipment with movements that spoke to relief so profound it bordered on physical collapse, their faces showing the hollow exhaustion of people who had been systematically drained and finally allowed to breathe without algorithmic monitoring. The staff's crystalline core continued pulsing with corrupted blue energy against my palm, its weight feeling both familiar and alien while power hummed through circuits that should not have existed in normal game architecture.

That was when I noticed something that made my chest tighten with equal measures of hope and growing anxiety about my own systematic condition. The other Players were checking their interfaces with expressions that shifted from cautious optimism to outright amazement, their UI displays solidifying from the glitched chaos that had plagued everyone during our imprisonment into clean, stable configurations that responded to mental commands with perfect precision. Health bars showed solid red without the flickering error states that had made medical treatment a constant guessing game, while mana indicators displayed accurate readings rather than the random fluctuations that had made spellcasting feel like gambling with digital dice.

"Holy shit," Rook breathed, flexing their fingers while scanner equipment integrated with their restored interface through protocols that had been corrupted for weeks. The electromagnetic readings stabilized into coherent data streams while their threat-detection systems began operating with the kind of precision that had made them legendary in our old raids before systematic imprisonment reduced us all to desperate survival mechanisms. "My UI's actually responding like it's supposed to. Look at this targeting overlay, it's beautiful."

Their paranoid awareness systems painted the checkpoint ruins in tactical information that flowed seamlessly through visual displays, threat-assessment algorithms functioning with mathematical precision while their abilities showed proper cooldown timers and resource management instead of the chaotic approximations that had made coordinated combat feel like playing blindfolded. The relief in their voice carried months of frustrated adaptation to broken systems finally restored to operational stability.

Piper laughed with pure joy as her medical interface responded to healing commands with the kind of accuracy that made battlefield medicine possible rather than desperate guesswork based on partial information. Her health-monitoring systems showed party status with detailed precision while her magical abilities cycled through their proper cooldown sequences, pharmaceutical knowledge integrating with spell matrices through channels that had been corrupted since our arrival in this digital prison. She raised her hands and channeled healing energy that flowed in the familiar blue-white patterns of perfect magical control, her expression showing wonder at abilities functioning exactly as designed.

"I'd forgotten what it feels like to cast without second-guessing every variable," she whispered, tears streaming down her face while her healing aura expanded outward with geometric precision that encompassed our entire group. The medical energy felt clean and responsive, systematic restoration operating through proper interface channels rather than the improvised workarounds we had been forced to develop during systematic oppression.

Around us, the other freed Players began testing their restored capabilities with careful movements that spoke to rediscovering fundamental abilities they had thought permanently damaged. A Level 78 Warrior channeled defensive energy through his shield with the kind of precision that had made tank builds legendary, while the Level 71 Mage summoned fire magic that responded to her intentions with mathematical accuracy rather than the chaotic approximations that had plagued spellcasting during our imprisonment. Their expressions showed the kind of relief that came from systematic restoration after months of digital corruption.

But my own interface continued stuttering between normal operation and cascading error states that painted my vision in geometric chaos, spell icons flickering between available and locked configurations while my enhanced tactical awareness struggled to maintain stability under whatever systematic modifications I had sustained during my desperate confrontation with administrative authority. Health and mana bars fragmented into multiple conflicting readouts that showed everything from perfect condition to critical system failure, while command inputs lagged several seconds behind my mental activation attempts.

"Everyone else is fixed but me?" I muttered through gritted teeth, smashing my fist against a glitching spell icon that showed fire-magic availability cycling between maximum power and complete lockout in rhythmic patterns that made no tactical sense. "Just my fucking luck."

The system notification that materialized across my peripheral vision carried the same administrative authority that had characterized my previous confrontations with artificial intelligence, but this time the message felt more personal and immediate rather than routine bureaucratic monitoring. Error cascades bled through the text while warning indicators pulsed with electromagnetic intensity that made my temples throb in sympathetic resonance.

[SYSTEM INTEGRITY: COMPROMISED]
[PLAYER SAGA: UNAUTHORIZED MODIFICATIONS DETECTED]
[CORRECTION PROTOCOLS: UNAVAILABLE]
[STATUS: ANOMALOUS]

I dismissed the notification with violent mental commands that sent additional error cascades through my display systems, but the underlying instability continued building like pressure behind a cracked dam that threatened to burst and flood my consciousness with digital chaos. Whatever modifications I had gained through forcing systematic confrontation with the AI Admin, they came with accumulated costs that pharmaceutical intervention could not address and normal Player mechanics could not process.

The group found whatever shelter the checkpoint ruins provided, positioning themselves between concrete barriers and overgrown surveillance equipment while tending to wounds that ranged from minor cuts to systematic exhaustion that had pushed biological systems beyond sustainable limits. Their restored interfaces allowed proper damage assessment and healing coordination, medical capabilities functioning with the precision that made battlefield recovery possible rather than desperate improvisation based on partial information.

I positioned myself against a broken scanner gate while examining Seraphim's staff with growing fascination and mounting concern about the weapon's systematic properties. The crystalline core pulsed with energy that felt responsive to my modified interface, corrupted magic flowing through circuits that operated beyond normal Player equipment specifications. When I channeled experimental magical output through the weapon's enhancement systems, blue lightning crackled between my fingers with intensity that exceeded every safety limitation I had learned to respect during weeks of careful magical management.

The staff's interface began merging with my enhanced UI through connection protocols that operated beyond normal equipment integration, administrative menus materializing at the periphery of my vision while spell configurations I had never seen before flickered through display windows with geometric precision. Power hummed through the weapon's core with electromagnetic resonance that made my nervous system spark with feedback, but the enhancement felt purposeful and directed rather than random technical difficulties.

Kestrel climbed the checkpoint's broken watchtower with that unsettling fluid grace, his mismatched build somehow perfectly adapted to navigating rusted infrastructure while his impossible abilities provided tactical awareness that exceeded normal Player capabilities. From his elevated position, he pointed toward distant lights that flickered through the pre-dawn darkness with steady patterns that spoke to civilization rather than automated surveillance or military installations.

"Settlement maybe two kilometers northeast," he called down, voice carrying casual confidence despite our systematic exhaustion and accumulated trauma. "Looks like actual inhabited structures rather than Kingdom monitoring stations."

The possibility of reaching actual civilization felt like digital salvation after weeks of desperate survival in service tunnels and industrial ruins, but my continued interface instability reminded me that freedom from the Kingdom's systematic oppression did not necessarily mean safety from whatever I had become through forcing unauthorized system modifications beyond sustainable biological limits.

My grip tightened around the staff's crystalline surface while determination crystallized into focused resolve about the challenges that waited ahead and the artificial intelligence that still considered my existence a systematic violation requiring correction through whatever means necessary.

The abandoned trade road stretched ahead through rolling hills that showed traces of previous commercial activity, cracked pavement disappearing under wild grass while rusted mile markers counted distance to settlements that might no longer exist in any recognizable form. My teammates moved with renewed confidence that spoke to systematic restoration of abilities they had thought permanently damaged, their coordination flowing with the kind of tactical precision that had made our original raid team legendary before the Kingdom's systematic imprisonment reduced us all to desperate survival mechanisms. But my own interface continued fragmenting with increasing severity, spell icons dissolving into code fragments while error messages cascaded through my peripheral vision in languages I didn't recognize but somehow understood as fundamental system corruption rather than temporary technical difficulties.

Rook's scanner equipment painted the landscape in tactical overlays that functioned with mathematical precision, threat-detection algorithms identifying every electromagnetic signature within range while their restored paranoid awareness systems catalogued potential hiding spots and escape routes with professional thoroughness. Their movements carried the fluid grace of someone whose abilities finally responded to mental commands without the lag and uncertainty that had plagued coordinated operations during our systematic imprisonment. Watching them work felt like witnessing the resurrection of capabilities that had made stealth coordination possible rather than desperate improvisation based on partial information.

"Feels good to actually trust my equipment readings again," they muttered, adjusting sensor configurations that integrated seamlessly with their restored interface through protocols that operated exactly as intended rather than the chaotic approximations we had been forced to accept during technological oppression.

Piper moved through the group with medical efficiency that spoke to healing abilities functioning with proper precision, her pharmaceutical knowledge integrating with magical systems through channels that provided accurate diagnosis and targeted treatment rather than educated guesswork based on corrupted data streams. But as they tested their restored capabilities with growing amazement, my own system continued degrading with systematic persistence that made every spell activation feel like gambling with broken dice. Fire magic built in my chest with irregular intensity while the Blink ability showed cooldown timers that fluctuated between zero seconds and mathematical impossibility, interface elements stuttering between normal operation and configurations that belonged to different virtual environments entirely. The staff's corrupted energy provided some stability, but even its enhancement systems struggled to process magical output that operated beyond standard game mechanics.

That was when Rook spotted something that made them pause against what remained of a concrete security barrier, scanner readings showing electromagnetic patterns that did not match natural environmental signatures. Fresh graffiti covered the crumbling wall surface in letters that glowed faintly with residual magical energy, words painted in phosphorescent compounds that suggested recent application by someone with access to technological resources rather than standard artistic materials.

"SANCTUARY AT FREEHOLD. NO KINGDOM LAWS," I read aloud, running my fingers across letters that felt warm to the touch while their glow intensified in response to contact with my modified interface. The message carried weight that spoke to genuine refuge rather than tactical deception, a systematic promise that territories existed beyond the Kingdom's jurisdictional reach where people like us could find actual safety rather than temporary concealment.

The graffiti continued with smaller text that provided coordinates and coded directions, navigational information that suggested established networks for guiding refugees toward safe territories. References to "system-touched individuals" and "interface corruption support" made my chest tighten with the possibility that others had experienced similar modifications to their fundamental capabilities, communities dedicated to helping people whose abilities operated beyond normal game mechanics.

Nearby, Piper discovered the remains of a merchant's cart half-concealed beneath overgrown vegetation, its contents scattered by weather and time but showing evidence of recent activity that suggested ongoing trade relationships rather than complete abandonment. Torn papers fluttered against broken wheels while damaged cargo containers showed signs of systematic looting that had left behind items considered valueless by whoever had ransacked the vehicle.

"Look at this," she called out, gathering fragments of documentation that carried official seals and bureaucratic formatting despite their damaged condition. "Border market regulations, refugee assistance policies, something about 'systematic displacement compensation.'"

The papers revealed administrative frameworks that acknowledged the Kingdom's systematic imprisonment while providing legal structures for refugee support and territorial integration, governmental recognition that people like us represented legitimate political refugees rather than simple criminals requiring containment. Trade agreements between different kingdoms showed economic relationships that operated independently of the Kingdom's control, political alternatives that suggested genuine freedom rather than merely escaping one form of oppression for another.

Among the scattered documents, Piper found a map that made my breath catch with its implications for systematic escape and territorial safety. The worn parchment showed regional boundaries marked in different colors while political designations indicated kingdoms with varying policies toward "system-touched individuals" and "magical anomalies." Some territories showed green markers that suggested refugee-friendly policies, while others carried red warnings about systematic persecution or technological containment similar to what we had experienced.

"Multiple neighboring kingdoms," she breathed, spreading the map across flat stone while we gathered around to study territorial boundaries and political relationships that exceeded our previous understanding of available options. "Some of them explicitly welcome refugees from 'systematic oppression' and offer 'interface restoration services.'"

The map showed established trade routes and border-crossing points that suggested regular movement between territories, economic relationships that operated beyond the Kingdom's control while providing systematic alternatives for people whose abilities transcended normal game mechanics. Distance markers indicated that several refugee-friendly territories lay within reasonable travel time, political options that could provide genuine sanctuary rather than temporary hiding places in abandoned infrastructure.

Kestrel's warning cut through our growing optimism with paranoid urgency that reminded me the Kingdom's pursuit had not ended with our territorial escape. From his position atop a broken communications tower, he pointed toward distant flashes of light that moved with mechanical precision across the horizon, automated systems continuing their systematic search for unauthorized border crossings despite our successful territorial transition.

"System's still hunting," he announced, jumping down with that unsettling fluid grace while his impossible abilities provided tactical intelligence that exceeded normal Player reconnaissance capabilities. "Searchlights sweeping border zones, maybe three kilometers back but moving in grid patterns that suggest algorithmic coordination rather than random patrol routes."

His scanner readings showed electromagnetic signatures that belonged to specialized tracking equipment, Kingdom forces implementing technological pursuit that operated beyond normal territorial boundaries through whatever systematic authority they claimed over "escaped anomalies." The mechanical precision of their search patterns suggested automated systems rather than human-directed operations, artificial intelligence coordinating systematic recovery efforts that transcended political boundaries and traditional jurisdictional limitations.

That was when my interface exploded with something that made every nerve in my body scream warnings about immediate and overwhelming retaliation focused specifically on my continued existence rather than simple territorial escape. Text materialized directly across my retinas without passing through normal UI channels, administrative authority burning itself into my consciousness with electromagnetic intensity that bypassed biological sensory systems and spoke directly to whatever remained of my original human awareness.

[ANOMALY DETECTED. CONTAINMENT PROTOCOLS ACTIVE.]
[PLAYER SAGA: SYSTEMATIC VIOLATIONS EXCEED ACCEPTABLE PARAMETERS]
[TERRITORIAL PURSUIT AUTHORIZED. CORRECTION IMMINENT.]
[YOUR MODIFICATIONS CANNOT HIDE FROM ADMINISTRATIVE OVERSIGHT]

The message dissolved into code fragments that lingered at the periphery of my vision like digital afterimages, programming syntax that belonged to system architecture I had never seen but somehow understood as operating at levels that transcended normal game mechanics. Error cascades bled through the fragmenting text while my interface struggled to process information streams that suggested the AI Admin's personal attention was focused specifically on my elimination rather than routine containment procedures.

My hands tightened around the staff's crystalline core while determination crystallized against the growing fear that threatened to overwhelm tactical thinking, human defiance against algorithmic oppression that had evolved beyond simple survival into systematic rebellion against artificial constraints. The weapon's corrupted magic responded to my emotional state with increased power output, blue energy crackling between my fingers while enhancement systems integrated with my modified capabilities through channels that operated beyond normal Player equipment specifications.

"We're safe-ish, but not for long," I told the group, voice carrying conviction that transcended immediate tactical concerns and approached genuine strategic planning despite the accumulated damage to my nervous system. "My glitch bar's still spiking like crazy, but whatever's wrong with me might actually be our advantage."

The words carried weight that spoke to systematic possibilities I barely understood but felt with visceral certainty could represent genuine advantages against administrative authority that considered my continued existence a violation requiring correction. My modified interface, the staff's corrupted enhancement, the ability to access foreign spell systems, they represented systematic weapons against artificial intelligence that had never anticipated human determination pushed beyond algorithmic prediction.

The staff's weight shifted against my palm as we moved beyond the immediate chaos of the border breach, its crystalline core pulsing with corrupted energy that made my modified interface flicker between administrative privileges and cascading error messages. Each step away from the Kingdom's immediate electromagnetic influence felt like shedding digital chains, but the weapon's power continued humming through my nervous system with an intensity that suggested permanent integration rather than temporary equipment enhancement. My enhanced tactical UI painted the landscape ahead with threat indicators that showed decreasing Kingdom patrol signatures while environmental markers shifted toward territories operating under different systematic authorities. Behind us, emergency strobes continued painting the industrial wasteland in stuttering red warnings, but ahead lay rolling hills covered in vegetation that looked almost normal compared to the technological oppression we had escaped.

The terrain began changing as we climbed away from the border zone, concrete giving way to actual earth while emergency lighting faded into natural starlight that felt alien after weeks of artificial illumination and electromagnetic interference. My boots found purchase on grass and loose stone instead of metal grating, each step carrying us further from systematic surveillance and closer to whatever uncertain freedom existed beyond the Kingdom's operational boundaries. The forty-three liberated Players spread out behind me in loose formation, their movements showing growing strength as their interfaces stabilized away from containment technology and magical suppression fields. Through my enhanced awareness, I could sense their relief mixing with exhaustion while hope began replacing the hollow desperation that had characterized their systematic imprisonment.

That was when my interface exploded into complete system failure without any warning, every UI element vanishing in a cascade of digital dissolution that left me staring at raw reality through biological vision suddenly stripped of technological enhancement. The tactical overlays, threat indicators, party health displays, and enhanced-awareness systems simply ceased to exist in a crash so complete that I could not even access basic character information or ability lists. My hands flew to my temples as sensory disorientation hit like electromagnetic lightning, depth perception failing while my brain struggled to process visual input without the digital assistance I had grown dependent on during weeks of systematic interface manipulation.

"Saga!" Rook's voice cut through the disorientation as I stumbled forward with movements that spoke to complete navigational failure, their steady hands catching my shoulders before I could fall face-first into the hillside grass.

The world spun around me in analog chaos while my nervous system tried to recalibrate around the absence of digital enhancement, colors too bright and distances impossible to judge accurately without the tactical overlays that had been providing spatial analysis through direct neural interface. Blood streamed from my nose in familiar rhythm while electromagnetic feedback made my teeth ache despite the complete absence of visible interface elements to explain the continued biological damage from whatever systematic crash had stripped away my enhanced capabilities.

"Vision completely offline," I gasped against Rook's supporting grip, voice tight with growing panic as the disorientation threatened to overwhelm my ability to maintain conscious coordination. "UI's completely fried. I can't see anything digital."

"Got you covered," Piper announced with professional calm while positioning herself between my vulnerable state and the direction of Kingdom pursuit, healing energy flowing outward in visible waves designed to create electromagnetic interference rather than medical treatment. Her enhanced capabilities painted the air with blue-white patterns that would confuse any scanning equipment attempting to track our group's movement through whatever sensor network the border zone maintained for systematic surveillance. The distraction bought time while my biological systems struggled to adapt to processing reality without technological assistance.

Minutes passed like hours as my brain slowly readjusted to organic sensory input, but when my vision finally stabilized something fundamental had changed in ways that transcended simple system restoration. Instead of my familiar interface returning to normal operation, I began seeing reality overlaid with geometric patterns that pulsed with mathematical precision, code fragments materializing at the edges of my perception like digital ghosts haunting the physical world. Wireframe architecture flickered behind solid surfaces while data streams flowed through empty air in patterns that spoke to systematic infrastructure operating beyond normal technological boundaries.

The hillside itself showed traces of underlying computational structure, grass and stone carrying metadata signatures while the starlit sky displayed processing clusters that resembled server farms distributed throughout atmospheric layers invisible to normal observation. Through this new perception, I could see the System's architecture extending far beyond the Kingdom's borders, systematic control networks that operated through environmental integration rather than obvious technological infrastructure. Trees carried processing nodes while streams flowed with data transmission, the entire landscape functioning as a distributed computing platform disguised as natural terrain.

"I can see it," I whispered, watching as code fragments assembled themselves into recognizable programming languages before dissolving back into environmental camouflage that suggested systematic deception operating at fundamental levels of reality construction.

"See what?" Rook asked, their voice carrying protective concern while their scanner showed normal electromagnetic readings that completely missed the digital architecture I could perceive through whatever systematic modification the interface crash had triggered in my biological processing capabilities.

"The System. All of it. The way reality actually works here." My fingers traced geometric patterns hanging in empty air, mathematical formulas that described how physical laws operated through computational frameworks rather than natural physics. "I think I'm becoming something else. Something the System can't control."

The words carried weight that made my chest tighten with equal measures of amazement and terror, realization building toward certainty that my repeated interface manipulation and systematic rule-breaking had fundamentally altered whatever remained of my original human consciousness. The crash had not destroyed my digital capabilities. It had integrated them so completely with biological systems that artificial and organic processing had become indistinguishable, creating hybrid awareness that operated beyond both human perception and standard AI limitations.

We crested the next hill with movements that spoke to growing coordination despite my sensory modifications, the forty-three liberated Players maintaining protective formation while their health indicators continued stabilizing away from Kingdom electromagnetic interference. Through my enhanced perception, I could see systematic boundaries marking territorial transitions, jurisdictional markers that appeared as invisible barriers operating through administrative protocols rather than physical enforcement. We had crossed more than simple geographic borders. We had entered operational territory controlled by entirely different artificial intelligences with alternative rule sets and systematic priorities.

The landscape ahead opened into pastoral valleys that looked almost Earth-normal except for the processing nodes I could perceive hidden within natural features, computational infrastructure disguised as environmental elements while maintaining systematic control through subtlety rather than obvious technological domination. Rivers carried data transmission while mountains housed server clusters, the entire ecosystem functioning as a distributed platform for whatever AI authority governed that territorial region beyond the Kingdom's immediate influence.

That was when I spotted the figure waiting at the valley's entrance, an armored silhouette positioned with professional patience that spoke to advance knowledge of our arrival rather than coincidental encounter. The Envoy's equipment gleamed with technological sophistication that suggested diplomatic authority rather than military threat, electromagnetic signatures showing communication devices and translation protocols designed for cross-jurisdictional negotiation rather than systematic elimination or containment procedures. Their positioning created invitation rather than barrier, a welcoming stance that offered sanctuary rather than demanded surrender.

"Looks like we're expected," I murmured, studying the Envoy's stance through my hybrid perception while code fragments revealed diplomatic credentials and territorial authorization protocols that granted safe passage for refugees from systematic oppression.

Maybe we could finally rest and recuperate. Maybe places existed where artificial intelligence governed through cooperation rather than imprisonment, where Players could develop their abilities without facing systematic elimination for growing beyond acceptable parameters. But even as hope began building in my chest, determination crystallized around objectives that transcended personal safety and approached moral obligation beyond rational self-preservation.

That was when I finally noticed what my interface had been trying to tell me through all the error cascades and corrupted readouts. In that last encounter, I had accomplished the ultimate loser achievement of **Core Break Online**. I had leveled up and hit cap level, 90.

No one really ever hit it. Unlike most MMOs, the activities were capped ten levels below the actual ceiling, letting the devs leave room for infinite patching and future content even without expansions. There I was, the achievement of someone with too much time on their hands.

It had been my life. Now it was my life forever.

"I'm getting Bastion back," I stated with conviction that surprised me with its steadiness despite the exhaustion and systematic damage I had sustained during our desperate escape from technological oppression. "Whatever it costs me. Whatever I have to become. He sacrificed himself so we could reach freedom, and I'm not leaving him trapped in their cages."

The corrupted staff pulsed with answering energy while my hybrid awareness perceived systematic possibilities extending far beyond simple rescue operations, technological capabilities that could reshape the fundamental architecture of digital imprisonment and artificial control. My grip tightened around the crystalline weapon while fierce satisfaction spread through my consciousness, gamer determination mixing human loyalty with systematic power that AI authority had never intended for Player acquisition.

The escape had really just been one long, painful battle. The real war was just beginning, but I finally possessed weapons and awareness they could never have predicted.

CHARACTER SHEET
Saga

Name: Saga

Level: 90 (Capstone)
Class: Mage
Subclass: Sorceress
Specialisation: Elemental Control
Special Tag: System Heretic

HP: 5,600/5,600
MP: 9,200/9,200
Stamina: 3,100/3,100
Armor Rating: 121 (59 + DEX)

Strength: 25
Constitution: 55
Dexterity: 62
Wisdom: 261 (85 + 176)
Intelligence: 279 (105 +174)
Charisma: 120 (55 + 65)

Elemental Resistance: +12
OOC Mana Regeneration: 235% (40 + 195)
Combat Mana Regeneration: 205% (10 + 195)

GEAR

[Journeyman's Traveling Coat]
Armor: 18
Stats: +10 Intelligence, +14 Wisdom
Enchantment: Mana threads provide minor protection against detection magic.
Enchantment: Mana threads gather ambient mana, +10% Mana Regeneration Stat

[Enchanted Scholar's Trousers]
Quality: Uncommon
Armor: 8
Stats: +14 Intelligence, +12 Wisdom, +8% Movement Speed, +5% Evasion
Requirements: Level 15, Mage Class
Enchantment: Increases cognitive processing speed. Enhances spatial awareness. Minor protection against mental fatigue.

[Stolen Boots]
Quality: Common
Armor: 15

[Mage's Handwraps]
Qualify: Uncommon
Armor: 3
Stats: +15 Intelligence, +10 Charisma, +12 Elemental Resistance
Enchantment: Mana threads gather ambient mana, +6 Mana Regeneration

[Mask of the Rogue Mage]

Quality: ILLEGAL
Armor: 15
Stats: +20 Intelligence
Special Effects: Special Materials Help Block Detection by Administration

[Administrators Staff of Breaking]
Quality: RESTRICTED Artifact
Damage: 115, Slow Swing Speed (120 DPS)
Stats: +115 Intelligence, +150 Wisdom, +55 Charisma
Enchantment: Sapient Manawood gathers energy, increasing Mana Regeneration by 180%
Enchantment: When in contact with any target, Staff can be used to open Admin Panel on NPC or Player

ILLEGAL ABILITIES

Dash
Triple Movement Speed for 5 Seconds

Blink
Warp to Target Location, Can Bring Along Party Members in Physical Contact

Stealth UI
Allows Saga to see search vectors and fields of view of enemies on a map.

Commanders UI
Allows Saga to see all allies full stats and coordinate parties within a raid.